ENTHRALLING MYSTERY STORIES

ENTHRALLING MYSTERY STORIES

OCTOPUS BOOKS

First published in 1981
This revised edition first published in 1988 by
Octopus Books Limited
Michelin House
81 Fulham Road
London
SW3 6RB

ISBN 0 7064 3274 6

This arrangement copyright © 1981, 1988 Octopus Books Limited
Line illustrations by Sam Thompson
Colour illustrations by Nicki Palin
Cover artwork by Philip Hood

Printed in Czechoslovakia
52163

Contents

Colour Illustrations

LOST HEARTS
M. R. James

It was, as far as I can ascertain, in September of the year 1811 that a post-chaise drew up before the door of Aswarby Hall, in the heart of Lincolnshire. The little boy who was the only passenger in the chaise, and who jumped out as soon as it had stopped, looked about him with the keenest curiosity during the short interval that elapsed between the ringing of the bell and the opening of the hall door. He saw a tall, square, red-brick house, built in the reign of Anne; a stone-pillared porch had been added in the purer classical style of 1790; the windows of the house were many, tall and narrow, with small panes and thick white woodwork. A pediment, pierced with a round window, crowned the front. There were wings to right and left, connected by curious glazed galleries, supported by colonnades, with the central block. These wings plainly contained the stables and offices of the house. Each was surmounted by an ornamental cupola with a gilded vane.

An evening light shone on the building, making the window-panes glow like so many fires. Away from the Hall in front stretched a flat park studded with oaks and fringed with firs, which stood out against the sky. The clock in the church-tower, buried in trees on the edge of the park, only its golden weather-cock catching the light, was striking six, and the sound came gently beating down the wind. It was altogether a pleasant impression, though tinged with the sort of melancholy appropriate to an evening in early autumn, that was conveyed to the mind of the boy who was standing in the porch waiting for the door to open to him.

The post-chaise had brought him from Warwickshire, where, some six months before, he had been left an orphan. Now, owing to the generous offer of his elderly cousin, Mr Abney, he had come to live at Aswarby. The offer was unexpected, because all who knew anything of Mr Abney looked upon him as a somewhat austere recluse, into whose steady-going household the advent of a small boy would import a new and, it seemed, incongruous element. The truth is that very little was known of Mr Abney's pursuits or temper. The Professor of Greek at Cambridge had been heard to say that no one knew more of the religious beliefs of the later pagans than did the owner of Aswarby. Certainly his library contained all the then available books bearing on the Mysteries, the Orphic poems, the worship of Mithras, and the Neo-Platonists. In the marble-paved hall stood a fine group of Mithras slaying a bull, which had been imported from the Levant at great expense by the owner. He had contributed a description of it to the *Gentleman's Magazine*, and he had written a remarkable series of articles in the *Critical Museum* on the superstitions of the Romans of the Lower Empire. He was looked upon, *in fine*, as a man wrapped up in his books, and it was a matter of great surprise among his neighbours that he could even have heard of his orphan cousin, Stephen Elliott, much more that he should have volunteered to make him an inmate of Aswarby Hall.

Whatever may have been expected by his neighbours, it is certain that Mr Abney – the tall, the thin, the austere – seemed inclined to give his young cousin a kindly reception. The moment the front door was opened he darted out of his study, rubbing his hands with delight.

'How are you, my boy? – how are you? How old are you?' said he – 'that is, you are not too much tired, I hope, by your journey to eat your supper?'

'No, thank you, sir,' said Master Elliott; 'I am pretty well.'

'That's a good lad,' said Mr Abney. 'And how old are you, my boy?'

It seemed a little odd that he should have asked the question twice in the first two minutes of their acquaintance.

'I'm twelve years old next birthday, sir,' said Stephen.

'And when is your birthday, my dear boy? Eleventh of September, eh?

The boy raised his arms in the air with an appearance of menace

That's well – that's very well. Nearly a year hence, isn't it? I like – ha, ha!. – I like to get these things down in my book. Sure it's twelve? Certain?'

'Yes, quite sure, sir.'

'Well, well! Take him to Mrs Bunch's room, Parkes, and let him have his tea – supper – whatever it is.'

'Yes, sir,' answered the staid Mr Parkes; and conducted Stephen to the lower regions.

Mrs Bunch was the most comfortable and human person whom Stephen had as yet met in Aswarby. She made him completely at home; they were great friends in a quarter of an hour: and great friends they remained. Mrs Bunch had been born in the neighbourhood some fifty-five years before the date of Stephen's arrival, and her residence at the Hall was of twenty years' standing. Consequently, if anyone knew the ins and outs of the house and the district, Mrs Bunch knew them; and she was by no means disinclined to communicate her information.

Certainly there were plenty of things about the Hall and the Hall gardens which Stephen, who was of an adventurous and inquiring turn, was anxious to have explained to him. 'Who built the temple at the end of the laurel walk? Who was the old man whose picture hung on the staircase, sitting at a table, with a skull under his hand?' These and many similar points were cleared up by the resources of Mrs Bunch's powerful intellect. There were others, however, of which the explanations furnished were less satisfactory.

One November evening Stephen was sitting by the fire in the housekeeper's room reflecting on his surroundings.

'Is Mr Abney a good man, and will he go to heaven?' he suddenly asked, with the peculiar confidence which children possess in the ability of their elders to settle these questions, the decision of which is believed to be reserved for other tribunals.

'Good? – bless the child!' said Mrs Bunch. 'Master's as kind a soul as ever I see! Didn't I never tell you of the little boy as he took in out of the street, as you may say, this seven years back? and the little girl, two years after I first come here?'

'No. Do tell me all about them, Mrs Bunch – now this minute!'

'Well,' said Mrs Bunch, 'the little girl I don't seem to recollect so much about. I know master brought her back with him from his walk one day, and give orders to Mrs Ellis, as was housekeeper then, as she should be

took every care with. And the pore child hadn't no one belonging to her –
she told me so her own self – and here she lived with us a matter of three
weeks it might be; and then, whether she were somethink of a gipsy in
her blood or what not, but one morning she out of her bed afore any of us
had opened an eye, and neither track nor yet trace of her have I set eyes on
since. Master was wonderful put about, and had all the ponds dragged;
but it's my belief she was had away by them gipsies, for there was singing
round the house for as much as an hour the night she went, and Parkes, he
declare as he heard them a-calling in the woods all that afternoon. Dear,
dear! a hodd child she was, so silent in her ways and all, but I was
wonderful taken up with her, so domesticated she was – surprising.'

'And what about the little boy?' said Stephen.

'Ah, that pore boy!' sighed Mrs Bunch. 'He were a foreigner – Jevanny
he called hisself – and he come a-tweaking his 'urdy-gurdy round and
about the drive one winter day, and master 'ad him in that minute, and
ast all about where he came from, and how old he was, and how he made
his way, and where was his relatives, and all as kind as heart could wish.
But it went the same way with him. They're a hunruly lot, them foreign
nations, I do suppose, and he was off one fine morning just the same as
the girl. Why he went and what he done was our question for as much as
a year after; for he never took his 'urdy-gurdy, and there it lays on the
shelf.'

The remainder of the evening was spent by Stephen in miscellaneous
cross-examination of Mrs Bunch and in efforts to extract a tune from the
hurdy-gurdy.

That night he had a curious dream. At the end of the passage at the top
of the house, in which his bedroom was situated, there was an old disused
bathroom. It was kept locked, but the upper half of the door was glazed,
and, since the muslin curtains which used to hang there had long been
gone, you could look in and see the lead-lined bath affixed to the wall on
the right hand, with its head towards the window.

On the night of which I am speaking, Stephen Elliott found himself, as
he thought, looking through the glazed door. The moon was shining
through the window, and he was gazing at a figure which lay in the bath.

His description of what he saw reminds me of what I once beheld
myself in the famous vaults of St Michan's Church in Dublin, which
possess the horrid property of preserving corpses from decay for

13

centuries. A figure inexpressibly thin and pathetic, of a dusty leaden colour, enveloped in a shroud-like garment, the thin lips crooked into a faint and dreadful smile, the hands pressed tightly over the region of the heart.

As he looked upon it, a distant almost inaudible moan seemed to issue from its lips, and the arms began to stir. The terror of the sight forced Stephen backwards, and he awoke to the fact that he was indeed standing on the cold boarded floor of the passage in the full light of the moon. With a courage which I do not think can be common among boys of his age, he went to the door of the bathroom to ascertain if the figure of his dream were really there. It was not, and he went back to bed.

Mrs Bunch was much impressed next morning by his story, and went so far as to replace the muslin curtain over the glazed door of the bathroom. Mr Abney, moreover, to whom he confided his experiences at breakfast, was greatly interested, and made notes of the matter in what he called 'his book'.

The spring equinox was approaching, as Mr Abney frequently reminded his cousin, adding that this had been always considered by the ancients to be a critical time for the young: that Stephen would do well to take care of himself, and to shut his bedroom window at night; and that Censorinus had some valuable remarks on the subject. Two incidents that occurred about this time made an impression upon Stephen's mind.

The first was after an unusually uneasy and oppressed night that he had passed – though he could not recall any particular dream that he had had.

The following evening Mrs Bunch was occupying herself in mending his nightgown.

'Gracious me, Master Stephen!' she broke forth rather irritably, 'how do you manage to tear your nightdress all to flinders this way? Look here, sir, what trouble you do give to poor servants that have to darn and mend after you!'

There was indeed a most destructive and apparently wanton series of slits or scorings in the garment, which would undoubtedly require a skilful needle to make good. They were confined to the left side of the chest – long, parallel slits, about six inches in length, some of them not quite piercing the texture of the linen. Stephen could only express his entire ignorance of their origin: he was sure they were not there the night before.

'But,' he said, 'Mrs Bunch, they are just the same as the scratches on the outside of my bedroom door; and I'm sure I never had anything to do with making *them*'.

Mrs Bunch gazed at him open-mouthed, then snatched up a candle, departed hastily fom the room, and was heard making her way upstairs. In a few minutes she came down.

'Well,' she said, 'Master Stephen, it's a funny thing to me how them marks and scratches can 'a' come there – too high up for any cat or dog to 'ave made 'em, much less a rat: for all the world like a Chinaman's finger-nails, as my uncle in the tea-trade used to tell us of when we was girls together. I wouldn't say nothing to master, not if I was you, Master Stephen, my dear; and just turn the key of the door when you go to your bed.'

'I always do, Mrs Bunch, as soon as I've said my prayers.'

'Ah, that's a good child: always say your prayers, and then no one can't hurt you.'

Herewith Mrs Bunch addressed herself to mending the injured nightgown, with intervals of meditation, until bedtime. This was on a Friday night in March 1812.

On the following evening the usual duet of Stephen and Mrs Bunch was augmented by the sudden arrival of Mr Parkes, the butler, who as a rule kept himself rather to himself in his own pantry. He did not see that Stephen was there: he was, moreover, flustered, and less slow of speech than was his wont.

'Master may get up his own wine, if he likes, of an evening,' was his first remark. 'Either I do it in the daytime or not at all, Mrs Bunch. I don't know what it may be: very like it's the rats, or the wind got into the cellars; but I'm not so young as I was, and I can't go through with it as I have done.'

'Well Mr Parkes, you know it is a surprising place for the rats, is the Hall.'

'I'm not denying that, Mrs Bunch; and, to be sure, many a time I've heard the tale from the men in the shipyards about the rat that could speak. I never laid no confidence in that before; but tonight, if I'd demeaned myself to lay my ear to the door of the further bin, I could pretty much have heard what they was saying.'

'Oh, there, Mr Parkes, I've no patience with your fancies! Rats talking

15

in the wine-cellar indeed!'

'Well, Mrs Bunch, I've no wish to argue with you: all I say is, if you choose to go to the far bin, and lay your ear to the door, you may prove my words this minute.'

'What nonsense you do talk, Mr Parkes – not fit for children to listen to! Why, you'll be frightening Master Stephen there out of his wits.'

'What! Master Stephen?' said Parkes, awaking to the consciousness of the boy's presence. 'Master Stephen knows well enough when I'm a-playing a joke with you, Mrs Bunch.'

In fact, Master Stephen knew much too well to suppose that Parkes had in the first instance intended a joke. He was interested, not altogether pleasantly, in the situation; but all his questions were unsuccessful in inducing the butler to give any more detailed account of his experiences in the wine-cellar.

★   ★   ★   ★

We have now arrived at 24 March 1812. It was a day of curious experiences for Stephen: a windy, noisy day, which filled the house and the gardens with a restless impression. As Stephen stood by the fence of the grounds, and looked out into the park, he felt as if an endless procession of unseen people were sweeping past him on the wind, borne on restlessly and aimlessly, vainly striving to stop themselves, to catch at something that might arrest their flight and bring them once again into contact with the living world of which they had formed a part. After luncheon that day Mr Abney said:

'Stephen, my boy, do you think you could manage to come to me tonight as late as eleven o'clock in my study? I shall be busy until that time, and I wish to show you something connected with your future life which it is most important that you should know. You are not to mention this matter to Mrs Bunch nor to anyone else in the house; and you had better go to your room at the usual time.'

Here was a new excitement added to life: Stephen eagerly grasped at the opportunity of sitting up until eleven o'clock. He looked in at the library door on his way upstairs that evening, and saw a brazier, which he had often noticed in the corner of the room, moved out before the fire; an old silver-gilt cup stood on the table, filled with red wine, and some written sheets of paper lay near it. Mr Abney was sprinkling some incense on the brazier from a round silver box as Stephen passed, but did not seem to notice his step.

The wind had fallen, and there was a still night and a full moon. At about ten o'clock Stephen was standing at the open window of his bedroom, looking out over the country. Still as the night was, the mysterious population of the distant moonlit woods was not yet lulled to rest. From time to time strange cries as of lost and despairing wanderers sounded from across the mere. They might be the notes of owls or water-birds, yet they did not quite resemble either sound. Were not they coming nearer? Now they sounded from the nearer side of the water, and in a few moments they seemed to be floating about among the shrubberies. Then they ceased; but just as Stephen was thinking of shutting the window and resuming his reading of *Robinson Crusoe*, he caught sight of two figures standing on the gravelled terrace that ran along the garden side of the Hall – the figures of a boy and girl, as it seemed; they stood side by side, looking up at the windows. Something in the form of the girl recalled irresistibly his dream of the figure in the bath. The boy inspired him with more acute fear.

Whilst the girl stood still, half smiling, with her hands clasped over her heart, the boy, a thin shape, with black hair and ragged clothing, raised his arms in the air with an appearance of menace and of unappeasable hunger and longing. The moon shone upon his almost transparent hands, and Stephen saw that the nails were fearfully long and that the light shone through them. As he stood with his arms thus raised, he disclosed a terrifying spectacle. On the left side of his chest there opened a black and gaping rent; and there fell upon Stephen's brain, rather than upon his ear, the impression of one of those hungry and desolate cries that he had heard resounding over the woods of Aswarby all that evening. In another moment this dreadful pair had moved swiftly and noiselessly over the dry gravel, and he saw them no more.

Inexpressibly frightened as he was, he determined to take his candle and go down to Mr Abney's study, for the hour appointed for their meeting was near at hand. The study or library opened out of the front hall on one side, and Stephen, urged on by his terrors, did not take long in getting there. To effect an entrance was not so easy. The door was not locked, he felt sure, for the key was on the outside of it as usual. His

17

repeated knocks produced no answer. Mr Abney was engaged: he was speaking. What! why did he try to cry out? and why was the cry choked in his throat? Had he, too, seen the mysterious children? But now everything was quiet, and the door yielded to Stephen's terrified and frantic pushing.

★　　　★　　　★　　　★

On the table in Mr Abney's study certain papers were found which explained the situation to Stephen Elliott when he was of an age to understand them. The most important sentences were as follows:

It was a belief very strongly and generally held by the ancients – of whose wisdom in these matters I have had such experience as induces me to place confidence in their assertions – that by enacting certain processes which to us moderns have something of a barbaric complexion, a very remarkable enlightenment of the spiritual faculties in man may be attained: that, for example, by absorbing the personalities of a certain number of his fellow-creatures, an individual may gain a complete ascendancy over those orders of spiritual beings which control the elemental forces of our universe.

It is recorded of Simon Magnus that he was able to fly in the air, to become invisible, or to assume any form he pleased, by the agency of the soul of a boy whom, to use the libellous phrase employed by the author of the *Clementine Recognitions*, he had 'murdered'. I find it set down, moreover, with considerable detail in the writings of Hermes Trismegistus, that similar happy results may be produced by the absorption of the hearts of not less than three human beings below the age of twenty-one years. To the testing of the truth of this receipt I have devoted the greater part of the last twenty years, selecting as the *corpora vilia* of my experiment such persons as could conveniently be removed without occasioning a sensible gap in society. The first step I effected by the removal of one Phoebe Stanley, a girl of gipsy extraction, on 24 March 1792. The second by the removal of a wandering Italian lad, named Giovanni Paoli, on the night of 23 March 1805. The final 'victim' – to employ a word repugnant in the highest degree to my feelings – must be my cousin, Stephen Elliott. His day must be this 24 March 1812.

The best means of effecting the required absorption is to remove the heart from the *living* subject, to reduce it to ashes, and to mingle them with about a pint of some red wine, preferably port. The remains of the first two subjects, at least, it will be well to conceal: a disused bathroom or wine-cellar will be found convenient for such a purpose. Some annoyance may be experienced from the psychic portion of the subjects, which popular language dignifies with the name of ghosts. But the man of philosophic temperament – to whom alone the experiment is appropriate – will be little prone to attach importance to the feeble efforts of these beings to wreak their vengeance on him. I contemplate with the liveliest satisfaction the enlarged and emancipated existence which the experiment, if successful, will confer on me; not only placing me beyond the reach of human justice (so-called), but eliminating to a great extent the prospect of death itself.

Mr Abney was found in his chair, his head thrown back, his face stamped with an expression of rage, fright, and mortal pain. In his left side was a terrible lacerated wound, exposing the heart. There was no blood on his hands, and a long knife that lay on the table was perfectly clean. A savage wild-cat might have inflicted the injuries. The window of the study was open, and it was the opinion of the coroner that Mr Abney had met his death by the agency of some wild creature. But Stephen Elliott's study of the papers I have quoted led him to a very different conclusion.

THE MUSIC ON THE HILL
Saki

Sylvia Seltoun ate her breakfast in the morning-room at Yessney with a
pleasant sense of ultimate victory, such as a fervent Ironside might have
permitted himself on the morrow of Worcester fight. She was scarcely
pugnacious by temperament, but belonged to that more successful class
of fighters who are pugnacious by circumstance. Fate had willed that her
life should be occupied with a series of small struggles, usually with the
odds slightly against her, and usually she had just managed to come
through winning. And now she felt that she had brought her hardest and
certainly her most important struggle to a successful issue. To have
married Mortimer Seltoun, 'Dead Mortimer' as his more intimate
enemies called him, in the teeth of the cold hostility of his family, and in
spite of his unaffected indifference to women, was indeed an
achievement that had needed some determination and adroitness to carry
through; yesterday she had brought her victory to its concluding stage
by wrenching her husband away from Town and its group of satellite
watering-places and 'settling him down,' in the vocabulary of her kind,
in this remote wood-girt manor farm which was his country house.

'You will never get Mortimer to go,' his mother had said carpingly, 'but if he once goes he'll stay; Yessney throws almost as much a spell over him as Town does. One can understand what holds him to Town, but Yessney—' and the dowager had shrugged her shoulders.

There was a sombre almost savage wildness about Yessney that was certainly not likely to appeal to town-bred tastes, and Sylvia, notwithstanding her name, was accustomed to nothing much more sylvan than leafy Kensington. She looked on the country as something excellent and wholesome in its way, which was apt to become troublesome if you encouraged it overmuch. Distrust of town-life had been a new thing with her, born of her marriage with Mortimer, and she had watched with satisfaction the gradual fading of what she called 'the Jermyn-Street-look' in his eyes as the woods and heather of Yessney had closed in on them yesternight. Her will-power and strategy had prevailed; Mortimer would stay.

Outside the morning-room windows was a triangular slope of turf, which the indulgent might call a lawn, and beyond its low hedge of neglected fuchsia bushes, a steeper slope of heather and bracken dropped down into cavernous combes overgrown with oak and yew. In its wild open savagery there seemed a stealthy linking of the joy of life with the terror of unseen things. Sylvia smiled complacently as she gazed with a School-of-Art appreciation at the landscape, and then of a sudden she almost shuddered.

'It is very wild,' she said to Mortimer, who had joined her; 'one could almost think that in such a place the worship of Pan had never quite died out.'

'The worship of Pan never has died out,' said Mortimer. 'Other newer gods have drawn aside his votaries from time to time, but he is the Nature-God to whom all must come back at last. He has been called the Father of all the Gods, but most of his children have been stillborn.'

Sylvia was religious in an honest, vaguely devotional kind of way, and did not like to hear her beliefs spoken of as mere aftergrowths, but it was at least something new and hopeful to hear Dead Mortimer speak with such energy and conviction on any subject.

'You don't really believe in Pan?' she asked incredulously.

'I've been a fool in most things,' said Mortimer quietly, 'but I'm not such a fool as not to believe in Pan when I'm down here. And if you're wise you won't disbelieve in him too boastfully while you're in his country.'

It was not until a week later, when Sylvia had exhausted the attractions of the woodland walks round Yessney, that she ventured on a tour of inspection of the farm buildings. A farmyard suggested in her mind a scene of cheerful bustle, with churns and flails and smiling dairymaids, and teams of horses drinking knee-deep in duck-crowded ponds. As she wandered among the gaunt grey buildings of Yessney manor farm, her first impression was one of crushing stillness and desolation, as though she had happened on some lone deserted homestead long given over to owls and cobwebs; then came a sense of furtive watchful hostility, the same shadow of unseen things that seemed to lurk in the wooded combes and coppices. From behind heavy doors and shuttered windows came the restless stamp of hoof or rasp of chain halter, and at times a muffled bellow from some stalled beast. From a distant corner a shaggy dog watched her with intent unfriendly eyes; as she drew near, it slipped quietly into its kennel, and slipped out again as noiselessly when she had passed by. A few hens, questing for food under a rick, stole away under a gate at her approach. Sylvia felt that if she had come across any human beings in this wilderness of barn and byre, they would have fled wraith-like from her gaze. At last, turning a corner quickly, she came upon a living thing that did not fly from her. Astretch in a pool of mud was an enormous sow, gigantic beyond the town-woman's wildest computation of swine-flesh, and speedily alert to resent and if necessary repel the unwonted intrusion. It was Sylvia's turn to make an unobtrusive retreat. As she threaded her way past rickyards and cowsheds and long blank walls, she started suddenly at a strange sound – the echo of a boy's laughter, golden and equivocal. Jan, the only boy employed on the farm, a tow-headed, wizen-faced yokel, was visibly at work on a potato clearing half-way up the nearest hillside, and Mortimer, when questioned, knew of no other probable or possible begetter of the hidden mockery that had ambushed Sylvia's retreat. The memory of that untraceable echo was added to her other impressions of a furtive sinister 'something' that hung around Yessney.

Of Mortimer she saw very little; farm and woods and trout-streams seemed to swallow him up from dawn till dusk. Once, following the direction she had seen him take in the morning, she came to an open space in a nut copse, further shut in by huge yew trees, in the centre of which stood a stone pedestal surmounted by a small bronze figure of a youthful Pan. It was a beautiful piece of workmanship, but her attention was chiefly held by the fact that a newly cut bunch of grapes had been placed as an offering at its feet. Grapes were none too plentiful at the manor house, and Sylvia snatched the bunch angrily from the pedestal. Contemptuous annoyance dominated her thoughts as she strolled slowly homeward, and then gave way to a sharp feeling of something that was very near fright; across a thick tangle of undergrowth a boy's face was scowling at her, brown and beautiful, with unutterably evil eyes. It was a lonely pathway, all pathways round Yessney were lonely for the matter of that, and she sped forward without waiting to give a closer scrutiny to this sudden apparition. It was not till she had reached the house that she discovered that she had dropped the bunch of grapes in her flight.

'I saw a youth in the wood today,' she told Mortimer that evening, 'brown-faced and rather handsome, but a scoundrel to look at. A gipsy lad, I suppose,'

'A reasonable theory,' said Mortimer, 'only there aren't any gipsies in these parts at present.'

'Then who was he?' asked Sylvia, and as Mortimer appeared to have no theory of his own, she passed on to recount her finding of the votive offering.

'I suppose it was your doing,' she observed; 'it's a harmless piece of lunacy, but people would think you dreadfully silly if they knew of it.'

'Did you meddle with it in any way?' asked Mortimer.

'I – I threw the grapes away. It seemed so silly,' said Sylvia, watching Mortimer's impassive face for a sign of annoyance.

'I don't think you were wise to do that,' he said reflectively. 'I've heard it said that the Wood Gods are rather horrible to those who molest them.'

'Horrible perhaps to those that believe in them, but you see I don't,' retorted Sylvia.

'All the same,' said Mortimer in his even, dispassionate tone, 'I should avoid the woods and orchards if I were you, and give a wide berth to the horned beasts on the farm.'

It was all nonsense, of course, but in that lonely wood-girt spot nonsense seemed able to rear a bastard brood of uneasiness.

'Mortimer,' said Sylvia suddenly, 'I think we will go back to Town some time soon.'

Her victory had not been so complete as she had supposed; it had carried her on to ground that she was already anxious to quit.

'I don't think you will ever go back to Town,' said Mortimer. He seemed to be paraphrasing his mother's prediction as to himself.

Sylvia noted with dissatisfaction and some self-contempt that the course of her next afternoon's ramble took her instinctively clear of the network of woods. As to the horned cattle, Mortimer's warning was scarcely needed for she had always regarded them as of doubtful neutrality at the best; her imagination unsexed the most matronly dairy cows and turned them into bulls liable to 'see red' at any moment. The ram who fed in the narrow paddock below the orchards she had adjudged, after ample and cautious probation, to be of docile temper; today, however, she decided to leave his docility untested, for the usually tranquil beast was roaming with every sign of restlessness from corner to corner of his meadow. A low, fitful piping, as of some reedy flute, was coming from the depth of a neighbouring copse, and there seemed to be some subtle connection between the animal's restless pacing and the wild music from the wood. Sylvia turned her steps in an upward direction and climbed the heather-clad slopes that stretched in rolling shoulders high above Yessney. She had left the piping notes behind her, but across the wooded combes at her feet the wind brought her another kind of music, the straining bay of hounds in full chase. Yessney was just on the outskirts of the Devon-and-Somerset country, and the hunted deer sometimes came that way. Sylvia could presently see a dark body, breasting hill after hill, and sinking again and again out of sight as he crossed the combes, while behind him steadily swelled that relentless chorus, and she grew tense with the excited sympathy that one feels for any hunted thing in whose capture one is not directly interested. And at last he broke through the outermost line of oak scrub and fern and stood panting in the open, a fat September stag carrying a well-furnished head. His obvious course was to drop down to the brown pools of Undercombe, and thence make his way towards the red deer's favoured sanctuary, the sea. To Sylvia's surprise, however, he turned his head to the upland slope and came lumbering resolutely onward over the heather. 'It will be dreadful,' she thought, 'the hounds will pull him down under my very eyes.' But the music of the pack seemed to have died away for a moment, and in its place she heard again that wild piping, which rose now on this side, now on that, as though urging the failing stag to a final effort. Sylvia stood well aside from his path, half hidden in a thick growth of whortle bushes, and watched him swing stiffly upward, his flanks dark with sweat, the coarse hair on his neck showing light by contrast. The pipe music suddenly shrilled around her, seeming to come from the bushes at her very feet, and at the same moment the great beast slewed round and bore directly down upon her. In an instant her pity for the hunted animal was changed to wild terror at her own danger; the thick heather roots mocked her scrambling efforts at flight, and she looked frantically downward for a glimpse of oncoming hounds. The huge antler spikes were within a few yards of her, and in a flash of numbing fear she remembered Mortimer's warning, to beware of horned beasts on the farm. And then with a quick throb of joy she saw that she was not alone; a human figure stood a few paces aside, knee-deep in the whortle bushes.

'Drive it off!' she shrieked. But the figure made no answering movement.

The antlers drove straight at her breast, the acrid smell of the hunted animal was in her nostrils, but her eyes were filled with the horror of something she saw other than her oncoming death. And in her ears rang the echo of a boy's laughter, golden and equivocal.

THE PHANTOM SHIP
Jean Morris

To hear my grandfather talk, you would have thought that the ruin of
our harbour had come about all in one night, with him watching every
minute of it. He made a good story of it, with the great storm battering
away our sea-wall, and the tide pouring through the breaches to mumble
and gnaw away whole streets of houses; and, since we always lost a few
houses to the sea every winter, even the youngest of us children could
picture it all happening.

But seaward of the town, on the estuary side, the mud-flats that had
silted up our deep-water anchorage stretched a mile and more at low tide,
and never a sign was to be seen of any sea-wall. My father, who was a
lettered man, and had his mate's ticket before he was lost when the
Martha B. went down with all hands, told me that the great storm had
been so long ago that not even my grandfather's grandfather could have
seen it, and that if there was anything left of the old sea-wall it was three
miles under the open sea now.

'We were a great port then,' he would say, and sigh.

'Well, and when we've built our new sea-wall,' I would say, parroting
my grandfather, 'we'll be a great port again'; and if I got any answer to
that it would be from my mother, snapping at me not to listen to those
fools of old men. Not that I took notice of her. The town in my day was a

little straggle of fishermen's houses, of which ours was the last, and even I remembered five to seaward which the sea had taken; but, since I had never seen anything finer, I thought we were the equal of any port on any shore: just, perhaps, a little struck with bad luck for a few years.

My father, while more patient with my grandfather, would grow short with me sometimes and tell me to use my head.

'They say they'll build a new sea-wall with our harbour-dues. What harbour-dues will we get until we've a deep-water anchorage? And how do we get a deep-water anchorage without a sea-wall?'

But no more than my grandfather did I let good sense interfere with my dreams. So when, one night in the spring when I was thirteen, I woke to see a drenching sea-mist hard up against my window, and just pricking through it the dead yellow sparks that could only be the riding-lights of a big ship – why, then I tumbled on my clothes and was out by way of the coal-house roof, determined to be in the middle of everything that was going on.

The tide was at springs, so I made for the little ramshackle jetty that was all the harbourage we had, and plugged along its hollow-sounding planks. I suppose I knew how little depth of water there was there even at best, and it did come to me that the mast-head light had seemed higher than any light I had ever seen before. But then a sea-mist is notoriously deceptive, and certainly from down here I could not see so much as a spar of her rigging; and since she was there, I couldn't say that that was impossible in our shallow channels, could I?

But I remember – oh, I *do* remember! – how her sides rose above me as I trotted on. She was clinker-built, her timbers all ashine with the wet. For there was nothing but the wet (was there?) to give them that fish-back glow.

I was even pleased to find myself alone, since it meant that I was first out. Not that I had the least notion that anyone would notice me, except to cuff me out of the way, or – by great good luck – send me on some errand. A boy thinking himself unnoticed can appear very bold. Very boldly I trotted along our jetty looking out for signs of the crew of this ship.

There were signs, but not very many, none of the bustle of a ship making a strange port and the officers singing out their orders. Every now and again a head would lift over the rail above me, and the pale blur of a face look down, and there was certainly a great scurry of feet and a frantic mutter of voices. I don't know what gave me the idea that all the mutters were about me, so that suddenly I felt shy and stopped where I was. One of the crew, I saw, wore a stocking cap, and because I wore one myself I waved at it; but it ducked down at once. Instead, I found myself looking at the Captain.

I never had any doubt but that he was the Captain, though I would not have expected him to be down at the rail. He was a big man, with a thick square beard all silvered by the mist, and something about his face, with its slitted eyes and short strong nose, made me fancy him perhaps German; and his accent when he hailed me had the throaty, jerky sound of those northern coasts. Not that I took much notice of that, for what he said was so absurd that it set me gaping.

'Harbour-master,' he said, 'have we your permission to land?'

Who in his senses could take a scrubby boy in a cut-down jersey for the harbour-master? And, though I knew little enough about it, that seemed to me a curious way for a ship's captain to speak. I stuttered in answering, saying something like 'No no, sir – the harbour-master will be here –' Perhaps he heard only my first little squeak of denial; and yet it seemed to me almost as if he heard nothing at all, as if he were playing out his side of a scene without realising that the moment for it was not come. With his deep abrupt voice sounding all hollow in the mist, he said over the rail, 'Will you come aboard, sir, and discuss it?'

Would I go aboard? – I should be the hero of every boy in the town if I had been aboard. But there is little a boy doesn't know about cunning, since he spends his days practising it, in joke or earnest, on his friends and his elders; and I knew that the Captain was being cunning with me in this invitation. But, since it was meant for the harbour-master, what harm could there be in my accepting it, since all I had to do was to explain matters? I looked around for a rope to swarm up, and then saw that they were actually putting out a gang-plank for me.

Again, I never quite saw them, though I sensed the scurrying and muttering, and once I saw a pale head looking at me over the rail. It must have been a bald man with a queer growth of beard, so fearful were the shadows in the cheeks. I looked for the stocking cap, being sure that it was a boy who wore it, and envying him his place. I never saw it, for the gang-plank grounded on the jetty and I stepped up it; only, just as I put

28

out my hand to take hold of the ship's rail, a boy's voice cried out. It cried out, no doubt, in a foreign tongue; but then *No!* cried high in outrage and warning sounds much the same in any language.

I believe I stopped dead, with my hand in the air above the rail. But there at the head of the gang-plank was the Captain, though I hadn't seen him coming, and so affable that for pure shame I had to put my hand to the rail and step down on deck. And though I could still see no crew, I heard their muttering still to one great soft sigh.

Welcome on board, sir,' said the Captain, and touched his cap. At close quarters he was a great grim man, with folds between his brows and folds from nose to mouth – and Lord save us, how wasted he was! The beard hid the worst of it, but if you can imagine a broad false smile on a naked skull, that was his face. And here he was behaving as if a boy were the grandest of visitors! Perhaps a grown man would have been flattered into believing in him; but inwardly I writhed with the shame of it.

'Cap'n sir –' I began, and he would not let me finish.

'Captain van der Decken, sir, at your service,' he said, though I noticed that he did not add the name of his ship and her home port.

'Captain van der Decken, sir – I'm truly not the harbour-master. He'll be coming, sir, he'll be here if you'll just be patient –'

'And then I don't doubt,' he said smiling – he said it without a blink, as if he had never mistaken me –, 'that you will give us leave to land. It will not trouble me to pay something over and above your harbour dues.'

Harbour dues? – for the building of the new sea-wall? My face must have shown my covetousness, for he smiled the easier, as if at last I were playing my proper part in his scene.

'Pray allow me,' he said, 'to show you something I fancy you will not have seen before.' And he linked his arm in mine and took me forrard. I was small for my age, so that he had to stoop to do it, and make believe that he did not know how grotesque a pair we made, so that I shrivelled inwardly with shame and could only go with him.

Now on such a ship I had expected to see spanking new paint, clean decks, and gleaming brass-work. The mist was still boiling thick, and they had only a couple of lanterns hanging lit and it seemed to me that it was more by the light of the ship itself that I saw the salt-bleached wood under the cracking paint, and the dead green-black of old brass. Under the poop-deck, I suppose, was the Captain's cabin, and though I had heard no orders given the crew were dragging something out through the door. You would have thought that now I could have made out more of the crew, but in that light all I could see was here an arm hauling, and there bare feet slipping on the deck with the weight of the burden. I looked out for the stocking cap, and thought I caught a friendly gleam from a boy's eye; but then they had all scurried away again, and it came into my head somehow that the scurrying sounded just like rats at their business behind a wainscoting.

'Now I venture to claim,' said the Captain magnificently, 'that this will surprise you. And once you have seen it I fancy that there will be no trouble about your harbour dues, and you will invite us to land.'

And he put his toe to the thing that stood there, as if trifling pleasantly with it, while it was plain on his face that he could hardly bear to be near it. It was a sea-chest, and when he at last tipped open its lid I could not help but gasp. It was three-quarters full of coin, all of it gold, and on top of the coin a tangle of jewels.

'And since you, sir,' he said carelessly, 'were so kind as to be first on board, allow me to offer you some trifles for your trouble.'

There was a jewel-hilted knife I lusted after, and a wonderful red ring I would have given my mother. How did he know? – he swept them up and put them into my hands.

'You see that we can pay our way,' he said, and he leant over me, and his voice grew hollower. 'You will surely invite us to land. How long do you think we have been at sea?'

How long? – well, how should I know? But he swept an arm around, and there were his crew, lining the rail with their backs to me, yearning for the land. I was a seaman's son; I knew how they felt; I had seen my own father come home again after months. There came over me a little cold shudder, because you must always take care what you make free of your home. But these were seamen like ourselves; it seemed only civil to say 'Why, sir, if your men wish a run on shore, I've no doubt but that in my town they will be –'

And then at last the stocking cap turned round, and the boy who wore it lifted his bare arms and let me see him.

I had never seen plague before, but I knew it when I saw it. It struck the fatal word dumb on my lips. The Captain gave a great cry of rage and struck at the boy, and I dropped the jewels and tried to stop the blow. I seemed not to touch anything, but a great jolt stung all my bones, and I fetched up on my knees on the deck, and bruised my hands on the jewels I had let fall. And as I knelt I saw that the blade of the knife I had wanted was crusted with old powdery blood, and that through the ring, very small and withered, were the bones of a finger.

So I knew what ship I had boarded, and I gave myself up for dead. I looked up, and through the boiling of the mist saw that in that dead calm the ship carried all sail set.

I said to the Captain, 'Cap'n sir, you are the Flying Dutchman.' Since I was lost body and soul, I found I could think and speak quite steady; and since he saw that, he could drop his falseness and be as he was, which was grim and unsmiling.

'I have been so called,' he said, and at the rail the crew had all turned my way, and every one of them bore the marks of plague.

'And this treasure you got by piracy and murder; and with it you got the plague; and now there is no harbour on earth will let you land.'

'And now not yours,' he said. 'We have been looking for one these three hundred years.'

But I was a boy who had been looking for a friend, and had found one. I looked at the boy in the stocking cap, who could not smile because he was in agony, and cried in outrage, 'But he is dying!'

The Captain said, 'He has been dying for three hundred years.'

Oh, I was angry! I went to the boy, and pulled his arm over my shoulder so that I could take his weight, and said to him, 'You come with me. You can have my bed, and you'll lie easier there.'

He sighed once, and slid away from me, and died on the deck.

I got up from his side after a time, and found that they were all around me, bare-headed, and not noticing me. The Captain said in a matter-of-fact way, 'Well, another of us gone. Three, is it now?'

'Three,' they agreed among themselves, nodding and counting them on their fingers. 'There was Jakob, and that girl who rowed out selling fruit. She'd have asked us ashore, but he said we weren't to fool her, and he fell asleep peaceful that night and never woke again. And there was Anders at the helm, who disobeyed orders that night we were steering for his home port, and next morning the helm was swinging free and he was dead aside it. And now little Jan. Well, Cap'n sir,' they said – God help them, they made a joke of it! – 'how many more years at this rate, do

31

you reckon?'

'Three tides short of the crack of doom,' the Captain returned grimly. 'And I'll be the last of you. The Captain stays with his ship until the end. Come on, lads, take him below and set him down trim in his hammock, and we'll bury him once we're in deep water.'

I watched them, while they went about this task, with my head in a mist of confusion. I might not have been there – did they even see me, now that I was of no further use to them? I took a stealing terrified step backwards, and then another and another, and felt the deathly cold of the rail under my hands; and still no one saw me.

I was over the rail in a flash, not caring how far I had to fall, tumbling into ten foot of sandy water and from it flailing my way under the shelter of the jetty. When I had recovered my breath and a very little of my courage I paddled to the edge of the shadow and peered out.

The tide was on the ebb and the mist thinning, and though there was no breath of wind I could see very faintly the masts of a ship with all sail set drawing away into the darkness. I pulled myself out of the water and knelt on the jetty to watch, and with all my heart I tried to feel forgiveness for the Captain and the crew. For I thought that if I could do that, they would all die in peace, and the ship would settle to the bottom, and the timbers and bones would mingle with the stones of our lost sea-wall.

But all I could think of was that, except for Jan, they had tried to fool me, and, except for Jan, they had tried to bribe me, and that though they had suffered three hundred years for it they were all pirates and murderers anyway.

So, for all I know, they are sailing still. And it is only sometimes that I wonder whose doing that is – theirs who did the wrong, or mine who would not forgive it.

Across a thick tangle of undergrowth a boy's face was scowling at her. (p.23)

There was a jewel-hilted knife I lusted after. (p.30)

THE BLADES

Joan Aiken

Right from the start they were enemies. Or at least on opposite sides. Maybe that was to be expected with two boys so diametrically different from each other as Jack Kettering and Will Donkine. Kettering was tall, or tallish, solidly built, with a flat, high-cheekboned, ruddy, handsome face, and a thick crop of burnished red-gold hair. His dad was a Master of Foxhounds, and when the older Kettering came to the school for speechdays you could see just what Jack would become in the course of time—solid, swaggering, red-faced, with his thatch of shining hair turned snowy white. Kettering excelled at all sports—cricket, football, rowing, swimming, athletics; and he was by no means a fool, either; had a knack of learning anything by heart that could be learned in that way, so grammar, mathematical and scientific formulae, dates, facts were always at his finger-tips, passing exams was no trouble to him; he was generally among the top four or five at the year's end. He could be funny, too, in a rather unsubtle way, and generous—at least to his friends—he had that sort of air about him which people like Francis Drake and Robin Hood must have carried, so that followers, as it were, flocked to his standard. Not that I mean to say he was an outlaw—oh dear, no. Law-abiding, on the whole, was Jack, more so as he went up the school; of course there was the odd quiet escapade, beer drunk behind the art studios and then whisky in the boat-house, dodging off to go to the Motor Show and a night on the spree in London, but these were just schoolboy capers, nothing nasty about them. He enjoyed the reputation of being a good-natured, easy-going fellow. His lot, there were about half a dozen of them, the Blades, they called themselves, were the same kind, and they stuck together all the way up the school.

Later on, when girls were admitted into the upper forms, they all acquired girlfriends to match: Kettering's girl was called Pamela Cassell, and she was big and blooming and bossy, with a head of brick-red hair to match Jack's copper-gold, always freshly shampooed and shining and crisp. Captain of the girls' hockey, she was, won the tennis cup three years running, and intended to run a ballroom-dancing school. She had that pink-and-white complexion often found in red-heads, and pale china-blue eyes; striking, people said she was, but I couldn't see it myself. If you didn't belong to Kettering's group her eyes passed over you in utter rejection, you might as well have been a garden bench.

Donkine, Will Donkine was, as I've said, in all ways the complete opposite of Jack. From the start, poor devil, he suffered from his name. Will was short for Willibald, which was a family name; some ancestor had come from Austria—Willibald Edvard Donkine, his full name was, so if he wasn't called the Hun, or Kraut, or Donk, or Donkey, it was Weed or Weedy because of his initials. He came to the school when he was twelve, and by the time he was fourteen the various nicknames had more or less settled down into Donk. Of course it cut no ice at all that his father, Sir Joel Donkine, was a well-known scientist, in line for the Nobel prize. Will Donkine was small and bony, with a pale hollow-eyed face, short-sighted serious dark-brown eyes (he had to wear steel-rimmed glasses which were always getting broken), and sparse no-colour hair like a crop of mousy moss on top of his undistinguished head. Being so short-sighted he was no use at games, and anyway his arms and legs were thin as sticks of celery so he couldn't run fast or catch balls or hit them; he was bright enough, but his wits had a habit of wandering, so that he didn't do particularly well in exams; when he ought to have been answering Question 2, he'd be looking out of the window trying to estimate the flight-speed of swifts, or wondering if it would be possible to turn a Black Hole inside out, or to compress Mars Bars to the size of dice for rapid and economic distribution. His conversation was always interesting—he knew a lot about codes, and ESP, and how people's discarded selves may come back to haunt them (he read books on psychology when most people were reading Biggles) and where you can still find bits of primeval forest in Europe, and what to do if you sit on a queen bee, but his knowledge wasn't very well applied; it never turned up when it was needed. I liked Donkine's company, but he wasn't a popular boy. Part of that was his own fault. He found most people boring; simply preferred his own thoughts. I expect they were more interesting than locker-room chat, but, just the same, if you don't want to have a dismal time at school you need to meet people half-way, display a bit of give-and-take. Donkine did nothing of that kind, so he was an outcast. His solitary state didn't worry him in the least, he spent his spare time reading in the library or measuring things in the lab, or working in his allotment. He was very keen on gardening.

It must be said that Kettering and the Blades gave him a fairly hard time, specially when we were all younger; every now and then they'd rough him up, not *too* much, of course, because they didn't want to spoil their reputation for being decent types; never anything that would show. To do Donkine justice, he never grassed on them; for a day or two he'd go about rather more silent and hunched over, shabbier and a trifle more moth-eaten-looking, that was all. What he did mind was when they messed up his garden; that really hit him in a tender spot. But, as luck would have it, old Postlethwaite the science master was out at three a.m. one night studying a comet and came on Kettering and McGeech systematically digging up Will's artichokes and celeriac, so there was a certain amount of fuss about that, and from then on they had to lay off the garden sabotage; it would have been too obvious that it was them, see? They had to think of other forms of persecution.

White Kettering and the Blades were acquiring girlfriends and boasting of their exploits, Will made friends with my sister Ceridwen, who was small and dark and cross-looking. Nothing romantic about their friendship: they were both interested in the same kinds of things. Ceridwen intended to do animal- and plant-breeding later on, and she was very impressed with Will's aptitude for growing things.

By the time we were in the lower Fifth, Will's father had invented his dust extractor, D.R.I.P., it was called, Dust Removal from Industrial and Institutional Premises. Of course it was shortened to DRIP. Don't ask me how it worked—it was a thermo-nuclear process, radioactivity came into it, and magnetic fields, and the earth's rotation and gravitational pull. Unlike many such processes, it was simple and economical to install. What it did was suck all the dust and grit and germs out of the air inside a building by means of vents on the floor, so that once a DRIP System was installed in your factory—or office block—or hospital—you need never sweep or dust or Hoover or scrub again. There have been similar systems in the past, of course, but expensive to run, and none were so efficient as Sir J. Donkine's. Apparently it really did remove every particle and molecule of anything nasty from the atmosphere so that the air you breathed into your lungs was 100% Simon-pure.

Naturally a process, an invention like this was nothing like so sensational as discovering penicillin or DNA or splitting the atom; but still there were articles about it in scientific journals, and old Corfe our headmaster mentioned it in a congratulatory way one morning at Assembly, and said we must all be proud that Sir J. was an Old Boy of our school and his son was our dear fellow-scholar, and we must hope that Will would invent something equally useful one day. I noticed Will give a kind of blink behind his glasses at that; he was not at all gratified by being singled out, and I knew why; of course for him it would mean extra hazing and sarcastic broadsides from the Blades for several weeks, till the news had settled down. Old Corfe, who never knew anything about what went on in the school, was unaware of that, naturally; and he was pleased as a dog with two tails about the publicity for the school.

Because of this connection, and before anyone had finished asking 'What About Side Effects?' our school, along with several hospitals and a Midland furniture factory, had taken the plunge and had the Donkine DRIP System installed. A demonstration of loyalty it was, on our part, to show our faith and pride in our Old Boy (though I bet that Mr Corfe managed to get the installation done at half price because of the public interest etc. etc.). Anyway, air vents were set into the floors of all rooms, in corners where they were not inconvenient, and suction pipes, and a big gleaming white tank down in the basement which housed the works. If you held your breath and nobody else was breathing in the room you could just catch the sound of a very faint hum, no more noise than a light-bulb makes when it's at the point of death. Nobody could say the DRIP System was loud or annoying. And the school certainly was clean! Not a speck of mud, no dust or fluff could lie on any surface for more than a moment, our clothes and books and bedding and towels all stayed cleaner longer, even substances like spilled jam or glue tended to vanish overnight if not wiped up; and at the end of the first term old Corfe announced with triumph that our health rate had improved by eighty per cent, practically no head colds, hay fever, or asthma, and all other infectious complaints much reduced.

The hospitals and furniture factory had reported the same good results; by now Sir Joel Donkine was on the high road to success, fame, fortune, and the Nobel prize. DripCo, the company formed to make the DRIP Systems, could hardly keep pace with the orders; every factory and hospital in the country wanted them now; they were being installed not only in public buildings but also in private homes. Buckingham Palace, if you can call that a private home, was first on the list, and Sir Joel got a decoration from the Palace as well as his Nobel.

What was his son Will doing all this time? Will, of course, had known about his father's intentions long ago, heard the subject discussed since he was nine or ten. His mother had died, when he was six, of an anti-immunity failure, so Sir Joel tended to talk to him a lot when they were together; one of the reasons why Will found most school conversation boring.

Will's main problem after Sir Joel's rise to fame was dodging retribution from the Society of Blades—what they called 'necessary discipline' to stop him from getting above himself. *Above himself*—poor Will sometimes looked as if he wished he was under the ground. Most of the Blades, by now, were big and tough as grown men, whereas Will, at fifteen, seemed to have stopped growing for good and was no bigger than a thirteen-year-old. It wasn't for lack of fresh air; he still spent hours every day tending his garden. Unfortunately the school allotments were isolated beyond a row of utility sheds, on the edge of the school grounds; he was much at risk there from the unwelcome attentions of the Blades.

'How's our little Drip today, how's our Weed?' they would say, clustering round him affectionately. 'We've come to remind you not to get too stuck up, just because your dad invented a giant Hoover.'

Once they painted him all over with Stockholm tar, which he'd been using on a peach tree he grew from a peach-stone; another time they dropped him, and all his tools, into the river; on a third occasion they removed tufts of hair from all over his head. The effect was a bit like a chessboard. That was a mistake, because it was quite visible; old Corfe made inquiries, sent for Kettering and the Blades, and gave them a severe tongue-lashing and various penalties, so their attentions abated for a while.

And Donkine went doggedly on his way, reading a lot, keeping up reasonably well with school work, showing fitful brilliance here and there, specially in chemistry and biology; working in his garden and trying to mind his own business. Whatever that was.

'Don't you ever want to get your own back on those pigs?' my sister Ceridwen asked him once. We are Welsh; I reckon that revenge comes more naturally to us. But Will just shrugged.

'What's the point?' he said. 'They'd only make it worse for me, after. You've got to think ahead. And I've got better things to do than conduct a feud. Besides, I have an idea that by and by . . .'

He didn't finish his sentence. His eyes had wandered, as they often did, towards two huge shiny pink potatoes he had just dug up, and a tussock of grass he had pulled out.

One thing he had discovered was that DRIP compost was marvellous for the garden.

I expect you have been wondering what happened to all the dirt and dust that was sucked out of the classrooms and offices and dormitories. It went into black plastic sacks that fitted over the outlet-vents and were removed at regular intervals. The stuff inside them was like stiff dark-brown prune jam, very thick and sticky. Will found that if this was diluted and watered on to the garden, or just spaded around in gooey lumps, like undercooked Christmas pudding, it worked wonders for growing plants. A few weeks of this treatment and Will's artichokes were big as footballs, his spinach-leaves the size of the *Daily Mirror* and his roses six inches in diameter.

Postlethwaite the science master (we called him Old Possum, of course, because he had big, wide-apart gentle eyes, and very little chin, and his thin hair wavered backwards like water-weeds), old Postlethwaite was absolutely delighted at this link-up between the activities of father and son, evidence of Will's independent research.

'Wonderful work, wonderful, my dear Donkine,' he kept saying. 'You may have hit on something of real importance there.' And he quoted: ' "Whoever could make two blades of grass grow where only one grew before, would deserve better of mankind than the whole race of politicians put together." Do you know who said that?'

'Swift,' said Will without hesitation. But his mind as usual seemed half astray. 'People wore wigs in Swift's day, didn't they, sir?'

'We must see if we can't get you the Wickenden Award for this,' Old Possum went on.

The Wickenden Cup was a school honour endowed by a past rich American parent; it was given from time to time for unusually original school work.

'Oh, *please*, sir, don't bother,' said Will, who knew that anything of the kind would only lead to more trouble with Kettering's group. 'If you could just ask Mr Corfe to give an order that the black sacks aren't to be taken away by the garbage trucks but left in a heap here by the allotments. Then everybody who wants to can use them.'

But nobody else took the trouble to do so. It's true the stuff did smell rather vile: sweet and rotten like malt and codliver oil.

By and by there began to be odd, apparently disconnected paragraphs in the newspapers: the Queen had been obliged to cancel all her engagements, as she was suffering from a virus cold; a hospital in the north was plagued by an epidemic of ringworm or possibly infectious alopecia; the staff of a Midland furniture factory were all out on strike for some mysterious reason; and the Prime Minister, in the middle of a visit to Moscow, returned to Britain hurriedly and unexpectedly.

Could there be a link between these incidents? The factory and the hospital were two which had been among the first to have the DRIP System installed.

At our school, though, we didn't read the papers a lot; interested in our own affairs, we weren't much concerned with outside news. Time had skidded on its way and by now we were working for our A-levels, up to the eyes in reading and revision. Still, even busy as we were, we couldn't help observing something that was happening right under our noses.

Ceridwen, my sharp-eyed sister, spotted it first.

'All the staff are going bald,' she said. 'Have you noticed?'

It was true. The men's hair was receding at a rapid rate, and the women teachers had taken to various ruses, buns, chignons, hair-pieces, to try and conceal the fact that their locks were becoming scantier and scantier. It seemed to affect older people faster, and dark people less than fair.

Then one morning there was a crisis in the girls' dormitory.

Hysterical shrieks were heard coming from the room of big red-headed Pamela Cassell (who by this time was a prefect and so entitled to a room of her own); she had locked herself in and refused to come out. When Mrs Budleigh the matron finally opened up with a master-key, it was said that she let out almost as loud a squawk as the frantic girl inside. For—Ceridwen told me and Will, then the news spread like lightning through the girls' dorm and so out and about the main school—all Pamela Cassell's thick glossy red hair, of which she had been so proud that she let it grow to waist length—all that hair had fallen out in the night and the wretched girl was now bald as an egg, while the hair lay in a tangled mess on her pillow.

Well! What a thing! Needless to say, Pamela was whisked away to a skin and hair specialist; and what he said was so unhelpful that she flatly refused to come back to school, as long as she was such a spectacle, so that was the last we saw of her. Will certainly wasn't sorry. In the old days she used sometimes to stand by and watch while the Blades did things to him.

Meanwhile the mysterious doom struck again: several other people became bald overnight in the same manner, while the hair of others began falling out at a frightening rate. Fair people were much worse affected than dark; I remember watching a blond boy called Titheredge combing his hair one day in the cloakroom, and it was like watching a Flymo go through a patch of hay—three quarters of the hair came away with the comb.

Jack Kettering's was a spectacular case. People from different forms read out the notices each day after Assembly. Tuesday it's the Fifth Formers. Kettering did it one Tuesday; he had a nervous habit, on public occasions, of brushing his hair back with his left hand, and when he did it this time the entire thick reddish-fair thatch fell right off on to the floor behind him. The whole school gasped in horrified amusement and then—reaction, I suppose—a roar of laughter went up. People were rocking from side to side, falling about—how could they help it? The startled Kettering ran his hands over his smooth bare scalp, glanced in appalled disbelief at the heap of hair on the floor behind him, then turned white as a rag and bolted from the school hall.

I noticed that Will Donkine was looking very thoughtful.

'Did *you* do that?' Ceridwen asked him, after Assembly was over. 'I mean—did you make his hair fall out?'

Both of us had a lot of respect for Donkine; we could quite believe that he was capable of it.

But—'No,' he answered slowly. 'No, I had nothing to do with it. Though I'm not surprised—I had an idea something like that was due. And I can't say I'm sorry—when I remember some of the things those big bullies did to me.'

He gave a reminiscent rub to his own meagre mouse-brown thatch— which, like everyone else's, was getting noticeably thinner. Ceridwen and I have black hair. It took longer than anybody's to go, but it went in the end.

'No; I didn't do it,' Will said. 'But I expect I'll be in trouble from Kettering's lot soon enough, if what I think is true.'

'What's that?'

'Why, it must be an effect of my father's dust extractor, don't you see? The Queen hasn't been out for ages—they had one in Buck House. And the P.M. had one at 10 Downing Street—and I'm sure she's been wearing a wig for weeks. Have you noticed the newspaper photographs? And then there's that hospital, and the Biffin factory—it'll be all over the country soon, I expect. Father's always a bit too hasty . . .'

Of course events have proved Will right. A few months more, and all the buildings which had installed DRIP Systems were populated by totally bald inhabitants.

In three weeks our school, which of course was among the first innovators, couldn't show a single hair among the six hundred students and the forty staff. Even Smokey, the school cat, had gone bald as a pig, and was rechristened Pinky. Even the mice, when seen, could be seen to be bald. Punk cuts, crew cuts, Afro heads, Rastafarian plaits, beehives, all had vanished, like snow-wreaths in thaw, as the poet says.

In a way, our all being companions in misfortune made the state easier to bear. I found it interesting to notice how school relationships and pecking orders had changed and reversed, now that our appearance was so different. At first we found it quite difficult to recognize one another; with no hair, just pale bald scalps, we all looked alike, you couldn't tell boys from girls, we seemed like members of some Eastern sect, ready to bang gongs or spin prayer-wheels; and the people who hitherto had prided themselves on their looks went round as humbly as anybody else.

Meanwhile there was a terrific public outcry and fuss. After a while, as Will had predicted, somebody put two and two together and traced the baldness to the Donkine DRIP System. Most of the purchasers of DRIP Systems thereupon switched them off, hoping that the hair of employees, patients, students, and nurses would begin to grow again. But it didn't. Some vital growing hormone, it seemed, had been sucked out for good; or at least, for a generation.

About this time Sir Joel Donkine came back to England from the Brazilian forests where he had been on a research expedition. Naturally he was aghast at what had happened and made a statement about it.

'I accept full blame and responsibility,' he said to the newspapers, before his lawyers could warn him not to, and in no time lawsuits and writs amounting to God knows how many millions were piling upon his doorstep.

'Dad's so impetuous,' Will said again thoughtfully. 'He sounds off without checking the probabilities.'

I thought how different his son was. But perhaps I was wrong.

People said Sir Joel ought to have his Nobel and C.B.E. taken away. He was probably the most unpopular man in Europe. What though his System had prevented hundreds of colds and other infections? All that was forgotten in the wave of fury. People marched with placards demanding, 'Give Us Back Our Hair!'

Unisex shops and barbers and the manufacturers of shampoos, conditioners, setting lotions, hairbrushes, combs, hairgrips, clasps, nets, ribbons, bathing caps, dyes, tints, and bleaches were all after Sir Joel's blood.

Taken away their livelihood he had, see?

Nobody thought to mention that, on the other side of the scale, makers of wigs, hairpieces, headsquares, hats, caps, hoods, and bonnets were doing a roaring trade. Tattoo artists stencilled ingenious hair designs over people's naked heads, or just drew pretty patterns; colourful head paint was invented; at least part of the population remembered that the Ancient Egyptians went bald from choice, and discovered that there were quite a few conveniences about the bald state.

But as an unusually hot summer drew on there were a few cases of sunstroke, and questions were asked in Parliament, and people began to say that Sir J. Donkine should be impeached, or hung, drawn, and quartered, or at least tried for causing grievous public harm.

An inquiry was proposed. But before its machinery could be set up—public inquiries are very slow-moving things—poor Sir Joel was dead. Heart failure, the Coroner's report announced. And I daresay that was correct. I'm pretty sure that he had died of a broken heart.

'Poor Father,' Will said sadly. 'All he wanted was to help people. He wanted to prevent their getting infections like the one that killed Mother. And so he landed himself in all this trouble. He never would think before he acted.'

Will grieved very much for his father—the more so as he had no other relations and would now have to become a Ward of Court.

After Sir Joel's death, Kettering's group had the grace to leave Will alone for a while; nobody these days had the spirit for recriminations. Also we were all working like Stakhanovites for our A-levels . . .

Will's results in those were fairly remarkable, considering all he had been through. He came top of our lot, way ahead of anybody else. And when we re-assembled in the autumn term he seemed in reasonably good shape. He had spent the summer with Mr Postlethwaite; the Old Possum had offered to put him up so he wouldn't have to go into Care. And apparently he had passed most of the holidays in biological research.

'Boy's got a really amazing mind,' I heard the Old Possum one day tell Mrs Budleigh in the cafeteria. 'Kind of results he's getting wouldn't disgrace those fellows in the Bickerden Labs at Cambridge. What he's working after, I do believe, is to make up for the harm his father did—or felt he had done, poor man.'

'The harm he did seems quite real enough to me,' replied the Matron coldly, adjusting her wig. 'If the boy thinks he can discover some way of making people's hair grow again, I consider that a very proper ambition.'

Will was wholly uncommunicative about his work. Most of it was carried out in the labs—he didn't have time for gardening these days—and it required buckets and buckets of the DRIP System compost which was still piled in black shiny sackfuls by the side of the allotments. He fiddled about with test tubes and cultures and filters, he painted black and brown grease on to mushrooms, and eggs, and frogs, and the bald school mice, and guinea pigs. Ceridwen helped him.

By and by he began to look more hopeful; a spark came back into his eye that had been missing for many months; and, strangely enough, he began to grow, quite suddenly shot up so tall and lanky that he overtopped Kettering and most of the Blades. By now that group had rather fallen apart; two or three of the Blades had left school after their undistinguished A-levels; Pamela, of course, departed after the loss of her hair, and Jack Kettering himself was fairly subdued these days. Becoming bald had changed him a lot. Whereas Will's hair was such a modest crop and unremarkable colour that its going made little difference to his looks—indeed, thin-faced, with dark, deepset eyes and newly acquired horn-rimmed glasses he now seemed quite impressive—Jack Kettering without any hair looked flat-faced, florid, and stupid, somewhere between a pig and a seal. And was nothing like so aggressive as he used to be.

Indeed I noticed that nowadays he was cautiously friendly and almost obsequious towards Will, went out of his way to address remarks to him, pass the sugar for his cereal at breakfast, and so forth. Will didn't take much notice, just went on his own way as usual.

One day he captured Pinky the cat (no problem, they had been friends for years) and bore him off to the lab. When next seen, Pinky's pale uncatlike exterior had been dyed all over a delicate rust brown.

'You think the Animal Protection League would approve of what you've done to that poor dumb animal?' demanded Mrs Budleigh, fixing Will with a sharp grey eye.

'Sure they would; it was done for his own good,' Will answered positively. 'But if you think it would be better I'll fix him up with an insulation jacket while I wait for results.' And Ceridwen helped him construct the cat a butter-muslin jacket, which was sewn up his back so he couldn't get it off. (Pinky showed no gratitude; Ceridwen's hands were quite badly scratched.)

The cat's head was left uncovered and, after a week, anybody gently rubbing under his chin or above his eyes could feel a faint stubble of something growing. This caused a sensation, as you can imagine; people rushed to Will to offer themselves as guinea-pigs for his treatment.

Old Corfe the headmaster was down on this.

'Donkine is working hard and I'm sure all our good wishes are with him, but I think it wholly inadvisable that any of the rest of you should submit yourselves as research material, at least without parental consent. We know by now—alas!—what disastrous effects the best intentioned work may produce.'

Anyway it seemed that Will didn't want guinea-pigs; he turned away all the people who tapped at the lab door and offered their bald heads for his process.

All but one.

'I've got Dad's consent!' Jack Kettering told him in an urgent whisper. 'I phoned home and asked him. He says I look so godawful now that anything could be better. Come on, now, Donk—be a sport! I know I've laughed at you a bit in the past, in a friendly way, but that's all over long ago—isn't it? We're good friends now, aren't we?'

He looked up beseechingly into Will's face. Will said, 'You realize it may not be just ordinary hair that grows back?'

'Anything, horsehair, sheep's wool, would be better than having a dome like an egg. I don't care *what* it is, just *do* it, old feller.'

So Donkine painted Jack's scalp a rusty brown, and Ceridwen stitched him a butter-muslin skull-cap to cover the painted area.

'What's that for?'

'To stop birds pecking it,' replied Will gravely.

'*Birds?*'

'Or anything else. You never know. Wear the cap till I tell you.'

Two weeks passed. Pinky the cat's muslin jacket seemed to be getting tight; perhaps he was growing.

One evening as we all sat at supper Pinky hurtled in through the open dining-room window carrying a struggling, cheeping sparrow. The cat had torn his jacket in the chase, it flapped loose, and one of the girls, rushing to the rescue of the sparrow, let out a quack of amazement.

'The cat's gone green!'

'Take off the remains of the jacket,' suggested old Postlethwaite.

Ceridwen pulled it off, tearing the tattered muslin with no trouble—
to reveal Pinky, erstwhile Smokey, wearing a fine coat of short velvety
green.

Someone said in an awed voice, 'That cat is covered with *grass*.'

'May I be utterly blessed!' muttered Old Possum. He gazed with
bulging eyes at the verdant animal. Will poured the cat a saucer of milk
and inspected him with serious satisfaction as he drank.

'It worked with the mice, and it seems to have worked with him. I
found it impossible, you see, sir, to grow hair on anything—but grass
responded very well—and, after all, it makes just as good a cover—'

Jack Kettering, who had come in late for tea, arrived in time to hear
this remark. Without a word, he spun on his heel and strode back into
the hall, where there is a big wall mirror, dragging off his muslin cap as
he went. We heard him let out a kind of astonished wail.

'*Grass . . . !*'

Will strolled out after him, and I could hear him say mildly, 'You did
tell me that anything would be better than having a dome like an egg—'

'I didn't bargain on *grass*!'

But by that time half the school were frothing around Will,
clamouring and begging: 'Do me, do me, do *me*! I'd *like* grass! Maybe
there could be a few buttercups as well? Or a daisy?'

'I shan't do anybody without parental permission,' Will said gravely.

I saw him glance, over the clustered shining bald heads, towards Old
Possum, with a kind of rueful resigned shrug and gesture of the head.
Postlethwaite's expression was still fairly stunned.

'After all, sir,' Will went on in a reasonable tone, 'you did say that to
make two blades of grass grow where one grew before was a good thing
to do. And I've made two blades grow where *none* grew before. Think
what a hay crop we'd get, off the heads of everyone here.'

But I could imagine what Old Possum was thinking, for I was
thinking it myself. After grass has been established for a while, you get
larger plants rooting, and then larger ones still, and then acorns which
sprout into oak trees . . .

Will was just as impulsive as his father. And who is going to deal with
the next lot of side effects?

THE MONKEY'S PAW
W. W. Jacobs

Without, the night was cold and wet, but in the small parlour of Lakesnam Villa the blinds were drawn and the fire burned brightly. Father and son were at chess, the former, who possessed ideas about the game involving radical changes, putting his king into such sharp and unnecessary perils that it even provoked comment from the white-haired old lady knitting placidly by the fire.

'Hark at the wind,' said Mr White, who, having seen a fatal mistake after it was too late, was amiably desirous of preventing his son from seeing it.

'I'm listening,' said the latter, grimly surveying the board as he stretched out his hand. 'Check.'

'I should hardly think that he'd come to-night,' said his father, with his hand poised over the board.

'Mate,' replied the son.

'That's the worst of living so far out,' bawled Mr White, with sudden and unlooked-for violence; 'of all the beastly, slushy, out-of-the-way places to live in, this is the worst. Pathway's a bog, and the road's a torrent. I don't know what people are thinking about. I suppose because only two houses on the road are let, they think it doesn't matter.'

'Never mind, dear,' said his wife soothingly; 'perhaps you'll win the next one.'

Mr White looked up sharply, just in time to intercept a knowing glance between mother and son. The words died away on his lips, and he hid a guilty grin in his thin grey beard.

'There he is,' said Herbert White, as the gate banged-to loudly and heavy footsteps came towards the door.

The old man rose with hospitable haste, and opening the door, was heard condoling the new arrival. The new arrival also condoled with himself, so that Mrs White said, 'Tut, tut!' and coughed gently as her husband entered the room, followed by a tall burly man, beady of eye and rubicund of visage.

'Sergeant-major Morris,' he said, introducing him.

The sergeant-major shook hands, and taking the proffered seat by the fire, watched contentedly while his host got out whisky and tumblers and stood a small copper kettle on the fire.

At the third glass his eyes got brighter, and he began to talk, the little family circle regarding with eager interest this visitor from distant parts, as he squared his broad shoulders in the chair and spoke of strange scenes and doughty deeds, of wars and plagues and strange peoples.

'Twenty-one years of it,' said Mr White, nodding at his wife and son. 'When he went away he was a slip of a youth in the warehouse. Now look at him.'

'He don't look to have taken much harm,' said Mrs White politely.

'I'd like to go to India myself,' said the old man, 'just to look round a bit, you know.'

'Better where you are,' said the sergeant-major, shaking his head. He put down the empty glass and, sighing softly, shook it again.

'I should like to see those old temples and fakirs and jugglers,' said the old man. 'What was that you started telling me the other day about a monkey's paw or something, Morris?'

'Nothing,' said the soldier hastily. 'Leastways, nothing worth hearing.'

'Monkey's paw?' said Mrs White curiously.

'Well, it's just a bit of what you might call magic, perhaps,' said the sergeant-major off-handedly.

His three listeners leaned forward eagerly. The visitor absent-mindedly put his empty glass to his lips and then set it down again. His host filled it for him.

The startled Kettering bolted from the school hall. (p.41)

Fierce faces, bearded and dark, shape themselves out of the mist. (p.65)

'To look at,' said the sergeant-major, fumbling in his pocket, 'it's just an ordinary little paw, dried to a mummy.'

He took something out of his pocket and proffered it. Mrs White drew back with a grimace, but her son, taking it, examined it curiously.

'And what is there special about it?' inquired Mr White, as he took it from his son and, having examined it, placed it upon the table.

'It had a spell put on it by an old fakir,' said the sergeant-major, 'a very holy man. He wanted to show that fate ruled people's lives, and that those who interfered with it did so to their sorrow. He put a spell on it so that three separate men could have three wishes from it.'

His manner was so impressive that his hearers were conscious that their light laughter jarred somewhat.

'Well, why don't you have three, sir?' said Herbert White cleverly.

The soldier regarded him in the way that middle age is wont to regard presumptuous youth. 'I have,' he said quietly, and his blotchy face whitened.

'And did you really have the three wishes granted?' asked Mrs White.

'I did,' said the sergeant-major, and his glass tapped against his strong teeth.

'And has anybody else wished?' inquired the old lady.

'The first man had his three wishes, yes,' was the reply. 'I don't know what the first two were, but the third was for death. That's how I got the paw.'

His tones were so grave that a hush fell upon the group.

'If you've had your three wishes, it's no good to you now, then, Morris,' said the old man at last. 'What do you keep it for?'

The soldier shook his head. 'Fancy, I suppose,' he said slowly. 'I did have some idea of selling it, but I don't think I will. It has caused enough mischief already. Besides, people won't buy. They think it's a fairy tale, some of them, and those who do think anything of it want to try it first and pay me afterwards.'

'If you could have another three wishes,' said the old man, eyeing him keenly, 'would you have them?'

'I don't know,' said the other. 'I don't know.'

He took the paw, and dangling it between his front finger and thumb, suddenly threw it upon the fire. White, with a slight cry, stooped down and snatched it off.

'Better let it burn,' said the soldier solemnly.

'If you don't want it, Morris,' said the old man, 'give it to me.'

'I won't,' said his friend doggedly. 'I threw it on the fire. If you keep it, don't blame me for what happens. Pitch it on the fire again, like a sensible man.'

The other shook his head and examined his new possession closely. 'How do you do it?' he inquired.

'Hold it up in your right hand and wish aloud,' said the sergeant-major, 'but I warn you of the consequences.'

'Sounds like the *Arabian Nights*,' said Mrs White, as she rose and began to set the supper. 'Don't you think you might wish for four pairs of hands for me?'

Her husband drew the talisman from his pocket and then all three burst into laughter as the sergeant-major, with a look of alarm on his face, caught him by the arm.

'If you must wish,' he said gruffly, 'wish for something sensible.'

Mr White dropped it back into his pocket, and placing chairs, motioned his friend to the table. In the business of supper the talisman was partly forgotten, and afterwards the three sat listening in an enthralled fashion to a second instalment of the soldier's adventures in India.

'If the tale about the monkey's paw is not more truthful than those he has been telling us,' said Herbert, as the door closed behind their guest, just in time for him to catch the last train, 'we shan't make much out of it.'

'Did you give him anything for it, Father?' inquired Mrs White, regarding her husband closely.

'A trifle,' said he, colouring slightly. 'He didn't want it, but I made him take it. And he pressed me again to throw it away.'

'Likely,' said Herbert, with pretended horror. 'Why, we're going to be rich, and famous, and happy. Wish to be an emperor, father, to begin with; then you can't be henpecked.'

He darted round the table, pursued by the maligned Mrs White armed with an antimacassar.

Mr White took the paw from his pocket and eyed it dubiously. 'I don't know what to wish for, and that's a fact,' he said slowly. 'It seems to me I've got all I want.'

'If you only cleared the house, you'd be quite happy, wouldn't you?'

said Herbert, with his hand on his shoulder. 'Well, wish for two hundred pounds, then; that'll just do it.'

His father, smiling shamefacedly at his own credulity, held up the talisman, as his son, with a solemn face somewhat marred by a wink at his mother, sat down at the piano and struck a few impressive chords.

'I wish for two hundred pounds,' said the old man distinctly.

A fine crash from the piano greeted the words, interrupted by a shuddering cry from the old man. His wife and son ran towards him.

'It moved,' he cried, with a glance of disgust at the object as it lay on the floor. 'As I wished it twisted in my hands like a snake.'

'Well, I don't see the money,' said his son, as he picked it up and placed it on the table, 'and I bet I never shall.'

'It must have been your fancy, Father,' said the wife, regarding him anxiously.

He shook his head. 'Never mind, though; there's no harm done, but it gave me a shock all the same.'

They sat down by the fire again while the two men finished their pipes. Outside, the wind was higher than ever, and the old man started nervously at the sound of a door banging upstairs. A silence unusual and depressing settled upon all three, which lasted until the old couple rose to retire for the night.

'I expect you'll find the cash tied up in a big bag in the middle of your bed,' said Herbert, as he bade them good-night, 'and something horrible squatting up on top of the wardrobe watching you as you pocket your ill-gotten gains.'

★　　　★　　　★　　　★

In the brightness of the wintry sun next morning as it streamed over the breakfast table, Herbert laughed at his fears. There was an air of prosaic wholesomeness about the room which it had lacked on the previous night, and the dirty, shrivelled little paw was pitched on the sideboard with a carelessness which betokened no great belief in its virtues.

'I suppose all old soldiers are the same,' said Mrs White. 'The idea of our listening to such nonsense! How could wishes be granted in these days? And if they could, how could two hundred pounds hurt you, Father?'

51

'Might drop on his head from the sky,' said the frivolous Herbert.

'Morris said the things happened so naturally,' said his Father, 'that you might, if you so wished, attribute it to coincidence.'

'Well, don't break into the money before I come back,' said Herbert, as he rose from the table. 'I'm afraid it'll turn you into a mean, avaricious man, and we shall have to disown you.'

His mother laughed, and following him to the door, watched him down the road, and returning to the breakfast table, was very happy at the expense of her husband's credulity. All of which did not prevent her from scurrying to the door at the postman's knock, nor prevent her from referring somewhat shortly to retired sergeant-majors of bibulous habits when she found that the post brought a tailor's bill.

'Herbert will have some more of his funny remarks, I expect, when he comes home,' she said, as they sat at dinner.

'I dare say,' said Mr White, pouring himself out some beer, 'but for all that, the thing moved in my hand; that I'll swear to.'

'You thought it did,' said the old lady soothingly.

'I say it did,' replied the other. 'There was no thought about it; I had just – What's the matter?'

His wife made no reply. She was watching the mysterious movements of a man outside, who, peering in an undecided fashion at the house, appeared to be trying to make up his mind to enter. In mental connection with the two hundred pounds, she noticed that the stranger was well-dressed and wore a silk hat of glossy newness. Three times he paused at the gate, and then walked on again. The fourth time he stood with his hand upon it, and then with sudden resolution flung it open and walked up the path. Mrs White at the same moment placed her hands behind her, and hurriedly unfastening the strings of her apron, put that useful article of apparel beneath the cushion of her chair.

She brought the stranger, who seemed ill at ease, into the room. He gazed furtively at Mrs White, and listened in a preoccupied fashion as the old lady apologised for the appearance of the room, and her husband's coat, a garment which he usually reserved for the garden. She then waited as patiently as her sex would permit for him to broach his business, but he was at first strangely silent.

'I – was asked to call,' he said at last, and stooped and picked a piece of cotton from his trousers. 'I come from Maw and Meggins.'

The old lady started. 'Is anything the matter?' she asked breathlessly. 'Has anything happened to Herbert? What is it? What is it?'

Her husband interposed. 'There, there, mother,' he said hastily. 'Sit down, and don't jump to conclusions. You've not brought bad news, I'm sure, sir,' and he eyed the other wistfully.

'I'm sorry–' began the visitor.

'Is he hurt?' demanded the mother.

The visitor bowed in assent. 'Badly hurt,' he said quietly, 'but he is not in any pain.'

'Oh, thank God!' said the old woman, clasping her hands. 'Thank God for that! Thank–'

She broke off suddenly as the sinister meaning of the assurance dawned upon her and she saw the awful confirmation of her fears in the other's averted face. She caught her breath, and turning to her slower-witted husband, laid her trembling old hand upon his. There was a long silence.

'He was caught in the machinery,' said the visitor at length, in a low voice.

'Caught in the machinery,' repeated Mr White, in a dazed fashion, 'yes.'

He sat staring blankly out at the window, and taking his wife's hand between his own, pressed it as he had been wont to do in their old courting days nearly forty years before.

'He was the only one left us,' he said, turning gently to the visitor. 'It is hard.'

The other coughed, and rising, walked slowly to the window. 'The firm wished me to convey their sincere sympathy with you in your great loss,' he said, without looking round. 'I beg that you will understand I am only their servant and merely obeying orders.'

There was no reply; the old woman's face was white, her eyes staring, and her breath inaudible; on the husband's face was a look such as his friend the sergeant might have carried into his first action.

'I was to say that Maw and Meggins disclaim all responsibility,' continued the other. 'They admit no liability at all, but in consideration of your son's services they wish to present you with a certain sum as compensation.'

Mr White dropped his wife's hand, and rising to his feet, gazed with a

The old man dropped to the floor

look of horror at his visitor. His dry lips shaped the words, 'How much?'

'Two hundred pounds,' was the answer.

Unconscious of his wife's shriek, the old man smiled faintly, put out his hands like a sightless man, and dropped, a senseless heap, to the floor.

★   ★   ★   ★

In the huge new cemetery, some two miles distant, the old people buried their dead, and came back to a house steeped in shadow and silence. It was all over so quickly that at first they could hardly realise it, and remained in a state of expectation as though of something else to happen – something else which was to lighten this load, too heavy for old hearts to bear. But the days passed, and expectation gave place to resignation – the hopeless resignation of the old, sometimes miscalled apathy. Sometimes they hardly exchanged a word, for now they had nothing to talk about, and their days were long to weariness.

It was about a week after that that the old man, waking suddenly in the night, stretched out his hand and found himself alone. The room was in darkness, and the sound of subdued weeping came from the window. He raised himself in bed and listened.

'Come back,' he said tenderly. 'You will be cold.'

'It is colder for my son,' said the old woman, and wept afresh.

The sound of her sobs died away on his ears. The bed was warm, and his eyes heavy with sleep. He dozed fitfully, and then slept until a sudden wild cry from his wife awoke him with a start.

'The monkey's paw!' she cried wildly. 'The monkey's paw!'

He started up in alarm. 'Where? Where is it? What's the matter?'

She came stumbling across the room towards him. 'I want it,' she said quietly. 'You've not destroyed it?'

'It's in the parlour, on the bracket,' he replied, marvelling. 'Why?'

She cried and laughed together, and bending over, kissed his cheek.

'I only just thought of it,' she said hysterically. 'Why didn't I think of it before? Why didn't you think of it?'

'Think of what?' he questioned.

'The other two wishes,' she replied rapidly. 'We've only had one.'

'Was not that enough?' he demanded fiercely.

'No,' she cried triumphantly; 'we'll have one more. Go down and get it quickly, and wish our boy alive again.'

The man sat up in bed and flung the bedclothes from his quaking limbs. 'Good God, you are mad!' he cried, aghast.

'Get it,' she panted; 'get it quickly, and wish – Oh, my boy, my boy!'

Her husband struck a match and lit the candle. 'Get back to bed,' he said unsteadily. 'You don't know what you are saying.'

'We had the first wish granted,' said the old woman feverishly; 'why not the second?'

'A coincidence,' stammered the old man.

'Go and get it and wish,' cried the old woman, and dragged him towards the door.

He went down in the darkness, and felt his way to the parlour, and then to the mantelpiece. The talisman was in its place, and a horrible fear that the unspoken wish might bring his mutilated son before him ere he could escape from the room seized upon him, and he caught his breath as he found that he had lost the direction of the door. His brow cold with sweat, he felt his way round the table, and groped along the wall until he found himself in the small passage with the unwholesome thing in his hand.

Even his wife's face seemed changed as he entered the room. It was white and expectant, and to his fears seemed to have an unusual look upon it. He was afraid of her.

'Wish!' she cried, in a strong voice.

'It is foolish and wicked,' he faltered.

'Wish!' repeated his wife.

He raised his hand. 'I wish my son alive again.'

The talisman fell to the floor, and he regarded it shudderingly. Then he sank trembling into a chair as the old woman, with burning eyes, walked to the window, and raised the blind.

He sat until he was chilled with the cold, glancing occasionally at the figure of the old woman peering through the window. The candle end, which had burnt below the rim of the china candlestick, was throwing pulsating shadows on the ceiling and walls, until, with a flicker larger than the rest, it expired. The old man, with an unspeakable sense of relief at the failure of the talisman, crept back to his bed, and a minute or two afterwards the old woman came silently and apathetically beside him.

Neither spoke, but both lay silently listening to the ticking of the clock. A stair creaked, and a squeaky mouse scurried noisily through the wall. The darkness was oppressive, and after lying for some time screwing up his courage, the husband took the box of matches, and striking one, went downstairs for a candle.

At the foot of the stairs the match went out, and he paused to strike another, and at the same moment a knock, so quiet and stealthy as to be scarcely audible, sounded on the front door.

The matches fell from his hand. He stood motionless, his breath suspended until the knock was repeated. Then he turned and fled swiftly back to his room, and closed the door behind him. A third knock sounded through the house.

'*What's that?*' cried the old woman, starting up.

'A rat,' said the old man, in shaking tones – 'a rat. It passed me on the stairs.'

His wife sat up in bed, listening. A loud knock resounded through the house.

'It's Herbert!' she screamed. 'It's Herbert!'

She ran to the door, but her husband was before her, and catching her by the arm, held her tightly.

'What are you going to do?' he whispered hoarsely.

'It's my boy: it's Herbert!' she cried, struggling mechanically. 'I forgot it was two miles away. What are you holding me for? Let go. I must open the door.'

'For God's sake don't let it in,' cried the old man, trembling.

'You're afraid of your own son,' she cried struggling. 'Let me go. I'm coming, Herbert; I'm coming.'

There was another knock, and another. The old woman with a sudden wrench broke free and ran from the room. Her husband followed to the landing, and called after her appealingly as she hurried downstairs. He heard the chain rattle back and the bottom bolt drawn slowly and stiffly from the socket. Then the old woman's voice strained and panting.

'The bolt,' she cried loudly. 'Come down. I can't reach it.'

But her husband was on his hands and knees groping wildly on the floor in search of the paw. If he could only find it before the thing outside got in. A perfect fusillade of knocks reverberated through the house, and he heard the scraping of a chair as his wife put it down in the passage against the door. He heard the creaking of the bolt as it came slowly back, and at the same moment, he found the monkey's paw, and frantically breathed his third and last wish.

The knocking ceased suddenly, although the echoes of it were still in the house. Heard the chair drawn back and the door opened. A cold wind rushed up the staircase, and a long loud wail of disappointment and misery from his wife gave him courage to run down to her side, and then to the gate beyond. The street lamp flickering opposite shone on a quiet and deserted road.

THE SILVER MIRROR
Sir Arthur Conan Doyle

Jan. 3 This affair of White and Wotherspoon's accounts proves to be a gigantic task. There are twenty thick ledgers to be examined and checked. Who would be a junior partner? However, it is the first big bit of business which has been left entirely in my hands. I must justify it. But it has to be finished so that the lawyers may have the result in time for the trial. Johnson said this morning that I should have to get the last figure out before the twentieth of the month. Good Lord! Well, have at it, and if human brain and nerve can stand the strain, I'll win out at the other side. It means office-work from ten to five, and then a second sitting from about eight to one in the morning. There's drama in an accountant's life. When I find myself in the still early hours, while all the world sleeps, hunting through column after column for those missing figures which will turn a respected alderman into a felon, I understand that it is not such a prosaic profession after all.

On Monday I came on the first trace of defalcation. No heavy game hunter ever got a finer thrill when first he caught sight of the trail of his quarry. But I look at the twenty ledgers and think of the jungle through which I have to follow him before I get my kill. Hard work – but rare sport, too, in a way! I saw that fat fellow once at a City dinner, his red face glowing above a white napkin. He looked at the little pale man at the end

59

of the table. He would have been pale too if he could have seen the task that would be mine.

Jan. 6   What perfect nonsense it is for doctors to prescribe rest when rest is out of the question! Asses! They might as well shout to a man who has a pack of wolves at his heels that what he wants is absolute quiet. My figures must be out by a certain date: unless they are so, I shall lose the chance of my lifetime, so how on earth am I to rest? I'll take a week or so after the trial.

Perhaps I was myself a fool to go to the doctor at all. But I get nervous and highly-strung when I sit alone at my work at night. It's not a pain – only a sort of fullness of the head with an occasional mist over the eyes. I thought perhaps some bromide, or chloral, or something of the kind might do me good. But stop work? It's absurd to ask such a thing. It's like a long-distance race. You feel queer at first and your heart thumps and your lungs pant, but if you have only the pluck to keep on, you get your second wind. I'll stick to my work and wait for my second wind. If it never comes – all the same, I'll stick to my work. Two ledgers are done, and I am well on in the third. The rascal has covered his tracks well, but I pick them up for all that.

Jan. 9   I had not meant to go to the doctor again. And yet I have had to. 'Straining my nerves, risking a complete breakdown, even endangering my sanity.' That's a nice sentence to have fired off at one. Well, I'll stand the strain and I'll take the risk, and so long as I can sit in my chair and move a pen, I'll follow the old sinner's slot.

By the way, I may as well set down here the queer experience which drove me this second time to the doctor. I'll keep an exact record of my symptoms and sensations, because they are interesting in themselves – 'A curious psycho-physiological study,' says the doctor – and also because I am perfectly certain that when I am through with them they will all seem blurred and unreal, like some queer dream betwixt sleeping and waking. So now, while they are fresh, I will just make a note of them, if only as a change of thought after the endless figures.

There's an old silver-framed mirror in my room. It was given me by a friend who had a taste for antiquities, and he, as I happened to know, picked it up at a sale and had no notion where it came from. It's a large thing – three feet across and two feet high – and it leans at the back of a side-table on my left as I write. The frame is flat, about three inches across, and very old; far too old for hall-marks or other methods of determining its age. The glass part projects, with a bevelled edge, and has the magnificent reflecting power which is only, as it seems to me, to be found in very old mirror. There's a feeling of perspective when you look into it such as no modern glass can ever give.

The mirror is so situated that as I sit at the table, I can usually see nothing in it but the reflection of the red window curtains. But a queer thing happened last night. I had been working for some hours, very much against the grain, with continual bouts of that mistiness of which I had complained. Again and again I had to stop and clear my eyes. Well, on one of these occasions I chanced to look at the mirror. It had the oddest appearance. The red curtains which should have been reflected in it were no longer there, but the glass seemed to be clouded and steamy, not on the surface, which glittered like steel, but deep down in the very grain of it. This opacity, when I stared hard at it, appeared to slowly rotate this way and that, until it was a thick white cloud swirling in heavy wreaths. So real and solid was it, and so reasonable was I, that I remember turning, with the idea that the curtains were on fire. But everything was deadly still in the room – no sound save the ticking of the clock, no movement save the slow gyration of that strange woolly cloud deep in the heart of the old mirror.

Then, as I looked, the mist, or smoke, or cloud, or whatever one may call it, seemed to coalesce and solidify at two points quite close together, and I was aware, with a thrill of interest rather than of fear, that these were two eyes looking out into the room. A vague outline of a head I could see – a woman's by the hair, but this was very shadowy. Only the eyes were quite distinct; such eyes – dark, luminous, filled with some passionate emotion, fury or horror, I could not say which. Never have I seen eyes which were so full of intense, vivid life. They were not fixed upon me, but stared out into the room. Then as I sat erect, passed my hand over my brow, and made a strong conscious effort to pull myself together, the dim head faded into the general opacity, the mirror slowly cleared, and there were the red curtains once again.

A sceptic would say, no doubt, that I had dropped asleep over my figures, and that my experience was a dream. As a matter of fact, I was never more vividly awake in my life. I was able to argue about it even as I looked at it, and to tell myself that it was a subjective impression – a

61

chimera of the nerves – begotten by worry and insomnia. But why this particular shape? And who is the woman, and what is the dreadful emotion which I read in those wonderful brown eyes? They come between me and my work. For the first time I have done less than the daily tally which I had marked out. Perhaps that is why I have had no abnormal sensations tonight. Tomorrow I must wake up, come what may.

Jan. 11 All well, and good progress with my work. I wind the net, coil after coil, round that bulky body. But the last smile may remain with him if my own nerves break over it. The mirror would seem to be a sort of barometer which marks my brain-pressure. Each night I have observed that it had clouded before I reached the end of my task.

Dr Sinclair (who is, it seems, a bit of a psychologist) was so interested in my account that he came round this evening to have a look at the mirror. I had observed that something was scribbled in crabbed old characters upon the metal-work at the back. He examined this with a lens, but could make nothing of it. 'Sanc. X. Pal.' was his final reading of it, but that did not bring us any farther. He advised me to put it away into another room; but after all, whatever I may see in it is, by his own account, only a symptom. It is in the cause that the danger lies. The twenty ledgers – not the silver mirror – should be packed away if I could only do it. I'm at the eighth now, so I progress.

Jan. 13 Perhaps it would have been wiser after all if I had packed away the mirror. I had an extraordinary experience with it last night. And yet I find it so interesting, so fascinating, that even now I will keep it in its place. What on earth is the meaning of it all?

I suppose it was about one in the morning, and I was closing my books preparatory to staggering off to bed, when I saw her there in front of me. The stage of mistiness and development must have passed unobserved, and there she was in all her beauty and passion and distress, as clear-cut as if she were really in the flesh before me. The figure was small, but very distinct – so much so that every feature, and every detail of dress, are stamped in my memory. She is seated on the extreme left of the mirror. A sort of shadowy figure crouches down beside her – I can dimly discern that it is a man – and then behind them is cloud, in which I see figures – figures which move. It is not a mere picture upon which I look. It is a scene in life, an actual episode. She crouches and quivers. The man beside her cowers down. The vague figures make abrupt movements and gestures. All my fears were swallowed up in my interest. It was maddening to see so much and not to see more.

But I can at least describe the woman to the smallest point. She is very beautiful and quite young – not more than five-and-twenty, I should judge. Her hair is of a very rich brown, with a warm chestnut shade fining into gold at the edges. A little flat-pointed cap comes to an angle in front, and is made of lace edged with pearls. The forehead is high, too high perhaps for perfect beauty; but one would not have it otherwise; as it gives a touch of power and strength to what would otherwise be a softly feminine face. The brows are most delicately curved over heavy eyelids, and then come those wonderful eyes – so large, so dark, so full of overmastering emotion, of rage and horror, contending with a pride of self-control which holds her from sheer frenzy! The cheeks are pale, the lips white with agony, the chin and throat most exquisitely rounded. The figure sits and leans forward in the chair, straining and rigid, cataleptic with horror. The dress is black velvet, a jewel gleams like a flame in the breast, and a golden crucifix smoulders in the shadow of a fold. This is the lady whose image still lives in the old silver mirror. What dire deed could it be which has left its impress there, so that now, in another age, if the spirit of a man be but worn down to it, he may be conscious of its presence?

One other detail: on the left side of the skirt of the black dress was, as I thought at first, a shapeless bunch of white ribbon. Then, as I looked more intently or as the vision defined itself more clearly, I perceived what it was. It was the hand of a man, clenched and knotted in agony, which held on with a convulsive grasp to the fold of the dress. The rest of the crouching figure was a mere vague outline, but the strenuous hand shone clear on the dark background, with a sinister suggestion of tragedy in its frantic clutch. The man is frightened – horribly frightened. That I can clearly discern. What has terrified him so? Why does he grip the woman's dress? The answer lies amongst those moving figures in the background. They have brought danger both to him and to her. The interest of the thing fascinated me. I thought no more of its relation to my own nerves. I stared and stared as if in a theatre. But I could get no farther. The mist thinned. There were tumultuous movements in which all the figures were vaguely concerned. Then the mirror was clear once more.

The doctor says I must drop work for a day, and I can afford to do so, for I have made good progress lately. It is quite evident that the visions depend entirely upon my own nervous state, for I sat in front of the mirror for an hour tonight, with no result whatsoever. My soothing day has chased them away. I wonder whether I shall ever penetrate what they all mean? I examined the mirror this evening under a good light, and besides the mysterious inscription 'Sanc. X. Pal.,' I was able to discern some signs of heraldic marks, very faintly visible upon the silver. They must be very ancient, as they are almost obliterated. So far as I could make out, they were three spear-heads, two above and one below. I will show them to the doctor when he calls tomorrow.

Jan. 14   Feel perfectly well again, and I intend that nothing else shall stop me until my task is finished. The doctor was shown the marks on the mirror and agreed that they were armorial bearings. He is deeply interested in all that I have told him, and cross-questioned me closely on the details. It amuses me to notice how he is torn in two by conflicting desires – the one that his patient should lose his symptoms, the other that the medium – for so he regards me – should solve this mystery of the past. He advised continued rest, but did not oppose me too violently when I declared that such a thing was out of the question until the ten remaining ledgers have been checked.

Jan. 17   For three nights I have had no experiences – my day of rest has borne fruit. Only a quarter of my task is left, but I must make a forced march, for the lawyers are clamouring for their material. I will give them enough and to spare. I have him fast on a hundred counts. When they realise what a slippery, cunning rascal he is, I should gain some credit from the case. False trading accounts, false balance-sheets, dividends drawn from capital, losses written down as profits, suppression of working expenses, manipulation of petty cash – it is a fine record!

Jan. 18   Headaches, nervous twitches, mistiness, fullness of the temples – all the premonitions of trouble, and the trouble came sure enough. And yet my real sorrow is not so much that the vision should come as that it should cease before all is revealed.

But I saw more tonight. The crouching man was as visible as the lady whose gown he clutched. He is a little swarthy fellow, with a black pointed beard. He has a loose gown of damask trimmed with fur. The prevailing tints of his dress are red. What a fright the fellow is in, to be sure! He cowers and shivers and glares back over his shoulder. There is a small knife in his other hand, but he is far too tremulous and cowed to use it. Dimly now I begin to see the figures in the background. Fierce faces, bearded and dark, shape themselves out of the mist. There is one terrible creature, a skeleton of a man, with hollow cheeks and eyes sunk in his head. He also has a knife in his hand. On the right of the woman stands a tall man, very young, with flaxen hair, his face sullen and dour. The beautiful woman looks up at him in appeal. So does the man on the ground. This youth seems to be the arbiter of their fate. The crouching man draws closer and hides himself in the woman's skirts. The tall youth bends and tries to drag her away from him. So much I saw last night before the mirror cleared. Shall I never know what it leads to and whence it comes? It is not a mere imagination, of that I am very sure. Somewhere, some time, this scene has been acted, and this old mirror has reflected it. But when – where?

Jan. 20 My work draws to a close, and it is time. I feel a tenseness within my brain, a sense of intolerable strain, which warns me that something must give. I have worked myself to the limit. But tonight should be the last night. With a supreme effort I should finish the final ledger and complete the case before I rise from my chair. I will do it. I will.

Feb. 7 I did. My God, what an experience! I hardly know if I am strong enough yet to set it down.

Let me explain in the first instance that I am writing this in Dr Sinclair's private hospital some three weeks after the last entry in my diary. On the night of January 20 my nervous system finally gave way, and I remembered nothing afterwards until I found myself three days ago in this home of rest. And I can rest with a good conscience. My work was done before I went under. My figures are in the solicitors' hands. The hunt is over.

And now I must describe that last night. I had sworn to finish my work, and so intently did I stick to it, though my head was bursting, that I would never look up until the last column had been added. And yet it was fine self-restraint, for all the time I knew that wonderful things were happening in the mirror. Every nerve in my body told me so. If I looked up there was an end of my work. So I did not look up until all was

65

finished. Then, when at last with throbbing temples I threw down my pen and raised my eyes, what a sight was there!

The mirror in its silver frame was like a stage, brilliantly lit, in which a drama was in progress. There was no mist now. The oppression of my nerves had wrought this amazing clarity. Every feature, every movement, was as clear-cut as in life. To think that I, a tired accountant, the most prosaic of mankind, with the account-books of a swindling bankrupt before me, should be chosen of all the human race to look upon such a scene!

It was the same scene and the same figures, but the drama had advanced a stage. The tall young man was holding the woman in his arms. She strained away from him and looked up at him with loathing in her face. They had torn the crouching man away from his hold upon the skirt of her dress. A dozen of them were round him – savage men, bearded men. They hacked at him with knives. All seemed to strike him together. Their arms rose and fell. The blood did not flow from him – it squirted. His red dress was dabbled in it. He threw himself this way and that, purple upon crimson, like an over-ripe plum. Still they hacked and still the jets shot from him. It was horrible – horrible! They dragged him kicking to the door. The woman looked over her shoulder at him and her mouth gaped. I heard nothing, but I knew that she was screaming. And then, whether it was this nerve-racking vision before me, or whether, my task finished, all the overwork of the past weeks came in one crushing weight upon me, the room danced round me, the floor seemed to sink away beneath my feet, and I remembered no more. In the early morning my landlady found me stretched senseless before the silver mirror, but I knew nothing myself until three days ago I awoke in the deep peace of the doctor's nursing home.

Feb. 9 Only today have I told Dr Sinclair my full experience. He had not allowed me to speak of such matters before. He listened with an absorbed interest. 'You don't identify this with any well-known scene in history?' he asked, with suspicion in his eyes. I assured him that I knew nothing of history. 'Have you no idea whence that mirror came and to whom it once belonged?' he continued. 'Have you?' I asked, for he spoke with meaning. 'It's incredible,' said he, 'and yet how else can one explain it? The scenes which you described before suggested it, but now it has gone beyond all range of coincidence. I will bring you some notes in the evening.'

Later He has just left me. Let me set down his words as closely as I can recall them. He began by laying several musty volumes upon my bed.

'These you can consult at your leisure,' said he. 'I have some notes here which you can confirm. There is not a doubt that what you have seen is the murder of Rizzio by the Scottish nobles in the presence of Mary, which occurred in March, 1566. Your description of the woman is accurate. The high forehead and heavy eyelids combined with great beauty could hardly apply to two women. The tall young man was her husband, Darnley. Rizzio, says the chronicle, "was dressed in a loose dressing-gown of furred damask; with hose of russet velvet." With one hand he clutched Mary's gown, with the other he held a dagger. Your fierce, hollow-eyed man was Ruthven, who was new-risen from a bed of sickness. Every detail is exact.'

'But why to me?' I asked, in bewilderment. 'Why of all the human race to me?'

'Because you were in the fit mental state to receive the impression. Because you chanced to own the mirror which gave the impression.'

'The mirror! You think, then, that it was Mary's mirror – that it stood in the room where the deed was done?'

'I am convinced that it was Mary's mirror. She had been Queen of France. Her personal property would be stamped with the Royal arms. What you took to be three spear-heads were the lilies of France.'

'And the inscription?'

' "Sanc. X. Pal." You can expand it into Sanctae Crucis Palatium. Some one has made a note upon the mirror as to whence it came. It was the Palace of the Holy Cross.'

'Holyrood!' I cried.

'Exactly. Your mirror came from Holyrood. You have had one very singular experience, and have escaped. I trust that you will never put yourself into the way of having such another.'

THE STOLEN CIGAR-CASE
Bret Harte

I found Hemlock Jones in the old Bank Street lodgings, musing before the fire. With the freedom of an old friend I at once threw myself in my old familiar attitude at his feet, and gently caressed his boot. I was induced to do this for two reasons; one that it enabled me to get a good look at his bent, concentrated face, and the other that it seemed to indicate my reverence for his superhuman insight. So absorbed was he, even then, in tracking some mysterious clue, that he did not seem to notice me. But therein I was wrong – as I always was in my attempt to understand that powerful intellect.

'It is raining,' he said, without lifting his head.

'You have been out then?' I said quickly.

'No. But I see that your umbrella is wet, and that your overcoat, which you threw off on entering, has drops of water on it.'

I sat aghast at his penetration. After a pause he said carelessly, as if dismissing the subject: 'Besides, I hear the rain on the window. Listen.'

I listened. I could scarcely credit my ears, but there was a soft pattering of drops on the pane. It was evident, there was no deceiving this man!

'Have you been busy lately?' I asked, changing the subject. 'What new problem – given up by Scotland Yard as inscrutable – has occupied that gigantic intellect?'

He drew back his foot slightly, and seemed to hesitate ere he returned it to its original position. Then he answered wearily: 'Mere trifles – nothing to speak of. The Prince Kopoli has been here to get my advice regarding the disappearance of certain rubies from the Kremlin; the Rajah of Pootibad, after vainly beheading his entire bodyguard, has been obliged to seek my assistance to recover a jewelled sword. The Grand Duchess of Pretzel-Brauntswig is desirous of discovering where her husband was on the night of the 14th of February, and last night' – he lowered his voice slightly – 'a lodger in this very house, meeting me on the stairs, wanted to know "Why they don't answer his bell".'

I could not help smiling – until I saw a frown gathering on his inscrutable forehead.

'Pray to remember,' he said coldly, 'that it was through such an apparently trivial question that I found out, "Why Paul Ferroll killed his Wife," and "What happened to Jones"!'

I became dumb at once. He paused for a moment, and then suddenly changing back to his usual pitiless, analytical style, he said: 'When I say these are trifles – they are so in comparison to an affair that is now before me. A crime has been committed, and, singularly enough, against myself. You start,' he said, 'you wonder who would have dared to attempt it! So did I; nevertheless, it has been done. *I have been robbed!*'

'*You* robbed – you, Hemlock Jones, the Terror of Peculators!' I gasped in amazement, rising and gripping the table as I faced him.

'Yes; listen. I would confess it to no other. But *you* who have followed my career, who know my methods; yea, for whom I have partly lifted the veil that conceals my plans from ordinary humanity; you, who have for years rapturously accepted my confidences, passionately admired my inductions and inferences, placed yourself at my beck and call, become my slave, grovelled at my feet, given up your practice except those few unremunerative and rapidly-decreasing patients to whom, in moments of abstraction over *my* problems, you have administered strychnine for quinine and arsenic for Epsom salts; you, who have sacrificed everything and everybody to me – *you* I make my confidant!'

I rose and embraced him warmly, yet he was already so engrossed in thought that at the same moment he mechanically placed his hand upon his watch chain as if to consult the time. 'Sit down,' he said; 'have a cigar?'

'I have given up cigar smoking,' I said.

'Why?' he asked.

I hesitated, and perhaps coloured. I had really given it up because, with my diminished practice, it was too expensive. I could only afford a pipe. 'I prefer a pipe,' I said laughingly. 'But tell me of this robbery. What have you lost?'

He rose, and planting himself before the fire with his hands under his coat tails, looked down upon me reflectively for a moment. 'Do you remember the cigar-case presented to me by the Turkish Ambassador for discovering the missing favourite of the Grand Vizier in the fifth chorus girl at the Hilarity Theatre? It was that one. It was encrusted with diamonds. I mean the cigar-case.'

'And the largest one had been supplanted by paste,' I said.

'Ah,' he said with a reflective smile, 'you know that?'

'You told me yourself. I remember considering it a proof of your extraordinary perception. But, by Jove, you don't mean to say you have lost it.'

He was silent for a moment. 'No; it has been stolen, it is true, but I shall still find it. And by myself alone! In your profession, my dear fellow, when a member is severely ill he does not prescribe for himself, but calls in a brother doctor. Therein we differ. I shall take this matter in my own hands.'

'And where could you find better?' I said enthusiastically. 'I should say the cigar case is as good as recovered already.'

'I shall remind you of that again,' he said lightly. 'And now, to show you my confidence in your judgment, in spite of my determination to pursue this alone, I am willing to listen to any suggestions from you.'

He drew a memorandum book from his pocket, and, with a grave smile, took up his pencil.

I could scarcely believe my reason. He, the great Hemlock Jones! accepting suggestions from a humble individual like myself! I kissed his hand reverently, and began in a joyous tone:

'First I should advertise, offering a reward; I should give the same intimation in handbills, distributed at the "pubs" and the pastry-cooks. I should next visit the different pawnbrokers; I should give notice at the police station. I should examine the servants. I should thoroughly search the house and my own pockets. I speak relatively,' I added with a laugh, 'of course, I mean *your* own.'

He gravely made an entry of these details.

'Perhaps,' I added, 'you have already done this?'

'Perhaps,' he returned enigmatically. 'Now, my dear friend,' he continued, putting the note-book in his pocket, and rising – 'would you excuse me for a few moments? Make yourself perfectly at home until I return; there may be some things,' he added with a sweep of his hand towards his heterogeneously filled shelves, 'that may interest you, and while away the time. There are pipes and tobacco in that corner and whiskey on the table.' And nodding to me with the same inscrutable face, he left the room. I was too well accustomed to his methods to think much of his unceremonious withdrawal, and made no doubt he was off to investigate some clue which had suddenly occurred to his active intelligence.

Left to myself, I cast a cursory glance over his shelves. There were a number of small glass jars, containing earthy substances labelled 'Pavement and road sweepings,' from the principal thoroughfares and suburbs of London, with the sub-directions 'For identifying foot tracks.' There were several other jars labelled 'Fluff from omnibus and road-car seats,' 'Coconut fibre and rope strands from mattings in public places,' 'Cigarette stumps and match ends from floor of Palace Theatre, Row A, 1 to 50.' Everywhere were evidences of this wonderful man's system and perspicacity.

I was thus engaged when I heard the slight creaking of a door, and I looked up as a stranger entered. He was a rough-looking man, with a shabby overcoat, a still more disreputable muffler round his throat, and a cap on his head. Considerably annoyed at his intrusion I turned upon him rather sharply, when, with a mumbled, growling apology for mistaking the room, he shuffled out again and closed the door. I followed him quickly to the landing and saw that he disappeared down the stairs.

With my mind full of the robbery, the incident made a singular impression on me. I knew my friend's habits of hasty absences from his room in his moments of deep inspiration; it was only too probable that with his powerful intellect and magnificent perceptive genius concentrated on one subject, he should be careless of his own belongings, and, no doubt, even forget to take the ordinary precaution of locking up his drawers. I tried one or two and found that I was right – although for

71

A rough-looking man in a shabby overall entered

some reason I was unable to open one to its fullest extent. The handles were sticky, as if someone had opened them with dirty fingers. Knowing Hemlock's fastidious cleanliness, I resolved to inform him of this circumstance, but I forgot it, alas! until – but I am anticipating my story.

His absence was strangely prolonged. I at last seated myself by the fire, and lulled by warmth and the patter of the rain on the window, I fell asleep. I may have dreamt, for during my sleep I had a vague semi-consciousness as of hands being softly pressed on my pockets – no doubt induced by the story of the robbery. When I came fully to my senses, I found Hemlock Jones sitting on the other side of the hearth, his deeply concentrated gaze fixed on the fire.

'I found you so comfortably asleep that I could not bear to waken you,' he said with a smile.

I rubbed my eyes. 'And what news?' I asked. 'How have you succeeded?'

'Better than I expected,' he said, 'and I think,' he added, tapping his note-book 'I owe much to *you*.'

Deeply gratified. I awaited more. But in vain. I ought to have remembered that in his moods Hemlock Jones was reticence itself. I told him simply of the strange intrusion, but he only laughed.

Later, when I rose to go, he looked at me playfully. 'If you were a married man,' he said, 'I would advise you not to go home until you had brushed your sleeve. There are a few short, brown seal-skin hairs on the inner side of the forearm – just where they would have adhered if your arm had encircled a seal-skin sacque with some pressure!'

'For once you are at fault,' I said triumphantly, 'the hair is my own as you will perceive; I have just had it cut at the hairdressers, and no doubt this arm projected beyond the apron.'

He frowned slightly, yet nevertheless, on my turning to go he embraced me warmly – a rare exhibition in that man of ice. He even helped me on with my overcoat and pulled out and smoothed down the flaps of my pockets. He was particular, too, in fitting my arm in my overcoat sleeve, shaking the sleeve down from the armhole to the cuff with his deft fingers. 'Come again soon!' he said, clapping me on the back.

'At any and all times,' I said enthusiastically. 'I only ask ten minutes twice a day to eat a crust at my office and four hours' sleep at night, and the rest of my time is devoted to you always – as you know.'

'It is, indeed,' he said, with his impenetrable smile.

Nevertheless I did not find him at home when I next called. One afternoon, when nearing my own home, I met him in one of his favourite disguises – a long, blue, swallow-tailed coat, striped cotton trousers, large turn-over collar, blacked face, and white hat, carrying a tambourine. Of course to others the disguise was perfect, although it was known to myself, and I passed him – according to an old understanding between us – without the slightest recognition, trusting to a later explanation. At another time, as I was making a professional visit to the wife of a publican at the East End, I saw him in the disguise of a broken-down artisan looking into the window of an adjacent pawnshop. I was delighted to see that he was evidently following my suggestions, and in my joy I ventured to tip him a wink; it was abstractedly returned.

Two days later I received a note appointing a meeting at his lodgings that night. That meeting, alas! was the one memorable occurrence of my life, and the last meeting I ever had with Hemlock Jones! I will try to set it down calmly, though my pulses still throb with the recollection of it.

I found him standing before the fire with that look upon his face which I had seen only once or twice in our acquaintance – a look which I may call an absolute concatenation of inductive and deductive ratiocination – from which all that was human, tender, or sympathetic, was absolutely discharged. He was simply an icy, algebraic symbol! Indeed his whole being was concentrated to that extent that his clothes fitted loosely, and his head was absolutely so much reduced in size by his mental compression that his hat tipped back from his forehead and literally hung on his massive ears.

After I had entered, he locked the doors, fastened the windows, and even placed a chair before the chimney. As I watched those significant precautions with absorbing interest, he suddenly drew a revolver and presenting it to my temple, said in low, icy tones:

'Hand over that cigar-case!'

Even in my bewilderment, my reply was truthful, spontaneous, and involuntary. 'I haven't got it,' I said.

He smiled bitterly, and threw down his revolver. 'I expected that reply! Then let me now confront you with something more awful, more deadly, more relentless and convincing than that mere lethal weapon –

the damning inductive and deductive proofs of your guilt!' He drew from his pocket a roll of paper and a note-book.

'But surely,' I gasped, 'you are joking! You could not for a moment believe–'

'Silence!' he roared. 'Sit down!'

I obeyed.

'You have condemned yourself,' he went on pitilessly. 'Condemned yourself on my processes – processes familiar to you, applauded by you, accepted by you for years! We will go back to the time when you first saw the cigar-case. Your expressions,' he said in cold, deliberate tones, consulting his paper, 'were: "How beautiful! I wish it were mine." This was your first step in crime – and my first indication. From "I *wish* it were mine" to "I *will* have it mine," and the mere detail, "How *can* I make it mine," the advance was obvious. Silence! But as in my methods, it was necessary that there should be an overwhelming inducement to the crime, that unholy admiration of yours for the mere trinket itself was not enough. You are a smoker of cigars.'

'But,' I burst out passionately, 'I told you I had given up smoking cigars.'

'Fool!' he said coldly, 'that is the *second* time you have committed yourself. Of course, you *told* me! what more natural than for you to blazon forth that prepared and unsolicited statement to *prevent* accusation. Yet, as I said before, even that wretched attempt to cover up your tracks was not enough. I still had to find that overwhelming, impelling motive necessary to affect a man like you. That motive I found in *passion*, the strongest of all impulses – love, I suppose you would call it,' he added bitterly 'that night you called! You had brought the damning proofs of it in your sleeve.'

'But,' I almost screamed.

'Silence,' he thundered. 'I know what you would say. You would say that even if you had embraced some young person in a sealskin sacque, what had that to do with the robbery? Let me tell you then, that that sealskin sacque represented the quality and character of your fatal entanglement If you are at all conversant with light sporting literature, you would know that a sealskin sacque indicates a love induced by sordid mercenary interests. You bartered your honour for it – that stolen cigar-case was the purchaser of the sealskin sacque! Without money, with a decreasing practice, it was the only way you could insure your passion being returned by that young person, whom, for your sake, I have not even pursued. Silence! Having thoroughly established your motive, I now proceed to the commission of the crime itself. Ordinary people would have begun with that – with an attempt to discover the whereabouts of the missing object. These are not my methods.'

So overpowering was his penetration, that although I knew myself innocent, I licked my lips with avidity to hear the further details of this lucid exposition of my crime.

'You committed that theft the night I showed you the cigar-case and after I had carelessly thrown it in that drawer. You were sitting in that chair, and I had risen to take something from that shelf. In that instant you secured your booty without rising. Silence! Do you remember when I helped you on with your overcoat the other night? I was particular about fitting your arm in. While doing so I measured your arm with a spring tape measure from the shoulder to the cuff. A later visit to your tailor confirmed that measurement. It proved to be *the exact distance between your chair and that drawer!*'

I sat stunned.

'The rest are mere corroborative details! You were again tampering with the drawer when I discovered you doing so. Do not start! The stranger that blundered into the room with the muffler on – was myself. More, I had placed a little soap on the drawer handles when I purposely left you alone. The soap was on your hand when I shook it at parting. I softly felt your pockets when you were asleep for further developments. I embraced you when you left – that I might feel if you had the cigar-case, or any other articles, hidden on your body. This confirmed me in the belief that you had already disposed of it in the manner and for the purpose I have shown you. As I still believed you capable of remorse and confession, I allowed you to see I was on your track twice, once in the garb of an itinerant negro minstrel, and the second time as a workman looking in the window of the pawnshop where you pledged your booty.'

'But,' I burst out, 'if you had asked the pawnbroker you would have seen how unjust–'

'Fool!' he hissed; 'that was one of *your* suggestions to search the pawnshops. Do you suppose I followed any of your suggestions – the suggestions of the thief? On the contrary, they told me what to avoid.'

'And I suppose,' I said bitterly, 'you have not even searched your drawer.'

'No,' he said calmly.

I was for the first time really vexed. I went to the nearest drawer and pulled it out sharply. It stuck as it had before, leaving a part of the drawer unopened. By working it, however, I discovered that it was impeded by some obstacle that had slipped to the upper part of the drawer, and held it firmly fast. Inserting my hand, I pulled out the impeding object. It was the missing cigar-case. I turned to him with a cry of joy.

But I was appalled at his expression. A look of contempt was now added to his acute, penetrating gaze. 'I have been mistaken,' he said slowly. 'I had not allowed for your weakness and cowardice. I thought too highly of you even in your guilt; but I see now why you tampered with that drawer the other night. By some incredible means – possibly another theft – you took the cigar-case out of pawn, and like a whipped hound restored it to me in this feeble, clumsy fashion. You thought to deceive me, Hemlock Jones: more, you thought to destroy my infallibility. Go! I give you your liberty. I shall not summon the three policemen who wait in the adjoining room – but out of my sight for ever.'

As I stood once more dazed and petrified, he took me firmly by the ear and led me into the hall, closing the door behind him. This re-opened presently wide enough to permit him to thrust out my hat, overcoat, umbrella and overshoes, and then close against me for ever!

I never saw him again. I am bound to say, however, that thereafter my business increased – I recovered much of my old practice – and a few of my patients recovered also. I became rich. I had a brougham and a house in the West End. But I often wondered, pondering on that wonderful man's penetration and insight, if, in some lapse of consciousness, I had not really stolen his cigar-case!

THE SIGNALMAN
Charles Dickens

'Halloa! Below there!'

When he heard a voice thus calling to him, he was standing at the door of his box, with a flag in his hand, furled round its short pole. One would have thought, considering the nature of the ground, that he could not have doubted from what quarter the voice came; but instead of looking up to where I stood on the top of the steep cutting nearly over his head, he turned himself about, and looked down the line. There was something remarkable in his manner of doing so, though I could not have said for my life what. But I know it was remarkable enough to attract my notice, even though his figure was foreshortened and shadowed, down in the deep trench, and mine was high above him, so steeped in the glow of an angry sunset that I had shaded my eyes with my hand before I saw him at all.

'Halloa! Below!'

From looking down the line, he turned himself about again, and, raising his eyes, saw my figure high above him.

'Is there any path by which I can come down and speak to you?'

He looked up at me without replying, and I looked down at him without pressing him too soon with a repetition of my idle question. Just then there came a vague vibration in the earth and air, quickly changing into a violent pulsation, and an oncoming rush that caused me to start back, as though it had force to draw me down. When such vapour as rose to my height from this rapid train had passed me, and was skimming away over the landscape, I looked down again, and saw him refurling the flag he had shown while the train went by.

I repeated my inquiry. After a pause, duing which he seemed to regard me with fixed attention, he motioned with his rolled-up flag towards a point on my level, some two or three hundred yards distant. I called down to him, 'All right!' and made for that point. There, by dint of looking closely about me, I found a rough zigzag descending path notched out, which I followed.

The cutting was extremely deep and unusually precipitate. It was made through a clammy stone that became oozier and wetter as I went down. For these reasons, I found the way long enough to give me time to recall a singular air of reluctance or compulsion with which he had pointed out the path.

When I came down low enough upon the zigzag descent to see him again, I saw that he was standing between the rails on the way by which the train had lately passed, in an attitude as if he were waiting for me to appear. He had his left hand at his chin, and that left elbow rested on his right hand, crossed over his breast. His attitude was one of such expectation and watchfulness that I stopped a moment, wondering at it.

I resumed my downward way, and stepping out upon the level of the railroad, and drawing nearer to him, saw that he was a dark sallow man, with a dark beard and rather heavy eyebrows. His post was in as solitary and dismal a place as ever I saw. On either side, a dripping-wet wall of jagged stone, excluding all view but a strip of sky; the perspective one way only a crooked prolongation of this great dungeon; the shorter perspective in the other direction terminating in a gloomy red light, and the gloomier entrance to a black tunnel, in whose massive architecture there was a barbarous, depressing and forbidding air. So little sunlight ever found its way to this spot that it had an earthy, deadly smell; and so much cold wind rushed through it that it struck chill to me, as if I had left the natural world.

Before he stirred, I was near enough to him to have touched him. Not even then removing his eyes from mine, he stepped back one step, and lifted his hand.

This was a lonesome post to occupy (I said), and it had riveted my attention when I looked down from up yonder. A visitor was a rarity, I should suppose; not an unwelcome rarity, I hoped? In me, he merely saw a man who had been shut up within narrow limits all his life, and who, being at last set free, had a newly-awakened interest in these great works. To such purpose I spoke to him; but I am far from sure of the terms I used; for, besides that I am not happy in opening any conversation, there was something in the man that daunted me.

He directed a most curious look towards the red light near the tunnel's mouth, and looked all about it, as if something were missing from it, and then looked at me.

That light was part of his charge? Was it not?

He answered in a low voice, 'Don't you know it is?'

The monstrous thought came into my mind, as I perused the fixed eyes and the saturnine face, that this was a spirit, not a man. I have speculated since, whether there may have been infection in his mind.

In my turn I stepped back. But in making the action, I detected in his eyes some latent fear of me. This put the monstrous thought to flight.

'You look at me,' I said, forcing a smile, 'as if you had a dread of me.'

'I was doubtful,' he returned, 'whether I had seen you before.'

'Where?'

He pointed to the red light he had looked at.

'There?' I said.

Intently watchful of me, he replied (but without sound), 'Yes.'

'My good fellow, what should I do there? However, be that as it may, I never was there, you may swear.'

'I think I may,' he rejoined. 'Yes; I am sure I may.'

His manner cleared, like my own. He replied to my remarks with readiness, and in well-chosen words. Had he much to do there? Yes; that was to say, he had enough responsibility to bear; but exactness and watchfulness were what was required of him, and of actual work – manual labour – he had next to none. To change that signal, to trim those lights, and to turn this iron handle now and then, was all he had to under that head.

Regarding those many long and lonely hours of which I seemed to make so much, he could only say that the routine of his life had shaped itself into that form, and he had grown used to it. He had taught himself a language down here – if only to know it by sight, and to have formed his own crude ideas of its pronunciation, could be called learning it. He had also worked at fractions and decimals, and tried a little algebra; but he was, and had been as a boy, a poor hand at figures. Was it necessary for him when on duty always to remain in that channel of damp air, and could he never rise into the sunshine from between those high stone walls? Why, that depended upon times and circumstances. Under some conditions there would be less upon the line than under others, and the same held good as to certain hours of the day and night. In bright weather, he did choose occasions for getting a little above those lower shadows; but, being at all times liable to be called by his electric bell, and at such times listening for it with redoubled anxiety, the relief was less than I would suppose.

He took me into his box, where there was a fire, a desk for an official book in which he had to make certain entries, a telegraphic instrument with its dial, face, and needles, and the little bell of which he had spoken. On my trusting that he would excuse the remark that he had been well educated, and (I hoped I might say without offence) perhaps educated above that station, he observed that instances of slight incongruity in such wise would rarely be found wanting among large bodies of men; that he had heard it was so in workhouses, in the police force, even in that last desperate resource, the army; and that he knew it was so, more or less, in any great railway staff. He had been, when young (if I could believe it, sitting in that hut – he scarcely could), a student of natural philosophy, and had attended lectures; but he had run wild, misused his opportunities, gone down, and never risen again. He had no complaint to offer about that. He had made his bed, and he lay upon it. It was far too late to make another.

All that I have here condensed he said in a quiet manner, with his grave dark regards divided between me and the fire. He threw in the word 'sir' from time to time, and especially when he referred to his youth – as though to request me to understand that he claimed to be nothing but what I found him. He was several times interrupted by the little bell, and had to read off messages and send replies. Once he had to stand without the door, and display a flag as a train passed, and make some verbal communication to the driver. In the discharge of his duties, I observed him to be remarkably exact and vigilant, breaking off his discourse at a syllable, and remaining silent until what he had to do was done.

In a word, I should have set this man down as one of the safest of men to be employed in that capacity, but for the circumstance that while he was speaking to me he twice broke off with a fallen colour, turned his face towards the little bell when it did *not* ring, opened the door of the hut (which was kept shut to exclude the unhealthy damp), and looked out towards the red light near the mouth of the tunnel. On both of those occasions he came back to the fire with the inexplicable air upon him which I had remarked, without being able to define, when we were so far asunder.

Said I, when I rose to leave him, 'You almost make me think that I have met with a contented man.'

(I am afraid I must acknowledge that I said it to lead him on.)

'I believe I used to be so,' he rejoined, in the low voice in which he had first spoken; 'but I am troubled sir, I am troubled.'

He would have recalled the words if he could. He had said them, however, and I took them up quickly.

'With what? What is your trouble?'

'It is very difficult to impart, sir. It is very, very difficult to speak of. If ever you make me another visit, I will try to tell you.'

'But I expressly intend to make you another visit. Say, when shall it be?'

'I go off early in the morning, and I shall be on again at ten tomorrow night, sir.'

'I will come at eleven.'

He thanked me, and went out at the door with me. 'I'll show my white light, sir,' he said in his peculiar low voice, 'till you have found the way up. When you have found it, don't call out! And when you are at the top, don't call out!'

His manner seemed to make the place strike colder to me, but I said no more than 'Very well.'

'And when you come down tomorrow night, don't call out! Let me ask you a parting question. What made you cry, "Halloa! Below there!" tonight?'

'Heaven knows,' said I, 'I cried something to that effect—'

'Not to that effect, sir. Those were the very words. I know them well.'

'Admit those were the very words. I said them, no doubt, because I saw you below.'

'For no other reason?'

'What other reason could I possibly have?'

'You have no feeling that they were conveyed to you in any supernatural way?'

'No.'

He wished me good-night, and held up his light. I walked by the side of the down line of rails (with a very disagreeable sensation of a train coming behind me) until I found the path. It was easier to mount than to descend, and I got back to my inn without any adventure.

★   ★   ★   ★

Punctual to my appointment, I placed my foot on the first notch of the zigzag next night as the distant clocks were striking eleven. He was waiting for me at the bottom, with his white light on. 'I have not called out,' I said, when we came close together; 'may I speak now?' 'By all means, sir.' 'Good-night, then, and here's my hand.' 'Good-night, sir, and here's mine.' With that we walked side by side to his box, entered it, closed the door, and sat down by the fire.

'I have made up my mind, sir,' he began, bending forward as soon as we were seated, and speaking in a tone but a little above a whisper, 'that you shall not have to ask me twice what troubles me. I took you for someone else yesterday evening. That troubles me.'

'That mistake?'

'No. That someone else.'

'Who is it?'

'I don't know.'

'Like me?'

'I don't know. I never saw the face. The left arm is across the face, and the right arm is waved – violently waved. This way.'

I followed his action with my eyes, and it was the action of an arm gesticulating, with the utmost passion and vehemence, 'For God's sake, clear the way!'

'One moonlight night,' said the man, 'I was sitting here, when I heard a voice cry, "Halloa! Below there!" I started up, looked from that door, and saw this someone else standing by the red light near the tunnel, waving as I just now showed you. The voice seemed hoarse with shouting, and it cried, "Look out! Look out!" And then again, "Halloa! Below there! Look out!" I caught up my lamp, turned it on red, and ran towards the figure, calling, "What's wrong? What has happened? Where?" It stood just outside the blackness of the tunnel. I advanced so close upon it that I wondered at its keeping the sleeve across its eyes. I ran right up at it, and had my hand stretched out to pull the sleeve away, when it was gone.'

'Into the tunnel?' said I.

'No. I ran on into the tunnel, five hundred yards. I stopped, and held my lamp above my head, and saw the figures of the measured distance, and saw the wet stains stealing down the walls and trickling through the arch. I ran out again faster than I had run in (for I had a mortal abhorrence of the place upon me), and I looked all round the red light with my own red light; and I went up the iron ladder to the gallery atop of it, and I came down again, and ran back here. I telegraphed both ways, "An alarm has been given. Is anything wrong?" The answer came back, both ways, "All well".'

Resisting the slow touch of a frozen finger tracing out my spine, I showed him how that this figure must be a deception of his sense of sight; and how that figures, originating in disease of the delicate nerves that minister to the functions of the eye, were known to have often troubled patients, some of whom had become conscious of the nature of their affliction, and had even proved it by experiments upon themselves. 'As to an imaginary cry,' said I, 'do but listen for a moment to the wind in this unnatural valley while we speak so low, and to the wild harp it makes of the telegraph wires.'

That was all very well, he returned, after we had sat listening for a while, and he ought to know something of the wind and the wires – he who so often passed long winter nights there, alone and watching. But he would beg to remark that he had not finished.

I asked his pardon, and he slowly added these words, touching my arm: 'Within six hours after the appearance, the memorable accident on this line happened, and within ten hours the dead and wounded were brought along the tunnel over the spot where the figure had stood.'

A disagreeable shudder crept over me, but I did my best against it. It was not to be denied, I rejoined, that this was a remarkable coincidence, calculated deeply to impress his mind. But it was unquestionable that remarkable coincidences did continually occur, and they must be taken into account in dealing with such a subject. Though to be sure I must admit, I added (for I thought I saw that he was going to bring the objection to bear upon me), men of common sense did not allow much for coincidences in making the ordinary calculations of life.

He again begged to remark that he had not finished.

I again begged his pardon for being betrayed into interruptions.

'This,' he said, again laying his hand upon my arm, and glancing over his shoulder with hollow eyes, 'was just a year ago. Six or seven months passed, and I had recovered from the surprise and shock, when one morning, as the day was breaking, I, standing at the door, looked towards the red light, and saw the spectre again.' He stopped, with a fixed look at me.

'Did it cry out?'

'No. It was silent.'

'Did it wave its arm?'

'No. It leaned against the shaft of the light with both hands before the face. Like this.'

Once more I followed his action with my eyes. It was an action of mourning. I have seen such an attitude on stone figures on tombs.

'Did you go up to it?'

'I came in and sat down, partly to collect my thoughts, partly because it had turned me faint. When I went to the door again, daylight was above me, and the ghost was gone.'

'But nothing followed? Nothing came of this?'

He touched me on the arm with his forefinger twice or thrice, giving a ghastly nod each time.

'That very day, as a train came out of the tunnel, I noticed, at a carriage window on my side, what looked like a confusion of hands and heads, and something waved. I saw it just in time to signal the driver "Stop!" He shut off, and put his brake on, but the train drifted past here a hundred and fifty yards or more. I ran after it, and, as I went along, heard terrible screams and cries. A beautiful young lady had died instantaneously in one of the compartments, and was brought in here, and laid down on this floor between us.'

Involuntarily I pushed my chair back, as I looked from the boards at which he pointed to himself.

'True, sir. True. Precisely as it happened, so I tell it you.'

I could think of nothing to say, to any purpose, and my mouth was very dry. The wind and the wires took up the story with a long lamenting wail.

He resumed. 'Now, sir, mark this, and judge how my mind is troubled. The spectre came back a week ago. Ever since, it has been there, now and again, by fits and starts.'

'At the light?'

'At the danger-light.'

'What does it seem to do?'

He repeated, if possible with increased passion and vehemence, that former gesticulation of 'For God's sake, clear the way!'

Then he went on. 'I have no peace or rest for it. It calls to me, for many minutes together, in an agonised manner. "Below there! Look out! Look out!" It stands waving to me. It rings my little bell –'

I caught at that. 'Did it ring your bell yesterday evening when I was here, and you went to the door?'

'Twice.'

'Why, see,' said I, 'how your imagination misleads you. My eyes were on the bell, and my ears were open to the bell, and if I am a living man, it did *not* ring at those times. No, nor at any other time, except when it was rung in the natural course of physical things by the station communicating with you.'

He shook his head. 'I have never made a mistake as to that yet, sir. I have never confused the spectre's ring with the man's. The ghost's ring is a strange vibration in the bell that it derives from nothing else, and I have not asserted that the bell stirs to the eye. I don't wonder that you failed to hear it. But *I* heard it.'

'And did the spectre seem to be there when you looked out?'

'It *was* there.'

'Both times?'

He repeated firmly: 'Both times.'

'Will you come to the door with me, and look for it now?'

He bit his lower lip as though he were somewhat unwilling, but arose.

I opened the door, and stood on the step, while he stood in the doorway. There was the danger-light. There was the dismal mouth of the tunnel. There were the high, wet stone walls of the cutting. There were the stars above them.

'Do you see it?' I asked him, taking particular note of his face. His eyes were prominent and strained, but not very much more so, perhaps, than my own had been when I had directed them earnestly towards the same spot.

'No,' he answered. 'It is not there.'

'Agreed,' said I.

We went in again, shut the door, and resumed our seats. I was thinking how best to improve this advantage, if it might be called one, when he took up the conversation in such a matter-of-course way, so assuming that there could be no serious question of fact between us, that I felt myself placed in the weakest of positions.

'By this time you will fully understand, sir,' he said, 'that what troubles me so dreadfully is the question: what does the spectre mean?'

I was not sure, I told him, that I did not fully understand.

'What is it warning against?' he said, ruminating, with his eyes on the fire, and only by times turning them on me. 'What is the danger? Where is the danger? There is danger overhanging somewhere on the line. Some dreadful calamity will happen. It is not to be doubted this third time, after what has gone before. But surely this is a cruel haunting of *me*. What can I do?'

He pulled out his handkerchief, and wiped the drops from his heated forehead.

'If I telegraph danger on either side of me, or on both, I can give no reason for it,' he went on, wiping the palms of his hands. 'I should get into trouble and do no good. They would think I was mad. This is the way it would work: Message: "Danger! Take care!" Answer: "What danger? Where?" Message: "Don't know. But for God's sake, take care!"

They would displace me. What else could they do?'

His pain of mind was most pitiable to see. It was the mental torture of a conscientious man, oppressed beyond endurance by an unintelligible responsibility involving life.

'When it first stood under the danger-light,' he went on, putting his dark hair back from his head, and drawing his hands outward across his

87

temples in an extremity of feverish distress, 'why not tell me where that accident was to happen – if it must happen? Why not tell me how it could be averted – if it could have been averted? When on its second coming it hid its face, why not tell me, instead. "She is going to die. Let them keep her at home"? If it came, on those two occasions, only to show me that its warnings were true, and so to prepare me for the third why not warn me plainly now? And I, Lord help me! A mere poor signalman on this solitary station! Why not go to somebody with credit to be believed, and power to act?'

When I saw him in this state, I saw that for the poor man's sake, as well as for the public safety, what I had to do for the time was to compose his mind. Therefore, setting aside all question of reality or unreality between us, I represented to him that whoever thoroughly discharged his duty must do well, and that at least it was his comfort that he understood his duty, though he did not understand these confounding appearances. In this effort I succeeded far better than in the attempt to reason him out of his conviction. He became calm; the occupations incidental to his post as the night advanced began to make larger demands on his attention: and I left him at two in the morning. I had offered to stay through the night, but he would not hear of it.

That I more than once looked back at the red light as I ascended the pathway, that I did not like the red light, and that I should have slept but poorly if my bed had been under it, I see no reason to conceal. Nor did I like the two sequences of the accident and the dead girl. I see no reason to conceal that either.

But what ran most in my thoughts was the consideration how ought I to act, having become the recipient of this disclosure? I had proved the man to be intelligent, vigilant, painstaking, and exact; but how long might he remain so, in his state of mind? Though in a subordinate position, still he held a most important trust, and would I (for instance) like to stake my own life on the chances of his continuing to execute it with precision?

Unable to overcome a feeling that there would be something treacherous in my communicating what he had told me to his superiors in the company, without first being plain with himself and proposing a middle course to him, I ultimately resolved to offer to accompany him (otherwise keeping his secret for the present) to the wisest medical practitioner we could hear of in those parts, and to take his opinion. A change in his time of duty would come round next night, he had apprised me, and he would be off an hour or two after sunrise, and on again soon after sunset. I had appointed to return accordingly.

       ★   ★   ★   ★

Next evening was a lovely evening, and I walked out early to enjoy it. The sun was not yet quite down when I traversed the field-path near the top of the deep cutting. I would extend my walk for an hour, I said to myself, half an hour on and half an hour back, and it would then be time to go to my signalman's box.

Before pursuing my stroll, I stepped to the brink, and mechanically looked down, from the point from which I had first seen him. I cannot describe the thrill that seized upon me, when, close at the mouth of the tunnel, I saw the appearance of a man, with his left sleeve across his eyes, passionately waving his right arm.

The nameless horror that oppressed me passed in a moment, for in a moment I saw that this appearance of a man was a man indeed, and that there was a little group of other men standing at a short distance, to whom he seemed to be rehearsing the gesture he made. The danger-light was not yet lit. Against its shaft a little low hut entirely new to me had been made of some wooden supports and tarpaulin. It looked no bigger than a bed.

With an irresistible sense that something was wrong – with a flashing self-reproachful fear that fatal mischief had come of my leaving the man there, and causing no one to be sent to overlook or correct what he did – I descended the notched path with all the speed I could make.

'What is the matter?' I asked the men.

'Signalman killed this morning, sir.'

'Not the man belonging to that box?'

'Yes, sir.'

'Not the man I know?'

'You will recognise him, sir, if you knew him,' said the man who spoke for all the others, solemnly uncovering his own head, and raising an end of the tarpaulin, 'for his face is quite composed.'

'Oh, how did this happen, how did this happen?' I asked, turning from one to another as the hut closed in again.

'He was cut down by an engine, sir. No man in England knew his work better. But somehow he was not clear of the outer rail. It was just at broad day. He had struck the light, and had the lamp in his hand. As the engine came out of the tunnel, his back was towards her, and she cut him down. That man drove her, and was showing how it happened. Show the gentleman, Tom.'

The man, who wore a rough dark dress, stepped back to his former place at the mouth of the tunnel.

'Coming round the curve in the tunnel, sir, he said. 'I saw him at the end, like as if I saw him down a perspective-glass. There was no time to check speed, and I knew him to be very careful. As he didn't seem to take heed of the whistle, I shut it off when we were running down upon him, and called to him as loud as I could call.'

'What did you say?'

"I said, "Below there! Look out! Look out! For God's sake, clear the way!"'

I started.

'Ah! it was a dreadful time, sir. I never left off calling to him. I put this arm before my eyes not to see, and I waved this arm to the last; but it was no use.

Without prolonging the narrative to dwell on any one of its curious circumstances more than on any other, I may, in closing it, point out the coincidence that the warning of the engine-driver included, not only the words which the unfortunate signalman had repeated to me as haunting him, but also the words which I myself – not he – had attached, and that only in my own mind, to the gesticulation he had imitated.

NULE

Jan Mark

The house was not old enough to be interesting, just old enough to be starting to fall apart. The few interesting things had been dealt with ages ago, when they first moved in. There was a bell-push in every room, somehow connected to a glass case in the kitchen which contained a list of names and an indicator which wavered from name to name when a button was pushed, before settling on one of them: *Parlour*; *Drawing Room*; *Master Bedroom*; *Second Bedroom*; *Back Bedroom*.

'What are they for?' said Libby one morning, after roving round the house and pushing all the buttons in turn. At that moment Martin pushed the button in the front room and the indicator slid up to *Parlour*, vibrating there while the bell rang. And rang and rang.

'To fetch up the maid,' said Mum.

'We haven't got a maid.'

'No, but you've got me,' said Mum, and tied an old sock over the bell, so that afterwards it would only whirr instead of ringing.

The mouse-holes in the kitchen looked interesting, too. The mice were bold and lounged about, making no effort at all to be timid and mouse-like. They sat on the draining board in the evenings and could scarcely be bothered to stir themselves when the light was switched on.

'Easy living has made them soft,' said Mum. 'They have a gaming-hall behind the boiler. They throw dice all day. They dance the can-can at night.'

'Come off it,' said Dad. 'You'll be finding crates of tiny gin bottles, next.'

'They dance the can-can,' Mum insisted. 'Right over my head they dance it. I can hear them. If you didn't sleep so soundly, you'd hear them too.'

'Oh, that. That's not mice,' said Dad, with a cheery smile. 'That's rats.'

Mum minded the mice less than the bells, until the day she found footprints in the frying-pan.

'Sorry, lads, the party's over,' she said to the mice, who were no doubt combing the dripping from their elegant whiskers at that very moment, and the mouse-holes were blocked up.

Dad did the blocking-up, and also some unblocking, so that after the bath no longer filled itself through the plug hole, the house stopped being interesting altogether; for a time.

Libby and Martin did what they could to improve matters. Beginning in the cupboard under the stairs, they worked their way through the house, up to the attic, looking for something; anything; tapping walls and floors, scouring cupboards, measuring and calculating, but there were no hidden cavities, no secret doors, no ambiguous bulges under the wallpaper, except where the damp got it. The cupboard below the stairs was full of old pickle jars, and what they found in the attic didn't please anyone, least of all Dad.

'That's dry rot,' he said. 'Thank god this isn't our house,' and went cantering off to visit the estate agents, Tench and Tench, in the High Street. Dad called them Shark and Shark. As he got to the gate he turned back and yelled, 'The Plague! The Plague! Put a red cross on the door!' which made Mrs Bowen, over the fence, lean right out of her landing window instead of hiding behind the curtains.

When Dad came back from the estate agents he was growling.

'Shark junior says that since the whole row is coming down inside two years, it isn't worth bothering about. I understand that the new by-pass is going to run right through the scullery.'

'What did Shark senior say?' said Mum.

'I didn't see him. I've never seen him. I don't believe that there is a Shark senior,' said Dad. 'I think he's dead. I think Young Shark keeps him in a box under the bed.'

'Don't be nasty,' said Mum, looking at Libby who worried about things under the bed even in broad daylight. 'I just hope we find a house of our own before this place collapses on our heads—and we shan't be buying it from the Sharks.'

She went back to her sewing, not in a good mood. The mice had broken out again. Libby went into the kitchen to look for them. Martin ran upstairs, rhyming:

> 'Mr Shark,
> In the Dark,
> Under the bed.
> Dead.'

When he came down again, Mum was putting away the sewing and Libby was parading around the hall in a pointed hat with a veil and a long red dress that looked rich and splendid unless you knew, as Martin did, that it was made of old curtains.

The hall was dark in the rainy summer afternoon, and Libby slid from shadow to shadow, rustling.

'What are you meant to be?' said Martin. 'An old witch?'

'I'm the Sleeping Beauty's mother,' said Libby, and lowering her head she charged along the hall, pointed hat foremost, like a unicorn.

Martin changed his mind about walking downstairs and slid down the bannisters instead. He suspected that he would not be allowed to do this for much longer. Already the bannister rail creaked, and who knew where the dreaded dry rot would strike next? As he reached the upright post at the bottom of the stairs, Mum came out of the back room, lugging the sewing-machine, and just missed being impaled on Libby's hat.

'Stop rushing up and down,' said Mum. 'You'll ruin those clothes and I've only just finished them. Go and take them off. And you,' she said, turning to Martin, 'stop swinging on that newel post. Do you want to tear it up by the roots?'

The newel post was supposed to be holding up the bannisters, but possibly it was the other way about. At the foot it was just a polished wooden post, but further up it had been turned on a lathe, with slender hips, a waist, a bust almost, and square shoulders. On top was a round ball, as big as a head.

There was another at the top of the stairs but it had lost its head. Dad called it Ann Boleyn; the one at the bottom was simply a newel post, but Libby thought that this too was its name; Nule Post, like Ann Boleyn or Libby Anderson.

Mrs Nule Post.

Lady Nule Post.

When she talked to it she just called it Nule.

The pointed hat and the old curtains were Libby's costume for the school play. Martin had managed to stay out of the school play, but he knew all of Libby's lines by heart as she chanted them round the house, up and down stairs, in a strained, jerky voice, one syllable per step.

'My-dear-we-must-in-vite-all-the-fair-ies-to-the-chris-ten-ing, Hullo, Nule, we-will-not-in-vite-the-wick-ed-fair-y!'

On the last day of term, he sat with Mum and Dad in the school hall and watched Libby go through the same routine on stage. She was word-perfect, in spite of speaking as though her shock absorbers had collapsed, but as most of the cast spoke the same way it didn't sound so very strange.

Once the holidays began Libby went back to talking like Libby, although she still wore the pointed hat and the curtains, until they began to drop to pieces. The curtains went for dusters, but the pointed hat was around for a long time until Mum picked it up and threatened, 'Take this thing away or it goes in the dustbin.'

Libby shunted up and down stairs a few times with the hat on her head, and then Mum called out that Jane-next-door had come to play. If Libby had been at the top of the stairs, she might have left the hat on her bed, but she was almost at the bottom so she plonked it down on Nule's cannon-ball head, and went out to fight Jane over whose turn it was to kidnap the teddy-bear. She hoped it was Jane's turn. If Libby were the kidnapper, she would have to sit about for ages holding Teddy to ransome behind the water tank, while Jane galloped round the garden on her imaginary pony, whacking the hydrangea bushes with a

94

broomstick.

The hat definitely did something for Nule. When Martin came in later by the front door, he thought at first that it was a person standing at the foot of the stairs. He had to look twice before he understood who it was. Mum saw it at the same time.

'I told Libby to put that object away or I'd throw it in the dustbin.'

'Oh, don't,' said Martin. 'Leave it for Dad to see.'

So she left it, but Martin began to get ideas. The hat made the rest of Nule look very undressed, so he fetched down the old housecoat that had been hanging behind the bathroom door when they moved in. It was purple, with blue paisleys swimming all over it, and very worn, as though it had been somebody's favourite housecoat. The sleeves had set in creases around arms belonging to someone they had never known.

Turning it front to back, he buttoned it like a bib round Nule's neck so that it hung down to the floor. He filled two gloves with screwed-up newspaper, poked them into the sleeves and pinned them there. The weight made the arms dangle and opened the creases. He put a pair of football boots under the hem of the housecoat with the toes just sticking out, and stood back to see how it looked.

As he expected, in the darkness of the hall it looked just like a person, waiting, although there was something not so much lifelike as deathlike in the hang of those dangling arms.

Mum and Libby first saw Nule as they came out of the kitchen together.

'Who on earth did this?' said Mum as they drew alongside.

'It wasn't me,' said Libby, and sounded very glad that it wasn't.

'It was you left the hat, wasn't it?'

'Yes, but not the other bits.'

'What do you think?' said Martin.

'Horrible thing,' said Mum, but she didn't ask him to take it down. Libby sidled round Nule and ran upstairs as close to the wall as she could get.

When Dad came home from work he stopped in the doorway and said, 'Hullo—who's that? Who . . .?' before Martin put the light on and showed him.

'An idol, I suppose,' said Dad. 'Nule, god of dry rot,' and he bowed low at the foot of the stairs. At the same time the hat slipped forward slightly, as if Nule had lowered its head in acknowledgement. Martin also bowed low before reaching up to put the hat straight.

Mum and Dad seemed to think that Nule was rather funny, so it stayed at the foot of the stairs. They never bowed to it again, but Martin did, every time he went upstairs, and so did Libby. Libby didn't talk to Nule any more, but she watched it a lot. One day she said, 'Which way is it facing?'

'Forwards, of course,' said Martin, but it was hard to tell unless you looked at the feet. He drew two staring eyes and a toothy smile on a piece of paper and cut them out. They were attached to the front of Nule's head with little bits of chewing-gum.

'That's better,' said Libby, laughing, and next time she went upstairs she forgot to bow. Martin was not so sure. Nule looked ordinary now, just like a newel post wearing a housecoat, football boots and the Sleeping Beauty's mother's hat. He took off the eyes and the mouth and rubbed away the chewing-gum.

'*That's* better,' he said, while Nule stared once more without eyes, and smiled without a mouth.

Libby said nothing.

At night the house creaked.

'Thiefly footsteps,' said Libby.

'It's the furniture warping,' said Mum.

Libby thought she said that the furniture was walking, and she could well believe it. The dressing-table had feet with claws; why shouldn't it walk in the dark, tugging fretfully this way and that because the clawed feet pointed in opposite directions? The bath had feet too. Libby imagined it galloping out of the bathroom and tobogganing downstairs on its stomach, like a great white walrus plunging into the sea. If someone held the door open, it would whizz up the path and crash into the front gate. If someone held the gate open, it would shoot across the road and hit the district nurse's car, which she parked under the street light, opposite.

Libby thought of headlines in the local paper—NURSE RUN OVER BY BATH—and giggled, until she heard the creaks again. Then she hid under the bedclothes.

In his bedroom Martin heard the creaks too, but he had a different reason for worrying. In the attic where the dry rot lurked, there was a big oak wardrobe full of old dead ladies' clothes. It was directly over his head. Supposing it came through?

Next day he moved the bed.

The vacuum cleaner had lost its casters and had to be helped, by Libby pushing from behind. It skidded up the hall and knocked Nule's football boots askew.

'The Hoover doesn't like Nule either,' said Libby. Although she wouldn't talk to Nule anymore she liked talking *about* it, as though that somehow made Nule safer.

'What's that?' said Mum.

'It knocked Nule's feet off.'

'Well, put them back,' said Mum, but Libby preferred not to. When Martin came in he set them side by side, but later they were kicked out of place again. If people began to complain that Nule was in the way, Nule would have to go. He got round this by putting the right boot where the left had been and the left boot on the bottom stair. When he left it, the veil on the hat was hanging down behind, but as he went upstairs after tea he noticed that it was now draped over Nule's right shoulder, as if Nule had turned its head to see where its feet were going.

That night the creaks were louder than ever, like a burglar on hefty tiptoe. Libby had mentioned thieves only that evening, and Mum had said, 'What have we got worth stealing?'

Martin felt fairly safe because he had worked out that if the wardrobe fell tonight, it would land on his chest of drawers and not on him, but what might it not bring down with it? Then he realized that the creaks were coming not from above but from below.

He held his breath. Downstairs didn't creak.

His alarm clock gleamed greenly in the dark and told him that it had gone two o'clock. Mum and Dad were asleep ages ago. Libby would sooner burst than leave her bed in the dark. Perhaps it *was* a burglar. Feeling noble and reckless he put on the bedside lamp, slid out of bed, trod silently across the carpet. He turned on the main light and opened the door. The glow shone out of the doorway and saw him as far as the landing light switch at the top of the stairs, but he never had time to turn it on. From the top of the stairs he could look down into the hall where the street light opposite shone coldly through the frosted panes of the front door.

It shone on the hall stand where the coats hung, on the blanket chest and the brass jug that stood on it, through the white coins of the honesty plants in the brass jug, and on the broody telephone that never rang at night. It did not shine on Nule. Nule was not there.

Nule was halfway up the stairs, one hand on the bannisters and one hand holding up the housecoat, clear of its boots. The veil on the hat drifted like smoke across the frosted glass of the front door. Nule creaked and came up another step.

Martin turned and fled back to the bedroom, and dived under the bedclothes, just like Libby who was three years younger and believed in ghosts.

'Were you reading in bed last night?' said Mum, prodding him awake next morning. Martin came out from under the pillow, very slowly.

'No, Mum.'

'You went to sleep with the light on. *Both* lights,' she said, leaning across to switch off the one by the bed.

'I'm sorry.'

'Perhaps you'd like to pay the next electricity bill?'

Mum had brought him a cup of tea, which meant that she had been down to the kitchen and back again, unscathed. Martin wanted to ask her if there was anything strange on the stairs, but he didn't quite know how to put it. He drank the tea, dressed, and went along the landing.

He looked down into the hall where the sun shone through the frosted glass of the front door, onto the hallstand, the blanket chest, the honesty plants in the brass jug, and the telephone that began to ring as he looked at it. It shone on Nule, standing with its back to him at the foot of the stairs.

Mum came out of the kitchen to answer the phone and Martin went down and stood three steps up, watching Nule and waiting for Mum to finish talking. Nule looked just as it always did. Both feet were back on ground level, side by side.

'I wish you wouldn't hang about like that when I'm on the phone,' said Mum, putting down the receiver and turning round. 'Eavesdropper. Breakfast will be ready in five minutes.'

She went back into the kitchen and Martin sat on the blanket chest, looking at Nule. It was time for Nule to go. He should walk up to Nule this minute, kick away the boots, rip off the housecoat, throw away the hat, but . . .

He stayed where he was, watching the motionless football boots, the dangling sleeves. The breeze from an open window stirred the hem of the housecoat and revealed the wooden post beneath, rooted firmly in the floor as it had been for seventy years.

There were no feet in the boots; no arms in the sleeves.

If he destroyed Nule, it would mean that he *believed* that he had seen Nule climbing the stairs last night, but if he left Nule alone, Nule might walk again.

He had a problem.

THE PICTURE OF DORIAN GRAY
Oscar Wilde

When young Dorian Gray sees the marvellous picture that Basil Hallward has painted of him, he exclaims that he would like the picture to grow old while he retains his incredible beauty and youth.

Under the amoral influence of Lord Henry Wooton, Dorian begins to lead a life of unsurpassed debauchery, leading others astray, and his prayer is answered — he retains his youth and the face in the portrait ages and becomes more despicable with every sin that Dorian commits.

It was on the ninth of November, the eve of his own thirty-eighth birthday, as he often remembered afterwards.

He was walking home about eleven o'clock from Lord Henry's, where he had been dining, and was wrapped in heavy furs, as the night was cold and foggy. At the corner of Grosvenor Square and South Audley Street a man passed him in the mist, walking very fast, and with the collar of his grey ulster turned up. He had a bag in his hand. Dorian recognised him. It was Basil Hallward. A strange sense of fear, for which he could not account, came over him. He made no sign of recognition, and went on quickly in the direction of his own house.

But Hallward had seen him. Dorian heard him first stopping on the pavement, and then hurrying after him. In a few moments his hand was on his arm.

'Dorian! What an extraordinary piece of luck! I have been waiting for you in your library ever since nine o'clock. Finally I took pity on your tired servant, and told him to go to bed, as he let me out. I am off to Paris by the midnight train, and I particularly wanted to see you before I left. I thought it was you, or rather your fur coat, as you passed me. But I wasn't quite sure. Didn't you recognise me?'

'In this fog, my dear Basil? Why, I can't even recognise Grosvenor Square. I believe my house is somewhere about here, but I don't feel at all certain about it. I am sorry you are going away, as I have not seen you for ages. But I suppose you will be back soon?'

'No: I am going to be out of England for six months. I intended to take a studio in Paris, and shut myself up until I have finished a great picture I have in my head. However, it wasn't about myself I wanted to talk. Here we are at your door. Let me come in for a moment. I have something to say to you.'

'I shall be charmed. But won't you miss your train?' said Dorian Gray, languidly, as he passed up the steps and opened the door with his latchkey.

The lamplight struggled out through the fog, and Hallward looked at his watch. 'I have heaps of time,' he answered. 'The train doesn't go until twelve-fifteen, and it is only just eleven. In fact, I was on my way to the club to look for you, when I met you. You see, I shan't have any delay about luggage, as I have sent on my heavy things. All I have with me is in this bag, and I can easily get to Victoria in twenty minutes.'

Dorian looked at him and smiled. 'What a way for a fashionable painter to travel! A Gladstone bag, and an ulster! Come in, or the fog will get into the house. And mind you don't talk about anything serious. Nothing is serious nowadays. At least nothing should be.'

Hallward shook his head as he entered, and followed Dorian into the library. There was a bright wood fire blazing in the large open hearth. The lamps were lit, and an open Dutch silver spirit-case stood, with some siphons of soda-water and large cut-glass tumblers, on a little marqueterie table.

'You see your servant made me quite at home, Dorian. He gave me everything I wanted, including your best gold-tipped cigarettes. He is a most hospitable creature. I like him much better than the Frenchman you used to have. What has become of the Frenchman, by the by?'

Dorian shrugged his shoulders. 'I believe he married Lady Radley's maid, and has established her in Paris as an English dressmaker. *Anglomanie* is very fashionable over there now, I hear. It seems silly of the French, doesn't it? But – do you know? – he was not at all a bad servant. I never liked him, but I had nothing to complain about. One often imagines things that are quite absurd. He was really devoted to me, and seemed quite sorry when he went away. Have another brandy-and-soda? Or would you like hock-and-seltzer? I always take hock-and-seltzer myself. There is sure to be some in the next room.'

'Thanks, I won't have anything more,' said the painter, taking his cap and coat off, and throwing them on the bag that he had placed in the corner. 'And now, my dear fellow, I want to speak to you seriously. Don't frown like that. You make it so much more difficult for me.'

'What is it all about?' cried Dorian, in his petulant way, flinging himself down on the sofa. 'I hope it is not about myself. I am tired of myself tonight. I should like to be somebody else.'

'It is about yourself,' answered Hallward, in his grave, deep voice, 'and I must say it to you. I shall only keep you half an hour.'

Dorian sighed, and lit a cigarette. 'Half an hour!' he murmured.

'It is not much to ask of you, Dorian, and it is entirely for your own sake that I am speaking. I think it right that you should know that the most dreadful things are being said against you in London.'

'I don't wish to know anything about them. I love scandals about other people, but scandals about myself don't interest me. They have not got the charm of novelty.'

'They must interest you, Dorian. Every gentleman is interested in his good name. You don't want people to talk of you as something vile and degraded. Of course you have your position, and your wealth, and all that kind of thing. But position and wealth are not everything. Mind you, I don't believe these rumours at all. At least, I can't believe them when I see you. Sin is a thing that writes itself across a man's face. It cannot be concealed. People talk sometimes of secret vices. There are no such things. If a wretched man has a vice, it shows itself in the lines of his mouth, the droop of his eyelids, the moulding of his hands even. Somebody – I won't mention his name, but you know him – came to me last year to have his portrait done. I had never seem him before, and had never heard anything about him at the time, though I have heard a good deal since. He offered an extravagant price. I refused him. There was something in the shape of his fingers that I hated. I know now that I was quite right in what I fancied about him. His life is dreadful. But you, Dorian, with your pure, bright, innocent face, and your marvellous untroubled youth – I can't believe anything against you. And yet I see you very seldom, and you never come down to the studio now, and when I am away from you, and I hear all these hideous things that people are whispering about you, I don't know what to say. Why is it, Dorian, that a man like the Duke of Berwick leaves the room of a club when you enter it? Why is it that so many gentlemen in London will neither go to your house nor invite you to theirs? You used to be a friend of Lord Staveley. I met him at dinner last week. Your name happened to come up in conversation, in connection with the miniatures you have lent to the exhibition at the Dudley. Staveley curled his lip, and said that you might have the most artistic tastes, but that you were a man whom no pure-minded girl should be allowed to know, and whom no chaste woman should sit in the same room with. I reminded him that I was a friend of yours, and asked him what he meant. He told me. He told me right out before everybody. It was horrible! Why is your friendship so fatal to young men? There was that wretched boy in the Guards who committed suicide. You were his great friend. There was Sir Henry Ashton, who had to leave England, with a tarnished name. You and he were inseparable. What about Adrian Singleton, and his dreadful end? What about Lord Kent's only son, and his career? I met his father yesterday in St James's Street. He seemed broken with shame and sorrow. What about the young Duke of Perth? What sort of life has he got now? What gentleman would associate with him?'

'Stop, Basil. You are talking about things of which you know nothing,' said Dorian Gray, biting his lip, and with a note of infinite contempt in his voice. 'You ask me why Berwick leaves a room when I enter it. It is because I know everything about his life, not because he knows anything about mine. With such blood as he has in his veins, how could his record be clean? You ask me about Henry Ashton and young Perth. Did I teach the one his vices, and the other his debauchery? If Kent's silly son takes his wife from the streets what is that to me? If Adrian Singleton writes his friend's name across a bill, am I his keeper? I know how people chatter in England. The middle classes air their moral prejudices over their gross dinner-tables, and whisper about what they call the profligacies of their betters in order to try and pretend that they are in smart society, and on intimate terms with the people they slander. In this country it is enough for a man to have distinction and brains for every common tongue to wag against him. And what sort of lives do these people, who pose as being moral, lead themselves? My dear fellow, you forget that we are in the native land of the hypocrite.'

'Dorian,' cried Hallward, 'that is not the question. England is bad enough, I know, and English society is all wrong. That is the reason why I want you to be fine. You have not been fine. One has a right to judge of a man by the effect he has over his friends. Yours seem to lose all sense of honour, of goodness, of purity. You have filled them with a madness for pleasure. They have gone down into the depths. You led them there. Yes: you led them there, and yet you can smile, as you are smiling now. And there is worse behind. I know you and Harry are inseparable. Surely for that reason, if for none other, you should not have made his sister's name a byword.'

'Take care, Basil. You go too far.'

'I must speak, and you must listen. You shall listen. When you met Lady Gwendolen, not a breath of scandal had ever touched her. Is there a single decent woman in London now who would drive with her in the Park? Why, even her children are not allowed to live with her. Then there are other stories – stories that you have been seen creeping at dawn out of dreadful houses and slinking in disguise into the foulest dens in London. Are they true? Can they be true? When I first heard them I laughed. I hear them now, and they make me shudder. What about your country house, and the life that is led there? Dorian, you don't know what is said about you. I won't tell you that I don't want to preach to you. I remember Harry saying once that every man who turned himself into an amateur curate for the moment always began by saying that, and then proceeded to break his word. I do want to preach to you. I want you to lead such a life as will make the world respect you. I want you to have a clean name and a fair record. I want you to get rid of the dreadful people you associate with. Don't shrug your shoulders like that. Don't be so indifferent. You have a wonderful influence. Let it be for good, not for evil. They say that you corrupt everyone with whom you become intimate, and that it is quite sufficient for you to enter a house, for shame of some kind to follow after. I don't know whether it is so or not. How should I know? But it is said of you. I am told things that it seems impossible to doubt. Lord Gloucester was one of my greatest friends at Oxford. He showed me a letter that his wife had written to him when she was dying alone in her villa at Mentone. Your name was implicated in the most terrible confession I ever read. I told him that it was absurd – that I knew you thoroughly, and that you were incapable of anything of the kind. Know you? I wonder do I know you? Before I could answer that, I should have to see your soul.'

'To see my soul!' muttered Dorian Gray, starting up from the sofa and turning almost white from fear.

'Yes,' answered Hallward, gravely, and with deep-toned sorrow in his voice – 'to see your soul. But only God can do that.'

A bitter laugh of mockery broke from the lips of the younger man. 'You shall see it yourself, tonight!' he cried, seizing a lamp from the table. 'Come: it is your own handiwork. Why shouldn't you look at it? You can tell the world all about it afterwards, if you choose. Nobody would believe you. If they did believe you, they would like me all the better for it. I know the age better than you do, though you will prate about it so tediously. Come, I tell you. You have chattered enough about corruption. Now you shall look on it face to face.'

There was the madness of pride in every word he uttered. He stamped his foot upon the ground in his boyish insolent manner. He felt a terrible joy at the thought that someone else was to share his secret, and that the man who had painted the portrait that was the origin of all his shame was to be burdened for the rest of his life with the hideous memory of what he had done.

'Yes,' he continued, coming closer to him, and looking steadfastly into his stern eyes. 'I shall show you my soul. You shall see the thing that you fancy only God can see.'

Hallward started back. 'This is blasphemy, Dorian!' he cried. 'You must not say things like that. They are horrible, and they don't mean anything.'

'You think so?' He laughed again.

'I know so. As for what I said to you tonight, I said it for your good. You know I have been always a staunch friend to you.'

'Don't touch me. Finish what you have to say.'

A twisted flash of pain shot across the painter's face. He paused for a moment, and a wild feeling of pity came over him. After all, what right had he to pry into the life of Dorian Gray? If he had done a tithe of what was rumoured about him, how much he must have suffered! Then he straightened himself up, and walked over to the fireplace, and stood there, looking at the burning logs with their frostlike ashes and their throbbing cores of flame.

'I am waiting, Basil,' said the young man, in a hard, clear voice.

He turned round. 'What I have to say is this,' he cried. 'You must give me some answer to these horrible charges that are made against you. If you tell me that they are absolutely untrue from beginning to end, I shall believe you. Deny them, Dorian, deny them! Can't you see what I am going through? My God! Don't tell me that you are bad, and corrupt, and shameful.'

Dorian Gray smiled. There was a curl of contempt in his lips. 'Come upstairs, Basil,' he said, quietly. 'I keep a diary of my life from day to day, and it never leaves the room in which it is written. I shall show it to you if you come with me.'

'I shall come with you, Dorian, if you wish it. I see I have missed my train. That makes no matter. I can go tomorrow. But don't ask me to read anything tonight. All I want is a plain answer to my question.'

'That shall be given to you upstairs. I could not give it here. You will not have to read long.'

*　　　*　　　*　　　*

He passed out of the room, and began the ascent, Basil Hallward following close behind. They walked softly, as men do instinctively at night. The lamp cast fantastic shadows on the wall and staircase. A rising wind made some of the windows rattle.

When they reached the top landing, Dorian set the lamp down on the floor, and taking out the key turned it in the lock. 'You insist on knowing, Basil?' he asked, in a low voice.

'Yes.'

'I am delighted,' he answered, smiling. Then he added, somewhat harshly, 'You are the one man in the world who is entitled to know everything about me. You have had more to do with my life than you think': and, taking up the lamp, he opened the door and went in. A cold current of air passed them, and the light shot up for a moment in a flame of murky orange. He shuddered. 'Shut the door behind you,' he whispered, as he placed the lamp on the table.

Hallward glanced round him, with a puzzled expression. The room looked as if it had not been lived in for years. A faded Flemish tapestry, a curtained picture, an old Italian *cassone*, and an almost empty bookcase – that was all that it seemed to contain, besides a chair and a table. As Dorian Gray was lighting a half-burned candle that was standing on the mantelshelf, he saw that the whole place was covered with dust, and that the carpet was in holes. A mouse ran scuffling behind the wainscoting. There was a damp odour of mildew.

'So you think that it is only God who sees the soul, Basil? Draw that curtain back, and you will see mine.'

The voice that spoke was cold and cruel. 'You are mad, Dorian, or playing a part,' muttered Hallward, frowning.

'You won't? Then I must do it myself,' said the young man; and he tore the curtain from its rod and flung it on the ground.

An exclamation of horror broke from the painter's lips as he saw in the dim light the hideous face on the canvas grinning at him. There was something in its expression that filled him with disgust and loathing. Good heavens! It was Dorian Gray's own face that he was looking at! The horror, whatever it was, had not yet entirely spoiled that marvellous beauty. There was still some gold in the thinning hair and some scarlet on the sensual mouth. The sodden eyes had kept something of the loveliness of their blue, the noble curves had not yet completely passed away from chiselled nostrils and from plastic throat. Yes, it was Dorian himself. But who had done it? He seemed to recognise his own brushwork, and the frame was his own design. The idea was monstrous, yet he felt afraid. He seized the lighted candle, and held it to the picture. In the left-hand corner was his own name, traced in long letters of bright vermilion.

It was some foul parody, some infamous, ignoble satire. He had never done that. Still, it was his own picture! He knew it, and he felt as if his blood had changed in a moment from fire to sluggish ice. His own picture! What did it mean? Why had it altered? He turned, and looked at Dorian Gray, with the eyes of a sick man. His mouth twitched, and his parched tongue seemed unable to articulate. He passed his hand across his forehead. It was dank with clammy sweat.

The young man was leaning against the mantelshelf, watching him with that strange expression that one sees on the faces of those who are absorbed in a play when some great artist is acting. There was neither real sorrow in it nor real joy. There was simply the passion of the spectator, with perhaps a flicker of triumph in his eyes. He had taken the flower out of his coat, and was smelling it, or pretending to do so.

'What does this mean?' cried Hallward, at last. His own voice sounded shrill and curious in his ears.

'Years ago, when I was a boy,' said Dorian Gray, crushing the flower in his hand, 'you met me, flattered me, and taught me to be vain of my good looks. One day you introduced me to a friend of yours, who explained to me the wonder of youth, and you finished the portrait of me that revealed to me the wonder of beauty. In a mad moment, that, even now, I don't know whether I regret or not, I made a wish, perhaps you would call it a prayer . . .'

'I remember it! Oh, how well I remember it! No, the thing is impossible! The room is damp. Mildew has got into the canvas. The paints I used had some wretched mineral poison in them. I tell you the thing is impossible.'

'Ah, what is impossible?' murmured the young man, going over to the window, and leaning his forehead against the cold, mist-stained glass.

'You told me you had destroyed it.'

'I was wrong. It has destroyed me.'

'I don't believe it is my picture.'

'Can't you see your ideal in it?' said Dorian, bitterly.

'My ideal, as you call it . . .'

'As you called it.'

'There was nothing evil in it, nothing shameful. You were to me such an ideal as I shall never meet again. This is the face of a satyr.'

'It is the face of my soul.'

'Christ! What a thing I must have worshipped! It has the eyes of a devil.'

'Each of us has Heaven and Hell in him, Basil,' cried Dorian, with a wild gesture of despair.

Hallward turned again to the portrait, and gazed at it. 'My God! If it is true,' he exclaimed, 'and this is what you have done with your life, why, you must be worse even than those who talk against you fancy you to be!' He held the light up again to the canvas, and examined it. The surface seemed to be quite undisturbed, and as he had left it. It was from within, apparently, that the foulness and horror had come. Through some strange quickening of inner life the leprosies of sin were slowly eating the thing away. The rotting of a corpse in a watery grave was not so fearful.

His hand shook, and the candle fell from its socket on the floor, and lay there sputtering. He placed his foot on it and put it out. Then he flung himself into the rickety chair that was standing by the table and buried his face in his hands.

'Good God, Dorian, what a lesson! What an awful lesson!' There was no answer, but he could hear the young man sobbing at the window. 'Pray, Dorian, pray,' he murmured. 'What is it that one was taught to say in one's boyhood? 'Lead us not into temptation. Forgive us our sins. Wash away our iniquities.' Let us say that together. The prayer of your pride has been answered. The prayer of your repentance will be answered also. I worshipped you too much. We are both punished.'

Dorian Gray turned slowly around, and looked at him with tear-dimmed eyes. 'It is too late, Basil,' he faltered.

'It is never too late, Dorian. Let us kneel down and try if we cannot remember a prayer. Isn't there a verse somewhere, "Though your sins be as scarlet, yet I will make them as white as snow"?'

'Those words mean nothing to me now.'

'Hush! Don't say that. You have done enough evil in your life. My God! Don't you see that accursed thing leering at us?'

Dorian Gray glanced at the picture, and suddenly an uncontrollable feeling of hatred for Basil Hallward came over him, as though it had been suggested to him by the image on the canvas, whispered into his ear by those grinning lips. The mad passions of a hunted animal stirred within him, and he loathed the man who was seated at the table, more than in his whole life he had ever loathed anything. He glanced wildly around. Something glimmered on the top of the painted chest that faced him. His eye fell on it. He knew what it was. It was a knife that he had brought up, some days before, to cut a piece of cord, and had forgotten to take away with him. He moved slowly towards it, passing Hallward as he did so. As soon as he got behind him, he seized it, and turned round. Hallward stirred in his chair as if he was going to rise. He rushed at him, and dug the knife into the great vein that is behind the ear, crushing the man's head down on the table, and stabbing again and again.

There was a stifled groan, and the horrible sound of someone choking with blood. Three times the outstretched arms shot up convulsively, waving grotesque stiff-fingered hands in the air. He stabbed him twice more, but the man did not move. Something began to trickle on the floor. He waited for a moment, still pressing the head down. Then he threw the knife on the table, and listened.

He could hear nothing but the drip, drip on the threadbare carpet. He opened the door and went out on the landing. The house was absolutely quiet. No one was about. For a few seconds he stood bending over the balustrade, and peering down into the black seething well of darkness. Then he took out the key and returned to the room, locking himself in as he did so.

The thing was still seated in the chair, straining over the table with bowed head, and humped back, and long fantastic arms. Had it not been for the red jagged tear in the neck, and the clotted black pool that was slowly widening on the table, one would have said that the man was simply asleep.

How quickly it had all been done! He felt strangely calm, and, walking over to the window, opened it, and stepped out on the balcony. The wind had blown the fog away, and the sky was like a monstrous peacock's tail, starred with myriads of golden eyes. He looked down, and saw the policeman going his rounds and flashing the long beam of his lantern on the doors of the silent houses. The crimson spot of a prowling hansom gleamed at the corner, and then vanished. A woman in a fluttering shawl was creeping slowly by the railings, staggering as she went. Now and then she stopped, and peered back. Once, she began to sing in a hoarse voice. The policeman strolled over and said something to her. She stumbled away, laughing. A bitter blast swept across the Square. The gas-lamps flickered, and became blue, and the leafless trees shook their black iron branches to and fro. He shivered, and went back, closing the window behind him.

Having reached the door, he turned the key, and opened it. He did not even glance at the murdered man. He felt that the secret of the whole thing was not to realise the situation. The friend who had painted the fatal portrait to which all his misery had been due had gone out of his life. That was enough.

Then he remembered the lamp. It was a rather curious one of Moorish workmanship, made of dull silver inlaid with arabesques of burnished steel, and studded with coarse turquoises. Perhaps it might be missed by his servant, and questions would be asked. He hesitated for a moment, then he turned back and took it from the table. He could not help seeing the dead thing. How still it was! How horribly white the long hands looked! It was like a dreadful wax image.

Having locked the door behind him, he crept quietly downstairs. The woodwork creaked, and seemed to cry out as if in pain. He stopped several times, and waited. No: everything was still. It was merely the sound of his own footsteps.

When he reached the library, he saw the bag and coat in the corner. They must be hidden away somewhere. He unlocked a secret press that was in the wainscoting, a press in which he kept his own curious disguises, and put them into it. He could easily burn them afterwards. Then he pulled out his watch. It was twenty minutes to two.

He sat down, and began to think. Every year – every month, almost – men were strangled in England for what he had done. There had been a madness of murder in the air. Some red star had come too close to the earth . . . And yet what evidence was there against him? Basil Hallward had left the house at eleven. No one had seen him come in again. Most of the servants were at Selby Royal. His valet had gone to bed . . . Paris! Yes. It was to Paris that Basil had gone, and by the midnight train, as he had intended. With his curious reserved habits, it would be months before any suspicions would be aroused. Months! Everything could be destroyed long before then.

A sudden thought struck him. He put on his fur coat and hat, and went out into the hall. There he paused, hearing the slow heavy tread of the policeman on the pavement outside, and seeing the flash of the bull's-eye reflected in the window. He waited, and held his breath.

After a few moments he drew back the latch, and slipped out, shutting the door very gently behind him. Then he began ringing the bell. In about five minutes his valet appeared half dressed, and looking very drowsy.

'I am sorry to have had to wake you up, Francis,' he said, stepping in;

111

'but I had forgotten my latchkey. What time is it?'

'Ten minutes past two, sir,' answered the man, looking at the clock and blinking.

'Ten minutes past two? How horribly late! You must wake me at nine tomorrow. I have some work to do.'

'All right, sir.'

'Did anyone call this evening?'

'Mr Hallward, sir. He stayed here until eleven, and then he went away to catch his train.'

'Oh! I am sorry I didn't see him. Did he leave any message?'

'No, sir, except that he would write to you from Paris, if he did not find you at the club.'

'That will do, Francis. Don't forget to call me at nine tomorrow.'

'No sir.'

The man shambled down the passage in his slippers.

Dorian Gray threw his hat and coat upon the table, and passed into the library. For a quarter of an hour he walked up and down the room biting his lip, and thinking. Then he took down the Blue Book from one of the shelves, and began to turn over the leaves. 'Alan Campbell, 152, Hertford Street, Mayfair.' Yes: that was the man he wanted.

*   *   *   *

Dorian blackmails Alan Campbell into disposing of the body. Unable to live with himself, Campbell commits suicide. Dorian goes to his country house, Selby Royal, and falls in love with a simple country girl. He returns to London to tell Lord Henry this and that he has decided to reform. Lord Henry tells Dorian that it is too late and Dorian leaves Lord Henry's house, having arranged to ride with him in the Park the following morning.

*   *   *   *

It was a lovely night, so warm that he threw his coat over his arm, and did not even put his silk scarf round his throat. As he strolled home, smoking his cigarette, two young men in evening dress passed him. He heard one of them whisper to the other, 'That is Dorian Gray.' He remembered how pleased he used to be when he was pointed out, or stared at, or

It was the action of an arm gesticulating, 'For God's sake, clear the way!' (p.83)

Nule creaked and came up another step. (p.98)

talked about. He was tired of hearing his own name now. Half the charm of the little village where he had been so often lately was that no one knew who he was. He had often told the girl whom he had lured to love him that he was poor, and she had believed him. He had told her once that he was wicked, and she had laughed at him, and answered that wicked people were always very old and very ugly. What a laugh she had! – just like a thrush singing. And how pretty she had been in her cotton dress and her large hats! She knew nothing, but she had everything that he had lost.

When he reached home, he found his servant waiting up for him. He sent him to bed, and threw himself down on the sofa in the library, and began to think over some of the things that Lord Henry had said to him.

Was it really true that one could never change? He felt a wild longing for the unstained purity of his boyhood – his rose-white boyhood, as Lord Henry had once called it. He knew that he had tarnished himself, filled his mind with corruption, and given horror to his fancy; that he had been an evil influence to others, and had experienced a terrible joy in being so; and that, of the lives that had crossed his own, it had been the fairest and the most full of promise that he had brought to shame. But was it all irretrievable? Was there no hope for him?

Ah! in what a monstrous moment of pride and passion he had prayed that the portrait should bear the burden of his days, and he keep the unsullied splendour of eternal youth! All his failure had been due to that. Better for him that each sin of his life had brought its sure, swift penalty along with it. There was purification in punishment. Not 'Forgive us our sins,' but 'Smite us for our iniquities,' should be the prayer of a man to a most just God.

The curiously carved mirror that Lord Henry had given to him, so many years ago now, was standing on the table, and the white-limbed Cupids laughed round it as of old. He took it up, as he had done on that night of horror, when he had first noted the change in the fatal picture, and with wild, tear-dimmed eyes looked into its polished shield. Once, someone who had terribly loved him had written to him a mad letter, ending with these idolatrous words: 'The world is changed because you are made of ivory and gold. The curves of your lips rewrite history.' The phrases came back to his memory, and he repeated them over and over to himself. Then he loathed his own beauty, and, flinging the mirror on the floor, crushed it into silver splinters beneath his heel. It was his beauty that had ruined him, his beauty and the youth that he had prayed for. But for those two things, his life might have been free from stain. His beauty had been to him but a mask, his youth but a mockery. What was youth at best? A green, an unripe time, a time of shallow moods and sickly thoughts. Why had he worn its livery? Youth had spoiled him.

It was better not to think of the past. Nothing could alter that. It was of himself, and of his own future, that he had to think. James Vane was hidden in a nameless grave in Selby Churchyard. Alan Campbell had shot himself one night in his laboratory, but had not revealed the secret that he had been forced to know. The excitement, such as it was, over Basil Hallward's disappearance would soon pass away. It was already waning. He was perfectly safe there. Nor, indeed, was it the death of Basil Hallward that weighed most upon his mind. It was the living death of his own soul that troubled him. Basil had painted the portrait that had marred his life. He could not forgive him that. It was the portrait that had done everything. Basil had said things to him that were unbearable, and that he had yet borne with patience. The murder had been simply the madness of a moment. As for Alan Campbell, his suicide had been his own act. He had chosen to do it. It was nothing to him.

A new life! That was what he wanted. That was what he was waiting for. Surely he had begun it already. He had spared one innocent thing, at any rate. He would never again tempt innocence. He would be good.

As he thought of Hetty Merton, he began to wonder if the portrait in the locked room had changed. Surely it was not still so horrible as it had been? Perhaps if his life became pure, he would be able to expel every sign of evil passion from the face. Perhaps the signs of evil had already gone away. He would go and look.

He took the lamp from the table and crept upstairs. As he unbarred the door a smile of joy flitted across his strangely young-looking face and lingered for a moment about his lips. Yes, he would be good, and the hideous thing that he had hidden away would no longer be a terror to him. He felt as if the load had been lifted from him already.

He went in quietly, locking the door behind him, as was his custom, and dragged the purple hanging from the portrait. A cry of pain and indignation broke from him. He could see no change save that in the eyes there was a look of cunning, and in the mouth the curved wrinkle of the hypocrite. The thing was still loathsome – more loathsome, if possible, than before – and the scarlet dew that spotted the hand seemed brighter, and more like blood newly spilt. Then he trembled. Had it been merely vanity that had made him do his one good deed? Or the desire for a new sensation, as Lord Henry had hinted, with his mocking laugh? Or that passion to act a part that sometimes makes us do things finer than we are ourselves? Or, perhaps, all these? And why was the red stain larger than it had been? It seemed to have crept like a horrible disease over the wrinkled fingers. There was blood on the painted feet, as though the thing had dripped – blood even on the hand that had not held the knife. Confess? Did it mean that he was to confess? To give himself up, and be put to death? He laughed. He felt that the idea was monstrous. Besides, even if he did confess, who would believe him? There was no trace of the murdered man anywhere. Everything belonging to him had been destroyed. He himself had burned what had been below-stairs. The world would simply say that he was mad. They would shut him up if he persisted in his story . . . Yet it was his duty to confess, to suffer public shame, and to make public atonement. There was a God who called upon men to tell their sins to earth as well as to heaven. Nothing that he could do would cleanse him until he had told his own sin. His sin? He shrugged his shoulders. The death of Basil Hallward seemed very little to him. He was thinking of Hetty Merton. For it was an unjust mirror, this mirror of his soul that he was looking at. Vanity? Curiosity? Hypocrisy? Had there been nothing more in his renunciation than that? There had been something more. At least he thought so. But who could tell? . . . No. There had been nothing more. Through vanity he had spared her. In hypocrisy he had worn the mask of goodness. For curiosity's sake he had tried the denial of self. He recognised that now.

But this murder – was it to dog him all his life? Was he always to be burdened by his past? Was he really to confess? Never. There was only one bit of evidence left against him. The picture itself – that was evidence. He would destroy it. Why had he kept it so long? Once it had given him pleasure to watch it changing and growing old. Of late he had felt no such pleasure. It had kept him awake at night. When he had been away, he had been filled with terror lest other eyes should look upon it. It had brought melancholy across his passions. Its mere memory had marred many moments of joy. It had been like conscience to him. Yes, it had been conscience. He would destroy it.

He looked round, and saw the knife that had stabbed Basil Hallward. He had cleaned it many times, until there was no stain left upon it. It was bright, and glistened. As it had killed the painter, so it would kill the painter's work, and all that that meant. It would kill the past and when that was dead he would be free. It would kill this monstrous soul-life, and, without its hideous warnings, he would be at peace. He seized the thing, and stabbed the picture with it.

There was a cry heard, and a crash. The cry was so horrible in its agony that the frightened servants woke, and crept out of their rooms. Two gentlemen, who were passing in the Square below, stopped, and looked up at the great house. They walked on until they met a policeman, and brought him back. The man rang the bell several times, but there was no answer. Except for a light in one of the top windows, the house was all dark. After a time, he went away and stood in an adjoining portico and watched.

'Whose house is that, constable?' asked the elder of the two gentlemen.

'Mr Dorian Gray's, sir,' answered the policeman.

They looked at each other, as they walked away, and sneered.

Inside, in the servants' part of the house, the half-clad domestics were talking in low whispers to each other. Old Mrs Leaf was crying and wringing her hands. Francis was as pale as death.

After about a quarter of an hour, he got the coachman and one of the footmen and crept upstairs. They knocked, but there was no reply. They called out. Everything was still. Finally, after vainly trying to force the door, they got on the roof, and dropped down on the balcony. The windows yielded easily; their bolts were old.

When they entered they found, hanging upon the wall, a splendid portrait of their master as they had last seen him, in all the wonder of his exquisite youth and beauty. Lying on the floor was a dead man, in evening dress, with a knife in his heart. He was withered, wrinkled, and loathsome of visage. It was not until they had examined the rings that they recognised who it was.

THE MYSTERIOUS MANSION
Honoré de Balzac

About a hundred yards from the town of Vendôme, on the borders of the Loire, there is an old grey house, surmounted by very high gables, and so completely isolated that neither tanyard nor shabby hostelry, such as you may find at the entrance to all small towns, exists in its immediate neighbourhood.

In front of this building, overlooking the river, is a garden, where the once well-trimmed box borders that used to define the walks now grow wild as they list. Several willows that spring from the Loire have grown as rapidly as the hedge that encloses it, and half conceal the house. The rich vegetation of those weeds that we call foul adorns the sloping shore. Fruit trees, neglected for the last ten years, no longer yield their harvest, and their shoots form coppices. The wall-fruit grows like hedges against the walls. Paths once gravelled are overgrown with moss, but, to tell the truth, there is no trace of a path. From the height of the hill, to which cling the ruins of the old castle of the Dukes of Vendôme, the only spot whence the eye can plunge into this enclosure, it strikes you that, at a time not easy to determine, this plot of land was the delight of a country gentleman, who cultivated roses and tulips and horticulture in general, and who was besides a lover of fine fruit. An arbor is still visible, or rather the débris of an arbor, where there is a table that time has not quite destroyed. The aspect of this garden of bygone days suggests the negative joys of peaceful, provincial life, as one might reconstruct the life of a worthy tradesman by reading the epitaph on his tombstone. As if to complete the sweetness and sadness of the ideas that possess one's soul, one of the walls displays a sun-dial decorated with the following commonplace Christian inscription: "Ultimam cogita!" The roof of this house is horribly dilapidated, the shutters are always closed, the balconies are covered with swallows' nests, the doors are perpetually shut, weeds have drawn green lines in the cracks of the flights of steps, the locks and bolts are rusty. Sun, moon, winter, summer, and snow have worn the panelling, warped the boards, gnawed the paint. The lugubrious silence which reigns there is only broken by birds, cats, martins, rats and mice, free to course to and fro, to fight and to eat each other. Everywhere an invisible hand has graven the word *mystery*.

Should your curiosity lead you to glance at this house from the side that points to the road, you would perceive a great door which the children of the place have riddled with holes. I afterward heard that this door had been closed for the last ten years. Through the holes broken by the boys you would have observed the perfect harmony that existed between the façades of both garden and courtyard. In both the same disorder prevails. Tufts of weed encircle the paving-stones. Enormous cracks furrow the walls, round whose blackened crests twine the thousand garlands of the pellitory. The steps are out of joint, the wire of the bell is rusted, the spouts are cracked. What fire from heaven has fallen here? What tribunal has decreed that salt should be strewn on this dwelling? Has God been blasphemed, has France been here betrayed? These are the questions we ask ourselves, but get no answer from the crawling things that haunt the place. The empty and deserted house is a gigantic enigma, of which the key is lost. In bygone times it was a small fief, and bears the name of the Grande Bretêche.

I inferred that I was not the only person to whom my good landlady had communicated the secret of which I was to be the sole recipient, and I prepared to listen.

'Sir,' she said, 'when the Emperor sent the Spanish prisoners of war and others here, the Government quartered on me a young Spaniard who had been sent to Vendôme on parole. Parole notwithstanding he went out every day to show himself to the sous-préfet. He was a Spanish grandee! Nothing less! His name ended in os and dia, something like Burgos de Férédia. I have his name on my books; you can read it if you like. Oh! but he was a handsome young man for a Spaniard; they are all said to be ugly. He was only five feet and a few inches high, but he was well-grown; he had small hands that he took such care of; ah! you should have seen! He had as many brushes for his hands as a woman for her whole dressing apparatus! He had thick black hair, a fiery eye, his skin was rather bronzed, but I liked the look of it. He wore the finest linen I have ever seen on any one, although I have had princesses staying here, and, among others, General Bertrand, the Duke and Duchess d'Abrantès, Monsieur Decazes, and the King of Spain. He didn't eat much; but his manners were so polite, so amiable, that one could not owe him a grudge. Oh! I was very fond of him, although he didn't open his lips four times in the day, and it was impossible to keep up a conversation with him. For if you spoke to him, he did not answer. It was a fad, a mania with them all, I heard say. He read his breviary like a priest, he went to Mass and to all the services regularly. Where did he sit? Two steps from the chapel of Madame de Merret. As he took his place there the first time he went to church, nobody suspected him of any intention in so doing. Besides, he never raised his eyes from his prayer-book, poor young man! After that, sir, in the evening he would walk on the mountains, among the castle ruins. It was the poor man's only amusement, it reminded him of his country. They say that Spain is all mountains! From the commencement of his imprisonment he stayed out late. I was anxious when I found that he did not come home before midnight; but we got accustomed to this fancy of his. He took the key of the door, and we left off sitting up for him. He lodged in a house of ours in the Rue des Casernes. After that, one of our stablemen told us that in the evening when he led the horses to the water, he thought he had seen the Spanish grandee swimming far down the river like a live fish. When he returned, I told him to take care of the rushes; he appeared vexed to have been seen in the water. At last, one day, or rather one morning, we did not find him in his room; he had not returned. After searching everywhere, I found some writing in the drawer of a table, where there were fifty gold pieces of Spain that are called doubloons and were worth about five thousand francs; and ten thousand francs' worth of diamonds in a small sealed box. The writing said, that in case he did not return, he left us the money and the diamonds, on condition of paying for Masses to thank God for his escape, and for his salvation. In those days my husband had not been taken from me; he hastened to seek him everywhere.

'And now for the strange part of the story. He brought home the Spaniard's clothes, that he had discovered under a big stone, in a sort of pilework by the river-side near the castle, nearly opposite to the Grande Bretêche. My husband had gone there so early that no one had seen him. After reading the letter, he burned the clothes, and according to Count Férédia's desire we declared that he had escaped. The sous-préfet sent all the gendarmerie in pursuit of him; but brust! they never caught him. Lepas believed that the Spaniard had drowned himself. I, sir, don't think so; I am more inclined to believe that he had something to do with the affair of Madame de Merret, seeing that Rosalie told me that the crucifix that her mistress thought so much of that she had it buried with her, was of ebony and silver. Now in the beginning of his stay here, Monsieur de Férédia had one in ebony and silver that I never saw him with later. Now, sir, don't you consider that I need have no scruples about the Spaniard's fifteen thousand francs, and that I have a right to them?'

'Certainly; but you haven't tried to question Rosalie?' I said.

'Oh, yes, indeed, sir; but to no purpose! the girl's like a wall. She knows something, but it is impossible to get her to talk.'

After exchanging a few more words with me, my landlady left me a prey to vague and gloomy thoughts, to a romantic curiosity, and a religious terror not unlike the profound impression produced on us when by night, on entering a dark church, we perceive a faint light under high arches; a vague figure glides by – the rustle of a robe or cassock is heard, and we shudder.

Suddenly the Grande Bretêche and its tall weeds, its barred windows, its rusty ironwork, its closed doors, its deserted apartments, appeared like a fantastic apparition before me. I essayed to penetrate the mysterious dwelling, and to find the knot of its dark story – the drama that had killed three persons. In my eyes Rosalie became the most interesting person in Vendôme. As I studied her, I discovered the traces of secret care, despite the radiant health that shone in her plump countenance.

There was in her the germ of remorse or hope; her attitude revealed a secret, like the attitude of a bigot who prays to excess, or of the infanticide who ever hears the last cry of her child. Yet her manners were rough and ingenious – her silly smile was not that of a criminal, and could you but have seen the great kerchief that encompassed her portly bust, framed and laced in by a lilac and blue cotton gown, you would have dubbed her innocent. No, I thought, I will not leave Vendôme without learning the history of the Grande Bretêche. To gain my ends I will strike up a friendship with Rosalie, if needs be.

'Rosalie,' said I, one evening.

'Sir?'

'You are not married?'

She started slightly.

'Oh, I can find plenty of men, when the fancy takes me to be made miserable,' she said, laughing.

She soon recovered from the effects of her emotion, for all women, from the great lady to the maid of the inn, possess a composure that is peculiar to them.

'You are too good-looking and well favoured to be short of lovers. But tell me, Rosalie, why did you take service in an inn after leaving Madame de Merret? Did she leave you nothing to live on?'

'Oh, yes! But, sir, my place is the best in all Vendôme.'

The reply was one of those that judges and lawyers would call evasive. Rosalie appeared to me to be situated in this romantic history like the square in the midst of a chessboard. She was at the heart of the truth and chief interest; she seemed to me to be bound in the very knot of it. The conquest of Rosalie was no longer to be an ordinary siege – in this girl was centred the last chapter of a novel, therefore from this moment Rosalie became the object of my preference.

One morning I said to Rosalie: 'Tell me all you know about Madame de Merret.'

'Oh!' she replied in terror, 'do not ask that of me, Monsieur Horace.'

Her pretty face fell – her clear, bright colour faded – and her eyes lost their innocent brightness.

'Well, then,' she said, at last, 'if you must have it so, I will tell you about it; but promise to keep my secret!'

'Done! my dear girl, I must keep your secret with the honour of a thief, which is the most loyal in the world.'

Were I to transcribe Rosalie's diffuse eloquence faithfully, an entire volume would scarcely contain it; so I shall abridge.

The room occupied by Madame de Merret at the Bretêche was on the ground floor. A little closet about four feet deep, built in the thickness of the wall, served as her wardrobe. Three months before the eventful evening of which I am about to speak, Madame de Merret had been so seriously indisposed that her husband had left her to herself in her own apartment, while he occupied another on the first floor. By one of those chances that it is impossible to foresee, he returned home from the club (where he was accustomed to read the papers and discuss politics with the inhabitants of the place) two hours later than usual. His wife supposed him to be at home, in bed and asleep. But the invasion of France had been the subject of a most animated discussion; the billiard-match had been exciting, he had lost forty francs, an enormous sum for Vendôme, where every one hoards, and where manners are restricted within the limits of a praiseworthy modesty, which perhaps is the source of the true happiness that no Parisian covets. For some time past Monsieur de Merret had been satisfied to ask Rosalie if his wife had gone to bed; and on her reply, which was always in the affirmative, had immediately gained his own room with the good temper engendered by habit and confidence. On entering his house, he took it into his head to go and tell his wife of his misadventure, perhaps by way of consolation. At dinner he found Madame de Merret most coquettishly attired. On his way to the club it had occurred to him that his wife was restored to health, and that her convalescence had added to her beauty. He was, as husbands are wont to be, somewhat slow in making this discovery. Instead of calling Rosalie, who was occupied just then in watching the cook and coachman play a difficult hand at brisque, Monsieur de Merret went to his wife's room by the light of a lantern that he deposited on the first step of the staircase. His unmistakable step resounded under the vaulted corridor. At the moment that the Count turned the handle of his wife's door, he fancied he could hear the door of the closet I spoke of close; but when he entered Madame de Merret was alone before the fireplace. The husband thought ingeniously that Rosalie was in the closet, yet a suspicion that jangled in his ear put him on his guard. He looked at his wife and saw in her eyes I know not what wild and hunted expression.

'You are very late,' she said. Her habitually pure, sweet voice seemed changed to him.

Monsieur de Merret did not reply, for at that moment Rosalie entered. It was a thunderbolt for him. He strode about the room, passing from one window to the other, with mechanical motion and folded arms.

'Have you heard bad news, or are you unwell?' inquired his wife timidly, while Rosalie undressed her.

He kept silent.

'You can leave me,' said Madame de Merret to her maid; 'I will put my hair in curl papers myself.'

From the expression of her husband's face she foresaw trouble, and wished to be alone with him. When Rosalie had gone, or was supposed to have gone (for she stayed in the corridor for a few minutes), Monsieur de Merret came and stood in front of his wife, and said coldly to her:

'Madame, there is someone in your closet!' She looked calmly at her husband and replied simply:

'No, sir.'

This answer was heartrending to Monsieur de Merret; he did not believe in it. Yet his wife had never appeared to him purer or more saintly than at that moment. He rose to open the closet door; Madame de Merret took his hand, looked at him with an expression of melancholy, and said in a voice that betrayed singular emotion:

'If you find no one there, remember this, all will be over between us!' The extraordinary dignity of his wife's manner restored the Count's profound esteem for her, and inspired him with one of those resolutions that only lack a vaster stage to become immortal.

'No,' said he, 'Josephine, I will not go there. In either case it would separate us for ever. Hear me, I know how pure you are at heart, and that your life is a holy one. You would not commit a mortal sin to save your life.'

At these words Madame de Merret turned a haggard gaze upon her husband.

'Here, take your crucifix,' he added. 'Swear to me before God that there is no one in there; I will believe you, I will never open that door.'

Madame de Merret took the crucifix and said:

'I swear.'

'Louder,' said the husband, 'and repeat "I swear before God that there is no one in that closet."'

She repeated the sentence calmly.

'That will do,' said Monsieur de Merret, coldly.

After a moment of silence:

'I never saw this pretty toy before,' he said, examining the ebony crucifix inlaid with silver, and most artistically chiseled.

'I found it at Duvivier's, who bought it off a Spanish monk when the prisoners passed through Vendôme last year.'

'Ah!' said Monsieur de Merret, as he replaced the crucifix on the nail, and he rang. Rosálie did not keep him waiting. Monsieur de Merret went quickly to meet her, led her to the bay window that opened on to the garden and whispered to her:

'Listen! I know that Gorenflot wishes to marry you, poverty is the only drawback, and you told him that you would be his wife if he found the means to establish himself as a master mason. Well! go and fetch him, tell him to come here with his trowel and tools. Manage not to awaken any one in his house but himself; his fortune will be more than your desires. Above all, leave this room without babbling, otherwise –' He frowned. Rosalie went away, he recalled her.

'Here, take my latchkey,' he said. 'Jean!' then cried Monsieur de Merret, in tones of thunder in the corridor. Jean, who was at the same time his coachman and his confidential servant, left his game of cards and came.

'Go to bed, all of you,' said his master, signing to him to approach; and the Count added, under his breath: 'When they are all asleep – *asleep*, d'ye hear? – you will come down and tell me.' Monsieur de Merret, who had not lost sight of his wife all the time he was giving his orders, returned quietly to her at the fireside and began to tell her of the game of billiards and the talk of the club. When Rosalie returned she found Monsieur and Madame de Merret conversing very amicably.

The Count had lately had all the ceilings of his reception rooms on the ground floor repaired. Plaster of Paris is difficult to obtain in Vendôme; the carriage raises its price. The Count had therefore bought a good deal, being well aware that he could find plenty of purchasers for whatever might remain over. This circumstance inspired him with the design he was about to execute.

'Sir, Gorenflot has arrived,' said Rosalie in low tones.

'Show him in,' replied the Count in loud tones.

Madame de Merret turned rather pale when she saw the mason.

'Gorenflot,' said her husband, 'go and fetch bricks from the coachhouse, and bring sufficient to wall up the door of this closet; you will use the plaster I have over to coat the wall with.' Then calling Rosalie and the workman aside:

'Listen, Gorenflot,' he said in an undertone, 'you will sleep here tonight. But tomorrow you will have a passport to a foreign country, to a town to which I will direct you. I shall give you six thousand francs for your journey. You will stay ten years in that town; if you do not like it, you may establish yourself in another, provided it be in the same country. You will pass through Paris, where you will await me. There I will insure you an additional six thousand francs by contract, which will be paid to you on your return, provided you have fulfilled the conditions of our bargain. This is the price for your absolute silence as to what you are about to do tonight. As to you, Rosalie, I will give you ten thousand francs on the day of your wedding, on condition of your marrying Gorenflot; but if you wish to marry, you must hold your tongues; or – no dowry.'

'Rosalie,' said Madame de Merret, 'do my hair.'

The husband walked calmly up and down, watching the door, the mason, and his wife, but without betraying any insulting doubts. Madame de Merret chose a moment when the workman was unloading bricks and her husband was at the other end of the room to say to Rosalie: 'A thousand francs a year for you, my child, if you can tell Gorenflot to leave a chink at the bottom.' Then out loud, she added coolly:

'Go and help him!'

Monsieur and Madame de Merret were silent all the time that Gorenflot took to brick up the door. This silence, on the part of the husband, who did not choose to furnish his wife with a pretext for saying things of a double meaning, had its purpose; on the part of Madame de Merret it was either pride or prudence. When the wall was about half-way up, the sly workman took advantage of a moment when the Count's back was turned, to strike a blow with his trowel in one of the glass panes of the closet-door. This act informed Madame de Merret that Rosalie had spoken to Gorenflot.

All three then saw a man's face; it was dark and gloomy with black hair and eyes of flame. Before her husband turned, the poor woman had time

All three saw the man's gloomy face

to make a sign to the stranger that signified: Hope!

At four o'clock, toward dawn, for it was the month of September, the construction was finished. The mason was handed over to the care of Jean, and Monsieur de Merret went to bed in his wife's room.

On rising the following morning, he said carelessly:

'The deuce! I must go to the Marie for the passport.' He put his hat on his head, advanced three steps toward the door, altered his mind and took the crucifix.

His wife trembled for joy. 'He is going to Duvivier,' she thought. As soon as the Count had left, Madame de Merret rang for Rosalie; then in a terrible voice:

'The trowel, the trowel!' she cried, 'and quick to work! I saw how Gorenflot did it; we shall have time to make a hole and to mend it again.'

In the twinkling of an eye, Rosalie brought a sort of mattock to her mistress, who with unparalleled ardor set about demolishing the wall. She had already knocked out several bricks and was preparing to strike a more decisive blow when she perceived Monsieur de Merret behind her. She fainted.

'Lay Madame on her bed,' said the Count coldly. He had foreseen what would happen in his absence and had set a trap for his wife; he had simply written to the mayor, and had sent for Duvivier. The jeweller arrived just as the room had been put in order.

'Duvivier,' inquired the Count, 'did you buy crucifixes off the Spaniards who passed through here?'

'No, sir.'

'That will do, thank you,' he said, looking at his wife like a tiger. 'Jean,' he added, 'you will see that my meals are served in the Countess's room; she is ill, and I shall not leave her until she has recovered.'

The cruel gentleman stayed with his wife for twenty days. In the beginning, when there were sounds in the walled closet, and Josephine attempted to implore his pity for the dying stranger, he replied, without permitting her to say a word:

'You have sworn on the cross that there is no one there.'

SWEETS FROM A STRANGER

Nicholas Fisk

First, the girl.

Tina Halliday, age eleven, almost black hair, waving at the ends. Brown eyes, tall for her age, quite pretty (but a nail-biter), good enough at most school subjects, very good at badminton (three trophies and, if she won tonight, possibly a fourth soon to come).

Next, the car. Black Jaguar saloon, recent model, fawn leather upholstery, paintwork shining in the drizzly evening light.

And last, the driver of the car.

No, but wait. We will meet him a little later.

★　　★　　★　　★

The black Jaguar was being driven slowly and badly. It lurched along the suburban street seeming to catch its breath, sneeze, then accelerate to all of fifteen miles an hour—then slow again. It came to a corner and took it in bites and nibbles, uncertainly, inexpertly.

Tina saw the car. She thought, That driver could be drunk. She moved closer to a low brick wall with a hedge. If the worst came to the

As soon as he got behind him he seized the knife and turned round. (p. 109)

'I need your help. I'm a friend! Help me!' (p.137)

worst—if the driver lost control—she could easily hop over the wall and be safe.

The car slowed. Now it seemed to be aiming at her: following her. Tina gripped her badminton racket tightly. She felt the first flutter of fear. The street was deserted. She thought, That car is coming for *me*.

The car almost stopped, right beside her, grating one wheel rim against the curb. Panic jumped into Tina's throat. When the car's window slid down, she thought, Shall I run? But her knees and legs felt weak.

A high-pitched voice, a man's voice, came through the open window. 'Little girl! Little girl! Do you want a ride in my car?'

Very loudly and distinctly, Tina said, 'No! I do not!' She thought, I'll give him 'little girl' if he tries anything on. 'Badminton Builds Bionic Biceps,' she murmured, and tried to smile.

The voice said, 'But—but it's a nice car. Wouldn't you like a ride?'

Tina said—almost shouted, 'No! Go away!'

The panic was leaving her. A part of her mind was giggling. If only Mum could see this! A classic scene! The thing she had been warned against even when she was tiny! 'Bad Stranger Man trying to get Nice Little Girl into Big Wicked Car!' Next thing, he'd be offering her a sweetie . . .

The Jaguar wheezed as the driver over-revved the engine. It lurched and bumbled along beside her. The man inside—she could not see his face—said, 'Little girl! Wouldn't you like a sweetie? I've got some sweeties!'

At this, Tina began laughing. She laughed so much that she bent over in the middle. 'You're too much!' she choked. 'Really you are! Sweeties! A nice ride, and you've got some *sweeties*, too!'

The man said something that stopped her laughing. '*Please*,' he said. '*Please!*'

There was complete despair in his voice.

'Don't go away!' he said. She could see a sort of agony in the way his body stretched towards her. 'Don't go away! I don't *understand* anything . . . I don't know what to *do* . . .'

Tina, knowing she was behaving foolishly, went closer to the car, bent down and looked through the window. Even now she could not see the man. The instrument lights showed her only that he was small.

Nothing else.

'They told me girls and boys liked sweets,' the man said, hopelessly. 'Crystallized fruits . . .' His voice was high and husky. 'They told me all sorts of things, but nothing helps. If only *you* would help . . .'

Tina told herself: You must be mad!—and got into the car.

Now she could see the man's head. It was turned away from her, bowed. Small man, small head.

'I don't know,' the man said. He made a gesture, a defeated throwing-out of his arm and hand. Tina saw the hand.

It was like a claw. It had only three fingers. There was skin that was not skin. There was dark, glossy hairiness.

The panic came back—leapt into her throat—choked her, froze her, numbed her.

'Nothing's working, nothing's going right,' the man said, in his high, rustling, despairing voice. Tina could not speak. She could only look at the hand, the dreadful hand.

He must have seen the whites of her eyes or the terrified O of her mouth, for he snatched his hand away, produced a glove and clumsily put it on. The glove had five fingers, Tina thought, Two of them must be padded. Still she could not move or speak. She made a gasping sound.

'I'm an invader,' the man said, as if replying to her sound. 'An invader. Come to conquer you. But it's not working.'

Tina coughed and forced her voice to work. 'An invader?' she said.

'Invading Earth,' the man said, dully. 'Your planet.'

'Where do you come from?' Tina said.

'Out there.' He waved his gloved hand vaguely upwards. 'Not from a planet: our home planet was finished thousands of years ago. We made our own world. We're having trouble with it. Not enough fuel, not enough ores and minerals, not enough of anything. Your planet has the things we need, so we're invading . . . But I don't know, I don't know . . .'

I'm not dreaming, Tina thought, This is real. It is happening. Escape! Run away! But she did not want to go.

'Look,' the man said. 'All I want to do is to stop being an invader. To go home. They told me things—told me what to do, what to say—but nothing fits, nothing goes right.'

'I don't see how I can help,' Tina said. 'I mean, what can *I* do?'

'Take me to a telephone. Get me a number, a particular number, I have it here——'

'But there's a telephone box just down the road, you passed it——'

'I couldn't make it work. They told me to use it, they told me how to use it; I did everything right, but it wouldn't work.'

'Come with me,' Tina said. Now she was no longer frightened, just very curious. 'Get out of the car. No, you must switch off the engine—— that's right. And don't leave the keys in. Stop shaking, there's nothing to be afraid of. No, get out *your* side, there's no need to climb over the seats. Now close the door. Try again. Give it a good slam. Good. Take my arm. Come on.'

They reached the telephone box. The man walked as if his legs made him uneasy. He shook and trembled. Tina had to hold him up. He was not as tall as she.

The telephone would not work. 'Out of order,' Tina said, with a shrug.

'What does that mean?' the man said.

'Only that it doesn't work.'

'They never told us about "Out of Order",' the man said, dully.

'Wait a second!' Tina saw there was a coin jammed in the little slot. She managed to force the jammed coin in. Now the telephone worked. She dialled the number the man gave her. A high-pitched voice answered. The man took the handset—he held it the wrong way round at first—and spoke.

'Mission completed,' he said. Then, 'What? Oh. Oh. Well, I *can't* complete it any more than I *have* completed it, I can't go on *any longer* . . . What? No, no, I don't care, it's no good telling me that. Completed or uncompleted, I'm going home.'

He put the receiver back on the hook, sighed, and said, 'Well, I'm not the only one. Several others have failed too and *they're* going home.'

Now Tina could see his face, for the first time, by the light of a street lamp. It was a horrible face, a waxwork mask—a face no more human than one of those plastic, jointed dolls. Though the mouth had lips, it was really only a movable hole. The skin—but it was not skin—was too tight over the cheek-bones, too loose at the ears. And the ears were waxen, unreal. The hair began and ended too sharply. It did not grow from the scalp; it was fitted to it. A wig.

She shuddered. '*Why?*' she demanded. 'Why did they dress you up like this? I mean, if you're an invader, why couldn't you look like an invader?—someone frightening and threatening and, what's the word, indomitable? You're just a—a mess. I'm sorry, but you are.'

'They—my masters—wanted us to be friendly invaders,' the man explained. 'Not monsters: people like yourselves. People who use telephones and drive cars and wear clothes. But it went wrong, of course. Everything's gone wrong.'

'What are you really like?' Tina said.

The man shifted uneasily. 'Probably you'd think us hideous,' he said. 'You might hate us if you saw us as we really are.'

'But you don't think *me* hideous?' Tina said, smiling. She knew she had a nice smile. Her smile faded as she saw the man's eyes (too big to fit the false eyelids) change, grow cautious and look away.

'Well . . .' he said. 'Well . . .'

'You *do* think me hideous? Tina said, amazed.

'You're so different, that's what it is. So very different from us. Your eyes are so small and pale, and your skin so white, and your hair grows in the wrong places—'

'I see,' Tina said, pursing her lips.

'I hope I haven't given offence?'

'Not at all. Do go on,' she said, stiffly.

'Different,' the man said. 'Things are so different where I come from! Perhaps a bit better. A lot better in some ways.' He began to speak enthusiastically. 'We don't need to use telephones when we want to speak to each other: we just tune into minds. We don't need these complicated great machines, these cars, to travel in. We don't cover ourselves with layers of fabric to keep the weather out—'

'You go naked, I suppose?' Tina said, acidly.

'Well, we don't find it necessary to wrap ourselves in coloured rags! But perhaps you do it because you'd be so ugly if you didn't—Oh, I beg your pardon—'

'Don't mind *me*,' Tina said, coldly. 'A pity, though, that you can't seem to cope in your superior world! Pity you have to go round invading people! Or,' she added spitefully, '*attempting* to invade them!'

'Our world must survive,' the man said quietly. 'It's a beautiful and wonderful world. It must be saved!'

Tina said, 'Hmm.'

'The most beautiful! The most wonderful!' the man insisted. 'If only you could see it for yourself! Then you'd understand!'

'I'm sure you're right,' Tina said, distantly. She looked at her watch. 'Lord! I'm late! I must go! The time!'

'On our world, we control time,' the man told her. 'We always have time . . .' A thought struck him. 'Come with me! See my world! Don't worry about time—stay as long as you like and I promise you'll be back here only a minute or so from now! Come with me!'

His dark eyes blazed at her from the mask of his face. The mask was stupid: the eyes were not.

For the second time Tina told herself: You must be mad! Out loud, she said, 'All right, then. Show me your world.'

She felt herself twisted, racked, stretched, flung apart and thought, This is the journey, then.

'This is my face,' he said. The mock-human mask was gone. Huge, dark, liquid eyes looked at her from the furred face—the face of a cat, but not a cat, not a seal, not an otter, not any Earth animal. She saw the neat, flowing body, covered in dense fur, dark grey and tipped with silver. She saw the high forehead, the mobile mouth (He's smiling! she thought, So that's how they look when they smile!). No tail. Useful three-fingered hands. A mobile, businesslike thumb.

'There is my world,' he said. Through the glassy bubble of nothingness that separated them from the stars, a world gleamed and glittered in the blackness, coming closer and closer impossibly fast—a huge, complicated globe, jewelled with a million tiny lights, sprinkled with clouds—

'Shana,' he said. 'That is Shana. I am a Shanad. In the heart of the world, there is a city called Ro-yil. Can you say those words?'

She found that she could. Her mouth spoke them for her in a tongue her brain did not know. She tried out this new gift. 'What is your name?'

'Talis,' he said.

'Rhymes with Palace,' Tina said, vaguely. There was so much to look at, the glittering world was rushing at them—

133

'There,' said Talis. 'We have landed. Get out. I will show you the city first.'

He hurried her to the edge of a vast square shaft, took her hand, and made her fall, endlessly, through a tunnel of lights and textures, fleeting shapes and sounds. She wanted to scream; but Talis's calm face was beside her, his hand held hers, his voice spoke to her.

They seemed to meet some sort of invisible cushion. The sensation was like that of being in a lift, slowing violently.

And then they were in the city of Ro-yil.

The city hung, a sphere within a sphere, from glistening filaments, pulsing with light. ('They are avenues,' Talis explained, matter-of-factly, 'rather like the one we are standing in.') Towers soared, glassy and magnificent. Plants taller than Earth trees sang softly. There were Shanads everywhere, many in glassy bubbles like that which had carried Tina and Talis from Earth. The bubbles seemed to move instantly from place to place. 'Hoverflies . . . fireflies,' Tina murmured.

'What?' Talis said.

'Beautiful,' she replied. 'Wonderful, beautiful, magnificent . . .!'

A crystal bubble drifted by. It was empty. 'Tsa!' said Talis; the bubble stopped by them. 'Ata-al!' he said and the side of the bubble split open. 'Get in,' he said. 'I'll take you to my home.'

Tina memorized the words and tried to understand how Talis drove the bubble. There was no time. The city hurtled for a split-second, then gently slowed. Tina gasped. Talis smiled. 'You like my city, then?' His voice had changed. Now it was confident, laughing, sure.

Tina could only reply, 'Marvellous!' Then, 'This bubble,' she said, 'it's the same as the one that brought us here, isn't it?'

'The same. It can take you anywhere! Anywhere in the universe! But who would want to leave *this*?' He swept his arm at the jewelled city, the crystalline towers of pearl and jet, aquamarine and turquoise, strung together with luminous silver threads . . .

'Home,' he said. 'Come.'

A door opened in a glassy golden wall.

She entered and saw humans.

The door closed and Talis was gone.

There were perhaps twenty of them. The room was not big enough.

They stared at her, silently. Then a raggedly dressed woman with a tired face came to Tina and said, 'Oh dear. Poor you. And so young.'

'But Talis said—Talis promised—'

'Oh, I dare say he did. I dare say he told you he can control time and all that . . . And you fell for it. Felt sorry for him, didn't you? Felt you had to help? Those big dark eyes of theirs . . . And you fell for it. So did I, years ago. I was a District Nurse. Do you know Hove? And Brighton—? That was where I was—'

A young man, his clothes falling to pieces, snorted, 'Never mind about Hove and Brighton. We've had enough of them.' He turned his back on the District Nurse and said, 'What's your name, then? Tina? Tina. You're right in it now. Up to the neck. Like the rest of us. There's lots of us, you know. Not just this room: the whole building.' He shrugged despairingly. To the District Nurse he said, 'You explain to her.'

'You're a hostage, dear,' the woman said. 'At least, that's the way we work it out. I mean, they want to invade Earth, but they can't. You see, they want metals and minerals and I-don't-know-what from Earth; but their weapons won't work *without* the metals and minerals and I-don't-know-whats. So they're stuck, aren't they?'

'What do you mean, hostages?' Tina said. Another man joined the group and answered. 'They're going to use us instead of weapons,' he said. 'They'll tell Earth they've got us. If Earth won't give them the things they want, they'll threaten to kill us, you see? They'll *barter* us! When they've got enough of us.'

Tina said, 'But—but they can't! I've got to go home!'

The young man told Tina, 'Cheer up, you're not dead yet. No good crying.'

Tina swallowed her sobs and said, 'How long have you been here?'

'He's been here longest,' the nurse said, pointing to a man huddled in a corner. 'Seven years. Old misery, he is. You won't get anything out of him. Given up speaking to anyone years ago.'

'Why don't you escape?' Tina said.

'Might be difficult, don't you think?' the young man said, cynically. 'I mean, we don't *look* much like them, do we? We'd be a bit *noticeable* outside, wouldn't we? Anyhow, if you think you can get out, have a go. Ah, food!'

A door in the wall opened: a gleaming box slid in. Immediately everyone—even the crouched man—came to life. They grabbed and gobbled, crammed their mouths, bargained noisily over swaps.

Tina thought, You're a shabby lot. She ate the food. It looked strange but tasted good. The things that looked like crystallized fruits were best of all. She saved some, hiding them in her pocket. She thought, They've given in; I won't. I'll learn everything I can, and hoard food and wait for the right moment: then I'll escape . . .

Nobody showed much interest when, three days later, Tina emptied the food box, climbed into it, and escaped the room.

Now she was at large in the city. The Shanad words she had learned from Talis were still in her mind. She had practised them and knew them well. But that was about all she knew.

Soon, she did not even know what she had hoped to gain by escaping. The Shanads thronging the city of Ro-yil neither helped nor hindered her. No sirens screamed, no vehicles dashed, no hard-faced law-enforcers pounced. The Shanads (to Tina, they all looked the same) ignored her. Their large, dark, intelligent eyes looked at her—then, deliberately, looked away.

'A bubble . . .' she said to herself. 'That's what I must have.' A bubble drifted beside her. 'Tsa!' she said. 'Ata-al!' She sat in the bubble, trying to find a knob or a lever or anything at all that would make it go. She failed. Shanads passed by, not looking or caring. She began to cry. She got out of the bubble and walked blindly, endlessly, through the gorgeous city.

She reached the shafts by accident. One shaft had brought her down from the surface of the world to the city; now she saw a twin shaft. Shanads walked into its entrance and went up. Up to the surface! 'One step nearer home,' Tina said, entered the shaft, and flew to the surface.

She found herself looking at white clouds in a green sky. Beyond, she saw darkness and in the darkness, stars and planets. 'One of you is Earth,' she said. She looked for a bubble. This time, she would not give up. This time, she would go home.

She saw a bubble. It was stationary. In front of it, two furry little things, charming, fat and jolly, rolled on the ground. They were smaller than Shanads, much smaller—

'Ah!' said Tina. '*Children!*'

'Tsa!' she hissed; and got into the bubble. The child Shanads rolled and squeaked, pounced and wrestled, outside. 'Ata-al!' she said. The magic word once again failed to have any effect. She knocked on the wall of the bubble to attract the children's attention. They looked up at her. Their eyes were beautiful.

Tina said—her mind and voice struggling for the words, 'I'm a friend. I need your help. I'm a friend! Help me!'

The children stared. One made a gurgling noise that must have been giggling.

'Look,' Tina said, 'I've got this lovely bubble, but I can't seem to work it. Wouldn't you like to show me how to work it?'

Both children giggled. Neither moved.

'Look, suppose you get in with me, and show me what to do, then we can go for a ride!'

The Shanad children linked paws and stared at her, still giggling.

Tina remembered the crystallized fruits in her pocket. 'I'll give you these!' she cried. 'One for each of you! *Two* each!'

And suddenly the Shanad children were running away, running very fast. They ran until they reached an adult Shanad, then stopped and pointed at Tina. She could hear what they were saying.

'. . . wanted to take us for a *ride*!' one said.

'In a nice bubble!' said the other.

'Offered us *sweets*!' said the first. 'Us! As if we'd take sweets from strangers!'

They pointed their fingers and giggled, loudly and scornfully. They jumped up and down, delighted with themselves.

And then Talis was there, with many other Shanads.

They took Tina back to the room.

★   ★   ★   ★

One day, perhaps, the Shanads will make contact with Earth. Until then, Tina will at least be fed. The things that look like crystallized fruits are delicious, at first.

Later, you grow tired of them.

THE MOONLIT ROAD
Ambrose Bierce

STATEMENT OF JOEL HETMAN, JR.

I AM the most unfortunate of men. Rich, respected, fairly well educated and of sound health – with many other advantages usually valued by those having them and coveted by those who have them not – I sometimes think that I should be less unhappy if they had been denied me, for then the contrast between my outer and my inner life would not be continually demanding a painful attention. In the stress of privation and the need of effort I might sometimes forget the sombre secret ever baffling the conjecture that it compels.

I am the only child of Joel and Julia Hetman. The one was a well-to-do country gentleman, the other a beautiful and accomplished woman to whom he was passionately attached with what I now know to have been a jealous and exacting devotion. The family home was a few miles from Nashville, Tennessee, a large, irregularly built dwelling of no particular order of architecture, a little way off the road, in a park of trees and shrubbery.

At the time of which I write I was nineteen years old, a student at Yale. One day I received a telegram from my father of such urgency that in compliance with its unexplained demand I left at once for home. At the railway station in Nashville a distant relative awaited me to apprise me of the reason for my recall: my mother had been barbarously murdered – why and by whom none could conjecture, but the circumstances were these:

My father had gone to Nashville, intending to return the next afternoon. Something prevented his accomplishing the business in hand, so he returned on the same night, arriving just before the dawn. In his testimony before the coroner he explained that having no latch-key and not caring to disturb the sleeping servants, he had, with no clearly defined intention, gone round to the rear of the house. As he turned an angle of the building, he heard a sound as of a door gently closed, and saw in the darkness, indistinctly, the figure of a man, which instantly disappeared among the trees of the lawn. A hasty pursuit and brief search of the grounds in the belief that the trespasser was someone secretly visiting a servant proving fruitless, he entered at the unlocked door and mounted the stairs to my mother's chamber. Its door was open, and stepping into black darkness he fell headlong over some heavy object on the floor. I may spare myself the details; it was my poor mother, dead of strangulation by human hands!

Nothing had been taken from the house, the servants had heard no sound, and excepting those terrible fingermarks upon the dead woman's throat – dear God! that I might forget them! – no trace of the assassin was ever found.

I gave up my studies and remained with my father, who, naturally, was greatly changed. Always of a sedate, taciturn disposition, he now fell into a so deep dejection that nothing could hold his attention, yet anything – a footfall, the sudden closing of a door – aroused in him a fitful interest; one might have called it an apprehension. At any small surprise of the senses he would start visibly and sometimes turn pale, then relapse into a melancholy apathy deeper than before. I suppose he was what is called a 'nervous wreck.' As to me, I was younger then than now – there is much in that. Youth is Gilead, in which is balm for every wound. Ah, that I might again dwell in that enchanted land! Unacquainted with grief, I knew not how to appraise my bereavement; I could not rightly estimate the strength of the stroke.

One night, a few months after the dreadful event, my father and I walked home from the city. The full moon was about three hours above the eastern horizon; the entire countryside had the solemn stillness of a summer night; our footfalls and the ceaseless song of the katydids were the only sound, aloof. Black shadows of bordering trees lay athwart the road, which, in the short reaches between, gleamed a ghostly white. As we approached the gate to our dwelling, whose front was in shadow, and in which no light shone, my father suddenly stopped and clutched my arm, saying, hardly above his breath:

'God! God! what is that?'

'I hear nothing,' I replied.

'But see – see!' he said, pointing along the road, directly ahead.

I said: 'Nothing is there. Come, father, let us go in – you are ill.'

He had released my arm and was standing rigid and motionless in the centre of the illuminated roadway, staring like one bereft of sense. His face in the moonlight showed a pallor and fixity inexpressibly distressing. I pulled gently at his sleeve, but he had forgotten my existence. Presently he began to retire backward, step by step, never for an instant removing his eyes from what he saw, or thought he saw. I turned half round to follow, but stood irresolute. I do not recall any feeling of fear, unless a sudden chill was its physical manifestation. It seemed as if an icy wind had touched my face and enfolded my body from head to foot; I could feel the stir of it in my hair.

At that moment my attention was drawn to a light that suddenly streamed from an upper window of the house: one of the servants, awakened by what mysterious premonition of evil who can say, and in obedience to an impulse that she was never able to name, had lit a lamp. When I turned to look for my father he was gone, and in all the years that have passed no whisper of his fate has come across the borderland of conjecture from the realm of the unknown.

STATEMENT OF CASPAR GRATTAN

Today I am said to live; to-morrow, here in this room, will lie a senseless shape of clay that all too long was I. If anyone lift the cloth from the face of that unpleasant thing it will be in gratification of a mere morbid curiosity. Some, doubtless, will go further and inquire, 'Who was he?' In this writing I supply the only answer that I am able to make – Caspar Grattan. Surely, that should be enough. The name has served my small need for more than twenty years of a life of unknown length. True, I gave it to myself, but lacking another I had the right. In this world one must have a name; it prevents confusion, even when it does not establish identity. Some, though, are known by numbers, which also seem inadequate distinctions.

One day, for illustration, I was passing along a street of a city, far from here, when I met two men in uniform, one of whom, half pausing and looking curiously into my face, said to his companion, 'That man looks like 767.' Something in the number seemed familiar and horrible. Moved by an uncontrollable impulse, I sprang into a side street and ran until I fell exhausted in a country lane.

I have never forgotten that number, and always it comes to memory attended by gibbering obscenity, peals of joyless laughter, the clang of iron doors. So I say a name, even if self-bestowed, is better than a number. In the register of the potter's field I shall soon have both. What wealth!

Of him who shall find this paper I must beg a little consideration. It is not the history of my life; the knowledge to write that is denied me. This is only a record of broken and apparently unrelated memories, some of them as distinct and sequent as brilliant beads upon a thread, others remote and strange, having the character of crimson dreams with interspaces blank and black – witch-fires glowing still and red in a great desolation.

Standing upon the shore of eternity, I turn for a last look landward over the course by which I came. There are twenty years of footprints fairly distinct, the impressions of bleeding feet. They lead through poverty and pain, devious and unsure, as of one staggering beneath a burden —

'Remote, unfriended, melancholy, slow.'

Ah, the poet's prophecy of Me – how admirable, how dreadfully admirable!

Backward beyond the beginning of this *via dolorosa* – this epic of suffering with episodes of sin – I see nothing clearly; it comes out of a cloud. I know that it spans only twenty years, yet I am an old man.

One does not remember one's birth – one has to be told. But with me it was different; life came to me full-handed and dowered me with all my faculties and powers. Of a previous existence I know no more than others, for all have stammering intimations that may be memories and may be dreams. I know only that my first consciousness was of maturity in body and mind – a consciousness accepted without surprise or conjecture. I merely found myself walking in a forest, half-clad, footsore, unutterably weary and hungry. Seeing a farmhouse, I approached and asked for food, which was given me by one who inquired my name. I did not know, yet knew that all had names. Greatly embarrrassed, I retreated, and night coming on, lay down in the forest and slept.

The next day I entered a large town which I shall not name. Nor shall I recount further incidents of the life that is now to end – a life of wandering, always and everywhere haunted by an overmastering sense of crime in punishment of wrong and of terror in punishment of crime. Let me see if I can reduce it to narrative.

I seem once to have lived near a great city, a prosperous planter, married to a woman whom I loved and distrusted. We had, it sometimes seems, one child, a youth of brilliant parts and promise. He is at all times a vague figure, never clearly drawn, frequently altogether out of the picture.

One luckless evening it occurred to me to test my wife's fidelity in a vulgar, commonplace way familiar to everyone who has acquaintance with the literature of fact and fiction. I went to the city, telling my wife that I should be absent until the following afternoon. But I returned before daybreak and went to the rear of the house, purposing to enter by a door with which I had secretly so tampered that it would seem to lock, yet not actually fasten. As I approached it, I heard it gently open and close, and saw a man steal away into the darkness. With murder in my heart, I sprang after him, but he had vanished without even the bad luck of identification. Sometimes now I cannot even persuade myself that it was a human being.

Crazed with jealousy and rage, blind and bestial with all the elemental passions of insulted manhood, I entered the house and sprang up the stairs to the door of my wife's chamber. It was closed, but having tampered with its lock also, I easily entered, and despite the black darkness soon stood by the side of her bed. My groping hands told me that although disarranged it was unoccupied.

'She is below,' I thought, 'and terrified by my entrance has evaded me in the darkness of the hall.'

With the purpose of seeking her I turned to leave the room, but took a wrong direction – the right one! My foot struck her, cowering in a corner of the room. Instantly my hands were at her throat, stifling a shriek, my knees were upon her struggling body; and there in the darkness, without a word of accusation or reproach, I strangled her till she died!

There ends the dream. I have related it in the past tense, but the present would be the fitter form, for again and again the sombre tragedy re-enacts itself in my consciousness – over and over I lay the plan, I suffer the confirmation, I redress the wrong. Then all is blank; and afterward the rains beat against the grimy window-panes, or the snows fall upon my scant attire, the wheels rattle in the squalid streets where my life lies in poverty and mean employment. If there is ever sunshine, I do not recall it; if there are birds, they do not sing.

There is another dream, another vision of the night. I stand among the shadows in a moonlit road. I am aware of another presence, but whose I cannot rightly determine. In the shadows of a great dwelling I catch the gleam of white garments; then the figure of a woman confronts me in the road – my murdered wife! There is death in the face; there are marks upon the throat. The eyes are fixed on mine with an infinite gravity which is not reproach, nor hate, nor menace, nor anything less terrible than recognition. Before this awful apparition I retreat in terror – a terror that is upon me as I write. I can no longer rightly shape the words. See! they—

Now I am calm, but truly there is no more to tell: the incident ends where it began – in darkness and in doubt.

Yes, I am again in control of myself: 'the captain of my soul.' But that is not respite; it is another stage and phase of expiation. My penance, constant in degree, is mutable in kind: one of its variants is tranquillity. After all, it is only a life-sentence. 'To Hell for life' – that is a foolish penalty: the culprit chooses the duration of his punishment. To-day my term expires.

To each and all, the peace that was not mine.

STATEMENT OF THE LATE JULIA HETMAN,
THROUGH THE MEDIUM BAYROLLES

I had retired early and fallen almost immediately into a peaceful sleep, from which I awoke with that indefinable sense of peril which is, I think, a common experience in that other, earlier life. Of its unmeaning character, too, I was entirely persuaded, yet that did not banish it. My husband, Joel Hetman, was away from home; the servants slept in another part of the house. But these were familiar conditions; they had never before distressed me. Nevertheless, the strange terror grew so insupportable that conquering my reluctance to move I sat up and lit the lamp at my bedside. Contrary to my expectation this gave me no relief; the light seemed rather an added danger, for I reflected that it would shine out under the door, disclosing my presence to what ever evil thing might lurk outside. You that are still in the flesh, subject to horrors of the imagination, think what a monstrous fear that must be which seeks in darkness security from malevolent existences of the night. That is to spring to close quarters with an unseen enemy – the strategy of despair!

Extinguishing the lamp, I pulled the bedclothing about my head and lay trembling and silent, unable to shriek, forgetful to pray. In this pitiable state I must have lain for what you call hours – with us there are no hours, there is no time.

At last it came – a soft, irregular sound of footfalls on the stairs! They were slow, hesitant, uncertain, as of something that did not see its way; to my disordered reason all the more terrifying for that, as the approach of some blind and mindless malevolence to which there is no appeal. I even thought that I must have left the hall lamp burning and the groping of this creature proved it a monster of the night. This was foolish and inconsistent with my previous dread of the light, but what would you have? Fear has no brains; it is an idiot. The dismal witness that it bears and the cowardly counsel that it whispers are unrelated. We know this well, we who have passed into the Realm of Terror, who skulk in eternal dusk among the scenes of our former lives, invisible even to ourselves, and one another, yet hiding forlorn in lonely places; yearning for speech with our loved ones, yet dumb, and as fearful of them as they of us. Sometimes the disability is removed, the law suspended: by the deathless power of love or hate we break the spell – we are seen by those whom we would warn, console, or punish. What form we seem to them to bear we know not; we know only that we terrify even those whom we most wish to comfort, and from whom we most crave tenderness and sympathy.

Forgive, I pray you, this inconsequent digression by what was once a woman. You who consult us in this imperfect way – you do not understand. You ask foolish questions about things unknown and things forbidden. Much that we know and could impart in our speech is meaningless in yours. We must communicate with you through a stammering intelligence in that small fraction of our language that you yourselves can speak. You think that we are of another world. No, we have knowledge of no world but yours, though for us it holds no sunlight, no warmth, no music, no laughter, no song of birds nor any companionship. O God! what a thing it is to be a ghost, cowering and shivering in an altered world, a prey to apprehension and despair!

No, I did not die of fright: the Thing turned and went away. I heard it go down the stairs, hurriedly, I thought, as if itself in sudden fear. Then I rose to call for help. Hardly had my shaking hand found the door-knob when – merciful heaven! – I heard it returning. Its footfalls as it remounted the stairs were rapid, heavy and loud; they shook the house. I fled to an angle of the wall and crouched upon the floor. I tried to pray. I tried to call the name of my dear husband. Then I heard the door thrown open. There was an interval of unconsciousness, and when I revived I felt a strangling clutch upon my throat – felt my arms feebly beating against something that bore me backward – felt my tongue thrusting itself from between my teeth! And then I passed into this life.

No, I have no knowledge of what it was. The sum of what we knew at death is the measure of what we know afterward of all that went before. Of this existence we know many things, but no new light falls upon any page of that; in memory is written all of it that we can read. Here are no heights of truth overlooking the confused landscape of that dubitable domain. We still dwell in the Valley of the Shadow, lurk in its desolate places, peering from brambles and thickets at its mad, malign inhabitants. How should we have new knowledge of that fading past?

What I am about to relate happened on a night. We know when it is night, for then you retire to your houses and we can venture from our places of concealment to move unafraid about our old homes, to look in at the windows, even to enter and gaze upon your faces as you sleep. I had lingered long near the dwelling where I had been so cruelly changed to what I am, as we do while any that we love or hate remain. Vainly I had sought some method of manifestation, some way to make my continued existence and my great love and poignant pity understood by my husband and son. Always if they slept they would wake, or if in my desperation I dared approach them when they were awake, would turn toward me the terrible eyes of the living, frightening me by the glances that I sought from the purpose that I held.

On this night I had searched for them without success, fearing to find them; they were nowhere in the house, nor about the moonlit lawn. For, although the sun is lost to us for ever, the moon, full-orbed or slender, remains to us. Sometimes it shines by night, sometimes by day, but always it rises and sets, as in that other life.

I left the lawn and moved in the white light and silence along the road, aimless and sorrowing. Suddenly I heard the voice of my poor husband in exclamations of astonishment, with that of my son in re-assurance and dissuasion; and there by the shadow of a group of trees they stood – near, so near! Their faces were toward me, the eyes of the elder man fixed upon mine. He saw me – at last, at last, he saw me! In the consciousness of that, my terror fled as a cruel dream. The death-spell was broken: Love had conquered Law! Mad with exultation I shouted – I *must* have shouted, 'He sees, he sees: he will understand!' Then, controlling myself, I moved forward, smiling and consciously beautiful, to offer myself to his arms, to comfort him with endearments, and, with my son's hand in mine, to speak words that should restore the broken bonds between the living and the dead.

Alas! alas! his face went white with fear. His eyes were as those of a hunted animal. He backed away from me, as I advanced, and at last turned and fled into the wood – whither, it is not given to me to know.

To my poor boy, left doubly desolate, I have never been able to impart a sense of my presence. Soon he, too, must pass to this Life Invisible and be lost to me for ever.

THE HITCH-HIKER

Roald Dahl

I had a new car. It was an exciting toy, a big B.M.W. 3.3 Li, which means 3.3 litre, long wheelbase, fuel injection. It had a top speed of 129 m.p.h. and terrific acceleration. The body was pale blue. The seats inside were darker blue and they were made of leather, genuine soft leather of the finest quality. The windows were electrically operated and so was the sun-roof. The radio aerial popped up when I switched on the radio, and disappeared when I switched it off. The powerful engine growled and grunted impatiently at slow speeds, but at sixty miles an hour the growling stopped and the motor began to purr with pleasure.

I was driving up to London by myself. It was a lovely June day. They were haymaking in the fields and there were buttercups along both sides of the road. I was whispering along at seventy miles an hour, leaning back comfortably in my seat, with no more than a couple of fingers resting lightly on the wheel to keep her steady. Ahead of me I saw a man thumbing a lift. I touched the footbrake and brought the car to a stop beside him. I always stopped for hitch-hikers. I knew just how it used to feel to be standing on the side of a country road watching the cars go by. I hated the drivers for pretending they didn't see me, especially the ones

147

in big cars with three empty seats. The large expensive cars seldom stopped. It was always the smaller ones that offered you a lift, or the old rusty ones, or the ones that were already crammed full of children and the driver would say 'I think we can squeeze in one more.'

The hitch-hiker poked his head through the open window and said, 'Going to London, guv'nor?'

'Yes,' I said, 'Jump in.'

He got in and I drove on.

He was a small ratty-faced man with grey teeth. His eyes were dark and quick and clever, like a rat's eyes, and his ears were slightly pointed at the top. He had a cloth cap on his head and he was wearing a greyish-coloured jacket with enormous pockets. The grey jacket, together with the quick eyes and the pointed ears, made him look more than anything like some sort of a huge human rat.

'What part of London are you headed for?' I asked him.

'I'm goin' right through London and out the other side,' he said. 'I'm goin' to Epsom, for the races. It's Derby Day today.'

'So it is,' I said. 'I wish I were going with you. I love betting on horses.'

'I never bet on horses,' he said. 'I don't even watch 'em run. That's a stupid silly business.

'Then why do you go?' I asked.

He didn't seem to like that question. His little ratty face went absolutely blank and he sat there staring straight ahead at the road, saying nothing.

'I expect you help to work the betting machines or something like that,' I said.

'That's even sillier,' he answered. 'There's no fun working them lousy machines and selling tickets to mugs. Any fool could do that.'

There was a long silence. I decided not to question him any more. I remembered how irritated I used to get in my hitch-hiking days when drivers kept asking *me* questions. Where are you going? Why are you going there? What's your job? Are you married? Do you have a girl-friend? What's her name? How old are you? And so on and so forth. I used to hate it.

'I'm sorry,' I said. 'It's none of my business what you do. The trouble is, I'm a writer, and most writers are terrible nosey parkers.'

'You write books?' he asked.

'Yes.'

'Writin' books is okay,' he said. 'It's what I call a skilled trade. I'm in a skilled trade too. The folks I despise is them that spend all their lives doin' crummy old routine jobs with no skill in 'em at all. You see what I mean?'

'Yes.'

'The secret of life,' he said, 'is to become very very good at somethin' that's very very 'ard to do.'

'Like you,' I said.

'Exactly. You and me both.'

'What makes you think that *I'm* any good at my job?' I asked. 'There's an awful lot of bad writers around.'

'You wouldn't be drivin' about in a car like this if you weren't no good at it,' he answered. 'It must've cost a tidy packet, this little job.'

'It wasn't cheap.'

'What can she do flat out?' he asked.

'One hundred and twenty-nine miles an hour,' I told him.

'I'll bet she won't do it.'

'I bet she will.'

'All car makers is liars,' he said. 'You can buy any car you like and it'll never do what the makers say it will in the ads.'

'This one will.'

'Open 'er up then and prove it,' he said. 'Go on, guv'nor, open 'er right up and let's see what she'll do.'

There is a roundabout at Chalfont St Peter and immediately beyond it there's a long straight section of dual cariageway. We came out of the roundabout on to the carriageway and I pressed my foot down on the accelerator. The big car leaped forward as though she'd been stung. In ten seconds or so, we were doing ninety.

'Lovely!' he cried. 'Beautiful! Keep goin'!'

I had the accelerator jammed right down against the floor and I held it there.

'One hundred!' he shouted . . . 'A hundred and five! . . . A hundred and ten! . . . A hundred and fifteen! Go on! Don't slack off!'

I was in the outside lane and we flashed past several cars as though they were standing still—a green Mini, a big cream-coloured Citroën, a white Land-Rover, a huge truck with a container on the back, an orange-coloured Volkswagen Minibus . . .

'A hundred and twenty!' my passenger shouted, jumping up and down. 'Go on! Go on! Get 'er up to one-two-nine!'

At that moment, I heard the scream of a police siren. It was so loud it seemed to be right inside the car, and then a policeman on a motor-cycle loomed up alongside us on the inside lane and went past us and raised a hand for us to stop.

'Oh, my sainted aunt!' I said. 'That's torn it!'

The policeman must have been doing about a hundred and thirty when he passed us, and he took plenty of time slowing down. Finally, he pulled into the side of the road and I pulled in behind him. 'I didn't know police motor-cycles could go as fast as that,' I said rather lamely.

'That one can,' my passenger said, 'It's the same make as yours. It's a B.M.W. R90S. Fastest bike on the road. That's what they're usin' nowadays.'

The policeman got off his motor-cycle and leaned the machine sideways on to its prop stand. Then he took off his gloves and placed them carefully on the seat. He was in no hurry now. He had us where he wanted us and he knew it.

'This is real trouble,' I said. 'I don't like it one bit.'

'Don't talk to 'im any more than is necessary, you understand,' my companion said. 'Just sit tight and keep mum.'

Like an executioner approaching his victim, the policeman came strolling slowly towards us. He was a big meaty man with a belly, and his blue breeches were skintight around his enormous thighs. His goggles were pulled up on the helmet, showing a smouldering red face with wide cheeks.

We sat there like guilty schoolboys, waiting for him to arrive.

'Watch out for this man,' my passenger whispered. 'Ee looks mean as the devil.'

The policeman came round to my open window and placed one meaty hand on the sill. 'What's the hurry?' he said.

'No hurry, officer,' I answered.

'Perhaps there's a woman in the back having a baby and you're rushing her to hospital? Is that it?'

'No, officer.'

'Or perhaps your house is on fire and you're dashing home to rescue the family from upstairs?' His voice was dangerously soft and mocking.

'My house isn't on fire, officer.'

'In that case,' he said, 'you've got yourself into a nasty mess, haven't you? Do you know what the speed limit is in this country?'

'Seventy,' I said.

'And do you mind telling me exactly what speed you were doing just now?'

I shrugged and didn't say anything.

When he spoke next, he raised his voice so loud that I jumped. '*One hundred and twenty miles per hour!*' he barked. 'That's *fifty* miles an hour over the limit!'

He turned his head and spat out a big gob of spit. It landed on the wing of my car and started sliding down over my beautiful blue paint. Then he turned back again and stared hard at my passenger. 'And who are you?' he asked sharply.

'He's a hitch-hiker,' I said. 'I'm giving him a lift.'

'I didn't ask you,' he said. 'I asked him.'

''Ave I done somethin' wrong?' my passenger asked. His voice was as soft and oily as haircream.

'That's more than likely,' the policeman answered. 'Anyway, you're a witness. I'll deal with you in a minute. Driving-licence,' he snapped, holding out his hand.

I gave him my driving-licence.

He unbuttoned the left-hand breast-pocket of his tunic and brought out the dreaded books of tickets. Carefully, he copied the name and address from my licence. Then he gave it back to me. He strolled round to the front of the car and read the number from the number-plate and wrote that down as well. He filled in the date, the time and the details of my offence. Then he tore out the top copy of the ticket. But before handing it to me, he checked that all the information had come through clearly on his own carbon copy. Finally, he replaced the book in his tunic pocket and fastened the button.

'Now you,' he said to my passenger, and he walked around to the other side of the car. From the other breast-pocket he produced a small black notebook. 'Name?' he snapped.

'Michael Fish,' my passenger said.

'Address?'

'Fourteen, Windsor Lane, Luton.'

'Show me something to prove this is your real name and address,' the policeman said.

My passenger fished in his pockets and came out with a driving-licence of his own. The policeman checked the name and address and handed it back to him. 'What's your job?' he asked sharply.

'I'm an 'od carrier.'

'A *what*?'

'An 'od carrier.'

'Spell it.'

'H-O-D-C-A- . . .'

'That'll do. And what's a hod carrier, may I ask?'

'An 'od carrier, officer, is a person 'oo carries the cement up the ladder to the bricklayer. And the 'od is what 'ee carries it in. It's got a long 'andle, and on the top you've got two bits of wood set at an angle . . .'

'All right, all right. Who's your employer?'

'Don't 'ave one. I'm unemployed.'

The policeman wrote all this down in the black notebook. Then he returned the book to its pocket and did up the button.

'When I get back to the station I'm going to do a little checking up on you,' he said to my passenger.

'Me? What've I done wrong?' the rat-faced man asked.

'I don't like your face, that's all,' the policeman said. 'And we just might have a picture of it somewhere in our files.' He strolled round the car and returned to my window.

'I suppose you know you're in serious trouble,' he said to me.

'Yes, officer.'

'You won't be driving this fancy car of yours again for a very long time, not after *we've* finished with you. You won't be driving *any* car again come to that for several years. And a good thing, too. I hope they lock you up for a spell into the bargain.'

'You mean prison?' I asked, alarmed.

'Absolutely,' he said, smacking his lips. 'In the clink. Behind bars. Along with all the other criminals who break the law. *And* a hefty fine into the bargain. Nobody will be more pleased about that than me. I'll see you in court, both of you. You'll be getting a summons to appear.'

He turned and walked over to his motor-cycle. He flipped the prop stand back into position with his foot and swung his leg over the saddle. Then he kicked the starter and roared off up the road out of sight.

'Phew!' I gasped. 'That's done it.'

'We was caught,' my passenger said. 'We was caught good and proper.'

'I was caught, you mean.'

'That's right,' he said. 'What you goin' to do now, guv'nor?'

'I'm going straight up to London to talk to my solicitor,' I said. I started the car and drove on.

'You mustn't believe what 'ee said to you about goin' to prison,' my passenger said. 'They don't put nobody in the clink just for speedin'.'

'Are you sure of that?' I asked.

'I'm positive,' he answered. 'They can take your licence away and they can give you a whoopin' big fine, but that'll be the end of it.'

I felt tremendously relieved.

'By the way,' I said, 'why did you lie to him?'

'Who, me?' he said. 'What makes you think I lied?'

'You told him you were an unemployed hod carrier. But you told *me* you were in a highly-skilled trade.'

'So I am,' he said. 'But it don't pay to tell everythin' to a copper.'

'So what *do* you do?' I asked him.

'Ah,' he said slyly. 'That'd be tellin', wouldn't it?'

'Is it something you're ashamed of?'

'Ashamed?' he cried. 'Me, ashamed of my job? I'm about as proud of it as anybody could be in the entire world!'

'Then why won't you tell me?'

'You writers really is nosey parkers, aren't you?' he said. 'And you ain't goin' to be 'appy, I don't think, until you've found out exactly what the answer is?'

'I don't really care one way or the other,' I told him, lying.

He gave me a craftly little ratty look out of the sides of his eyes. 'I think you do care,' he said. 'I can see it in your face that you think I'm in some kind of a very peculiar trade and you're just achin' to know what it is.'

I didn't like the way he read my thoughts. I kept quiet and stared at the road ahead.

'You'd be right, too,' he went on. 'I *am* in a very peculiar trade. I'm in the queerest peculiar trade of 'em all.'

I waited for him to go on.

'That's why I 'as to be extra careful 'oo I'm talkin' to, you see. 'Ow am I to know, for instance, you're not another copper in plain clothes?'

'Do I look like a copper?'

'No,' he said. 'You don't. And you ain't. Any fool could tell that.'

He took from his pocket a tin of tobacco and a packet of cigarette papers and started to roll a cigarette. I was watching him out of the corner of one eye, and the speed with which he performed this rather difficult operation was incredible. The cigarette was rolled and ready in about five seconds. He ran his tongue along the edge of the paper, stuck it down and popped the cigarette between his lips. Then, as if from nowhere, a lighter appeared in his hand. The lighter flamed. The cigarette was lit. The lighter disappeared. It was altogether a remarkable performance.

'I've never seen anyone roll a cigarette as fast as that,' I said.

'Ah,' he said, taking a deep suck of smoke. 'So you noticed.'

'Of course I noticed. It was quite fantastic.'

He sat back and smiled. It pleased him very much that I had noticed how quickly he could roll a cigarette. 'You want to know what makes me able to do it?' he asked.

'Go on then.'

'It's because I've got fantastic fingers. These fingers of mine,' he said, holding up both hands high in front of him, 'are quicker and cleverer than the fingers of the best piano player in the world!'

'Are you a piano player?'

'Don't be daft,' he said. 'Do I look like a piano player?'

I glanced at his fingers. They were so beautifully shaped, so slim and long and elegant, they didn't seem to belong to the rest of him at all. They looked more like the fingers of a brain surgeon or a watchmaker.

'My job,' he went on, 'is a hundred times more difficult than playin' the piano. Any twerp can learn to do that. There's titchy little kids learnin' to play the piano in almost any 'ouse you go into these days. That' right, ain't it?'

'More or less,' I said.

'Of course it's right. But there's not one person in ten million can learn to do what I do. Not one in ten million! 'Ow about that?'

'Amazing,' I said.

'You're darn right it's amazin',' he said.

'I think I know what you do,' I said. 'You do conjuring tricks. You're a conjurer.'

'Me?' he snorted. 'A conjurer? Can you picture me goin' round crummy kids' parties makin' rabbits come out of top 'ats?'

'Then you're a card player. You get people into card games and deal yourself marvellous hands.'

'Me! A rotten card-sharper!' he cried. 'That's a miserable racket if ever there was one.'

'All right. I give up.'

I was taking the car along slowly now, at no more than forty miles an hour, to make quite sure I wasn't stopped again. We had come on to the main London–Oxford road and were running down the hill towards Denham.

Suddenly, my passenger was holding up a black leather belt in his hand. 'Ever seen this before?' he asked. The belt had a brass buckle of unusual design.

'Hey!' I said. 'That's mine, isn't it? It *is* mine! Where did you get it?'

He grinned and waved the belt gently from side to side. 'Where d'you think I got it?' he said. 'Off the top of your trousers, of course.'

I reached down and felt for my belt. It was gone.

'You mean you took it off me while we've been driving along?' I asked, flabbergasted.

He nodded, watching me all the time with those little black ratty eyes.

'That's impossible,' I said. 'You'd have to undo the buckle and slide the whole thing out through the loops all the way round. I'd have seen you doing it. And even if I hadn't seen you, I'd have felt it.'

'Ah, but you didn't, did you?' he said, triumphant. He dropped the belt on his lap, and now all at once there was a brown shoelace dangling from his fingers. 'And what about this, then?' he exclaimed, waving the shoelace.

'What about it?' I said.

'Anyone round 'ere missin' a shoelace?' he asked, grinning.

I glanced down at my shoes. The lace of one of them was missing.

'Good grief!' I said. 'How did you do that? I never saw you bending down.'

'You never saw nothin',' he said proudly. 'You never even saw me move an inch. And you know why?'

'Yes,' I said. 'Because you've got fantastic fingers.'

'Exactly right!' he cried. 'You catch on pretty quick, don't you?' He said back and sucked away at his home-made cigarette, blowing the smoke out in a thin stream against the windshield. He knew he had impressed me greatly with those two tricks, and this made him very happy. 'I don' want to be late,' he said. 'What time is it?'

'There's a clock in front of you,' I told him.

'I don't trust car clocks,' he said. 'What does your watch say?'

I hitched up my sleeve to look at the watch on my wrist. It wasn't there. I looked at the man. He looked back at me, grinning.

'You've taken that, too,' I said.

He held out his hand and there was my watch lying in his palm. 'Nice bit of stuff, this,' he said. 'Superior quality. Eighteen-carat gold. Easy to flog, too. It's never any trouble gettin' rid of quality goods.'

'I'd like it back, if you don't mind,' I said rather huffily.

He placed the watch carefully on the leather tray in front of him. 'I wouldn't nick anything from you, guv'nor,' he said. 'You're my pal. You're giving me a lift.'

'I'm glad to hear it,' I said.

'All I'm doin' is answerin' your questions,' he went on. 'You asked me what I did for a livin' and I'm showin' you.'

'What else have you got of mine?'

He smiled again, and now he started to take from the pocket of his jacket one thing after another that belonged to me—my driving licence, a key-ring with four keys on it, some pound notes, a few coins, a letter from my publishers, my diary, a stubby old pencil, a cigarette-lighter, and last of all, a beautiful old sapphire ring with pearls around it belonging to my wife. I was taking the ring up to the jeweller in London because one of the pearls was missing.

'Now *there's* another lovely piece of goods,' he said, turning the ring over in his fingers. 'That's eighteenth century, if I'm not mistaken, from the reign of King George the Third.'

'You're right,' I said, impressed. 'You're absolutely right.'

He put the ring on the leather tray with the other items.

'So you're a pickpocket,' I said.

'I don't like that word,' he answered. 'It's a coarse and vulgar word. Pickpockets is coarse and vulgar people who only do easy little amateur jobs. They lift money from blind old ladies.'

'What do you call yourself, then?'

'Me? I'm a fingersmith. I'm a professional fingersmith.' He spoke the words solemnly and proudly, as though he were telling me he was the President of the Royal College of Surgeons or the Archbishop of Canterbury.

'I've never heard that word before,' I said. 'Did you invent it?'

'Of course I didn't invent it,' he replied. 'It's the name given to them who's risen to the very top of the profession. You've 'eard of a goldsmith and a silversmith, for instance. They're experts with gold and silver. I'm an expert with my fingers, so I'm a fingersmith.'

'It must be an interesting job.'

'It's a marvellous job,' he answered. 'It's lovely.'

'And that's why you go to the races?'

'Race meetings is easy meat,' he said. 'You just stand around after the race, watchin' for the lucky ones to queue up and draw their money. And when you see someone collectin' a big bundle of notes, you simply follows after 'im and 'elps yourself. But don't get me wrong, guv'nor. I never takes nothin' from a loser. Nor from poor people neither. I only go after them as can afford it, the winners and the rich.'

'That's very thoughtful of you.' I said. 'How often do you get caught?'

'Caught?' he cried, disgusted. '*Me* get caught? It's only pickpockets get caught. Fingersmiths never. Listen, I could take the false teeth out of your mouth if I wanted to and you wouldn't even catch me!'

'I don't have false teeth,' I said.

'I know you don't,' he answered. 'Otherwise I'd 'ave 'ad 'em out long ago!'

I believed him. Those long slim fingers of his seemed able to do anything.

We drove on for a while without talking.

'That policeman's going to check up on you pretty thoroughly,' I said. 'Doesn't that worry you a bit?'

'Nobody's checkin' up on me,' he said.

'Of course they are. He's got your name and address written down most carefully in his black book.'

The man gave me another of his sly, ratty little smiles. 'Ah,' he said. 'So 'ee 'as. But I'll bet 'ee ain't got it all written down in 'is memory as well. I've never known a copper yet with a decent memory. Some of 'em can't even remember their own names.'

'What's memory got to do with it?' I asked. 'It's written down in his book, isn't it?'

'Yes, guv'nor, it is. But the trouble is, 'ee's lost the book. 'Ee's lost both books, the one with my name in it *and* the one with yours.'

In the long delicate fingers of his right hand, the man was holding up in triumph the two books he had taken from the policeman's pockets. 'Easiest job I ever done,' he announced proudly.

I nearly swerved the car into a milk-truck, I was so excited.

'That copper's got nothin' on either of us now,' he said.

'You're a genius!' I cried.

''Ee's got no names, no addresses, no car number, no nothin',' he said.

'You're brilliant!'

'I think you'd better pull in off this main road as soon as possible,' he said. 'Then we'd better build a little bonfire and burn these books.'

'You're a fantastic fellow,' I exclaimed.

'Thank you, guv'nor,' he said. 'It's always nice to be appreciated.'

TWO MURDER MYSTERIES
Alice Monaghan

MADELAINE SMITH

In the late autumn of 1856, a tall, elegant young woman entered John Currie's pharmacy in Sauchihall Street in Glasgow. When asked what she required, the lady replied, 'Arsenic. To kill some rats.'

On hearing this, Mr Currie himself stepped forward and tried to convince the woman that another poison would do just as well. She insisted, gently, that she would rather have arsenic as she believed it to be the most efficient rat poison. Currie then explained that before he would sell it to her she would have to sign her name in the poison book. Would the young lady have any objections to doing so. 'No. None at all.'

Currie was impressed by the air of respectability and the openness of the young lady's manner, so he decided to go ahead with the sale. He carefully measured out one ounce of the arsenic and the young lady signed her name in the book, 'M. H. Smith.'

In June of the following year, the same M. H. Smith appeared in the High Court of Judiciary in Edinburgh on three charges; two of administering poison with intent to kill Pierre Emile L'Angelier and one of murdering the same man by poison.

The trial attracted a large amount of publicity and when the heavy wooden doors of the court swung open there was a rush for seats in the public gallery. The case had all the ingredients of the romantic novels that were so popular at the time. The daughter of a respectable and well-established architect had fallen in love with a penniless, young Frenchman of much lower social rank. However, her ardour had died and when she realised that he was not going to release her from her unofficial engagement in order that she could marry one of her own class, without threatening scandal, she had, with malice aforethought, decided to end his life in the most convenient manner.

The public waited expectantly for the trial to begin.

Two hours and twenty-five minutes after the public had been admitted, the clerk of the court's voice rang around the room. 'Court.'

The public in their benches and the legal gentlemen in the well of the court rose to their feet as the three judges moved in stately procession to their judicial chairs. They were Lord John Hope (The Lord Justice-Clerk), Lord Handside and Lord Ivory; dour, legal gentlemen not far above the accused in social rank, but well-known for their scrupulous fairness in matters judicial.

The public's eyes moved from the judges to a trapdoor in the floor. The door was opened and from the gloomy steps below there appeared a policeman followed by the accused. A murmur of sympathy swept around the court, and a few catcalls as well. The public were divided in their opinion of the attractive, slender young woman who had been described as a beauty.

Certainly, she was tall and graceful. Her dress was of elegant cut and colour, matching the rich, brown hair that was partially covered by a fashionable, veiled bonnet. When she raised the veil, the public saw that she was not beautiful. Handsome was a more appropriate description. Her nose was a trifle too large for true beauty, but her eyes were brilliant and her mouth was perfectly shaped.

The three charges were read out to her. She replied to each one in a steady, unemotional voice which was heard at the back of the crowded court.

'Not guilty.'

Again an audible whisper swept along the public gallery.

Over the next few days the story of Madelaine Smith and her romantic involvement with L'Angelier gradually unfolded.

A slender, attractive woman appeared from the gloomy steps

L'Angelier was not as 'French' as his name implied. He had been born on Jersey of French extraction. In his youth he drifted across Europe and eventually ended up, penniless, in Glasgow. He managed to find employment as a £50-a-year clerk in a local firm where he supervised the packing and despatch of the firm's goods. How he met Madelaine we do not know but he did meet her and the two became lovers.

Over a period of some months, a series of letters passed between the two. When these were read out in court, the public was astonished at the intimacy of the language used and several times Madelaine looked relieved when the Lord Advocate ordered that certain passages be omitted.

'Beloved Husband [!]' she wrote in one, 'This time last night you were with me. Tonight I am all alone . . . I love you more than ever . . . You are the only being I love.'

In another she wrote 'Beloved and best of husbands . . . the man I love and adore.'

For an impoverished clerk to receive such letters from the daughter of a wealthy architect, must have meant to him that his days of poverty would soon be over and that he would be married to his young lover. How his hopes must have been dashed when Madelaine became engaged to one of her own class, William Minnoch.

Madelaine wrote to L'Angelier breaking off their secret engagement. His reply was such to make Madelaine write, 'On my bended knees I write to you and ask you, as you hope for mercy at the judgement day, do not inform on me . . . Write to no one, Papa or any other . . . Do not make me a public shame.'

When L'Angelier had arrived in Glasgow he found lodgings at the home of David Jenkins, a joiner, and his wife Anne.

Anne Jenkins' evidence gave a graphic description of L'Angelier's illness. It seems that one day in February she had found the 'Frenchman' in bed suffering from violent nausea. She asked him why he had not called her and was told that he had been seized with such violent pain in the stomach that he had had to lie down to take his clothes off, crawl to bed, and was literally unable to summon up the energy to ring the bell.

Throughout the month he became ill again and again. The kindly Mrs Jenkins called a doctor to whom she said, 'He seems to become ill after being out. I must ask him the cause.' But before she could do so,

L'Angelier died – on 23rd March.

A post mortem revealed that L'Angelier had 82 grains of arsenic in his stomach. Dr Frederick Penny, Professor of Chemistry at Glasgow University replied 'four to six grains are generally regarded as sufficient to destroy life.'

Even more sensational evidence was given by a small, elderly spinster, Mary Perry, who attended the same church as L'Angelier and claimed to have acted as go-between for the two lovers. Under oath she told the court that L'Angelier said that during his secret visits to Madelaine, she served him chocolate and coffee as refreshment and that it was after taking these drinks that he became ill. On one occasion L'Angelier had told Mary Perry that 'if she, Madelaine, were to poison me I would forgive her. When Mary asked him why Madelaine would want to poison him, he replied, 'Perhaps she might not be sorry to be rid of me.'

Mr Currie's evidence that it was Madelaine Smith, sitting calmly in the box, who had purchased arsenic from him was, the prosecution claimed, conclusive that Smith had patched up her quarrel with L'Angelier having cold-bloodedly decided to murder him while pretending to be in love with him.

The prosecution had a strong case and one damning letter read out in court seemed to condemn Madelaine in her own words. 'You did look bad, Sunday night and Monday moring. I think that you got sick walking home so late – and the long want of food, so the next time we meet, I shall make you eat a loaf of bread.'

Would anyone planning poison have the cool nerve to implicate herself so clearly? Madelaine was certainly cool. As the evidence against her built up she remained totally calm, only once showing any sign of emotion, and that was when the Lord Advocate ruled certain parts of her letters as 'objectionable.'

Also, Madelaine admitted buying the arsenic. But would anyone planning murder openly sign her own name knowing that the purchase could be so easily traced?

When Madelaine was questioned by the police as to why she had bought arsenic she confessed that it was not for destroying rats, but for cosmetic reasons. Arsenic was a 'fashionable' cosmetic aid. Diluted down it was said to be good for the skin. Madelaine claimed that she was told about this by an old school friend, Augusta Guibeli. But Miss

Guibeli denied this under oath. The case against Madelaine seemed sure.

The prosecution summed up the case against her. She had written damning and indiscreet letters to her lover and in order to maintain her reputation and ensure her marriage to Minnoch she decided to kill him. She had purchased arsenic and given this to her lover in cups of coffee and chocolate. She had changed her story as to why she bought the arsenic. 'There is,' said Lord Advocate Moncrieff to the jury, 'but one course open to you, and that is to return a verdict of guilty.'

Madelaine's father had engaged as defence counsel, the Dean of the Faculty of Advocates. The Scottish legal system is different from that in England. An advocate is similar to a barrister and the Dean of the Faculty would be one of the leading and most prestigious lawyers of his day. The Dean's defence speech was masterly. He stressed that Madelaine was a girl of good family who had never, before she met L'Angelier, been the subject of even the merest whisper of gossip. He admitted that her affair had been corrupt and degrading, 'but would, without temptation, without evil teachers, a young girl fall into such depths of degradation?' Such influence, he claimed, could only come from one source – L'Angelier. The Dean painted him as a wastrel who had wormed his way into Madelaine's affections. There was evidence that L'Angelier had frequently suffered from stomach complaints. There was evidence, too, that he had boasted of being an arsenic eater. There was *circumstantial* evidence against Madelaine but the prosecution had failed to prove that Madelaine had been with the Frenchman on any occasion during the final bouts.

The judge summed up the case and the jury filed out. Less than half an hour later they returned. On the first charge of attempted murder she was found not guilty. Madelaine remained totally calm. The charge of attempted murder was found not proven as was the actual charge of murder. [Not Proven is a peculiarly Scottish verdict. It is generally taken to mean that the jury consider the accused guilty, but that the prosecution has failed to prove it. A prisoner is freed after such a verdict is returned.]

Madelaine gracefully accepted the congratulations of those in court who believed her innocent and seemed oblivious to the hoots of derision of those who thought her guilty.

The question as to whether Madelaine Smith was innocent or guilty has always fascinated those interested in crime. We shall never know for sure who killed L'Angelier. After the trial, Madelaine went to London where she married an artist. When he died she went to live in the United States where she died in 1927, aged 91.

JACK THE RIPPER

'It was too harrowing to be described . . . the most gruesome memory of the whole of my police career.' The writer was Detective Drew of the Metropolitan Police in London who later became famous as the policeman who arrested the infamous Doctor Crippen. The event he was writing about was the grisly murder of Mary Jeannette Kelly whose body was discovered on Saturday, 9th November, at quarter to eleven.

Mary Kelly was aged 25. She was Irish and she was a widow.

At about half past three on that Saturday morning two women who lived near Mary's small, ground-floor room at 13 Miller's Court in Whitechapel in London, heard the cry of 'Murder' but they paid little attention. When her body was discovered seven hours later the scene in the room well justified Detective Drew's comments. Her face had been mutilated in the most horrible manner and her throat had been cut. Parts of her body had been removed from her corpse and were spread around the room. In the opinion of Sir Melville Macnaughten, Head of Criminal Investigation, the murderer must have taken at least two hours over his 'hellish' job. Word soon spread around Whitechapel – Jack the Ripper had struck again.

★ ★ ★ ★

Whitechapel, in the East End of London, was as notorious as it was squalid. It was an area of sordid lodging houses and dirty pubs. Even in the sunshine of a sunny autumn day it had a threatening air about it, but at night when the mists blew off the river and swirled round the gas lamps, when the sound of raucous laughter and bawdy songs filled the damp and foggy gloom, when around each street corner there were women offering a few hours friendship for a few pennies, it was a place of threat and darkness. It was here that the terror of Jack the Ripper reigned for a few short weeks in the autumn of 1888.

In the cool hours of the early morning of Friday, 31st August, the body of Mary Anne Nichols was found. Her death was no loss to anyone for she was a 42-year-old penniless drunk; but the manner of her death shocked even the hardened mortuary attendant who 'dressed' the body. He was so sickened that he became violently ill. Mary Nichols' throat had been cut and there were severe abdominal injuries. Despite the horror of the crime, the police at first thought that it was 'just another murder' in an area where murder and brutal attack were not uncommon.

Then, eight days later, just before six o'clock in the morning of Saturday, 8th September, the body of 47-year-old Annie Chapman was found in the back yard of 29 Hanbury Street. Her injuries were almost identical to those of the luckless Mary Nichols, one difference being that several of Annie Chapman's internal organs had been removed – and removed with surgical skill!

The police suddenly realised that they had a madman on their hands. Horrified Londoners began to read the sensational headlines in the popular press. The residents of Whitechapel, hardened as they were to crime and violence, began to think twice about going out on their own at night and the population of London began to ask themselves questions about the handling of the case. Why were the bodies of the two victims not examined until after they had been washed and, perhaps, vital clues been lost? Why had Sir Charles Warren, the man in charge of the investigation, ordered that a recently chalked message be removed from the wall next to the scene of the crime? He justified this by claiming that he was protecting the public peace. Was he, Londoners asked, protecting more than the peace? Was the identity of the killer known to him, but if revealed would the ensuing scandal rock the establishment? Rumours began to fly around. It was said that the killer was none other than the Duke of Clarence, eldest son of the Prince of Wales and heir to the throne on his father's death! The duke was known to be 'unstable' and prone to fits of violence. Was Sir Charles protecting the monarchy? No one knows, but his handling of the case was such that he was forced to resign. But not before the murderer struck again.

Unfortunately Elizabeth Stride, known as 'Long Liz' was not one to think twice about going out alone at night. Her body was found on the last day of September by Louis Diemschutz whose horse shied at something in the road. The 'something' was the bleeding body of 'Long.

The 'something' was the bleeding body of Long Liz Stride

Liz'. So recently had she been murdered that blood was still warm from her gashed throat. Had the murderer been interrupted before he could begin to mutilate the body? The police believed so and chalked up murder number three to the Whitechapel killer.

A few hours after Louis Diemschutz had come upon Long Liz Stride's body, a fourth mutilated corpse was found. It was Catherine Eddows, a 43-year-old advanced alcoholic who suffered from Bright's disease. This disease affects the kidneys and those who suffer from it can easily be recognised by their peculiar bloated appearance.

Interestingly enough, as well as having had her throat cut and her body badly cut up, one of Catherine Eddows' kidneys had been removed! The police began to ask whether the murderer was a medical person, perhaps doing research into Bright's disease. Was the murderer familiar with his (or her) victim? Suspicion fell on Alexander Pedachenko.

He was a Russian doctor who worked in a clinic in the East End. Three of the murderer's victims had attended that clinic. He was questioned but was freed. However, many people, including Sir Basil Thomson, who was head of CID some years later, believed that he was guilty. Was it coincidence that shortly after he was released he returned to his native Russia and spent his last years in an asylum for the criminally insane having killed a Russian woman? Sir Basil believed not.

By the time that Elizabeth Stride and Catherine Eddows met their ghastly deaths the police had received a confession! Two days before these brutal murders the first of a series of callous letters was delivered at the Central News Agency. The letter finished with a dreadful poem:

> I'm not a butcher, I'm not a kid,
> Nor yet a foreign skipper,
> But I'm your own true loving friend,
> Yours truly – JACK THE RIPPER.

Within hours the name Jack the Ripper was being whispered in hushed, terrified tones in Whitechapel and soon spread into the rest of London. Who was this Jack the Ripper? The question was being asked in bars and shops, on buses and trains, and even in the fashionable drawing rooms of London society.

For the entire month of October, the Ripper was quiet. And then Mary Kelly's body was found. The Ripper had struck again – as he boasted in another letter to the Central News Agency.

Police investigations continued and one month later stopped as suddenly as the Ripper had struck. In December the body of a young lawyer, Montague John Druitt, was fished out of the River Thames. Druitt came from a good family who believed him to be insane. His name is mentioned in Sir Melville's files and all police investigations ceased on Druitt's suicide.

But was Druitt indeed the Ripper? There were plenty of other suspects. The Duke of Clarence was rumoured to be the killer. Certainly when he died in 1892 it was widely believed that he was demented and certain aspects of the police investigation have led 'Ripper hunters' to believe that there was a cover up of some sort being organised by the police. Were the police under orders from the Government, or even from the Palace, to hide the identity of the killer? Perhaps, but one fact has emerged from investigations – the Duke of Clarence could not have killed all the victims. When three of the Ripper's victims were murdered the duke was either shooting at Sandringham in Norfolk, or was in Scotland.

Several years after the Ripper had ceased to kill, a Doctor Thomas Neil Cream was tried and convicted of poisoning. On the scaffold he said 'I am Jack the . . ." but before he could finish the sentence the rope closed around his neck and squeezed the life out of him. But Cream could not have been the Ripper as he was in prison while the Ripper was active.

Chief Inspector Abberline, one of the detectives working on the case, was convinced that the Ripper was Severin Klosowski (who later changed his name to George Chapman). Klosowski was a Polish barber who worked in Whitechapel. As a barber, he would have been used to working with the cut-throat razors that the police believed were used to cut the victims' throats. But Klosowski's guilt could never be proved.

Sir Basil Thompson was equally convinced that the Russian, Pedachenko, was the Ripper. After all he had had contact with three of the victims. As a doctor he would have had the skill to cut up the victims in the way in which they were dissected and, also, he may have been sufficiently interested in Bright's disease to remove a kidney from Catherine Eddows' body for examination.

There was also evidence against a deranged shoemaker called Kosminski. This was based on the fact that a leather apron similar to the ones that he wore, was found next to Annie Chapman's body.

169

Whoever it was, one thing is clear. We shall never know, for sure, exactly who Jack the Ripper was. Certainly, there were no more murders after Druitt's sodden body was dragged from the Thames. Was he the Ripper? If so, he took his dark secret to the murky depths of the river with him. If not, then someone else took the secret to his grave – for the only person who could know for sure the identity of Jack the Ripper was Jack the Ripper himself..

THE DREAM WOMAN
William Wilkie Collins

I had not been settled much more than six weeks in my country practice, when I was sent for to a neighbouring town to consult with the resident medical man there, on a case of very dangerous illness.

My horse had come down with me, at the end of a long ride the night before, and had hurt himself, luckily, much more than he had hurt his master. Being deprived of the animal's services, I started for my destination by the coach (there were no railways at that time); and I hoped to get back again, towards the afternoon, in the same way.

After the consultation was over I went to the principal inn of the town to wait for the coach. When it came up, it was full inside and out. There was no resource left me, but to get home as cheaply as I could, by hiring a gig. The price asked for this accommodation struck me as being so extortionate, that I determined to look out for an inn of inferior pretensions, and to try if I could not make a better bargain with a less prosperous establishment.

I soon found a likely-looking house, dingy and quiet, with an old-fashioned sign, that had evidently not been repainted for many years past. The landlord, in this case, was not above making a small profit; and as soon as we came to terms, he rang the yard-bell to order the gig.

'Has Robert not come back from that errand?' asked the landlord appealing to the waiter, who answered the bell.

'No, sir, he hasn't.'

'Well, then, you must wake up Isaac.'

'Wake up Isaac?' I repeated; 'that sounds rather odd. Do your ostlers go to bed in the day-time?'

'This one does,' said the landlord, smiling to himself in rather a strange way.

'And dreams, too,' added the waiter.

'Never you mind about that,' retorted his master; 'you go and rouse Isaac up. The gentleman's waiting for his gig.'

The landlord's manner and the waiter's manner expressed a great deal more than they either of them said. I began to suspect that I might be on the trace of something professionally interesting to me, as a medical man; and I thought I should like to look at the ostler, before the waiter awakened him.

'Stop a minute,' I interposed; 'I have rather a fancy for seeing this man before you wake him up. I am a doctor; and if this queer sleeping and dreaming of his comes from anything wrong in his brain, I may be able to tell you what to do with him.'

'I rather think you will find his complaint past all doctoring, sir,' said the landlord. 'But if you would like to see him, you're welcome, I'm sure.'

He led the way across a yard and down a passage to the stables; opened one of the doors; and waiting outside himself, told me to look in.

I found myself in a two-stall stable. In one of the stalls, a horse was munching his corn. In the other, an old man was lying asleep on the litter.

I stooped, and looked at him attentively. It was a withered, woebegone face. The eyebrows were painfully contracted; the mouth was fast set, and drawn down at the corners. The hollow wrinkled cheeks, and the scanty grizzled hair, told their own tale of past sorrow or suffering. He was drawing his breath convulsively when I first looked at him; and in a moment more he began to talk in his sleep.

'Wake up!' I heard him say, in a quick whisper, through his clenched teeth. 'Wake up, there! Murder.'

He moved one lean arm slowly until it rested over his throat, shuddered a little, and turned on the straw. Then the arm left his throat, the hand stretched itself out, and clutched at the side towards which he had turned, as if he fancied himself to be grasping at the edge of something. I saw his lips move, and bent lower over him. He was still talking in his sleep.

'Light grey eyes,' he murmured, 'and a droop in the left eyelid – flaxen hair, with a gold-yellow streak in it – all right, mother – fair white arms, with a down on them – little lady's hand, with a reddish look under the finger-nails. The knife – always the cursed knife – first on one side, then on the other. Aha! you she-devil, where's the knife?'

At the last word his voice rose, and he grew restless on a sudden. I saw him shudder on the straw; his withered face became distorted, and he threw up both his hands with a quick hysterical gasp. They struck against the bottom of the manger under which he lay, and the blow awakened him. I had just time to slip through the door, and close it, before his eyes were fairly open, and his senses his own again.

'Do you know anything about that man's past life?' I said to the landlord.

'Yes, sir, I know pretty well all about it,' was the answer, 'and an uncommon queer story it is. Most people don't believe it. It's true, though, for all that. Why, just look at him,' continued the landlord, opening the stable door again. 'Poor devil! he's so worn out with his restless nights, that he's dropped back into his sleep already.'

'Don't wake him,' I said, 'I'm in no hurry for the gig. Wait until the other man comes back from his errand. And in the meantime, suppose I have some lunch, and a bottle of sherry; and suppose you come and help me to get through it.'

The heart of mine host, as I had anticipated, warmed to me over his own wine. He soon became communicative on the subject of the man asleep in the stable; and by little and little, I drew the whole story out of him. Extravagant and incredible as the events must appear to everybody, they are related here just as I heard them, and just as they happened.

*   *   *   *

Some years ago there lived in the suburbs of a large seaport town, on the west coast of England, a man in humble circumstances, by the name of Isaac Scatchard. His means of subsistence were derived from any employment he could get as an ostler, and occasionally, when times went

173

well with him, from temporary engagements in service as stable-helper in private houses. Though a faithful, steady, and honest man, he got on badly in his calling. His ill-luck was proverbial among his neighbours. He was always missing good opportunities by no fault of his own; and always living longest in service with amiable people who were not punctual payers of wages. 'Unlucky Isaac' was his nickname in his own neighbourhood – and no one could say that he did not richly deserve it.

With far more than one man's fair share of adversity to endure, Isaac had but one consolation to support him – and that was of the dreariest and most negative kind. He had no wife and children to increase his anxieties and add to the bitterness of his various failures in life. It might have been from mere insensibility, or it might have been from generous unwillingness to involve another in his own unlucky destiny – but the fact undoubtedly was, that he had arrived at the middle term of life without marrying; and, what is much more remarkable, without once exposing himself, from eighteen to eight-and-thirty, to the genial imputation of ever having had a sweetheart.

When he was out of service, he lived alone with his widowed mother. Mrs Scatchard was a woman above the average in her lowly station, as to capacity and manners. She had seen better days, as the phrase is; but she never referred to them in the presence of curious visitors; and, though perfectly polite to every one who approached her, never cultivated any intimacies among her neighbours. She contrived to provide, hardly enough, for her simple wants, by doing rough work for the tailors; and always managed to keep a decent home for her son to return to, whenever his ill-luck drove him out helpless into the world.

One bleak autumn, when Isaac was getting on fast towards forty, and when he was, as usual, out of place through no fault of his own, he set forth from his mother's cottage on a long walk inland to a gentleman's seat, where he had heard that a stable-helper was required.

It wanted then but two days of his birthday; and Mrs Scatchard, with her usual fondness, made him promise, before he started, that he would be back in time to keep that anniversary with her, in as festive a way as their poor means would allow. It was easy for him to comply with this request, even supposing he slept a night each way on the road.

· He was to start from home on Monday morning; and whether he got the new place or not, he was to be back for his birthday dinner on

Wednesday at two o'clock.

Arriving at his destination too late on the Monday night to make application for the stable-helper's place, he slept at the village inn, and, in good time on the Tuesday morning, presented himself at the gentleman's house, to fill the vacant situation. Here again, his ill-luck pursued him as inexorably as ever. The excellent written testimonials to his character which he was able to produce, availed him nothing; his long walk had been taken in vain – only the day before, the stable-helper's place had been given to another man.

Isaac accepted this new disappointment resignedly, and as a matter of course. Naturally slow in capacity, he had the bluntness of sensibility and phlegmatic patience of disposition which frequently distinguish men with sluggishly-working mental powers. He thanked the gentleman's steward with his usual quiet civility, for granting him an interview, and took his departure with no appearance of unusual depression in his face or manner.

Before starting on his homeward walk, he made some inquiries at the inn, and ascertained that he might save a few miles on his return by following a new road. Furnished with full instructions, several times repeated, as to the various turnings he was to take, he set forth on his homeward journey, and walked on all day with only one stoppage for bread and cheese. Just as it was getting towards dark, the rain came on and the wind began to rise; and he found himself, to make matters worse, in a part of the country with which he was entirely unacquainted, though he knew himself to be some fifteen miles from home. The first house he found to inquire at was a lonely roadside inn, standing on the outskirts of a thick wood. Solitary as the place looked, it was welcome to a lost man who was also hungry, thirsty, footsore, and wet. The landlord was civil and respectable-looking, and the price he asked for a bed was reasonable enough. Isaac therefore decided on stopping comfortably at the inn for that night.

He was constitutionally a temperate man. His supper simply consisted of two rashers of bacon, a slice of homemade bread, and a pint of ale. He did not go to bed immediately after this moderate meal, but sat up with the landlord, talking about his bad prospects and his long run of ill-luck, and diverging from these topics to the subjects of horseflesh and racing. Nothing was said either by himself, his host, or the few labourers who strayed into the tap-room, which could, in the slightest degree, excite the very small and very dull imaginative faculty which Isaac Scatchard possessed.

At a little after eleven the house was closed. Isaac went round with the landlord, and held the candle while the doors and lower windows were being secured. He noticed with surprise the strength of the bolts, bars, and iron-sheathed shutters.

'You see, we are rather lonely here,' said the landlord. 'We never have had any attempts made to break in yet, but it's always as well to be on the safe side. When nobody is sleeping here I am the only man in the house. My wife and daughter are timid, and the servant-girl takes after her missuses. Another glass of ale, before you turn in? – No! – Well, how such a sober man as you comes to be out of place, is more than I can make out, for one. – Here's where you're to sleep. You're the only lodger tonight, and I think you'll say my missus has done her best to make you comfortable. You're quite sure you won't have another glass of ale? – very well. Good night.'

It was half-past eleven by the clock in the passage as they went upstairs to the bedroom, the window of which looked on to the wood at the back of the house.

Isaac locked the door, set his candle on the chest of drawers, and wearily got ready for bed. The bleak autumn wind was still blowing, and the solemn surging moan of it in the wood was dreary and awful to hear through the night-silence. Isaac felt strangely wakeful. He resolved, as he lay down in bed, to keep the candle alight until he began to grow sleepy for there was something unendurably depressing in the bare idea of lying awake in the darkness, listening to the dismal, ceaseless moan of the wind in the wood.

Sleep stole on him before he was aware of it. His eyes closed, and he fell off insensibly to rest, without having so much as thought of extinguishing the candle.

The first sensation of which he was conscious, after sinking into slumber, was a strange shivering that ran through him suddenly from head to foot, and a dreadful sinking pain at the heart, such as he had never felt before. The shivering only disturbed his slumbers – the pain woke him instantly. In one moment he passed from a state of sleep to a state of wakefulness – his eyes wide open – his mental perceptions cleared on a sudden as if by a miracle.

The candle had burnt down nearly to the last morsel of tallow, but the top of the unsnuffed wick had just fallen off, and the light in the little room was, for the moment, fair and full.

Between the foot of the bed and the closed door, there stood a woman with a knife in her hand, looking at him.

He was stricken speechless with terror, but he did not lose the preternatural clearness of his faculties; and he never took his eyes off the woman. She said not a word as they stared each other in the face; but she began to move slowly towards the left-hand side of the bed.

His eyes followed her. She was a fair fine woman, with yellowish flaxen hair, and light grey eyes, with a droop in the left eyelid. He noticed these things and fixed them on his mind, before she was round at the side of the bed. Speechless, with no expression in her face, with no noise following her footfall, she came closer and closer – stopped – and slowly raised the knife. He laid his right arm over his throat to save it; but, as he saw the knife coming down, threw his hand across the bed to the right side, and jerked his body over that way, just as the knife descended on the mattress within an inch of his shoulder.

His eyes fixed on her arm and hand, as she slowly drew her knife out of the bed. A white, well-shaped arm, with a pretty down lying lightly over the fair skin. A delicate, lady's hand, with the crowning beauty of a pink flush under and round the finger-nails.

She drew the knife out, and passed back again slowly to the foot of the bed; stopped there for a moment looking at him; then came on – still speechless, still with no expression on the beautiful face, still with no sound following the stealthy foot-falls – came on to the right side of the bed where he now lay.

As she approached, she raised the knife again, and he drew himself away to the left side. She struck, as before, right into the mattress, with a deliberate, perpendicularly downward action to the arm. This time his eyes wandered from her to the knife. It was like the large clasp-knives which he had often seen labouring men use to cut their bread and bacon with. Her delicate little fingers did not conceal more than two-thirds of the handle; he noticed that it was made of buckhorn, clean and shining as the blade was, and looking like new.

For the second time she drew the knife out, concealed it in the wide

She drew the knife out and passed to the foot of the bed

sleeve of her gown, then stopped by the bedside, watching him. For an instant he saw her standing in that position – then the wick of the spent candle fell over into the socket. The flame diminished to a little blue point, and the room grew dark.

A moment, or less if possible, passed so – and then the wick flamed up, smokily, for the last time. His eyes were still looking eagerly over the right-hand side of the bed when the final flash of light came, but they discerned nothing. The fair woman with the knife was gone.

The conviction that he was alone again, weakened the hold of the terror that had struck him dumb up to this time. The preternatural sharpness which the very intensity of his panic had mysteriously imparted to his faculties, left them suddenly. His brain grew confused – his heart beat wildly – his ears opened for the first time since the appearance of the woman, to a sense of the woeful, ceaseless moaning of the wind among the trees. With the dreadful conviction of the reality of what he had seen still strong within him, he leapt out of bed, and screaming – 'Murder! – Wake up there, wake up!' – dashed headlong through the darkness to the door.

It was fast locked, exactly as he had left it on going to bed.

His cries, on starting up, had alarmed the house. He heard the terrified, confused exclamations of women; he saw the master of the house approach along the passage, with his burning rush-candle in one hand and his gun in the other.

'What is it?' asked the landlord, breathlessly.

Isaac could only answer in a whisper. 'A woman, with a knife in her hand,' he gasped out. 'In my room – a fair, yellow-haired woman; she jabbed at me with the knife, twice over.'

The landlord's pale cheek grew paler. He looked at Isaac eagerly by the flickering light of his candle; and his face began to get red again – his voice altered too, as well as his complexion.

'She seems to have missed you twice,' he said.

'I dodged the knife as it came down', Isaac went on, in the same scared whisper. 'It struck the bed each time.'

The landlord took his candle into the bedroom immediately. In less than a minute he came out again into the passage in a violent passion.

'The devil fly away with you and your woman with the knife! There isn't a mark in the bed-clothes anywhere. What do you mean by coming into a man's place and frightening his family out of their wits by a dream?'

'I'll leave your house,' said Isaac, faintly. 'Better out on the road, in rain and dark, on my way home, than back again in that room, after what I've seen in it. Lend me a light to get my clothes by, and tell me what I'm to pay.'

'Pay!' cried the landlord, leading the way with his light sulkily into the bedroom. 'You'll find your score on the slate when you go downstairs. I wouldn't have taken you in for all the money you've got about you, if I'd known your dreaming, screeching ways beforehand. Look at the bed. Where's the cut of a knife in it? Look at the window – is the lock bursted? Look at the door (which I heard you fasten yourself) – is it broke in? A murdering woman with a knife in my house! You ought to be ashamed of yourself!'

Isaac answered not a word. He huddled on his clothes; and then they went down the stairs together.

'Nigh on twenty minutes past two!' said the landlord, as they passed the clock. 'A nice time in the morning to frighten honest people out of their wits!'

Isaac paid his bill, and the landlord let him out at the front door, asking, with a grin of contempt, as he undid the strong fastenings, whether 'the murdering woman got in that way?'

They parted without a word on either side. The rain had ceased; but the night was dark, and the wind bleaker than ever. Little did the darkness, or the cold, or the uncertainty about the way home matter to Isaac. If he had been turned out into the wilderness in a thunderstorm, it would have been a relief, after what he had suffered in the bedroom of the inn.

What was the fair woman with the knife? The creature of a dream, or that other creature from the unknown world, called among men by the name of ghost? He could make nothing of the mystery – had made nothing of it, even when it was midday on Wednesday, and when he stood, at last, after many times missing his road, once more on the doorstep of home.

*   *   *   *

His mother came out eagerly to receive him. His face told her in a moment that something was wrong.

'I've lost the place; but that's my luck. I dreamed an ill dream last night, mother – or, maybe, I saw a ghost. Take it either way, it scared me out of my senses, and I'm not my own man again yet.'

'Isaac! your face frightens me. Come in to the fire. Come in, and tell mother all about it.'

He was as anxious to tell as she was to hear; for it had been his hope, all the way home, that his mother, with her quicker capacity and superior knowledge, might be able to throw some light on the mystery which he could not clear up for himself. His memory of the dream was still mechanically vivid, though his thoughts were entirely confused by it.

His mother's face grew paler and paler as he went on. She never interrupted him by so much as a single word; but when he had done, she moved her chair close to his, put her arm around his neck, and said to him:

'Isaac, you dreamed your ill dream on this Wednesday morning. What time was it when you saw the fair woman with the knife in her hand?'

Isaac reflected on what the landlord had said when they had passed by the clock on his leaving the inn – allowed nearly as he could for the time that must have elapsed between the unlocking of his bedroom door and the paying of his bill just before going away, and answered:

'Somewhere about two o'clock in the morning.'

His mother suddenly quitted her hold on his neck, and struck her hands together with a gesture of despair.

'This Wednesday is your birthday, Isaac; and two o'clock in the morning is the time when you were born!'

Isaac's capacities were not quick enough to catch the infection of his mother's superstitious dread. He was amazed, and a little startled also, when she suddenly rose from her chair, opened her old writing-desk, took pen, ink, and paper, and then said to him:

'Your memory is but a poor one, Isaac, and now I'm an old woman, mine's not much better. I want all about this dream of yours to be as well known to both of us, years hence, as it is now. Tell me over again all you told me a minute ago, when you spoke of what the woman with the knife looked like.'

Isaac obeyed, and marvelled much as he saw his mother carefully set

181

down on paper the very words that he was saying.

'Light grey eyes,' she wrote as they came to the descriptive part, 'with a droop in the left eyelid. Flaxen hair, with a gold-yellow streak in it. White arms, with a down upon them. Little lady's hand, with a reddish look about the finger-nails. Clasp-knife with a buckhorn handle, that seemed as good as new.' To these particulars, Mrs Scatchard added the year, month, day of the week, and time in the morning, when the woman of the dream appeared to her son. She then locked up the paper carefully in her writing-desk.

Neither on that day, nor on any day after, could her son induce her to return to the matter of the dream. She obstinately kept her thoughts about it to herself, and even refused to refer again to the paper in her writing-desk. Ere long, Isaac grew weary of attempting to make her break her resolute silence; and time, which sooner or later wears out all things, gradually wore out the impression produced on him by the dream. He began by thinking of it carelessly, and he ended by not thinking of it at all.

This result was the more easily brought about by the advent of some important changes for the better in his prospects, which commenced not long after his terrible night's experience at the inn. He reaped at last the reward of his long and patient suffering under adversity, by getting an excellent place, keeping it for seven years, and leaving it, on the death of his master, not only with an excellent character, but also with a comfortable annuity bequeathed to him as a reward for saving his mistress's life in a carriage accident. Thus it happened that Isaac Scatchard returned to his old mother, seven years after the time of the dream at the inn, with an annual sum of money at his disposal, sufficient to keep them both in ease and independence for the rest of their lives.

The mother, whose health had been bad of late years, profited so much by the care bestowed on her and by freedom from money anxieties, that when Isaac's birthday came round, she was able to sit up comfortably at table and dine with him.

On that day, as the evening drew on, Mrs Scatchard discovered that a bottle of tonic medicine – which she was accustomed to take, and in which she had fancied that a dose or more was still left – happened to be empty. Isaac immediately volunteered to go to the chemist's and get it filled again. It was as rainy and bleak an autumn night as on the

182

memorable past occasion when he lost his way and slept at the road-side inn.

On going in to the chemist's shop, he was passed hurriedly by a poorly-dressed woman coming out of it. The glimpse he had of her face struck him, and he looked back after her as she descended the door-steps.

'You're noticing that woman?' said the chemist's apprentice behind the counter. 'It's my opinion there's something wrong with her. She's been asking for laudanum to put to a bad tooth. Master's out for half an hour; and I told her I wasn't allowed to sell poison to strangers in his absence. She laughed in a queer way, and said she would come back in half an hour. If she expects master to serve her, I think she'll be disappointed. It's a case of suicide, sir, if ever there was one yet.'

These words added immeasurably to the sudden interest in the woman which Isaac had felt at the first sight of her face. After he had got the medicine bottle filled, he looked about anxiously for her, as soon as he was out in the street. She was walking slowly up and down on the opposite side of the road. With his heart, very much to his own surprise, beating fast, Isaac crossed over and spoke to her.

He asked if she was in any distress. She pointed to her torn shawl, her scanty dress, her crushed, dirty bonnet – then moved under a lamp so as to let the light fall on her stern, pale, but still most beautiful face.

'I look like a comfortable, happy woman – don't I?' she said, with a bitter laugh.

She spoke with a purity of intonation which Isaac had never heard before from other than ladies' lips. Her slightest actions seemed to have the easy, negligent grace of a thorough-bred woman. Her skin, for all its poverty-stricken paleness, was as delicate as if her life had been passed in the enjoyment of every social comfort that wealth can purchase. Even her small, finely-shaped hands, gloveless as they were, had not lost their whiteness.

Little by little, in answer to his questions, the sad story of the woman came out. There is no need to relate it here; it is told over and over again in police reports and paragraphs descriptive of attempted suicides.

'My name is Rebecca Murdoch,' said the woman, as she ended. 'I have ninepence left, and I thought of spending it at the chemist's over the way in securing a passage to the other world. Whatever it is, it can't be worse to me than this – so why should I stop here?'

Besides the natural compassion and sadness moved in his heart by what he heard, Isaac felt within him some mysterious influence at work all the time the woman was speaking, which utterly confused his ideas and almost deprived him of his powers of speech. All that he could say in answer to her last reckless words was, that he would prevent her from attempting her own life, if he followed her about all night to do it. His rough, trembling earnestness seemed to impress her.

'I won't occasion you that trouble,' she answered, when he repeated his threat. 'You have given me a fancy for living by speaking kindly to me. No need for the mockery of protestations and promises. You may believe me without them. Come to Fuller's Meadow tomorrow at twelve, and you will find me alive, to answer for myself. No! – no money. My ninepence will do to get me as good a night's lodging as I want.'

She nodded and left him. He made no attempt to follow – he felt no suspicion that she was deceiving him.

'It's strange, but I can't help believing her,' he said to himself, and walked away bewildered towards home.

On entering the house, his mind was still so completely absorbed by its new subject of interest, that he took no notice of what his mother was doing when he came in with the bottle of medicine. She had opened her old writing-desk in his absence, and was now reading a paper attentively that lay inside it. On every birthday of Isaac's since she had written down the particulars of his dream from his own lips, she had been accustomed to read that same paper, and ponder over it in private.

The next day he went to Fuller's Meadow.

He had done only right in believing her so implicitly – she was there, punctual to a minute, to answer for herself. The last-left faint defences in Isaac's heart, against the fascination which a word or look from her began inscrutably to exercise over him, sank down and vanished before her for ever on that memorable morning.

When a man, previously insensible to the influence of women, forms an attachment in middle life, the instances are rare indeed, let the warning circumstances be what they may, in which he is found capable of freeing himself from the tyranny of the new ruling passion. The charm of being spoken to familiarly, fondly, and gratefully by a woman whose language and manners still retain enough of their early refinement to hint at the high social station that she had lost, would have been a dangerous luxury to a man of Isaac's rank at the age of twenty. But it was far more than that – it was certain ruin to him – now that his heart was opening unworthily to a new influence at that middle time of life when strong feelings of all kinds, once implanted, strike root most stubbornly in a man's moral nature. A few more stolen interviews after that first morning in Fuller's Meadow completed his infatuation. In less than a month from the time when he first met her, Isaac Scatchard had consented to give Rebecca Murdoch a new interest in existence, and a chance of recovering the character she had lost, by promising to make her his wife.

She had taken possession not of his passions only, but of his faculties as well. All the mind he had he put into her keeping. She directed him on every point, even instructing him how to break the news of his approaching marriage in the safest manner to his mother.

'If you tell her how you met me and who I am at first,' said the cunning woman, 'she will move heaven and earth to prevent our marriage. Say I am the sister of one of your fellow-servants – ask her to see me before you go into any more particulars – and leave it to me to do the rest. I mean to make her love me next best to you, Isaac, before she knows anything of who I really am.'

The motive of the deceit was sufficient to sanctify it to Isaac. The stratagem proposed relieved him of his one great anxiety, and quieted his uneasy conscience on the subject of his mother. Still, there was something wanting to perfect his happiness, something that he could not realise, something mysteriously untraceable, and yet something that perpetually made itself felt – not when he was absent from Rebecca Murdoch, but, strange to say, when he was actually in her presence! She was kindness itself with him; she never made him feel his inferior capacities and inferior manners; she showed the sweetest anxiety to please him in the smallest trifles; but, in spite of all these attractions, he never could feel quite at his ease with her. At their first meeting, there had mingled with his admiration when he looked in her face, a faint involuntary feeling of doubt whether that face was entirely strange to him. No after-familiarity had the slightest effect on this inexplicable, wearisome uncertainty.

Concealing the truth, as he had been directed, he announced his marriage engagement precipitately and confusedly to his mother, on the day when he contracted it. Poor Mrs Scatchard showed her perfect confidence in her son by flinging her arms round his neck, and giving him joy of having found at last, in the sister of one of his fellow-servants, a woman to comfort and care for him after his mother was gone. She was all eagerness to see the woman of her son's choice; and the next day was fixed for the introduction.

It was a bright sunny morning, and the little cottage parlour was full of light, as Mrs Scatchard, happy and expectant, dressed for the occasion in her Sunday gown, sat waiting for her son and her future daughter-in-law.

Punctual to the appointed time, Isaac hurriedly and nervously led his promised wife into the room. His mother rose to receive her – advanced a few steps, smiling – looked Rebecca full in the eyes – and suddenly stopped. Her face, which had been flushed the moment before, turned white in an instant – her eyes lost their expression of softness and kindness, and assumed a blank look of terror – her outstretched hands fell to her sides, and she staggered back a few steps with a low cry to her son.

'Isaac!' she whispered, clutching him fast by the arm, when he asked alarmedly if she was taken ill, 'Isaac! does that woman's face remind you of nothing?'

Before he could answer, before he could look round to where Rebecca stood, astonished and angered by her reception, at the lower end of the room, his mother pointed impatiently to her writing-desk and gave him the key.

'Open it,' she said, in a quick, breathless whisper.

'What does this mean? Why am I treated as if I had no business here? Does your mother want to insult me?' asked Rebecca, angrily.

'Open it, and give me the paper in the left-hand drawer. Quick! quick! for heaven's sake!' said Mrs Scatchard, shrinking further back in terror.

Isaac gave her the paper. She looked it over eagerly for a moment – then followed Rebecca, who was now turning away haughtily to leave the room, and caught her by the shoulder – abruptly raised the long, loose sleeve of her gown – and glanced at her hand and arm. Something like fear began to steal over the angry expression of Rebecca's face, as she shook herself free from the old woman's grasp. 'Mad!' she said to herself, 'and Isaac never told me.' With those few words she left the room.

Isaac was hastening after her, when his mother turned and stopped his further progress. It wrung his heart to see the misery and terror in her face as she looked at him.

'Light grey eyes,' she said, in low, mournful, awe-struck tones, pointing towards the open door. 'A droop in the left eyelid; flaxen hair with a gold-yellow streak in it; white arms with a down on them; little lady's hand, with a reddish look under the finger-nails. *The Dream Woman! –* Isaac, the Dream Woman!'

That faint cleaving doubt which he had never been able to shake off in Rebecca Murdoch's presence, was fatally set at rest for ever. He *had* seen her face, then, before – seven years before, on his birthday, in the bedroom of the lonely inn.

'Be warned! Oh, my son, be warned! Isaac! Isaac! let her go, and do you stop with me!'

Something darkened the parlour window as those words were said. A sudden chill ran through him, and he glanced sidelong at the shadow. Rebecca Murdoch had come back. She was peering in curiously at them over the low window-blind.

'I have promised to marry, mother,' he said, 'and marry I must.'

The tears came into his eyes as he spoke, and dimmed his sight; but he could just discern the fatal face outside, moving away again from the window.

His mother's head sank lower.

'Are you faint?' he whispered.

'Broken-hearted, Isaac.'

He stooped down and kissed her. The shadow, as he did so, returned to the window; and the fatal face peered in curiously once more.

*   *   *   *

Three weeks after that day Isaac and Rebecca were man and wife. All that was hopelessly dogged and stubborn in the man's moral nature, seemed to have closed round his fatal passion, and to have fixed it unassailably in his heart.

After that first interview in the cottage parlour, no consideration could induce Mrs Scatchard to see her son's wife again, or even talk of her when Isaac tried hard to plead her cause after their marriage.

This course of conduct was not in any degree occasioned by a discovery of the degradation in which Rebecca had lived. There was no question of that between mother and son. There was no question of anything but the fearfully exact resemblance between the living, breathing woman, and the spectre-woman of Isaac's dream.

Rebecca, on her side, neither felt nor expressed the slightest sorrow at the estrangement between herself and her mother-in-law. Isaac, for the sake of peace, had never contradicted her first idea that age and long illness had affected Mrs Scatchard's mind. He even allowed his wife to upbraid him for not having confessed this to her at the time of their marriage engagement, rather than risk anything by hinting at the truth. The sacrifice of his integrity before his one all-mastering delusion, seemed but a small thing, and cost his conscience but little, after the sacrifices he had already made.

The time of waking from his delusion – the cruel and rueful time – was not far off. After some quiet months of married life, as the summer was ending, and the year was getting on towards the month of his birthday, Isaac found his wife altering towards him. She grew sullen and contemptuous: she formed acquaintances of the most dangerous kind, in defiance of his objections, his entreaties, and his commands; and, worst of all, she learnt, ere long, after every fresh difference with her husband, to seek the deadly self-oblivion of drink. Little by little, after the first miserable discovery that his wife was keeping company with drunkards, the shocking certainty forced itself on Isaac that she had grown to be a drunkard herself.

He had been in a sadly desponding state for some time before the occurrence of these domestic calamities. His mother's health, as he could but too plainly discern every time he went to see her at the cottage, was failing fast; and he upbraided himself in secret as the cause of the bodily and mental suffering she endured. When to his remorse on his mother's account was added the shame and misery occasioned by the discovery of his wife's degradation, he sank under the double trial, his face began to alter fast, and he looked, what he was, a spirit-broken man.

His mother, still struggling bravely against the illness that was hurrying her to the grave, was the first to notice the sad alteration in him, and the first to hear of his last, worst trouble with his wife. She could only weep bitterly, on the day when he made his humiliating confession; but on the next occasion when he went to see her, she had taken a resolution, in reference to his domestic afflictions, which astonished, and even alarmed him. He found her dressed to go out, and on asking the reason, received this answer:

'I am not long for this world, Isaac,' she said; 'and I shall not feel easy on my death-bed, unless I have done my best to the last to make my son happy. I mean to put my own fears and my own feelings out of the question, and to go with you to your wife, and try what I can do to reclaim her. Give me your arm, Isaac and let me do the last thing I can in this world to help my son, before it is too late.'

He could not disobey her; and they walked together slowly towards his miserable home.

It was only one o'clock in the afternoon when they reached the cottage where he lived. It was their dinner hour, and Rebecca was in the kitchen. He was thus able to take his mother quietly into the parlour, and then prepare his wife for the interview. She had fortunately drank but little at that early hour, and she was less sullen and capricious than usual.

He returned to his mother, with his mind tolerably at ease. His wife soon followed him into the parlour, and the meeting between her and Mrs Scatchard passed off better than he had ventured to anticipate, though he observed with secret apprehension that his mother, resolutely as she controlled herself in other respects, could not look his wife in the face when she spoke to her. It was a relief to him, therefore, when Rebecca began to lay the cloth.

She laid the cloth, brought in the bread-tray, and cut a slice from the loaf for her husband, then returned to the kitchen. At that moment, Isaac, still anxiously watching his mother, was startled by seeing the same ghastly change pass over her face which had altered it so awfully on the morning when Rebecca and she first met. Before he could say a word, she whispered with a look of horror;

'Take me back! – home, home again, Isaac! Come with me, and never go back again!'

He was afraid to ask for an explanation; he could only sign her to be silent, and help her quickly to the door. As they passed the bread-tray on the table, she stopped and pointed to it.

'Did you see what your wife cut your bread with?' she asked in a low whisper.

'No, mother; I was not noticing. What was it?'

189

'Look!'

He did look. A new clasp-knife, with a buckhorn handle, lay with the loaf in the bread-tray. He stretched out his hand, shudderingly, to possess himself of it; but at the same time, there was a noise in the kitchen, and his mother caught at his arm.

'The knife of the dream! Isaac, I'm faint with fear – take me away, before she comes back!'

He was hardly able to support her. The visible, tangible reality of the knife struck him with a panic, and utterly destroyed any faint doubts he might have entertained up to this time, in relation to the mysterious dream-warning of nearly eight years before. By a last desperate effort, he summoned self-possession enough to help his mother out of the house – so quietly, that the 'Dream Woman' (he thought of her by that name now) did not hear their departure.

'Don't go back, Isaac, don't go back!' implored Mrs Scatchard, as he turned to go away, after seeing her safely seated again in her own room.

'I must get the knife,' he answered under his breath. His mother tried to stop him again; but he hurried out without another word.

On his return, he found that his wife had discovered their secret departure from the house. She had been drinking, and was in a fury of passion. The dinner in the kitchen was flung under the grate; the cloth was off the parlour table. Where was the knife?

Unwisely, he asked for it. She was only too glad of the opportunity of irritating him, which the request afforded her. 'He wanted the knife, did he? Could he give her a reason why? – No? Then he should not have it – not if he went down on his knees to ask for it.' Further recriminations elicited the fact that she bought it a bargain, and that she considered it her own especial property. Isaac saw the uselessness of attempting to get the knife by fair means, and determined to search for it later in the day, in secret. The search was unsuccessful. Night came on, and he left the house to walk about the streets. He was afraid now to sleep in the same room with her.

Three weeks passed. Still sullenly enraged with him, she would not give up the knife; and still that fear of sleeping in the same room with her possessed him. He walked about at night, or dozed in the parlour, or sat watching by his mother's bed-side. Before the expiration of the first week in the new month his mother died. It wanted then but ten days of her son's birthday. She had longed to live until that anniversary. Isaac was present at her death; and her last words in this world were addressed to him:

'Don't go back, my son – don't go back!'

He was obliged to go back, if it were only to watch his wife. Exasperated to the last degree by his distrust of her, she had revengefully sought to add a sting to his grief, during the last days of his mother's illness, by declaring that she would assert her right to attend the funeral. In spite of all that he could do or say, she held with wicked pertinacity to her words and, on the day appointed for the burial, forced herself – inflamed and shameless with drink – into her husband's presence, and delared that she would walk in the funeral procession to his mother's grave.

This last worst outrage, accompanied by all that was most insulting in word and look, maddened him for the moment. He struck her.

The instant the blow was dealt, he repented it. She crouched down, silent, in a corner of the room, and eyed him steadily; it was a look that cooled his hot blood, and made him tremble. But there was no time now to think of a means of making atonement. Nothing remained, but to risk the worst until the funeral was over. There was but one way of making sure of her. He locked her into her bedroom.

When he came back, some hours after, he found her sitting, very much altered in look and bearing, by the bedside, with a bundle on her lap. She rose, and faced him quietly, and spoke with a strange stillness in her voice, a strange repose in her eyes, a strange composure in her manner.

'No man has ever struck me twice,' she said; 'and my husband shall have no second opportunity. Set the door open and let me go. From this day forth we see each other no more.'

Before he could answer she passed him, and left the room. He saw her walk away up the street.

Would she return?

All that night he watched and waited; but no footstep came near the house. The next night, overcome by fatigue, he lay down in bed in his clothes, with the door locked, the key on the table, and the candle burning. His slumber was not disturbed. The third night, the fourth, the fifth, the sixth passed, and nothing happened. He lay down on the seventh, still in his clothes, still with the door locked, the key on the table, and the candle burning; but easier in his mind.

Easier in his mind, and in perfect health of body, when he fell off to sleep. But his rest was disturbed. He woke twice, without any sensation of uneasiness. But the third time it was that never-be-forgotten shivering of the night at the lonely inn, that dreadful sinking pain at the heart, which once more aroused him in an instant.

His eyes opened towards the left-hand side of the bed, and there stood – The Dream Woman again? No! His wife; the living reality, with the dream-spectre's face – in the dream-spectre's attitude: the fair arm up; the knife clasped in the delicate white hand.

He sprang upon her, almost at the instant of seeing her, and yet not quickly enough to prevent her from hiding the knife. Without a word from him, without a cry from her, he pinioned her in the chair. With one hand he felt up her sleeve; and there, where the Dream Woman had hidden the knife, his wife had hidden it – the knife with the buckhorn handle, that looked like new.

In the despair of that fearful moment his brain was steady, his heart was calm. He looked at her fixedly, with the knife in his hand, and said these last words:

'You told me we should see each other no more, and you have come back. It is my turn now to go, and to go for ever. I say that we shall see each other no more; and *my* word shall not be broken.'

He left her, and set forth into the night. There was a bleak wind abroad, and the smell of recent rain was in the air. The distant church clocks chimed the quarter as he walked rapidly beyond the last houses in the suburb. He asked the first policeman he met, what hour that was, of which the quarter past had just struck.

The man referred sleepily to his watch, and answered, 'Two o'clock.' Two in the morning. What day of the month was this day that had just begun? He reckoned it up from the date of his mother's funeral. The fatal parallel was complete – it was his birthday!

Had he escaped the mortal peril which his dream foretold? or had he only received a second warning?

As this ominous doubt forced itself on his mind, he stopped, reflected, and turned back again towards the city. He was still resolute to hold his word, and never to let her see him more; but there was a thought now in his mind of having her watched and followed. The knife was in his possession; the world was before him; but a new distrust of her – a vague, unspeakable, superstitious dread – had overcome him.

'I must know where she goes, now she thinks I have left her,' he said to himself, as he stole back wearily to the precincts of his house.

It was still dark. He had left the candle burning in the bedchamber; but when he looked up to the window of the room now, there was no light in it. He crept cautiously to the house door. On going away, he remembered to have closed it; on trying it now, he found it open.

He waited outside, never losing sight of the house until daylight. Then he ventured indoors – listened, and heard nothing – looked into kitchen, scullery, parlour; and found nothing; went up at last into the bedroom – it was empty. A picklock lay on the floor, betraying how she had gained entrance in the night, and that was the only trace of her.

Whither had she gone? No mortal tongue could tell him. The darkness had covered her flight; and when the day broke, no man could say where the light found her.

Before leaving the house and the town for ever, he gave instructions to a friend and neighbour to sell his furniture for anything that it would fetch, and to apply the proceeds towards employing the police to trace her. The directions were honestly followed, and the money was all spent; but the inquiries led to nothing. The picklock on the bedroom floor remained the last useless trace of the Dream Woman.

*　　*　　*　　*

At this part of the narrative the landlord paused; and, turning towards the window of the room in which we were sitting, looked in the direction of the stable-yard.

'So far,' he said, 'I tell you what was told to me. The little that remains to be added, lies within my own experience. Between two and three months after the events I have just been relating, Isaac Scatchard came to me, withered and old-looking before his time, just as you saw him today. He had his testimonials to character with him, and he asked me for employment here. Knowing that my wife and he were distantly related, I gave him a trial, in consideration of that relationship, and liked him in spite of his queer habits. He is as sober, honest, and willing a man as there is in England. As for his restlessness at night, and his sleeping away his

193

leisure time in the day, who can wonder at it after hearing his story? Besides, he never objects to being roused up, when he's wanted, so there's not much inconvenience to complain of, after all.'

'I suppose he is afraid of a return of that dreadful dream, and of waking out of it in the dark?'

'No,' returned the landlord. 'The dream comes back to him so often, that he has got to bear with it by this time resignedly enough. It's his wife keeps him waking at night, as he often told me.'

'What! Has she never been heard of yet?'

'Never. Isaac himself has the one perpetual thought that she is alive and looking for him. I believe he wouldn't let himself drop off to sleep towards two in the morning, for a king's ransom. Two in the morning, he says, is the time she will find him, one of these days. Two in the morning is the time, all the year round, when he likes to be most certain that he has got the clasp-knife safe about him. He does not mind being alone, as long as he is awake, except on the night before his birthday, when he firmly believes himself to be in peril of his life. The birthday has only come round once since he has been here, and then he sat up along with the night-porter. "She's looking for me," is all he says, when anybody speaks to him about the one anxiety of his life; "she's looking for me." He may be right. She *may* be looking for him. Who can tell?'

'Who can tell?' said I.

THE MASQUE OF THE RED DEATH
Edgar Allan Poe

The 'Red Death' had long devastated the country. No pestilence had ever been so fatal, or so hideous. Blood was its Avatar and its seal – the redness and horror of blood. There were sharp pains, and sudden dizziness, and then profuse bleeding at the pores, with dissolution. The scarlet stains upon the body and especially upon the face of the victim, were the pest ban which shut him out from the aid and from the sympathy of his fellow-men. And the whole seizure, progress, and termination of the disease, were the incidents of half an hour.

But the Prince Prospero was happy and dauntless and sagacious. When his dominions were half-depopulated, he summoned to his presence a thousand hale and light-hearted friends from among the knights and dames of his court, and with these retired to the deep seclusion of one of his castellated abbeys. This was an extensive and magnificent structure, the creation of the prince's own eccentric yet august taste. A strong and lofty wall girdled it in. This wall had gates of iron. The courtiers, having entered, brought furnaces and massy hammers and welded the bolts. They resolved to leave means neither of ingress nor egress to the sudden impulses of despair or of frenzy from within. The abbey was amply provisioned. With such precautions the courtiers might bid defiance to contagion. The external world could take care of itself. In the meantime it was folly to grieve, or to think. The prince had provided all the appliances of pleasure. There were buffoons, there were improvisatori, there were ballet-dancers, there were musicians, there was Beauty, there was wine. All these and security were within. Without was the 'Red Death'.

It was toward the close of the fifth or sixth month of his seclusion, and while the pestilence raged most furiously abroad, that the Prince Prospero entertained his thousand friends at a masked ball of the most unusual magnificence.

It was a voluptuous scene, that masquerade. But first let me tell of the rooms in which it was held. These were seven – an imperial suite. In many palaces, however, such suites form a long and straight vista, while the folding doors slide back nearly to the walls on either hand, so that the view of the whole extent is scarcely impeded. Here the case was very different, as might have been expected from the duke's love of the *bizarre*. The apartments were so irregularly disposed that the vision embraced but little more than one at a time. There was a sharp turn at every twenty or thirty yards, and at each turn a novel effect. To the right and left, in the middle of each wall, a tall and narrow Gothic window looked out upon a closed corridor which pursued the windings of the suite. These windows were of stained glass whose colour varied in accordance with the prevailing hue of the decorations of the chamber into which it opened. That at the eastern extremity was hung, for example, in blue – and vividly blue were its windows. The second chamber was purple in its ornaments and tapestries, and here the panes were purple. The third was green throughout, and so were the casements. The fourth was furnished and lighted with orange – the fifth with white – the sixth with violet. The seventh apartment was closely shrouded in black velvet tapestries that hung all over the ceiling and down the walls, falling in heavy folds upon a carpet of the same material and hue. But in this chamber only, the colour of the windows failed to correspond with the decorations. The panes here were scarlet – a deep blood colour. Now, in no one of the seven apartments was there any lamp or candelabrum, amid the profusion of golden ornaments that lay scattered to and fro or depended from the roof. There was no light of any kind emanating from lamp or candle within the suite of chambers. But in the corridors that followed the suite there stood, opposite to each window, a heavy tripod, bearing a brazier of fire, that projected its rays through the tinted glass and so glaringly illumined the room. And thus were produced a multitude of gaudy and fantastic appearances. But in the western or black chamber the effect of the firelight that streamed upon the dark hangings through the blood-tinted panes was ghastly in the extreme, and produced so wild a look upon the countenances of those who entered that there were few of the company bold enough to set foot within its precincts at all.

It was in this apartment, also, that there stood against the western wall, a gigantic clock of ebony. Its pendulum swung to and fro with a dull, heavy, monotonous clang; and when the minute-hand made the circuit of the face, and the hour was to be stricken, there came from the brazen lungs of the clock a sound which was clear and loud and deep and exceedingly musical, but of so peculiar a note and emphasis that, at each lapse of an hour, the musicians of the orchestra were constrained to pause, momentarily, in their performance, to harken to the sound; and thus the waltzers perforce ceased their evolutions; and there was a brief disconcert of the whole gay company; and, while the chimes of the clock yet rang, it was observed that the giddiest grew pale, and the more aged and sedate passed their hands over their brows as if in confused reverie or meditation. But when the echoes had fully ceased, a light laughter at once pervaded the assembly; the musicians looked at each other and smiled as if at their own nervousness and folly, and made whispering vows, each to the other, that the next chiming of the clock should produce in them no similar emotion; and then, after the lapse of sixty minutes (which embrace three thousand and six hundred seconds of the Time that flies), there came yet another chiming of the clock, and then were the same disconcert and tremulousness and meditation as before.

But, in spite of these things, it was a gay and magnificent revel. The tastes of the duke were peculiar. He had a fine eye for colours and effects. He disregarded the *decora* of mere fashion. His plans were bold and fiery, and his conceptions glowed with barbaric lustre. There are some who would have thought him mad. His followers felt that he was not. It was necessary to hear and see and touch him to be *sure* that he was not.

He had directed, in great part, the movable embellishments of the seven chambers, upon occasion of this great *fête*; and it was his own guiding taste which had given character to the masqueraders. Be sure

197

they were grotesque. There were much glare and glitter and piquancy and phantasm – much of what has been since seen in *Hernani*. There were arabesque figures with unsuited limbs and appointments. There were delirious fancies such as the madman fashions. There were much of the beautiful, much of the wanton, much of the *bizarre*, something of the terrible, and not a little of that which might have excited disgust. To and fro in the seven chambers there stalked, in fact, a multitude of dreams. And these – the dreams – writhed in and about, taking hue from the rooms, and causing the wild music of the orchestra to seem as the echo of their steps. And, anon, there strikes the ebony clock which stands in the hall of the velvet. And then, for a moment, all is still, and all is silent save the voice of the clock. The dreams are stiff-frozen as they stand. But the echoes of the chime die away – they have endured but an instant – and a light, half-subdued laughter floats after them as they depart. And now again the music swells, and the dreams live, and writhe to and fro more merrily than ever, taking hue from the many-tinted windows through which stream the rays from the tripods. But to the chamber which lies most westwardly of the seven there are now none of the maskers who venture; for the night is waning away; and there flows a ruddier light through the blood-coloured panes; and the blackness of the sable drapery appals; and to him whose foot falls upon the sable carpet, there comes from the near clock of ebony a muffled peal more solemnly emphatic than any which reaches *their* ears who indulged in the more remote gaieties of the other apartments.

But these other apartments were densely crowded, and in them beat feverishly the heart of life. And the revel went whirlingly on, until at length there commenced the sounding of midnight upon the clock. And then the music ceased, as I have told; and the evolutions of the waltzers were quieted; and there was an uneasy cessation of all things as before. But now there were twelve strokes to be sounded by the bell of the clock; and thus it happened, perhaps, that more of thought crept, with more of time, into the meditations of the thoughtful among those who revelled. And thus too, it happened, perhaps, that before the last echoes of the last chime had utterly sunk into silence, there were many individuals in the crowd who had found leisure to become aware of the presence of a masked figure which had arrested the attention of no single individual before. And the rumour of this new presence having spread itself whisperingly around, there arose at length from the whole company a buzz, or murmur, expressive of disapprobation and surprise – then, finally, of terror, of horror, and of disgust.

In an assembly of phantasms such as I have painted, it may well be supposed that no ordinary appearance could have excited such sensation. In truth the masquerade licence of the night was nearly unlimited; but the figure in question had out-Heroded Herod, and gone beyond the bounds of even the prince's indefinite decorum. There are chords in the hearts of the most reckless which cannot be touched without emotion. Even with the utterly lost, to whom life and death are equally jests, there are matters of which no jest can be made. The whole company, indeed, seemed now deeply to feel that in the costume and bearing of the stranger neither wit nor propriety existed. The figure was tall and gaunt, and shrouded from head to foot in the habiliments of the grave. The mask which concealed the visage was made so nearly to resemble the countenance of a stiffened corpse that the closest scrutiny must have had difficulty in detecting the cheat. And yet all this might have been endured, if not approved, by the mad revellers around. But the mummer had gone so far as to assume the type of the Red Death. His vesture was dabbled in *blood* – and his broad brow, with all the features of the face, was besprinkled with the scarlet horror.

When the eyes of Prince Prospero fell upon this spectral image (which, with a slow and solemn movement, as if more fully to sustain its *rôle*, stalked to and fro among the waltzers) he was seen to be convulsed in the first moment with a strong shudder either of terror or distaste; but, in the next, his brow reddened with rage.

'Who dares,' – he demanded hoarsely of the courtiers who stood near him – 'who dares insult us with this blasphemous mockery? Seize him and unmask him – that we may know whom we have to hang, at sunrise, from the battlements!'

It was in the eastern or blue chamber in which stood the Prince Prospero as he uttered these words. They rang throughout the seven rooms loudly and clearly, for the prince was a bold and robust man, and the music had become hushed at the waving of his hand.

It was in the blue room where stood the prince, with a group of pale courtiers by his side. At first, as he spoke, there was a slight rushing movement of this group in the direction of the intruder, who at the moment was also near at hand, and now, with deliberate and stately step, made closer approach to the speaker. But from a certain nameless awe with which the mad assumptions of the mummer had inspired the whole party, there were found none who put forth hand to seize him; so that, unimpeded, he passed within a yard of the prince's person; and while the vast assembly, as if with one impulse, shrank from the centres of the rooms to the walls, he made his way uninterruptedly, but with the same solemn and measured step which had distinguished him from the first, through the blue chamber to the purple – through the purple to the green – through the green to the orange – through this again to the white – and even thence to the violet, ere a decided movement had been made to arrest him. It was then, however, that the Prince Prospero, maddening with rage and the shame of his own momentary cowardice, rushed hurriedly through the six chambers, while none followed him on account of a deadly terror that had seized upon all. He bore aloft a drawn dagger, and had approached, in rapid impetuosity, to within three or four feet of the retreating figure, when the latter, having attained the extremity of the velvet apartment, turned suddenly and confronted his pursuer. There was a sharp cry – and the dagger dropped gleaming upon the sable carpet, upon which, instantly afterward, fell prostrate in death the Prince Prospero. Then, summoning the wild courage of despair, a throng of the revellers at once threw themselves into the black apartment, and, seizing the mummer, whose tall figure stood erect and motionless within the shadow of the ebony clock, gasped in unutterable horror at finding the grave cerements and corpse-like mask, which they handled with so violent a rudeness, untenanted by any tangible form.

And now was acknowledged the presence of the Red Death. He had come like a thief in the night. And one by one dropped the revellers in the blood-bedewed halls of their revel, and died each in the despairing posture of his fall. And the life of the ebony clock went out with that of the last of the gay. And the flames of the tripods expired. And darkness and Decay and the Red Death held illimitable dominion over all.

THE HORLA
Guy De Maupassant

8th May. What a lovely day! I have spent all the morning lying in the grass in front of my house, under the enormous plane tree that shades the whole of it. I like this part of the country and I like to live here because I am attached to it by old associations, by those deep and delicate roots which attach a man to the soil on which his ancestors were born and died, which attach him to the ideas and usages of the place as well as to the food, to local expressions, to the peculiar twang of the peasants, to the smell of the soil, of the villages, and of the atmosphere itself.

I love my house in which I grew up. From my windows I can see the Seine which flows alongside my garden, on the other side of the high road, almost through my grounds, the great and wide Seine, which goes to Rouen and Le Havre, and is covered with boats passing to and fro.

On the left, down yonder, lies Rouen, that large town, with its blue roofs, under its pointed Gothic towers. These are innumerable, slender or broad, dominated by the spire of the cathedral, and full of bells which sound through the blue air on fine mornings, sending their sweet and distant iron clang even as far as my home; that song of the metal, which the breeze wafts in my direction, now stronger and now weaker, according as the wind is stronger or lighter.

What a delicious morning it was!

About eleven o'clock, a long line of boats drawn by a steam tug as big as a fly, and which scarcely puffed while emitting its thick smoke, passed my gate.

After two English schooners, whose red flag fluttered in space, there came a magnificent Brazilian three-master; she was perfectly white, and wonderfully clean and shining. I saluted her, I hardly knew why, except that the sight of the vessel gave me great pleasure.

12th May. I have had a slight feverish attack for the last few days, and I feel ill, or rather I feel low-spirited.

Whence come those mysterious influences which change our happiness into discouragement, and our self-confidence into diffidence? One might almost say that the air, the invisible air, is full of unknowable Powers whose mysterious presence we have to endure. I wake up in the best spirits, with an inclination to sing. Why? I go down to the edge of the water and suddenly, after walking a short distance, I return home wretched, as if some misfortune were awaiting me there. Why? Is it a cold shiver which, passing over my skin, has upset my nerves and given me low spirits? Is it the form of the clouds, the colour of the sky, or the colour of the surrounding objects, which is so changeable, that has troubled my thoughts as they passed before my eyes? Who can tell? Everything that surrounds us, everything that we see, without looking at it, everything that we touch, without knowing it, everything that we handle, without feeling it, all that we meet, without clearly distinguishing it, has a rapid, surprising and inexplicable effect upon us and upon our senses, and, through them, on our ideas and on our heart itself.

How profound that mystery of the Invisible is! We cannot fathom it with our miserable senses, with our eyes which are unable to perceive what is either too small or too great, too near to us, or too far from us – neither the inhabitants of a star nor a drop of water; nor with our ears that deceive us, for they transmit to us the vibrations of the air in sonorous notes. They are fairies who work the miracle of changing these vibrations into sound, and by that metamorphosis give birth to music, which makes the silent motion of nature musical . . . with our sense of smell which is less keen than that of a dog . . . with our sense of taste which can scarcely distinguish the age of a wine!

Oh! If we only had other organs which would work other miracles in our favour, what a number of fresh things we might discover around us!

16th May. I am ill, decidedly! I was so well last month! I am feverish, horribly feverish, or rather I am in a state of feverish enervation, which makes my mind suffer as much as my body. I have, continually, that horrible sensation of some impending danger, that apprehension of some coming misfortune, or of approaching death; that presentiment which is, no doubt an attack of some illness which is still unknown, which germinates in the flesh and in the blood.

17th May. I have just come from consulting my physician, for I could no longer get any sleep. He said my pulse was rapid, my eyes dilated, my nerves highly strung, but there were no alarming symptoms. I must take a course of shower baths and of bromide of potassium.

25th May. No change! My condition is really very peculiar. As the evening comes on, an incomprehensible feeling of disquietude seizes me, just as if night concealed some threatening disaster. I dine hurriedly, and then try to read, but I do not understand the words, and can scarcely distingush the letters. Then I walk up and down my drawing-room, oppressed by a feeling of confused and irresistible fear, the fear of sleep and fear of my bed.

About ten o'clock I go up to my room. As soon as I enter it I double-lock and bolt the door; I am afraid – of what? Up to the present time I have been afraid of nothing . . . I open my cupboards, and look under my bed; I listen – to what? How strange it is that a simple feeling of discomfort, impeded or heightened circulation, perhaps the irritation of a nerve filament, a slight congestion, a small disturbance in the imperfect delicate functioning of our living machinery, may turn the most light-hearted of men into a melancholy one, and make a coward of the bravest? Then I go to bed, and wait for sleep as a man might wait for the executioner. I wait for its coming with dread, and my heart beats and my legs tremble, while my whole body shivers beneath the warmth of the bedclothes, until all at once I fall asleep, as though one should plunge into a pool of stagnant water in order to drown. I do not feel it coming on as I did formerly, this perfidious sleep which is close to me and watching me, which is going to seize me by the head, to close my eyes and annihilate me.

I sleep – a long time – two or three hours perhaps – then a dream – no – a nightmare lays hold on me. I feel that I am in bed and asleep . . . I feel it and I know it . . . and I feel also that somebody is coming close to me, is looking at me, touching me, is getting on my bed, is kneeling on my chest, is taking my neck between his hands and squeezing it . . . squeezing it with all his might in order to strangle me.

I struggle, bound by that terrible sense of powerlessness which paralyses us in our dreams; I try to cry out – but I cannot; I want to move – I cannot do so; I try, with the most violent efforts and breathing hard, to turn over and throw off this being who is crushing and suffocating me – I cannot!

And then, suddenly, I wake up, trembling and bathed in perspiration; I light a candle and find that I am alone, and after that crisis, which occurs every night, I at length fall asleep and slumber tranquilly until morning.

2nd June. My condition has grown worse. What is the matter with me? The bromide does me no good, and the shower baths have no effect. Sometimes, in order to tire myself thoroughly, I am fatigued enough already, I go for a walk in the forest of Roumare. I used to think at first that the fresh light and soft air, impregnated with the odour of herbs and leaves, would instil new blood into my veins and impart fresh energy to my heart. I turned into a broad hunting road, and then turned towards La Bouille, through a narrow path, between two rows of exceedingly tall trees, which placed a thick green, almost black, roof between the sky and me.

A sudden shiver ran through me, not a cold shiver, but a strange shiver of agony, and I hastened my steps, uneasy at being alone in the forest, afraid, stupidly and without reason, of the profound solitude. Suddenly it seemed to me as if I were being followed, as if somebody were walking at my heels, close, quite close to me, near enough to touch me.

I turned round suddenly, but I was alone. I saw nothing behind me except the straight, broad path, empty and bordered by high trees, horribly empty; before me it also extended until it was lost in the distance, and looked just the same – terrible.

I closed my eyes. Why? And then I began to turn round on one heel very quickly, just like a top. I nearly fell down, and opened my eyes; the trees were dancing round me and the earth heaved; I was obliged to sit down. Then, ah! I no longer remembered how I had come! What a strange idea! What a strange, strange idea! I did not in the least know. I started off to the right, and got back into the avenue which had led me into the middle of the forest.

3rd June. I have had a terrible night. I shall go away for a few weeks, for no doubt a journey will set me up again.

2nd July. I have come back, quite cured, and have had a most delightful trip into the bargain. I have been to Mont Saint-Michel, which I had not seen before.

What a sight, when one arrives as I did, at Avranches towards the end of the day! The town stands on a hill, and I was taken into the public garden at the extremity of the town. I uttered a cry of astonishment. An extraordinarily large bay lay extended before me, as far as my eyes could reach, between two hills which were lost to sight in the mist; and in the middle of this immense yellow bay, under a clear, golden sky, a peculiar hill rose up, sombre and pointed in the midst of the sand. The sun had just disappeared, and under the still flaming sky appeared the outline of that fantastic rock which bears on its summit a fantastic monument.

At daybreak I went out to it. The tide was low, as it had been the night before, and I saw that wonderful abbey rise up before me as I approached it. After several hours' walking, I reached the enormous mass of rocks which supports the little town, dominated by the great church. Having climbed the steep and narrow street, I entered the most wonderful Gothic building that has ever been built to God on earth, as large as a town, full of low rooms which seem buried beneath vaulted roofs, and lofty galleries supported by delicate columns.

I entered this gigantic gem, which is as light as a bit of lace, covered with towers, with slender belfries with spiral staircases, which raise their strange heads that bristle with chimeras, with devils, with fantastic animals, with monstrous flowers, to the blue sky by day, and to the black sky by night, and are connected by finely carved arches.

When I had reached the summit I said to the monk who accompanied me: 'Father, how happy you must be here!' And he replied: 'It's very windy here, monsieur'; and so we began to talk while watching the rising tide, which ran over the sand and covered it as with a steel cuirass.

And then the monk told me stories, all the old stories belonging to the place, legends, nothing but legends.

One of them struck me forcibly. The country people, those belonging to the Mount, declare that at night one can hear voices talking on the sands, and that one then hears two goats bleating, one with a strong, the

The flower raised itself three yards from my eyes

other with a weak voice. Incredulous people declare that it is nothing but the cry of the sea birds, which occasionally resembles bleatings, and occasionally, human lamentations; but belated fishermen swear that they have met an old shepherd wandering between tides on the sands around the little town. His head is completely concealed by his cloak and he is followed by a billy goat with a man's face, and a nanny goat with a woman's face, both having long, white hair, and talking incessantly and quarrelling in an unknown tongue. Then suddenly they cease and begin to bleat with all their might.

'Do you believe it?' I asked the monk. 'I scarcely know,' he replied, and I continued: 'If there are other beings besides ourselves on this earth, how comes it that we have not known it long since, or why have *you* not seen them? How is it that *I* have not seen them?' He replied: 'Do we see the hundred-thousandth part of what exists? Look here; there is the wind, which is the strongest force in nature, which knocks down men, and blows down buildings, uproots trees, raises the sea into mountains of water, destroys cliffs and casts great ships on the rocks; the wind which kills, which whistles, which sighs, which roars – have you ever seen it, and can you see it? It exists for all that, however.'

I was silent before this simple reasoning. That man was a philosopher, or perhaps a fool; I could not say which exactly, so I held my tongue. What he had said had often been in my own thoughts.

3rd July. I have slept badly; certainly there is some feverish influence here, for my coachman is suffering in the same way as I am. Whan I went back home yesterday, I noticed his singular paleness, and I asked him: 'What is the matter with you, Jean?' 'The matter is that I never get any rest, and my nights devour my days. Since your departure, monsieur, there has been a spell over me.'

However, the other servants are all well, but I am very much afraid of having another attack myself.

4th July. I am decidedly ill again; for my old nightmares have returned. Last night I felt somebody leaning on me and sucking my life from between my lips. Yes, he was sucking it out of my throat, like a leech. Then I got up, satiated, and I woke up, so exhausted, crushed and weak that I could not move. If this continues for a few days, I shall certainly go away again.

5th July. Have I lost my reason? What happened last night is so strange that my head wanders when I think of it!

I had locked my door, as I do now every evening, and then, being thirsty, I drank half a glass of water, and accidentally noticed that the water bottle was full up to the cutglass stopper.

Then I went to bed and fell into one of my terrible sleeps, from which I was aroused in about two hours by a still more frightful shock.

Picture to yourself a sleeping man who is being murdered and who wakes up with a knife in his lung, and whose breath rattles, who is covered with blood, and who can no longer breathe and is about to die, and does not understand – there you have it.

Having recovered my senses, I was thirsty again, so I lit a candle and went to the table on which stood my water bottle. I lifted it up and tilted it over my glass, but nothing came out. It was empty! It was completely empty! At first I could not understand it at all, and then suddenly I was seized by such a terrible feeling that I had to sit down, or rather I fell into a chair! Then I sprang up suddenly to look about me; then I sat down again, overcome by astonishment and fear, in front of the transparent glass bottle! I looked at it with fixed eyes, trying to conjecture, and my hands trembled! Somebody had drunk the water, but who? I? I, without any doubt. It could surely only be I. In that case I was a somnambulist; I lived, without knowing it, that mysterious double life which makes us doubt whether there are not two beings in us, or whether a strange, unknowable and invisible being does not at such moments, when our soul is in a state of torpor, animate our captive body, which obeys this other being, as it obeys us, and more than it obeys ourselves.

Oh! Who will understand my horrible agony? Who will understand the emotion of a man who is sound in mind, wide awake, full of common sense, who looks in horror through the glass of a water bottle for a little water that disappeared while he was asleep? I remained thus until it was daylight, without venturing to go to bed again.

6th July. I am going mad. Again all the contents of my water bottle have been drunk during the night – or rather, I have drunk it!

But is it I? Is it I? Who could it be? Who? Oh, God! Am I going mad? Who will save me?

10th July. I have just been through some surprising ordeals. Decidedly I am mad! And yet!

On 6th July, before going to bed, I put some wine, milk, water, bread

My foot struck her, cowering in a corner of the room. (p.143)

The hitch-hiker poked his head through the open window. (p.148)

and strawberries on my table. Somebody drank – I drank – all the water and a little of the milk, but neither the wine, bread, nor the strawberries were touched.

On the seventh of July I renewed the same experiment, with the same results, and on the 8th July, I left out the water and the milk, and nothing was touched.

Lastly, on 9th July I put only water and milk on my table, taking care to wrap up the bottles in white muslim and to tie down the stoppers. Then I rubbed my lips, my beard and my hands with pencil lead, and went to bed.

Irresistible sleep seized me, which was soon followed by a terrible awakening. I had not moved, and there was no mark of lead on the sheets. I rushed to the table. The muslim round the bottles remained intact; I undid the string, tembling with fear. All the water had been drunk, and so had the milk! Ah! Great God . . .

I must start for Paris immediately.

12th July. Paris. I must have lost my head during the last few days! I must be the plaything of my enervated imagination, unless I am really a somnambulist, or perhaps I have been under the power of one of those hitherto unexplained influences which are called suggestions. In any case, my mental state bordered on madness, and twenty-four hours of Paris sufficed to restore my equilibrium.

Yesterday, after doing some business and paying some visits which instilled fresh and invigorating air into my soul, I wound up the evening at the *Théâtre-Français.* A play by Alexandre Dumas the younger was being acted and his active and powerful imagination completed my cure. Certainly solitude is dangerous for active minds. We require around us men who can think and talk. When we are alone for a long time, we people space with phantoms.

I returned along the boulevards to my hotel in excellent spirits. Amid the jostling of the crowd I thought, not without irony, of my terrors and surmises of the previous week, because I had believed – yes, I had believed – that an invisible being lived beneath my roof. How weak our brains are, and how quickly they are terrified and led into error by a small incomprehensible fact.

Instead of saying simply: 'I do not understand because I do not know the cause,' we immediately imagine terrible mysteries and supernatural powers.

14th July. Fête of the Republic. I walked through the streets, amused as a child at the firecrackers and flags. Still it is very foolish to be merry on a fixed date, by Government decree. The populace is an imbecile flock of sheep, now stupidly patient, and now in ferocious revolt. Say to it: 'Amuse yourself,' and it amuses itself. Say to it: 'Go and fight with your neighbour,' and it goes and fights. Say to it: 'Vote for the Emperor,' and it votes for the Emperor, and then say to it: 'Vote for the Republic,' and it votes for the Republic.

Those who direct it are also stupid; only, instead of obeying men, they obey principles which can only be stupid, sterile, and false, for the very reason that they are principles, that is to say, ideas which are considered as certain and unchangeable in this world where one is certain of nothing, since light is an illusion and noise is an illusion.

16th July. I saw some things yesterday that troubled me very much.

I was dining at the house of my cousin, Madame Sablé, whose husband is colonel of the 76th Chasseurs at Limoges. There were two young women there, one of whom had married a medical man, Dr Parent, who devotes much attention to nervous diseases and to the remarkable manifestations taking place at this moment under the influence of hypnotism and suggestion.

He related to us at some length the wonderful results obtained by English scientists and by the doctors of the Nancy school; and the facts which he adduced appeared to me so strange that I declared that I was altogether incredulous.

'We are,' he declared, 'on the point of discovering one of the most important secrets of nature; I mean to say, one of its most important secrets on this earth, for there are certainly others of a different kind of importance up in the stars, yonder. Ever since man has thought, ever since he has been able to express and write down his thoughts, he has felt himself close to a mystery which is impenetrable to his gross and imperfect senses, and he endeavours to supplement through his intellect the inefficiency of his senses. As long as that intellect remained in its elementary stage, these apparitions of invisible spirits assumed forms that were commonplace, though terrifying. Thence sprang the popular belief in the supernatural, the legends of wandering spirits, of fairies, of gnomes, ghosts, I might even say the legend of God; for our conceptions

210

of the workman-creator, from whatever religion they may have come down to us, are certainly the most mediocre, the most stupid and the most incredible inventions that ever sprang from the terrified brain of any human beings. Nothing is truer than what Voltaire says: "God made man in His own image, but man has certainly paid Him back in his own coin."

'However, for rather more than a century men seem to have had a presentiment of something new. Mesmer and some others have put us on an unexpected track, and, especially within the last two or three years, we have arrived at really surprising results.'

My cousin, who is also very incredulous, smiled, and Dr Parent said to her: 'Would you like me to try to send you to sleep, madame?' 'Yes, certainly.'

She sat down in an easy chair, and he began to look at her fixedly, so as to fascinate her. I suddenly felt myself growing uncomfortable, my heart beating rapidly and a choking sensation in my throat. I saw Madame Sablé's eyes becoming heavy, her mouth twitching and her bosom heaving, and at the end of ten minutes she was asleep.

'Go behind her,' the doctor said to me, and I took a seat behind her. He put a visiting card into her hands, and said to her: 'This is a looking-glass; what do you see in it?' And she replied: 'I see my cousin.' What is he doing?' 'He is twisting his moustache.' 'And now?' 'He is taking a photograph out of his pocket.' 'Whose photograph is it?' 'His own.'

That was true, and the photograph had been given me that same evening in the hotel.

'What is his attitude in this portrait?' 'He is standing up with his hat in his hand.'

She saw, therefore, on that card, on that piece of white pasteboard, as if she had seen it in a mirror.

The young women were frightened and exclaimed. 'That is enough! Quite, quite enough!'

But the doctor said to Madame Sablé authoritatively: 'You will rise at eight o'clock tomorrow morning; then you will go and call on your cousin at his hotel and ask him to lend you five thousand francs which your husband demands of you, and which he will ask for when he sets out on his coming journey.'

Then he woke her up.

On returning to my hotel, I thought over this curious séance, and I was assailed by doubts, not as to my cousin's absolute and undoubted good faith, for I had known her well as if she were my own sister ever since she was a child, but as to a possible trick on the doctor's part. Had he not, perhaps, kept a glass hidden in his hand, which he showed to the young woman in her sleep, at the same time as he did the card? Professional conjurors do things that are just as singular.

So I went home and to bed, and this morning, at about half-past eight, I was awakened by my valet, who said to me: 'Madame Sablé has asked to see you immediately, monsieur.' I dressed hastily and went to her.

She sat down in some agitation, with her eyes on the floor, and without raising her veil she said to me: 'My dear cousin, I am going to ask a great favour of you.' 'What is it, cousin?' 'I do not like to tell you, and yet I must. I am in absolute need of five thousand francs.' 'What, you?' 'Yes I, or rather my husband, who has asked me to procure them for him.'

I was so thunderstruck that I stammered out my answers. I asked myself whether she had not really been making fun of me with Dr Parent, if it was not merely a well-acted farce which had been rehearsed beforehand. On looking at her attentively, however, all my doubts disappeared. She was trembling with grief, so painful was this step to her, and I was convinced that her throat was full of sobs.

I knew that she was very rich and I continued: 'What! Has not your husband five thousand francs at his disposal? Come, think. Are you sure that he commissioned you to ask me for them?'

She hesitated for a few seconds, as if she were making a great effort to search her memory, and then she replied: 'Yes . . . yes, I am quite sure of it.' 'He has written to you?'

She hesitated again and reflected, and I guessed the torture of her thoughts. She did not know. She only knew that she was to borrow five thousand francs off me for her husband. So she told a lie. 'Yes, he has written to me.' 'When, pray? You did not mention it to me yesterday,' 'I received his letter this morning.' 'Can you show it me?' 'No . . . no . . . no . . . it contains private matters . . . things too personal to ourselves . . . I burned it.' 'So your husband runs into debt?'

She hesitated again, and then murmured: 'I do not know.' 'Thereupon I said bluntly: 'I have not five thousand francs at my disposal at this moment, my dear cousin.'

She uttered a kind of cry as if she were in pain and said: 'Oh! oh! I beseech you, I beseech you to get them for me . . .'

She got excited and clasped her hands as if she were praying to me! I heard her voice change its tone; she wept and stammered, harassed and dominated by the irresistible order that she had received.

'Oh! oh! I beg you to . . . if you knew what I am suffering . . . I want them today.'

I had pity on her: 'You shall have them by and by, I swear to you.' 'Oh! thank you! thank you! How kind you are.'

I continued; 'Do you remember what took place at your house last night!' 'Yes.' 'Do you remember that Dr Parent sent you to sleep?' 'Yes.' 'Oh! Very well, then; he ordered you to come to me this morning to borrow five thousand francs, and at this moment you are obeying that suggestion.'

She considered for a few moments, and then replied: 'But as it is my husband who wants them –'

For a whole hour I tried to convince her, but could not succeed, and when she had gone I went to the doctor. He was just going out, and he listened to me with a smile, and said; 'Do you believe now?' 'Yes, I cannot help it.' 'Let us go to your cousin's.'

She was already half asleep on a reclining chair, overcome with fatigue. The doctor felt her pulse, looked at her for some time with one hand raised towards her eyes, which she closed by degrees under the irresistible power of this magnetic influence, and when she was asleep, he said:

'Your husband does not require the five thousand francs any longer! You must, therefore, forget that you asked your cousin to lend them to you, and, if he speaks to you about it, you will not understand him.'

Then he woke her up, and I took out a pocketbook and said: 'Here is what you asked me for this morning, my dear cousin.' But she was so surprised that I did not venture to persist; nevertheless, I tried to recall the circumstance to her, but she denied it vigorously, thought I was making fun of her, and, in the end, very nearly lost her temper.

There! I have just come back, and I have not been able to eat any lunch, for this experiment has altogether upset me.

19th July. Many people to whom I told the adventure laughed at me. I no longer know what to think. The wise man says: 'It may be!'

21st July. I dined at Bougival, and then I spent the evening at a boatman's ball. Decidedly everything depends on place and surroundings. It would be the height of folly to believe in the supernatural on the Ile de la Grenouilliere . . . but on the top of Mount Saint-Michel? . . . and in India? We are terribly influenced by our surroundings. I shall return home next week.

30th July. I came back to my own house yesterday. Everything is going well.

2nd August. Nothing new, it is splendid weather, and I spend my days in watching the Seine flowing past.

4th August. Quarrels among my servants. They declare that the glasses are broken in the cupboards at night. The footman accuses the cook, who accuses the seamstress, who accuses the other two. Who is the culprit? It is a clever person who can tell.

6th August. This time I am not mad. I have seen . . . I have seen . . . I have seen! . . . I can doubt no longer . . . I have seen it! . . .

I was walking at two o'clock among my rose trees, in the full sunlight . . . in the walk bordered by autumn roses which are beginning to fall. As I stopped to look at a Géant de Batille, which had three splendid blossoms, I distinctly saw the stalk of one of the roses near me bend, as if an invisible hand had bent it, and then break, as if that hand had picked it! Then the flower raised itself, following the curve which a hand would have described in carrying it towards a mouth, and it remained suspended in the transparent air, all alone and motionless, a terrible red spot, three yards from my eyes. In desperation I rushed at it to take it! I found nothing; it had disappeared. Then I was seized with furious rage against myself, for a reasonable and serious man should not have such hallucinations.

But was it an hallucination? I turned round to look for the stalk, and I found it at once, on the bush, freshly broken, between two other roses which remained on the branch. I returned home then, my mind greatly disturbed; for I am certain now, as certain as I am of the alternation of day and night, that there exists close to me an invisible being that lives on milk and water, that can touch objects, take them and change their places; that is, consequently, endowed with a material nature, although it is imperceptible to our senses, and that lives as I do, under my roof.

7th August. I slept tranquilly. He drank the water out of my decanter, but did not disturb my sleep.

I wonder if I am mad. As I was walking just now in the sun by the riverside, doubts as to my sanity arose in me; not vague doubts such as I have had hitherto, but definite, absolute doubts. I have seen mad people, and I have known some who have been quite intelligent, lucid, even clear-sighted at every concern of life, except on one point. They spoke clearly, readily, profoundly on everything, when suddenly their mind struck upon the shoals of their madness and broke to pieces there, and scattered and foundered in that furious and terrible sea, full of rolling waves, fogs and squalls, which is called *madness*.

I certainly should think that I was mad, absolutely mad, if I were not conscious, did not perfectly know my condition, did not fathom it by analysing it with the most complete lucidity, I should, in fact, be only a rational man who was labouring under an hallucination. Some unknown disturbance must have arisen in my brain, one of those disturbances which physiologists of the present day try to note and to verify; and that disturbance must have caused a deep gap in my mind and in the sequence and logic of my ideas. Similar phenomena occur in dreams which lead us among the most unlikely phantasmagoria, without causing us any surprise, because our verifying apparatus and our organ of control are asleep, while our imaginative faculty is awake and active. Is it not possible that one of the imperceptible notes of the cerebral keyboard has been paralysed in me? Some men lose the recollection of proper names, of verbs, or of numbers, or merely of dates, in consequence of an accident. The localisation of all the variations of thought has been established nowadays; why, then, should it be surprising if my faculty of controlling the unreality of certain hallucinations were dormant in me for the time being?

I thought of all this as I walked by the side of the water. The sun shone brightly on the river and made earth delightful, while it filled me with a love for life, for the swallows, whose agility always delights my eye, for the plants by the riverside, the rustle of whose leaves is a pleasure to my ears.

By degrees, however, an inexplicable feeling of discomfort seized me. It seemed as if some unknown force were numbing and stopping me, were preventing me from going farther, and were calling me back. I felt that painful wish to return which oppresses you when you have left a beloved invalid at home, and when you are seized with a presentiment that he is worse.

I, therefore, returned in spite of myself, feeling certain that I should find some bad news awaiting me, a letter or a telegram. There was nothing, however, and I was more surprised and uneasy than if I had had another fantastic vision.

8th August. I spent a terrible evening yesterday. He does not show himself any more, but I feel that he is near me, watching me, looking at me, penetrating me, dominating me, and more redoubtable when he hides himself thus than if he were to manifest his constant and invisible presence by supernatural phenomena. However, I slept.

9th August. Nothing; but I am afraid.

10th August. Nothing; what will happen tomorrow?

11th August. Still nothing; I cannot stop at home with this fear hanging over me and these thoughts in my mind; I shall go away.

12th August. Ten o'clock at night. All day long I have been trying to get away, and have not been able. I wished to accomplish this simple and easy act of freedom – to go out – to get into my carriage in order to go to Rouen – and I have not been able to do it. What is the reason?

13th August. When we are attacked by certain maladies, all the springs of our physical being appear to be broken, all our energies destroyed, all our muscles relaxed; our bones, too, have become as soft as flesh, and our bodies as liquid as water. I am experiencing these sensations in my moral being in a strange and distressing manner. I have no longer any strength, any courage, any self-control, not even any power to set my own will in motion. I have no power left to will anything; but someone does it for me and I obey.

14th August. I am lost! Somebody possesses my soul and dominates it. Somebody orders all my acts, all my movements, all my thoughts. I am no longer anything in myself, nothing except an enslaved and terrified spectator of all the things I do. I wish to go out; I cannot. He does not wish to, and so I remain, trembling and distracted, in the armchair in which he keeps me sitting. I merely wish to get up and to rouse myself; I cannot! I am riveted to my chair, and my chair adheres to the ground in such a manner that no power could move us.

Then, suddenly, I must, I must go to the bottom of my garden to pick some strawberries and eat them, and I go there. I pick the strawberries and eat them! Oh, my God! My God! Is there a God? If there be one, deliver me! Save me! Succour me! Pardon! Pity! Mercy! Save me! Oh, what sufferings! What torture! What horror!

15th August. This is certainly the way in which my poor cousin was possessed and controlled when she came to borrow five thousand francs off me. She was under the power of a strange will which had entered into her, like another soul, like another parasitic and dominating soul. Is the world coming to an end?

But who is he, this invisible being that rules me? This unknowable being, this rover of a supernatural race?

Invisible beings exist, then! How is it then, that since the beginning of the world they have never manifested themselves precisely as they do to me? I have never read of anything that resembles what goes on in my house. Oh, if I could only leave it, if I could only go away, escape, and never return! I should be saved, but I cannot.

16th August. I managed to escape today for two hours, like a prisoner who finds the door of his dungeon accidentally open. I suddenly felt that I was free and that he was far away, and so I gave orders to harness the horses as quickly as possible, and I drove to Rouen. Oh, how delightful to be able to say to a man who obeys you: 'Go to Rouen!'

I made him pull up before the library, and I begged them to lend me Dr Herrmann Herestauss' treatise on the unknown inhabitants of the ancient and modern world.

Then, as I was getting into my carriage, I intended to say: 'To the railway station!' but instead of this I shouted – I did not say, but I shouted – in such a loud voice that all the passers-by turned round: 'Home!' and I fell back on the cushion of my carriage, overcome by mental agony. He had found me again and regained possession of me.

17th August. Oh, what a night! What a night! And yet it seems to me that I ought to rejoice. I read until one o'clock in the morning! Herestauss, doctor of philosophy and theogony, wrote the history of the manifestation of all those invisible beings which hover around man, or of whom he dreams. He describes their origin, their domain, their power; but none of them resembles the one which haunts me. One might say that man, ever since he began to think, has had a foreboding fear of a new being, stronger than himself, his successor in this world, and that, feeling his presence, and not being able to foresee the nature of that master, he has, in his terror, created the whole race of occult beings, of vague phantoms born of fear.

Having therefore, read until one o'clock in the morning, I went and sat down at the open window, in order to cool my forehead and my thoughts, in the calm night air. It was very pleasant and warm! How I should have enjoyed such a night formerly!

There was no moon, but the stars darted out their rays in the dark heavens. Who inhabits those worlds? What forms, what living beings, what animals are there yonder? What do the thinkers in those distant worlds know more than we do? What can they do more than we can? What do they see which we do not know? Will not one of them, some day or other, traversing space, appear on our earth to conquer it, just as the Norsemen formerly crossed the sea in order to subjugate nations more feeble than themselves?

We are so weak, so defenceless, so ignorant, so small, we who live on this particle of mud which revolves in a drop of water.

I fell asleep, dreaming thus in the cool night air, and when I had slept for about three-quarters of an hour, I opened my eyes without moving, awakened by I know not what confused and strange sensation. At first I saw nothing, and then suddenly it appeared to me as if a page of a book which had remained open on my table turned over of its own accord. Not a breath of air had come in at my window, and I was surprised, and waited. In about four minutes, I saw, I saw, yes saw with my own eyes, another page lift itself up and fall down on the others, as if a finger had turned it over. My armchair was empty, appeared empty, but I knew that he was there, he, and sitting in my place, and that he was reading. With a furious bound, the bound of an enraged wild beast that springs at its tamer, I crossed my room to seize him, to strangle him, to kill him! But before I could reach it, the chair fell over as if somebody had run away from me – my table rocked, my lamp fell and went out, and my window closed as if some thief had been surprised and had fled out into the night, shutting it behind him.

So he had run away; he had been afraid; he, afraid of me!

But – but – tomorrow – or later – some day or other – I should be able to hold him in my clutches and crush him against the ground! Do not dogs occasionally bite and strangle their masters?

18th August. I have been thinking the whole day long. Oh yes, I will obey him, follow his impulses, fulfil all his wishes, show myself humble, submissive, a coward. He is the stronger; but the hour will come –

19th August. I know – I know – I know all! I have just read the following in the *Revue du Monde Scientifique*: 'A curious piece of news comes to us from Rio de Janeiro. Madness, an epidemic of madness, which may be compared to that contagious madness which attacked the people of Europe in the Middle Ages, is at this moment raging in the Province of San-Paolo. The terrified inhabitants are leaving their houses, saying that they are pursued, possessed, dominated like human cattle by invisible, though tangible, beings, a species of vampires, which feed on their life while they are asleep, and which, besides, drink water and milk without appearing to touch any other nourishment.

'Professor Don Pedro Henriques, accompanied by several medical savants, has gone to the Province of San-Paolo, in order to study the origin and the manifestations of this surprising madness on the spot, and to propose such measures to the Emperor as may appear to him to be most fitted to restore the mad population to reason.'

Ah! I remember now that fine Brazilian three-master which passed in front of my windows as she was going up the Seine, on the 8th day of last May! I thought she looked so pretty, so white and bright! That Being was on board of her, coming from there, where its race originated. And it saw me! It saw my house which was also white, and it sprang from the ship on to the land. Oh, merciful heaven!

Now I know, I can divine. The reign of man is over and he has come. He who was feared by primitive man; whom disquieted priests exorcised; whom sorcerers evoked on dark nights, without having seen him appear, to whom the imagination of the transient masters of the world lent all the monstrous or graceful forms of gnomes, spirits, genii, fairies, and familiar spirits. After the coarse conceptions of primitive fear, more clear-sighted men foresaw it more clearly. Mesmer divined it, and ten years ago physicians accurately discovered the nature of his power, even before he exercised it himself. They played with this new weapon of the Lord, the sway of a mysterious will over the human soul, which had become a slave. They called it magnetism, hypnotism, suggestion – what do I know? I have seen them amusing themselves like rash children with this horrible power! Woe to us! Woe to man! He has come, the – the –

what does he call himself – the – I fancy that he is shouting out his name to me and I do not hear him – the – yes – he is shouting it out – I am listening – I cannot – he repeats it – the – Horla – I hear – the Horla – it is he – the Horla – he has come!

Ah! the vulture has eaten the pigeon; the wolf has eaten the lamb; the lion has devoured the sharp-horned buffalo; man has killed the lion with an arrow, with a sword, with gunpowder; but the Horla will make of man what we have made of the horse and of the ox; his chattel, his slave, and his food, by the mere power of his will. Woe to us!

But nevertheless, the animal sometimes revolts and kills the man who has subjugated it. I should also like – I shall be able to – but I must know him, touch him, see him! Scientists say that animals' eyes, being different from ours, do not distinguish objects as ours do. And my eye cannot distinguish this newcomer who is oppressing me.

Why? Oh, now I remember the words of the monk at Mont Saint-Michel: 'Can we see the hundred-thousandth part of what exists? See her: there is the wind, which is the strongest force in nature, which knocks men down, and wrecks buildings, uproots trees, raises the sea into mountains of water, destroys cliffs and casts great ships on the breakers; the wind which kills, which whistles, which sighs, which roars – have you ever seen it, and can you see it? It exists for all that, however!'

And I went on thinking: my eyes are so weak, so imperfect, that they do not even distinguish hard bodies, if they are as transparent as glass! If a glass without tinfoil behind it were to bar my way, I should run into it, just as a bird which has flown into a room breaks its head against the window-panes. A thousand things, moreover, deceive man and lead him astray. Why should it then be surprising that he cannot perceive an unknown body through which the light passes?

A new being! Why not? It was assuredly bound to come! Why should we be the last? We do not distinguish it any more than all the others created before us! The reason is, that its nature is more perfect, its body finer and more finished than ours, that ours is so weak, so awkwardly constructed, encumbered with organs that are always tired, always on the strain like machinery that is too complicated, which lives like a plant and like a beast, nourishing itself with difficulty on air, herbs, and flesh, an animal machine which is pray to maladies, to malformations, to decay; broken-winded, badly regulated, simple and eccentric, ingeniously badly made, at once a coarse and a delicate piece of workmanship, the rough sketch of a being that might become intelligent and grand.

We are only a few, so few in this world, from the oyster up to man. Why should there not be one more, once that period is passed which separates the the successive apparitions from all the different species?

Why not one more? Why not, also, other trees with immense, splendid flowers, perfuming whole regions? Why not other elements besides fire, air, earth, and water? There are four, only four, those nursing fathers of various beings! What a pity! Why are there not forty, four hundred, four thousand? How poor everything is, how mean and wretched! grudgingly produced, roughly constructed, clumsily made! Ah the elephant and the hippopotamus, what grace! And the camel, what elegance!

But the butterfly, you will say, a flying flower! I dream of one that should be as large as a hundred worlds, with wings whose shape, beauty, colour and motion I cannot even express. But I see it – it flutters from star to star, refreshing them with the light and harmonious breath of its flight! And the people up there look at it as it passes in an ecstasy of delight!

*   *   *   *

What is the matter with me? It is he, the Horla, who haunts me, and who makes me think of these foolish things! He is within me, he is becoming my soul; I shall kill him!

29th August. I shall kill him. I have seen him! Yesterday I sat down at my table and pretended to write very assiduously. I knew quite well that he would come prowling round me, quite close to me, so close that I might perhaps be able to touch him, to seize him. And then – then I should have the strength of desperation; I should have my hands, my knees, my chest, my forehead, my teeth to strangle him, to crush him, to bite him, to tear him to pieces. And I watched for him with all my over-excited senses.

I had lighted my two lamps and the eight wax candles on my

mantelpiece, as if with this light I could discover him.

My bedstead, my old oak post bedstead, stood opposite to me; on my right was the fireplace; on my left, the door which was carefully closed, after I had left it open for some time in order to attract him; behind me was a very high wardrobe with a looking-glass in it, before which I stood to shave and dress every day, and in which I was in the habit of glancing at myself from head to foot every time I passed it.

I pretended to be writing in order to deceive him, for he also was watching me, and I felt – I was certain that he was reading over my shoulder, that he was there, touching my ear.

I got up, my hands extended, and turned round so quickly that I almost fell. Eh! well? It was as bright as at midday, but I did not see my reflection in the mirror! It was empty, clear, profound, full of light! But my figure was not reflected in it – and I, I was opposite to it! I saw the large, clear glass from top to bottom, and I looked at it with unsteady eyes; and I did not dare to advance; I did not venture to make a movement, feeling that he was there, but that he would escape me again, he whose imperceptible body had absorbed my reflection.

How frightened I was! And then, suddenly, I began to see myself in a mist in the depths of the looking-glass, in a mist as it were a sheet of water; and it seemed to me as if this water were flowing clearer every moment. It was like the end of an eclipse. Whatever it was that hid me did not appear to possess any clearly defined outlines, but a sort of opaque transparency which gradually grew clearer.

At last I was able to distinguish myself completely, as I do every day when I look at myself.

I had seen it! And the horror of it remained with me, and makes me shudder even now.

30th August. How could I kill it, as I could not get hold of it? Poison? But it would see me mix it with the water; and then, would our poisons have any effect on its impalpable body? No – no – no doubt about the matter – Then – then?–

31st August. I sent for a blacksmith from Rouen, and ordered iron shutters for my room such as some private hotels in Paris have on the gound floor, for fear of burglars, and he is going to make me an iron door as well. I have made myself out a coward, but I do not care about that!

10th September. Rouen, Hotel Continental. It is done – it is done – but is he dead? My mind is thoroughly upset by what I have seen.

Well, then, yesterday, the locksmith having put on the iron shutters and door, I left everything open until midnight, although it was getting cold.

Suddenly I felt that he was there, and joy, mad joy, took possession of me. I got up softly, and walked up and down for some time, so that he might not suspect anything; then I fastened the iron shutters, and, going back to the door, quickly double-locked it with a padlock, putting the key into my pocket.

Suddenly I noticed that he was moving restlessly round me, that in his turn he was frightened and was ordering me to let him out. I nearly yielded; I did not, however, but, putting my back to the door, I half opened it, just enough to allow me to go out backward, and as I am very tall my head touched the casing. I was sure that he had not been able to escape, and I shut him up quite alone, quite alone. What happiness! I had him fast. Then I ran downstairs; in the drawing-room, which was under my bedroom, I took the two lamps and I poured all the oil on the carpet, the furniture, everywhere; then I set fire to it and made my escape, after having carefully double-locked the door.

I went and hid myself at the bottom of the garden, in a clump of laurel bushes. How long it seemed! How long it seemed! Everything was dark, silent, motionless, not a breath of air and not a star, but heavy banks of clouds which one could not see, but which weighed, oh, so heavily on my soul.

I looked at my house and waited. How long it was! I already began to think that the fire had gone out of its own accord, or that he had extinguished it, when one of the lower windows gave way under the violence of the flames, and a long, soft, caressing sheet of red flame mounted up the white wall, and enveloped it as far as the roof. The light fell on the trees, the branches, and the leaves, and a shiver of fear pervaded them also! The birds awoke, a dog began to howl, and it seemed to me as if the day were breaking! Almost immediately two other windows flew into fragments, and I saw that the whole of the lower part of my house was nothing but a terrible furnace. But a cry, a horrible, shrill, heart-rending cry, a woman's cry, sounded through the night, and two garret windows were opened! I had forgotten the servants! I saw their terror-stricken faces, and their arms waving frantically.

Then, overwhelmed with horror, I set off to run to the village, shouting: 'Help! help! fire! fire!' I met some people who were already coming to the scene, and I returned with them.

By this time the house was nothing but a horrible and magnificent funeral pile, a monstrous funeral pile which lit up the whole country, a funeral pile where men were burning, and where he was burning also, He, He, my prisoner, that new Being, the new master, the Horla!

Suddenly the whole roof fell in between the walls, and a volcano of flames darted up to the sky. Through all the windows which opened on the furnace, I saw the flames darting, and I thought that he was there, in that kiln, dead.

Dead? Perhaps. – His body? Was not his body, which was transparent, indestructible by such means as would kill ours?

If he were not dead? – Perhaps time alone has power over that Invisible and Redoubtable Being. Why this transparent, unrecognizable body, this body belonging to a spirit, if it also has to fear ills, infirmities and premature destruction?

Premature destruction? All human terror spring from that! After man, the Horla. After him who can die every day, at any hour, at any moment, by any accident, comes the one who will die only at his own proper hour, day, and minute, because he has touched the limits of his existence!

No – no – without any doubt – he is not dead – Then – then – I suppose I must kill *myself!* . . .

The figure was tall and gaunt and shrouded from head to foot. (p. 199)

He was about two metres under, and he was on his back, with his eyes open; and his mouth. (p.235)

THE DEVIL'S LAUGHTER

Jan Needle

There was a typhoid scare on when the Boyd family flew out for their Greek island holiday, and everyone in England was being nervous, and getting jabs, and being silly as usual. The Boyds, who had travelled a lot, and to some pretty hairy places, laughed. All those Greeks, plus a few million tourists, and a mere three people had contracted the disease— what was the panic? You had more chance of getting trampled by an elephant at the zoo.

Danny Boyd's grandmother, however, was perturbed. 'He's only seven,' she protested. 'And he's such a beautiful little boy. You'd never forgive yourselves if anything happened to him.'

Danny blushed, because even at that age he did not like to be described as beautiful. It did not help that his two sisters laughed at him, and pointed their fingers.

'Beautiful, Beautiful!' squawked Sarah, who was thirteen and horrible. 'Don't worry, Grandma, no self-respecting typhoid germ would go anywhere near that dirty little boy!'

Grandma, who was quite old, and rather posh, looked 'vexed' as she would call it. 'Too beautiful to live,' she muttered.

But the family chuckled at her, in a friendly way. They were not bothering.

'No harm will come to Danny,' said Dad, ruffling his blonde, curly hair. 'Will it, Dan? It would take more than dirty water to kill this one.'

'He's afraid of ghosts,' said Vicky. She was nicer than Sarah, Danny thought. She was eleven and liked rough games. 'But I suppose you don't get them out there. Too hot.'

This caused a discussion, because to Sarah and Dad it seemed wrong that you couldn't have ghosts in a hot climate. But Mum, Danny, Grandma and Vicky were certain. For ghosts, you needed ruined houses, and howling winds, and cold, dripping cellars. The idea of a sunshine spook was crazy. Nobody howled eerily in the Mediterranean nights. Above a certain temperature, Vicky insisted, ghosts were impossible.

'You're safe then, Danny,' said Sarah. 'Pity really. It would be doing the world a service if you were spirited away!'

'Sarah!' said Gran. 'If you joke about *everything* something bad will happen. It's bound to.'

Danny, for no rational reason at all, felt a stir of fear.

When their plane touched down at the airport on Zakinthos, all these things had been forgotten. They arrived in the afternoon, and their parents' friend Nikos was waiting for them. He festooned their luggage all over the car, chatted to Dad, kissed Mum and hugged the children, and thundered off along the coast road to Akrotiri in a style that made the girls and Danny gasp, but which the adults appeared to accept as normal. The last two kilometres were up rough country lanes of dried mud, through acres and acres of bent and stunted trees which mother said bore olives. Even over the noise of the engine, and Nikos, they were aware of a weird sound—a harsh, high-pitched chirping. When they halted by a small white house and the engine was switched off, it almost overwhelmed them.

'But what *is* it?' said Danny. 'It sounds like a hundred babies saying choo-choo! A thousand babies! All the babies in the world!'

'It is cicadas,' said Nikos. 'Here in the olive trees there are millions of them. You get used to it.'

The whole family listened, amazed, for quite a while. The noise was loud, and insistent, and constant. It did sound something like Danny had said, but only something. It was indescribable.

'Don't they ever stop?' asked Danny.

'At night,' replied Nikos. 'They like the sun on them. From evening until the sun is well up in the morning they are silent. Look, I'll show you one.'

Danny and Vicky and Sarah followed him to a tree.

'Look,' said Nikos. 'Who can find one first?'

They stared and stared, but could see nothing. Yet the noise was so loud that their ears were ringing with it.

'No,' said Vicky. 'Are you certain there are any in this tree?'

Nikos pointed a brown stubby finger at the rough bark. When it was almost touching the tree, Danny squeaked.

'I can see it! It's *horrible!*'

It was like a cross between a huge wasp and a very fat fly, and it was beautifully camouflaged. As they stared, it started up its noise, without apparently moving or opening its mouth. It gazed glassily at them with brown bright eyes, as if indifferent.

The noise was irregular for a moment or two, until the creature had picked up the rhythm of the other cicadas in the tree. Which was the rhythm of them all. The noise surged upwards to a crescendo. Thousands, millions, of cicadas making the same harsh, rhythmic double note.

'It's like laughter,' said Danny. He looked sickened, fearful. 'It's like some horrible, nasty laughter.'

Sarah put on a face.

'Devil's laughter,' she said. She made a claw of her hand and snatched at Danny's eyes. 'It's long-dead souls. They'll climb into your hair at nightime and suck your brains out through your ears.'

Danny, to the embarrassment of Nikos, burst into tears and rushed into the house.

'They're completely harmless,' he told the girls, as if apologizing. 'They just sit in the trees all day and make this noise, I don't know why. They do not seem to have a purpose.'

Before he left the family to it, the Greek shared a glass of wine and a chat with the grown-ups. Mum and Dad had been to Zakinthos before, on business and pleasure, and they knew several of the locals. The children listened to some of the talk, but not seriously. It all sounded pretty routine.

'Oh,' said Nikos, as he walked into the sunshine. 'Dino. Things are bad with him.'

'Dino?' said mother.

'You know,' said Dad. 'The shepherd. What's up with him?'

'His son,' replied Nikos. 'Cristos. He is dead. He died three months ago.'

'Oh *no*,' said Mum. 'But he was only . . .'

'Seven years old,' said Nikos, gravely. 'The same age as your Daniel I remember. The same month even, I think.'

'Yes,' said father. 'February. What did the little chap die of?'

'He . . . I do not know,' said Nikos. 'He seemed to . . . to waste away somehow. He faded. Like a . . . like a flower. Then he died.'

The children were studying the faces of their parents. In the fly-buzzing warmth of the small white-washed kitchen, the atmosphere was oddly cold. There was nothing said for many seconds. The grinding rasp of the cicadas filled the air.

'Poor Cristos,' said Mother. 'Poor Dino.'

'He has taken it cruelly,' said Nikos. 'I must warn you. He is changed. Be careful.'

Again the sense of chill.

'Careful?' said Mum. 'How do you mean exactly?'

'I do not know, exactly,' said Nikos. 'I am sorry. I am spoiling your day. But . . . be careful.'

'But Dino is such a . . .' began Mother.

'Lovely, fantastic, man,' said Dad.

'To lose a son, in this country,' said Nikos. He gave a half smile to the girls. 'A daughter, for a man like Dino, would have been not . . . not quite so . . .'

'Poor Dino,' said mother. 'Thank you, Nikos. Thank you for telling us.'

By the time the shepherd turned up one morning, four days later, Danny, Sarah and Vicky had come to adore the little house, and the countryside, and the places they had seen.

The house was not like anything they knew at home. It was single storey, and very small, with two tiny bedrooms and a tinier place yet where Danny slept. It had neither water nor electricity, nor any form of plumbing. At first the children were thrown by this, quite put out. But their parents laughed at them, and told them they were talking like tourists. If they wanted to see another country properly, and experience how completely *different* it was, what was the point of staying in a hotel that could have been in Margate? The children, catching the logic, took the toilet roll and the spade into the olive grove when they needed to— and ended up enjoying it.

They soon became expert cicada spotters, and if the noise got too insistent in the heat of the afternoon, they would patrol the trees nearest the house and touch the lethargic fat creatures with the tip of a stick until they'd buzzed off—literally—to a more distant perch. This way they could cut the noise level considerably, and the 'devil's laughter' would be less fearsome, if just as eerie. They hunted up scorpions at the well, and had competitions every day to see who could surprise the biggest lizard basking on a rock.

Best of all they liked the beaches. Their parents hired a Citroën Pony, a type of mini-jeep with an open top and clattering engine, and they zoomed all over the place. By British standards the beaches they visited were empty, and each one had a taverna where they had beer and kebabs and ice-cream and gallons of lemonade. The water was clear and warm, and the sunshine lasted till well after Danny's bedtime. Despite the heat and the mosquitos—kept at bay with odd green spirals which smoked and smouldered redly beside their beds all night, the children slept like logs.

It was a Sunday morning that they met Dino, and he came past the house while they were still in bed. They heard him first, by the flat clanking of sheep bells, and a peculiar, mournful noise of music. Romantic Vicky thought it must be pan pipes, which she'd read about in *The Wind in the Willows*. When it got nearer, though, the noise revealed itself as a very cheap old tranny, playing the sort of stuff appropriate to a Sunday. Sarah laughed, of course.

Danny was still mouldering in his pit, so the parents and the girls went outside to greet the shepherd. At first they saw only sheep, big, skinny, rangy animals quite unlike anything they'd come across in England, more like goats in fact, which nibbled energetically at the dried-up grass they found at the bases of the trees. When Dino detached himself from the gnarled old olive trunk he had been leaning against Sarah and Vicky jumped. He'd been like part of it.

The shepherd came slowly forward, his face expressionless. He was a tall, gaunt man, with brown-burnt skin and drifts of hair wisping out from underneath an odd leather hat. He wore blue trousers, sandals, and a stained brown open shirt. His massive chest was covered in curly white hair. As he approached, an aura of quiet, wistful music emanated from somewhere about him, some pocket where the tiny radio was hidden.

'Dino,' said father quietly, then spoke in Greek for a while. The shepherd did not smile, although his eyes gazed directly at them. His eyes were very brown; and, to the girls, almost unbearably sad.

Mother spoke to the shepherd then, and Dad once more. Vicky and Sarah glanced at each other. Was this going to get embarrassing? Why did this huge, sad man not answer? Was he going to merely stare at them until they smarted, then go on his way? Father and mother stopped talking. Dad shifted his weight uneasily from one leg to the other. The cicadas found a crescendo. The harsh double note began to batter at their ears, each one of the millions perfectly in time. It was uncomfortably mocking, peculiarly deliberate.

Then Danny appeared in the doorway, pushing sleepily between his sisters onto the step, blinking blindly in the powerful sunshine. Danny, small and beautiful, with a mass of golden curls, with one sandal on and a pair of dirty white shorts, nothing else. The cicadas, as if by magic, stopped. The noise faded almost to nothing. In the quiet chirrupping that was left, the shepherd spoke.

'Boy,' he said. His voice was choked, emotional. They all looked at him, startled, except Danny, who was half asleep, still blinking. 'Oh, boy. Boy. Boy.'

His face was terrifying, racked with pain. His mouth was half open, and his eyes were liquid and beseeching. In the trees behind him the cicadas found a new rhythm. The noise built up to a new, violent, beating laughter.

'Dino,' said mother uncertainly. 'This is our son. Our Daniel.' She pushed him further forward, onto the step, into the sun.

'Danny. Say hello. It's Dino. He's the shepherd.'

Dino left them then, with hardly another word being spoken. But he returned that evening, with a large bottle of his own rough white wine, and a bundle of cheese and olives. They all sat out on the step and Dino talked to them. He was a changed man.

His English was not perfect, but he spoke it with a fluid humour that was completely charming. He knew how to turn a phrase to make the English laugh, and he could speak rapidly and fluently when he needed to, bringing the funny parts of his stories into comic relief. He also had a superb knack of knowing what the children liked to hear. If Sarah and Vicky were enthralled, Danny was bewitched.

The shepherd told comic tales of the characters he had known on the island, and bizarre tales of the war—like the hurling of sixty men and women off the cliff at Kampi because they had collaborated with the Germans. He told them stories of fishing in great storms, of visitations of dread diseases, of the eccentric behaviour of the tourists since the jet planes started flying them in. He was relaxed, and friendly, and laughing, his eyes no longer sad, no longer haunting. When he stood up to go it was pitch dark, and the cicadas had long been silent. Now the sounds were the sighing of the wind in the olive groves, and the occasional crackle as the fire they had built died down. Dino shook hands with mother and father, and bowed gravely at the girls.

Then he touched Danny lightly on the cheek.

'Perhaps you would like to come with me tomorrow? To help me tend the sheep?'

Mother gave a light laugh.

'Oh I don't think so, Dino,' she said. 'We're off to the beach near Volime tomorrow. It would take wild horses to keep him away from there.'

Danny surprised them all.

'I don't want to go swimming, Mum,' he said. 'I want to go with Dino.'

Dino bent and kissed him lightly among the curls on the top of his head.

'Good,' he said. 'I will call you at six o'clock.'

'Six!' said Sarah. 'But little sleepyhead won't . . .'

'I'll be up,' said Danny. 'Leave me alone, Sarah.'

When Dino left, the girls tried to rib him about it, but it didn't work.

Somehow they felt uncomfortable. Everybody did.

Except Danny.

And when they arose next morning, he was gone. The dawn was still red in the sky.

That evening, Dino brought Danny home at eight o'clock. He was carrying him, and Danny was asleep. The big shepherd laid him onto the pile of rugs that was his bed, while the family looked on like strangers. Mother, unable to stop herself, shook Danny's head gently, and woke him.

'Did you have a nice time, darling?' she asked, strangely anxious.

Danny's eyes were dazed, but his smile was radiant.

'Yes,' he said. 'I want to go again tomorrow.'

He fell asleep again immediately, and Dino sat down at the rough wood table to chat. Mother seemed absurdly curious to know what they had done all day. The Greek smiled slowly.

'We followed the sheep,' he said. 'We talked. It was like old times.'

Long into the night, Sarah and Vicky heard their parents talking in the room next door. Quietly but anxiously. The girls could not understand what they were worried about.

'If the daft little twit wants to sit on a rock all day and listen to stories, that's his lookout,' said Sarah. 'At least it keeps him out of *our* hair, doesn't it?'

'I wonder what he meant,' mused Vicky. 'It was like old times?'

'Oh shut up, Vick,' said Sarah. 'You're as bad as mum and dad you are. There's no mystery. They just like each other, that's all. Old Dino likes our baby brother. I can't *imagine* why!'

'His son was seven,' said Vicky. 'I wonder if that's what he meant. The one that died.'

'You could always ask him, Nosy,' replied her sister. 'Now shut up, will you? I'm asleep.'

Next day, although he woke up early, Danny was surprised to find his mother already in the kitchen. She told him that he was not going out with Dino that day, that she and his father had discussed it and decided on a family outing to the beach. Danny grinned and shrugged.

'All right,' he said. 'Great.'

Mum felt a complete idiot. She'd expected tears, or fury, or a fight. Why? She blushed.

'You can go with Dino some other day, of course,' she said. 'How will that do?'

'Yeah,' said Danny. 'Let's dig the girls out shall we? We can get to Tsilivi earlier than *anybody* else! You wake Dad up!'

The change was subtle, but complete. Within six days the girls were rattled, father was looking strained, and mum was getting desperate. Something was wrong, something terrible was happening. But what? And why? And how? There was nothing to catch hold of, nothing visible. But something awful was taking place. Something dreadful was being done.

It was noticeable, although not obvious, by the end of the day at Tsilivi. Danny, during the morning, had been his usual delirious self at the seaside. He'd played ball with the Greek children, he'd swum through the surf for hours on the Lilo, he'd explored the rocky pools at the headlands, he'd eaten ice-cream and drunk coke. But during the afternoon, he became listless, bored. Dad, swimming along the shore, had come across him on the Lilo, just floating, not moving a muscle, lying on his back with his eyes open, staring at the sky. And he had spoken to him—from the side of the air bed—three times before Danny had replied.

That evening, Dino turned up, and chatted and enchanted them as before. He brought wine and fresh local cheese, and a small gift for the girls and Danny—lovely little wooden figures that he had carved himself. At the end of the evening he asked if Danny could go with him next day, to tend the sheep, and Danny bubbled over with excitement.

What could his parents say? Dino was warm, and smiling, and friendly and they'd had a superb evening because of him. They said yes, of course. But don't keep him out so late this time, Dino, please. It did not suit him.

'No,' said Dino. 'Home by six o'clock. For the English tea!'

Everybody laughed. But in bed, even Sarah was uneasy. When Vicky raised the subject, she almost bit her head off. . . .

On his return the next evening, Danny was too sleepy, much too sleepy, for 'the English tea'. Dino, as before, put him to bed. This time he kissed him on the cheek and spoke to him, quietly, in Greek. Danny smiled, and answered. He was also speaking Greek. But when Sarah squeaked, and remarked on this phenomenon, Dino did not smile. He looked at her quite coldly. He stayed only a few minutes more, then left. He did not ask if Danny could accompany him tomorrow.

Three days later the first really frightening thing occurred. Danny almost drowned. And if it had not been so ridiculous, the family might have admitted to themselves that it seemed in a horrible way inevitable. Even . . . deliberate.

It happened at the rocky beach near Volimes. They had gone there because up to now it had been their favourite. Especially Danny's. They had snorkels and flippers, and the beach was so isolated that they always swum in the nude, the lot of them. There was a tiny cafe there, a tumbledown house among the rocks, owned by an old lady who served only eggs fried in deep olive oil and warm beer in dirty glasses. The road down was ridiculous, a dusty rutted track so steep that mother had to sit on the bonnet of the Pony going back up to give the front-wheel drive some weight to grip with. Nobody else went there at all. They'd never seen a soul.

They went there this time because it was Danny's favourite place, where he'd once even seen a small octopus lurking in the rocks. They hoped desperately it might interest him, might take his mind off the night before. Might make him behave like part of them again, like the happy, normal little boy they knew and—even Sarah would admit it now—loved.

They had had a row the evening before, in which Danny had behaved in a way that had shocked and frightened them. It had started, inevitably, with Dino. He had spent the evening with the family, and it had been disastrous. Mother, by now, could hardly talk to him without trembling, and father seemed on the point of anger all the time. The girls, polite and lost, still listened to his stories, but they were most uncomfortable, almost afraid. Dino was not talking to them any more. Or to their parents. He was talking to Danny. The two of them were in a world enclosed, they were alone in the company, they were a pair who deliberately shut the others out.

When Dino had gone, and Danny was lying in his bed, he announced that he was going to the hills again tomorrow.

'Who says?' snapped father. 'I don't recall hearing that arranged.'

'I arranged it,' said Danny. 'With Dino. With my *patera*.'

Although the girls did not understand it, this seemed to be a key word. Father's tanned face became abruptly pale, and mother let out a squawk. Within seconds there was bellowing, Danny was out of bed and scratching and biting at his parents, and Vicky was in tears. It was horrible and unsettling, and the upshot was that Danny was made to sleep in with his parents because he refused to say that he would not slip out of the house before dawn. Before they passed into unhappy and exhausted sleep, Sarah got Vicky to look up the word in her Greek dictionary. It meant father.

Danny almost drowned after he paddled the Lilo off among the rocks all by himself. He was pale and sick-looking this morning, but he—like the rest of the family—chose to ignore last night, chose to pretend that nothing had happened. When asked where he was going on the Lilo, he said, 'To look for that octopus again'. His father, smiling a strained smile, said, 'Fine. Make sure he doesn't have you for his breakfast!'

And fifteen minutes later, quite by accident, totally by luck, Sarah and Vicky happened to be standing on a high rock, and they saw their brother underwater—drowning.

He did not have his face mask on, nor his flippers. He was about two metres under, and he was on his back, with his eyes open; and his mouth. A small, naked boy with blonde hair streaming in the blue water, drifting slowly downwards into the deep, dark shadows among the jagged rocks. Through the distortion of the water he appeared to be looking at his sisters on the rock. He appeared to be smiling.

There was more than fear in the screams of Vicky and Sarah. There was a certain kind of horror. When they got back to the house, the cicadas were almost silent. Then, suddenly, they produced a raucous, blastingly loud burst of rhythmic noise. The laughter. It was terribly like laughter. Vicky cried uncontrollably for ten minutes before Dad could calm her down.

It was mother, a brilliant swimmer, who rescued Danny and gave him mouth-to-mouth, and it was mother, a rock once her mind was made up, who got them off the island the very next day, who cut short the holiday, and cut their losses, and booked them a flight to anywhere and damn the expense. She did not tell her husband until she had done it, and she did not tell the children at all. When they returned from the rocky beach, and Danny had been put to bed, she took the Pony and drove to the town. The girls half guessed what she had done, though, and they were glad. They were almost overwhelmed.

Danny was asleep all day, and watched all night. But he did get out, at about three in the morning, when Dad must have nodded off for a time. This time there was no pretending. The girls were woken up and made to search. The four of them, with torches, made towards the knoll above the olive groves where Danny often sat with Dino. They searched with silent determination, and moved fast and fiercely through the sparse, dry, grass. Vicky found her brother, not hiding, but sitting beside a rock, looking at the stars. He was crying, very quietly, and he allowed himself to be led by the hand back to his bed. He would not let his father carry him, or anybody else.

But he had to be carried onto the plane next day. He collapsed at lunchtime when the plan to fly out from Zakinthos was revealed to him. He turned so white, and breathed so shallowly, that he looked dead. The officials at the airport were anxious, thinking he might have some illness. There was still the typhoid scare, they pointed out. The typhoid scare? The family were bemused. It all seemed light years away. They smiled unhappily, and explained. No, not an illness. Their little boy was . . . well, he was not ill, at least.

As they stared through the small square window of the plane, Sarah and Vicky thought they spotted Dino. There was a tall, gaunt figure at the wire fence, in blue and brown. But it was too far to tell, really; much too far. He had a small child with him, a little boy, in shorts and tee shirt, with shining hair. So it could not be Dino, could it? As the jet accelerated, a haze of heat from the engines blotted out the figures.

About two months later, the family received a letter from Zakinthos, from Nikos. It was a long letter, full of news, and regret at their so-sudden parting, which they had half explained in a note. It ended with a peculiar piece of news. Dino the shepherd was dead. He had drowned himself in a lonely, rocky bay near Volimes.

Mother, who was reading the letter aloud, stopped. She looked at her husband, and at Sarah and Vicky. There was silence for some while. Then mother continued to read.

'. . . the most odd is, the old woman who saw him jump into the sea, said there was a child with him, a little boy. She said she even saw him in the water, drifting down and drowning. She insists.'

Mother's voice had almost died away. It was hardly audible.

'But she was wrong, of course. Dino, as you know, had lost his son. And there was no other body found, except for Dino's. It was odd, though, wasn't it? Drifting down, she said, with his hair trailing out like grass. And smiling. She insisted . . .'

After a crushing silence, mother said, 'Ought we to tell Danny, do you think? When we visit on Thursday?'

Sarah and Vicky said nothing. Father sighed.

'I don't know,' he said. 'Will it help, do you think? To know that Dino and . . . to know that Dino's dead? Will it help?'

In the quiet, Vicky spoke loudly. A smile was growing on her face, as if the strain of weeks was being smoothed away. It was a wonderful, shining smile. Her voice was shaky with excitement.

'The cicadas,' she said. 'In my head. They've gone. I can't hear them any more. Oh Mum! Oh Dad! I can't hear them any more!'

Sarah knew what she meant, even if her parents did not. Vicky had not wanted to burden them with her small troubles, this constant laughter in her brain. Sarah smiled.

'Don't worry, Mum,' said Sarah. 'She's not gone mad. Look—let's see Dan tomorrow, can we? Let's not wait till Thursday?'

The girls' elation was infectious. There was a stirring in all four of them. A heady, crazy feeling. Of hope.

'Yes,' said father. 'Why not?'

'Oh Danny,' said Mum. 'My poor lost boy.'

'We're going to find him, Mum,' said Vicky. 'Tomorrow.'

The laughter had gone.

THE SAILOR-BOY'S TALE
Karen Blixen

The barque *Charlotte* was on her way from Marseille to Athens, in grey weather, on a high sea, after three days' heavy gale. A small sailor-boy, named Simon, stood on the wet, swinging deck, held on to a shroud, and looked up towards the drifting clouds, and to the upper top-gallant yard of the main-mast.

A bird, that had sought refuge upon the mast, had got her feet entangled in some loose tackle-yard of the halliard, and, high up there, struggled to get free. The boy on the deck could see her wings flapping and her head turning from side to side.

Through his own experience of life he had come to the conviction that in this world everyone must look after himself, and expect no help from others. But the mute, deadly fight kept him fascinated for more than an hour. He wondered what kind of bird it would be. These last days a number of birds had come to settle in the barque's rigging: swallows, quails, and a pair of peregrine falcons; he believed that this bird was a peregrine falcon. He remembered how, many years ago, in his own country and near his home, he had once seen a peregrine falcon quite close, sitting on a stone and flying straight up from it. Perhaps this was the same bird. He thought: 'That bird is like me. Then she was there, and now she is here.'

At that a fellow-feeling rose in him, a sense of common tragedy; he stood looking at the bird with his heart in his mouth. There were none of the sailors about to make fun of him; he began to think out how he might go up by the shrouds to help the falcon out. He brushed his hair back and pulled up his sleeves, gave the deck round him a great glance, and climbed up. He had to stop a couple of times in the swaying rigging.

It was indeed, he found when he got to the top of the mast, a peregrine falcon. As his head was on a level with hers, she gave up her struggle, and looked at him with a pair of angry, desperate, yellow eyes. He had to take hold of her with one hand while he got his knife out, and cut off the tackle-yarn. He was scared as he looked down, but at the same time he felt that he had been ordered up by nobody, but that this was his own venture, and this gave him a proud, steadying sensation, as if the sea and the sky, the ship, the bird and himself were all one. Just as he had freed the falcon, she hacked him in the thumb, so that the blood ran, and he nearly let her go. He grew angry with her, and gave her a clout on the head, then he put her inside his jacket and climbed down again.

When he reached the deck the mate and the cook were standing there, looking up; they roared to him to ask what he had had to do in the mast. He was so tired that the tears were in his eyes. He took the falcon out and showed her to them, and she kept still within his hands. They laughed and walked off. Simon set the falcon down, stood back and watched her. After a while he reflected that she might not be able to get up from the slippery deck, so he caught her once more, walked away with her and placed her upon a bolt of canvas. A little after she began to trim her feathers, made two or three sharp jerks forward, and then suddenly flew off. The boy could follow her flight above the troughs of the grey sea. He thought: 'There flies my falcon.'

When the *Charlotte* came home, Simon signed aboard another ship, and two years later he was a light hand on the schooner *Hebe* lying at Bodø, high up the coast of Norway, to buy herrings.

To the great herring-markets of Bodø ships came together from all corners of the world; here were Swedish, Finnish and Russian boats, a forest of masts, and on shore a turbulent, irregular display of life, with many languages spoken, and mighty fights. On the shore booths had been set up, and the Lapps, small yellow people, noiseless in their movements, with watchful eyes, whom Simon had never seen before,

239

came down to sell bead-embroidered leather-goods. It was April, the sky and the sea were so clear that it was difficult to hold one's eyes up against them – salt, infinitely wide, and filled with bird-shrieks – as if someone were incessantly whetting invisible knives, on all sides, high up in heaven.

Simon was amazed at the lightness of these April evenings. He knew no geography, and did not assign it to the latitude, but he took it as a sign of an unwonted good-will in the Universe, a favour. Simon had been small for his age all his life, but this last winter he had grown, and had become strong of limb. That good luck, he felt, must spring from the very same source as the sweetness of the weather, from a new benevolence in the world. He had been in need of such encouragement, for he was timid by nature; now he asked for no more. The rest he felt to be his own affair. He went about slowly, and proudly.

One evening he was ashore with land-leave, and walked up to the booth of a small Russian trader, a Jew who sold gold watches. All the sailors knew that his watches were made from bad metal, and would not go, still they bought them, and paraded them about. Simon looked at these watches for a long time, but did not buy. The old Jew had diverse goods in his shop, and amongst others a case of oranges. Simon had tasted oranges on his journeys; he bought one and took it with him. He meant to go up on a hill, from where he could see the sea, and suck it there.

As he walked on, and had got to the outskirts of the place, he saw a little girl in a blue frock, standing at the other side of a fence and looking at him. She was thirteen or fourteen years old, as slim as an eel, but with a round, clear, freckled face, and a pair of long plaits. The two looked at one another.

'Who are you looking out for?' Simon asked, to say something. The girl's face broke into an ecstatic, presumptuous smile. 'For the man I am going to marry, of course,' she said. Something in her countenance made the boy confident and happy; he grinned a little at her. 'That will perhaps be me,' he said. 'Ha, ha,' said the girl, 'he is a few years older than you, I can tell you.' 'Why,' said Simon, 'you are not grown up yourself.' The little girl shook her head solemly. 'Nay,' she said, 'but when I grow up I will be exceedingly beautiful, and wear brown shoes with heels, and a hat.' 'Will you have an orange?' asked Simon, who could give her none of

240

the things she had named. She looked at the orange and at him. 'They are very good to eat,' said he. 'Why do you not eat it yourself then?' she asked. 'I have eaten so many already,' said he, 'when I was in Athens. Here I had to pay a mark for it.' 'What is your name?' asked she. 'My name is Simon,' said he. 'What is yours?' 'Nora,' said the girl. 'What do you want for your orange now, Simon?'

When he heard his name in her mouth, Simon grew bold. 'Will you give me a kiss for the orange?' he asked. Nora looked at him gravely for a moment. 'Yes,' she said, 'I should not mind giving you a kiss.' He grew as warm as if he had been running quickly. When she stretched out her hand for the orange he took hold of it. At that moment somebody in the house called out for her. 'That is my father,' said she, and tried to give him back the orange, but he would not take it. 'Then come again tomorrow,' she said quickly, 'then I will give you a kiss.' At that she slipped off. He stood and looked after her, and a little later went back to his ship.

Simon was not in the habit of making plans for the future, and now he did not know whether he would be going back to her or not.

The following evening he had to stay aboard, as the other sailors were going ashore, and he did not mind that either. He meant to sit on the deck with the ship's dog, Balthasar, and to practise upon a concertina that he had purchased some time ago. The pale evening was all round him, the sky was faintly roseate, the sea was quite calm, like milk-and-water, only in the wake of the boats going inshore it broke into streaks of vivid indigo. Simon sat and played; after a while his own music began to speak to him so strongly that he stopped, got up and looked upwards. Then he saw that the full moon was sitting high on the sky.

The sky was so light that she hardly seemed needed there; it was as if she had turned up by a caprice of her own. She was round, demure and presumptuous. At that he knew that he must go ashore, whatever it was to cost him. But he did not know how to get away, since the others had taken the yawl with them. He stood on the deck for a long time, a small lonely figure of a sailor-boy on a boat, when he caught sight of a yawl coming in from a ship farther out, and hailed her. He found that it was the Russian crew from a boat named *Anna* going ashore. When he could make himself understood to them, they took him with them; they first asked him for money for his fare, then, laughingly, gave it back to him. He thought: 'These people will be believing that I am going in to town, wenching.' And then he felt, with some pride, that they were right, although at the same time they were infinitely wrong, and knew nothing about anything.

When they came ashore they invited him to come in and drink in their company, and he would not refuse, because they had helped him. One of the Russians was a giant, as big as a bear; he told Simon that his name was Ivan. He got drunk at once, and then fell upon the boy with a bear-like affection, pawed him, smiled and laughed into his face, made him a present of a gold watch chain, and then kissed him on both cheeks. At that Simon reflected that he also ought to give Nora a present when they met again, and as soon as he could get away from the Russians he walked up to a booth that he knew of, and bought a small blue silk handkerchief, the same colour as her eyes.

It was Saturday evening, and there were many people amongst the houses; they came in long rows, some of them singing, all keen to have some fun that night. Simon, in the midst of this rich, bawling life under the clear moon, felt his head light with the flight from the ship and the strong drinks. He crammed the handkerchief in his pocket; it was silk which he had never touched before, a present for his girl.

He could not remember the path up to Nora's house, lost his way, and came back to where he had started. Then he grew deadly afraid that he should be too late, and began to run. In a small passage between two wooden huts he ran straight into a big man, and found that it was Ivan once more. The Russian folded his arms round him and held him. 'Good! Good!' he cried in high glee, 'I have found you my little chicken. I have looked for you everywhere, and poor Ivan has wept because he lost his friend.' 'Let me go, Ivan,' cried Simon. 'Oho,' said Ivan, 'I shall go with you and get what you want. My heart and my money are all yours, all yours; I have been seventeen years old myself, a little lamb of God, and I want to be so again tonight.' 'Let me go,' cried Simon, 'I am in a hurry.' Ivan held him so that it hurt, and patted him with his other hand. 'I feel it, I feel it,' he said. 'Now trust to me, my little friend. Nothing shall part you and me. I hear the others coming; we will have such a night together as you will remember when you are an old grandpapa.'

Suddenly he crushed the boy to him, like a bear that carries off a sheep. He thought of Nora waiting, like a slender ship in the dim air, and of himself, here, in the hot embrace of a hairy animal. He struck Ivan with

242

He drove the knife into the big man's arm

all his might. 'I shall kill you, Ivan,' he cried out, 'if you do not let me go.' 'Oh, you will be thankful to me later on,' said Ivan, and began to sing. Simon fumbled in his pocket for his knife, and got it opened. He could not lift his hand, but he drove the knife, furiously, in under the big man's arm. Almost immediately he felt the blood spouting out, and running down in his sleeve. Ivan stopped short in the song, let go his hold of the boy and gave two long deep grunts. The next second he tumbled down on his knees. 'Poor Ivan, poor Ivan,' he groaned. He fell straight on his face. At that moment Simon heard the other sailors coming along, singing, in the by-street.

He stood still for a minute, wiped his knife, and watched the blood spread into a dark pool underneath the big body. Then he ran. As he stopped for a second to choose his way, he heard the sailors behind him scream out over their dead comrade. He thought: 'I must get down to the sea, where I can wash my hand.' But at the same time he ran the other way. After a little while he found himself on the path that he had walked on the day before, and it seemed as familiar to him as if he had walked it many hundred times in his life.

He slackened his pace to look round, and suddenly saw Nora standing on the other side of the fence; she was quite close to him when he caught sight of her in the moonlight. Wavering and out of breath he sank down on his knees. For a moment he could not speak. The little girl looked down at him. 'Good evening, Simon,' she said in her small coy voice. 'I have waited for you a long time,' and after a moment she added: 'I have eaten your orange.'

'Oh, Nora,' cried the boy. 'I have killed a man.' She stared at him, but did not move. 'Why did you kill a man?' she asked after a moment. 'To get here,' said Simon. 'Because he tried to stop me. But he was my friend.' Slowly he got on to his feet. 'He loved me!' the boy cried out, and at that burst into tears. 'Yes,' said she slowly and thoughtfully. 'Yes, because you must be here on time.' 'Can you hide me?' he asked. 'For they are after me.'

'Nay,' said Nora, 'I cannot hide you. For my father is the parson here at Bodø, and he would be sure to hand you over to them, if he knew that you had killed a man.' 'Then,' said Simon, 'give me something to wipe my hands on.' 'What is the matter with your hands?' she asked and took a little step forward. He stretched out his hands to her. 'Is that your own blood?' she asked. 'No,' said he, 'it is his.' She took the step back again. 'Do you hate me now?' he asked. 'No, I do not hate you,' said she. 'But do put your hands at your back.'

As he did so she came up close to him, at the other side of the fence, and clasped her arms around his neck. She pressed her young body to his, and kissed him tenderly. He felt her face, cool as the moonlight, upon his own, and when she released him, his head swam, and he did not know if the kiss had lasted a second or an hour. Nora stood up straight, her eyes wide open. 'Now,' she said slowly and proudly, 'I promise you that I will never marry anybody, as long as I live.' The boy kept standing with his hands at his back, as if she had tied them there. 'And now,' she said, 'you must run, for they are coming.' They looked at one another. 'Do not forget Nora,' said she. He turned and ran.

He leaped over a fence, and when he was down amongst the houses he walked. He did not know at all where to go. As he came to a house, from where music and noise streamed out, he slowly went through the door. The room was full of people; they were dancing in here. A lamp hung from the ceiling, and shone down on them; the air was thick and brown with the dust rising from the floor. There were some women in the room, but many of the men danced with each other, and gravely or laughingly stamped the floor. A moment after Simon had come in the crowd withdrew to the walls to clear the floor for two sailors, who were showing a dance from their own country.

Simon thought: 'Now, very soon, the men from the boat will come round to look for their comrade's murderer, and from my hands they will know that I have done it.' These five minutes during which he stood by the wall of the dancing-room, in the midst of the gay, sweating dancers, were of great significance to the boy. He himself felt it, as if during this time he grew up, and became like other people. He did not entreat his destiny, nor complain. Here he was, he had killed a man, and had kissed a girl. He did not demand any more from life, nor did life now demand more from him. He was Simon, a man like the men round him, and going to die, as all men are going to die.

He only became aware of what was going on outside him, when he saw that a woman had come in, and was standing in the midst of the cleared floor, looking round her. She was a short, broad old woman, in the clothes of the Lapps, and she took her stand with such majesty and

245

fierceness, as if she owned the whole place. It was obvious that most of the people knew her, and were a little afraid of her, although a few laughed; the din of the dancing-room stopped when she spoke.

'Where is my son?' she asked in a high shrill voice, like a bird's. The next moment her eyes fell on Simon himself, and she steered through the crowd, which opened up before her, stretched out her old skinny, dark hand, and took him by the elbow. 'Come home with me now,' she said. 'You need not dance here tonight. You may be dancing a high enough dance soon.'

Simon drew back, for he thought that she was drunk. But as she looked him straight in the face with her yellow eyes, it seemed to him that he had met her before, and that he might do well in listening to her. The old woman pulled him with her across the floor, and he followed her without a word. 'Do not birch your boy too badly, Sunniva, one of the men in the room cried to her. 'He has done no harm, he only wanted to look at the dance.'

At the same moment as they came out through the door, there was an alarm in the street, a flock of people came running down it, and one of them, as he turned into the house, knocked against Simon, looked at him and the old woman, and ran on.

While the two walked along the street, the old woman lifted up her skirt, and put the hem of it into the boy's hand. 'Wipe your hand on my skirt,' she said. They had not gone far before they came to a small wooden house, and stopped; the door to it was so low that they must bend to get through it. As the Lapp woman went in before Simon, still holding on to his arm, the boy looked up for a moment. The night had grown misty; there was a wide ring round the moon.

The old woman's room was narrow and dark, with but one small window to it; a lantern stood on the floor and lighted it up dimly. It was all filled with reindeer skins and wolf skins, and with reindeer horn, such as the Lapps use to make their carved buttons and knife-handles, and the air in here was rank and stifling. As soon as they were in, the woman turned to Simon, took hold of his head, and with her crooked fingers parted his hair and combed it down in Lapp fashion. She clapped a Lapp cap on him and stood back to glance at him. 'Sit down on my stool, now,' she said. 'But first take out your knife.' She was so commanding in voice and manner that the boy could not but choose to do as she told him; he sat

246

down on the stool, and he could not take his eyes off her face, which was flat and brown, and as if smeared with dirt in its net of fine wrinkles. As he sat there he heard many people come along outside, and stop by the house; then someone knocked at the door, waited a moment and knocked again. The old woman stood and listened, as still as a mouse.

'Nay,' said the boy and got up. 'This is no good, for it is me that they are after. It will be better for you to let me go out to them.' 'Give me your knife,' said she. When he handed it to her, she stuck it straight into her thumb, so that the blood spouted out, and she let it drip all over her skirt. 'Come in, then,' she cried.

The door opened, and two of the Russian sailors came and stood in the opening; there were more people outside. 'Has anybody come in here?' they asked. 'We are after a man who has killed our mate, but he has run away from us. Have you seen or heard anybody this way?' The old Lapp woman turned upon them, and her eyes shone like gold in the lamplight. 'Have I seen or heard anyone?' she cried, 'I have heard you shriek murder all over the town. You frightened me, and my poor silly boy there, so that I cut my thumb as I was ripping the skin-rug that I sew. The boy is too scared to help me, and the rug is all ruined. I shall make you pay me for that. If you are looking for a murderer, come in and search my house for me, and I shall know you when we meet again.' She was so furious that she danced where she stood, and jerked her head like an angry bird of prey.

The Russian came in, looked round the room, and at her and her blood-stained hand and skirt. 'Do not put a curse on us now, Sunniva,' he said timidly. 'We know that you can do many things when you like. Here is a mark to pay you for the blood you have spilled.' She stretched out her hand, and he placed a piece of money in it. She spat on it. 'Then go, and there shall be no bad blood between us,' said Sunniva, and shut the door after them. She stuck her thumb in her mouth, and chuckled a little.

The boy got up from his stool, stood straight up before her and stared into her face. He felt as if he were swaying high up in the air, with but a small hold. 'Why have you helped me?' he asked her. 'Do you not know?' she answered. 'Have you not recognised me yet? But you will remember the peregrine falcon which was caught in the tackle-yarn of your boat, the *Charlotte*, as she sailed in the Mediterranean. That day you climbed up by the shrouds of the top-gallant mast to help her out, in a stiff wind, and

247

with a high sea. That falcon was me. We Lapps often fly in such a manner, to see the world. When I first met you I was on my way to Africa, to see my younger sister and her children. She is a falcon too, when she chooses. By that time she was living at Takaunga, within an old ruined tower, which down there they call a minaret.' She swathed a corner of her skirt round her thumb, and bit at it. 'We do not forget,' she said. 'I hacked your thumb, when you took hold of me; it is only fair that I should cut my thumb for you tonight.'

She came close to him, and gently rubbed her two brown, claw-like fingers against his forehead. 'So you are a boy,' she said, 'who will kill a man rather than be late to meet your sweetheart? We hold together, the females of this earth. I shall mark your forehead now, so that the girls will know of that, when they look at you, and they will like you for it.' She played with the boy's hair, and twisted it round her finger.

'Listen now, my little bird,' said she. 'My great-grandson's brother-in-law is lying with his boat by the landing-place at this moment; he is to take a consignment of skins out to a Danish boat. He will bring you back to your boat, in time, before your mate comes. The *Hebe* is sailing tomorrow morning, is it not so? But when you are aboard give him back my cap for me.' She took up his knife, wiped it in her skirt and handed it to him. 'Here is your knife,' she said. 'You will stick it into no more men; you will not need to, for from now you will sail the seas like a faithful seaman. We have enough trouble with our sons as it is.'

The bewildered boy began to stammer his thanks to her. 'Wait,' said she, 'I shall make you a cup of coffee, to bring back your wits, while I wash your jacket.' She went and rattled an old copper kettle upon the fireplace. After a while she handed him a hot, strong, black drink in a cup without a handle to it. 'You have drunk with Sunniva now,' she said; 'you have drunk down a little wisdom, so that in the future all your thoughts shall not fall like raindrops into the salt sea.'

When he had finished and set down the cup, she led him to the door and opened it for him. He was surprised to see that it was almost clear morning. The house was so high up that the boy could see the sea from it, and a milky mist about it. He gave her his hand to say goodbye.

She stared into his face. 'We do not forget,' she said. 'And you, you knocked me on the head there, high up in the mast. I shall give you that blow back.' With that she smacked him on the ear as hard as she could, so that his head swam. 'Now we are quits,' she said, gave him a great, mischievous, shining glance, and a little push down the doorstep, and nodded to him.

In this way the sailor-boy got back to his ship, which was to sail the next morning, and lived to tell the story.

JULIA CAHILL'S CURSE
George Moore

'And what has become of Margaret?'

'Ah, didn't her mother send her to America as soon as the baby was born? Once a woman is wake here she has to go. Hadn't Julia to go in the end, and she the only one that ever said she didn't mind the priest?'

'Julia who?' said I.

'Julia Cahill.'

The name struck my fancy, and I asked the driver to tell me her story.

'Wasn't it Father Madden who had her put out of the parish, but she put her curse on it, and it's on it to this day.'

'Do you believe in curses?'

'Bedad I do, sir. It's a terrible thing to put a curse on a man, and the curse that Julia put on Father Madden's parish was a bad one, the divil a worse. The sun was up at the time, and she on the hilltop raising both her hands. And the curse she put on the parish was that every year a roof must fall in and a family go to America. That was the curse, your honour, and every word of it has come true. You'll see for yourself as soon as we cross the mearing.'

'And what has become of Julia's baby?'

'I never heard she had one, sir.'

He flicked his horse pensively with his whip, and it seemed to me that

250

the disbelief I had expressed in the power of the curse disinclined him for further conversation.

'But,' I said, 'who is Julia Cahill, and how did she get the power to put a curse upon the village'

'Didn't she go into the mountains every night to meet the fairies, and who else could've given her the power to put a curse upon the village?'

'But she couldn't walk so far in one evening.'

'Them that's in league with the fairies can walk that far and much farther in an evening, your honour. A shepherd saw her; and you'll see the ruins of the cabins for yourself as soon as we cross the mearing, and I'll show you the cabin of the blind woman that Julia lived with before she went away.'

'And how long is it since she went?'

'About twenty year, and there hasn't been a girl the like of her in these parts since. I was only a gossoon at the time, but I've heard tell she was as tall as I'm myself, and as straight as a poplar. She walked with a little swing in her walk, so that all the boys used to be looking after her, and she had fine black eyes, sir, and she was nearly always laughing. Father Madden had just come to the parish; and there was courting in these parts then, for aren't we the same as other people – we'd like to go out with a girl well enough if it was the custom of the country. Father Madden put down the ball alley because he said the boys stayed there instead of going into Mass, and he put down the cross-road dances because he said dancing was the cause of many a sorrow, and he wanted none in his parish. Now there was no dancer like Julia; the boys used to gather about to see her dance, and whoever walked with her under the hedges in the summer could never think about another woman. The village was cracked about her. There was fighting, so I suppose the priest was right: he had to get rid of her. But I think he mightn't have been as hard on her as he was.

'One evening he went down to the house. Julia's people were well-to-do people, they kept a grocery-store in the village; and when he came into the shop who should be there but the richest farmer in the country, Michael Moran by name, trying to get Julia for his wife. He didn't go straight to Julia, and that's what swept him. There are two counters in that shop, and Julia was at the one on the left hand as you go in. And many's the pound she had made for her parents at that counter.

Michael Moran says to the father, "Now, what fortune are you going to give with Julia?" And the father says there was many a man who would take her without any; and that's how they spoke, and Julia listening quietly all the while at the opposite counter. For Michael didn't know what a spirited girl she was, but went on arguing until he got the father to say fifty pounds, and thinking he had got him so far he said, "I'll never drop a flap to her unless you give the two heifers." Julia never said a word, she just sat listening. It was then that the priest came in. And over he goes to Julia. "And now," says he, "aren't you proud to hear that you'll have such a fine fortune, and it's I that'll be glad to see you married, for I can't have any more of your goings-on in my parish. You're the encouragement of the dancing and courting here, but I'm going to put an end to it." Julia didn't answer a word, and he went over to them that were arguing about the sixty pounds. "Now, why not make it fifty-five?" says he. So the father agreed to that, since the priest had said it, and all three of them thought the marriage was settled. "Now what will you be taking, Father Tom?" says Cahill, "and you, Michael?" Sorra one of them thought of asking her if she was pleased with Michael; but little did they know what was passing in her mind, and when they came over to the counter to tell her what they had settled, she said, "Well, I've just been listening to you, and 'tis well for you to be wasting your time talking about me," and she tossed her head, saying she would just pick the boy out of the parish that pleased her best. And what angered the priest most of all was her way of saying it – that the boy that would marry her would be marrying herself and not the money that would be paid when the book was signed or when the first baby was born. Now it was agin girls marrying according to their fancy that Father Madden had set himself. He had said in his sermon the Sunday before that young people shouldn't be allowed out by themselves at all, but that the parents should make up the marriages for them. And he went fairly wild when Julia told him the example she was going to set. He tried to keep his temper, sir, but it was getting the better of him all the while. And Julia said, "My boy isn't in the parish now, but maybe he is on his way here, and he may be here tomorrow or the next day." And when Julia's father heard her speak like that he knew that no one would turn her from what she was saying, and he said, "Michael Moran, my good man, you may go your way: you will never get her." Then he went back to hear what Julia was saying to the priest, but it was the priest that was talking. "Do you think," says he, "I am going to let you go on turning the head of every boy in the parish? Do you think," says he, "I'm going to see you gallivanting with one and then with the other? Do you think I am going to see fighting and quarreling for your like? Do you think I am going to hear stories like I heard last week about poor Patsy Carey, who has gone out of his mind, they say, on account of your treatment? No," says he, "I'll have no more of that. I'll have you out of my parish, or I'll have you married." Julia didn't answer the priest; she tossed her head, and went on making up parcels of tea and sugar, and getting the steps and taking down candles, though she didn't want them, just to show the priest that she didn't mind what he was saying. And all the while her father trembling, not knowing what would happen, for the priest had a big stick, and there was no saying that he wouldn't strike her. Cahill tried to quiet the priest, he promising him that Julia shouldn't go out any more in the evenings, and bedad, sir, she was out the same evening with a young man and the priest saw them, and the next evening she was out with another and the priest saw them, nor was she minded at the end of the month to marry any of them. Then the priest went down to the shop to speak to her a second time, and he went down again a third time, though what he said the third time no one knows, no one being there at the time. And next Sunday he spoke out, saying that a disobedient daughter would have the worst devil in hell to attend on her. I've heard tell that he called her the evil spirit that set men mad. But most of the people that were there are dead or gone to America, and no one rightly knows what he did say, only that the words came out of his mouth, and the people when they saw Julia crossed themselves, and even the boys that were the most mad after Julia were afraid to speak to her. Cahill had to put her out.'

'Do you mean to say that the father put his daughter out?'

'Sure, didn't the priest threaten to turn him into a rabbit if he didn't, and no one in the parish would speak to Julia, they were so afraid of Father Madden, and if it hadn't been for the blind woman that I was speaking about a while ago, sir, it is to the Poor House she'd have to go. The blind woman has a little cabin at the edge of the bog – I'll point it out to you, sir; we do be passing it by – and she was with the blind woman for nearly two years disowned by her own father. Her clothes wore out, but she was as beautiful without them as with them. The boys were told not

253

As the sun rose he saw her curse the village

to look back, but sure they couldn't help it.

'Ah, it was a long while before Father Madden could get shut of her. The blind woman said she wouldn't see Julia thrown out on the roadside, and she was as good as her word for well-nigh two years, until Julia went to America, so some do be saying, sir, whilst others do be saying she joined the fairies. But 'tis for sure, sir, that the day she left the parish Pat Quinn heard a knocking at his window and somebody asking if he would lend his cart to go to the railway station. Pat was a heavy sleeper and he didn't get up, and it is thought that it was Julia who wanted Pat's cart to take her to the station; it's a good ten mile; but she got there all the same!'

'You said something about a curse?'

'Yes, sir. You'll see the hill presently. And a man who was taking some sheep to the fair saw her there. The sun was just getting up and he saw her cursing the village, raising both her hands, sir, up to the sun, and since that curse was spoken every year a roof has fallen in, sometimes two or three.'

I could see he believed the story, and for the moment I, too, believed in an outcast Venus becoming the evil spirit of a village that would not accept her as divine.

'Look, sir, the woman coming down the road is Bridget Coyne. And that's her house,' he said, and we passed a house built of loose stone without mortar, but a little better than the mud cabins I had seen in Father MacTurnan's parish.

'And now, sir, you will see the loneliest parish in Ireland.'

And I noticed that though the land was good, there seemed to be few people on it, and, what was more significant, that the untilled fields were the ruins, for they were not the cold ruins of twenty, or thirty, or forty years ago when the people were evicted and their tillage turned into pasture – the ruins I saw were the ruins of cabins that had been lately abandoned, and I said:

'It wasn't the landlord who evicted the people.'

'Ah, it's the landlord who would be glad to have them back, but there's no getting them back. Every one here will have to go, and 'tis said that the priest will say Mass in an empty chapel, sorra a one will be there but Bridget, and she'll be the last he'll give communion to. It's said, your honour, that Julia has been seen in America, and I'm going there this autumn. You may be sure I'll keep a lookout for her.'

'But all this is twenty years ago. You won't know her. A woman changes a good deal in twenty years.'

'There will be no change in her, your honour. Sure, hasn't she been with the fairies?'

THE MUMMY'S FOOT
Théophile Gautier

I had entered, in an idle mood, the shop of one of those curiosity-venders, who are called *marchands de bric-à-brac* in that Parisian *argot* which is so perfectly unintelligible elsewhere in France.

You have doubtless glanced occasionally through the windows of some of these shops, which have become so numerous now that it is fashionable to buy antiquated furniture, and that every petty stockbroker thinks he must have his *chambre au moyen âge*.

There is one thing there which clings alike to the shop of the dealer in old iron, the wareroom of the tapestry-maker, the laboratory of the chemist, and the studio of the painter – in all those gloomy dens where a furtive daylight filters in through the window-shutters, the most manifestly ancient thing is dust; – the cobwebs are more authentic than the guimp laces; and the old pear-tree furniture on exhibition is actually younger than the mahogany which arrived but yesterday from America.

The warehouse of my *bric-à-brac* dealer was a veritable Capharnaum; all ages and all nations seemed to have made their rendezvous there; an Etruscan lamp of red clay stood upon a Boule cabinet, with ebony panels, brightly striped by lines of inlaid brass; a duchess of the court of Louis XV nonchalantly extended her fawn-like feet under a massive table of the time of Louis XIII with heavy spiral supports of oak, and carven designs of chimeras and foliage intermingled.

Upon the denticulated shelves of several sideboards glittered immense Japanese dishes with red and blue designs relieved by gilded hatching; side by side with enamelled works by Bernard Palissy, representing serpents, frogs, and lizards in relief.

From disembowelled cabinets escaped cascades of silver-lustrous Chinese silks and waves of tinsel, which an oblique sunbeam shot through with luminous beads; while portraits of every era, in frames more or less tarnished, smiled through their yellow varnish.

The striped breastplate of a damascened suit of Milanese armour glittered in one corner; Loves and Nymphs of porcelain; Chinese Grotesques, vases of *céladon* and crackle-ware; Saxon and old Sèvres cups encumbered the shelves and nooks of the apartment.

The dealer followed me closely through the tortuous way contrived between the piles of furniture; warding off with his hand the hazardous sweep of my coat-skirts; watching my elbows with the uneasy attention of an antiquarian and a usurer.

It was a singular face, that of the merchant – an immense skull, polished like a knee, and surrounded by a thin aureole of white hair, which brought out the clear salmon tint of his complexion all the more strikingly, lent him a false aspect of patriarchal *bonhomie*, counteracted, however, by the scintillation of two little yellow eyes which trembled in their orbits like two louis-d'or upon quicksilver. The curve of his nose presented an aquiline silhouette, which suggested the Oriental or Jewish type. His hands – thin, slender, full of nerves which projected like strings upon the finger-board of a violin, and armed with claws like those on the terminations of bats' wings – shook with senile trembling; but those convulsively agitated hands became firmer than steel pincers or lobsters' claws when they lifted any precious article – an onyx cup, a Venetian glass, or a dish of Bohemian crystal. This strange old man had an aspect so thoroughly rabbinical and cabalistic that he would have been burnt on the mere testimony of his face three centuries ago.

'Will you not buy something from me today, sir? Here is a Malay kreese with a blade undulating like flame: look at those grooves contrived for the blood to run along, those teeth set backwards so as to tear out the entrails in withdrawing the weapon – it is a fine character of ferocious arm, and will look well in your collection: this two-handed sword is very beautiful – it is the work of Josepe de la Hera; and this *colichemarde*, with its fenestrated guard – what a superb specimen of handicraft!'

'No; I have quite enough weapons and instruments of carnage – I want a small figure, something which will suit me as a paper-weight; for I cannot endure those trumpery bronzes which the stationers sell, and which may be found on everybody's desk.'

The old gnome foraged among his ancient wares, and finally arranged before me some antique bronzes – so-called, at least; fragments of malachite; little Hindoo or Chinese idols – a kind of poussah toys in jadestone, representing the incarnations of Brahma or Vishnoo, and wonderfully appropriate to the very undivine office of holding papers and letters in place.

I was hesitating between a porcelain dragon, all constellated with warts – its mouth formidable with bristling tusks and ranges of teeth – and an abominable little Mexican fetish, representing the god Zitziliputzili *au naturel*, when I caught sight of a charming foot, which I at first took for a fragment of some antique Venus.

It had those beautiful ruddy and tawny tints that lend to Florentine bronze that warm living look so much preferable to the gray-green aspect of common bronzes, which might easily be mistaken for statues in a state of putrefaction: satiny gleams played over its rounded forms, doubtless polished by the amorous kisses of twenty centuries; for it seemed a Corinthian bronze, a work of the best era of art – perhaps molded by Lysippus himself.

'That foot will be my choice,' I said to the merchant, who regarded me with an ironical and saturnine air, and held out the object desired that I might examine it more fully.

I was surprised at its lightness; it was not a foot of metal, but in sooth a foot of flesh – an embalmed foot – a mummy's foot: on examining it still more closely the very grain of the skin, and the almost imperceptible lines impressed upon it by the texture of the bandages, became perceptible. Those toes were slender and delicate, and terminated by perfectly formed nails, pure and transparent as agates; the great toe, slightly separated from the rest, afforded a happy contrast, in the antique style, to the position of the other toes, and lent it an aerial lightness – the grace of a bird's foot – the sole, scarcely streaked by a few almost imperceptible cross lines, afforded evidence that it had never touched the bare ground, and had only come in contact with the finest matting of Nile rushes, and the softest carpets of panther skin.

'Ha, ha! – you want the foot of the Princess Hermonthis,' – exclaimed the merchant, with a strange giggle, fixing his owlish eyes upon me – 'ha, ha, ha! – for a paper-weight! – an original idea! – artistic idea! Old Pharaoh would certainly have been surprised had someone told him that the foot of his adored daughter would be used for a paper-weight after he had had a mountain of granite hollowed out as a receptacle for the triple coffin, painted and gilded – covered with hieroglyphics and beautiful paintings of the Judgment of Souls,' – continued the queer little merchant, half audibly, as though talking to himself!

'How much will you charge me for this mummy fragment?'

'Ah, the highest price I can get; for it is a superb piece: if I had the match of it you could not have it for less than five hundred francs; – the daughter of a Pharaoh! nothing is more rare.'

'Assuredly that is not a common article; but, still, how much do you want? In the first place let me warn you that all my wealth consists of just five louis: I can buy anything that costs five louis, but nothing dearer – you might search my vest pockets and most secret drawers without even finding one poor five-franc piece more.'

'Five louis for the foot of the Princess Hermonthis! that is very little, very little indeed; 'tis an authentic foot,' muttered the merchant, shaking his head, and imparting a peculiar rotary motion to his eyes. 'Well, take it, and I will give you the bandages into the bargain,' he added, wrapping the foot in an ancient damask rag – 'very fine! real damask – Indian damask which has never been redyed; it is strong, and yet it is soft,' he mumbled, stroking the frayed tissue with his fingers, through the trade-acquired habit which moved him to praise even an object of so little value that he himself deemed it only worth the giving away.

He poured the gold coins into a sort of mediaeval alms-purse hanging at his belt, repeating:

'The foot of the Princess Hermonthis, to be used for a paper-weight!'

Then turning his phosphorescent eyes upon me, he exclaimed in a voice strident as the crying of a cat which has swallowed a fish-bone:

'Old Pharaoh will not be well pleased; he loved his daughter – the dear man!'

'You speak as if you were a contemporary of his: you are old enough, goodness knows! but you do not date back to the Pyramids of Egypt,' I answered, laughingly, from the threshold.

I went home, delighted with my acquisition.

With the idea of putting it to profitable use as soon as possible, I placed the foot of the divine Princess Hermonthis upon a heap of papers scribbled over with verses, in themselves an undecipherable mosaic work of erasures; articles freshly begun; letters forgotten, and posted in the table drawer instead of the letter-box – an error to which absent-minded people are peculiarly liable. The effect was charming, bizarre, and romantic.

Well satisfied with this embellishment, I went out with the gravity and pride becoming one who feels that he has the ineffable advantage over all the passers-by whom he elbows, of possessing a piece of the Princess Hermonthis, daughter of Pharaoh.

I looked upon all who did not possess, like myself, a paper-weight so authentically Egyptian, as very ridiculous people; and it seemed to me that the proper occupation of every sensible man should consist in the mere fact of having a mummy's foot upon his desk.

Happily I met some friends, whose presence distracted me in my infatuation with this new acquisition: I went to dinner with them; for I could not very well have dined with myself.

When I came back that evening, with my brain slightly confused by a few glasses of wine, a vague whiff of Oriental perfume delicately titillated my olfactory nerves: the heat of the room had warmed the natron, bitumen, and myrrh in which the *paraschistes*, who cut open the bodies of the dead, had bathed the corpse of the princess – it was a perfume at once sweet and penetrating – a perfume that four thousand years had not been able to dissipate.

The Dream of Egypt was Eternity: her odours have the solidity of granite, and endure as long.

I soon drank deeply from the black cup of sleep: for a few hours all remained opaque to me; Oblivion and Nothingness inundated me with their sombre waves.

Yet light gradually dawned upon the darkness of my mind; dreams commenced to touch me softly in their silent flight.

The eyes of my soul were opened; and I beheld my chamber as it actually was; I might have believed myself awake, but for a vague consciousness which assured me that I slept, and that something fantastic was about to take place.

The odour of the myrrh had augmented in intensity: and I felt a slight headache, which I very naturally attributed to several glasses of champagne that we had drunk to the unknown gods and our future fortunes.

I peered through my room with a feeling of expectation which I saw nothing to justify: every article of furniture was in its proper place; the lamp, softly shaded by its globe of ground crystal, burned upon its bracket; the water-color sketches shone under their Bohemian glass; the curtains hung down languidly; everything wore an aspect of tranquil slumber.

After a few moments, however, all this calm interior appeared to become disturbed; the woodwork cracked stealthily; the ash-covered log suddenly emitted a jet of blue flame; and the disks of the pateras seemed like great metallic eyes, watching, like myself, for the things which were about to happen.

My eyes accidentally fell upon the desk where I had placed the foot of the Princess·Hermonthis.

Instead of remaining quiet – as behooved a foot which had been embalmed for four thousand years – it commenced to act in a nervous manner; contracted itself, and leaped over the papers like a startled frog – one would have imagined that it had suddenly been brought into contact with a galvanic battery: I could distinctly hear the dry sound made by its little heel, hard as the hoof of a gazelle.

I became rather discontented with my acquisition, inasmuch as I wished my paper-weights to be of a sedentary disposition, and thought it very unnatural that feet should walk about without legs; and I commenced to experience a feeling closely akin to fear.

Suddenly I saw the folds of my bed-curtain stir; and heard a bumping sound, like that caused by some person hopping on one foot across the floor. I must confess I became alternately hot and cold; that I felt a strange wind chill my back; and that my suddenly rising hair caused my nightcap to execute a leap of several yards.

The bed-curtains opened and I beheld the strangest figure imaginable before me.

I beheld the strangest figure imaginable

It was a young girl of a very deep coffee-brown complexion, like the bayadère Amani, and possessing the purest Egyptian type of perfect beauty: her eyes were almond-shaped and oblique, with eyebrows so black that they seemed blue; her nose was exquisitely chiselled, almost Greek in its delicacy of outline; and she might indeed have been taken for a Corinthian statue of bronze, but for the prominence of her cheekbones and the slightly African fullness of her lips, which compelled one to recognise her as belonging beyond all doubt to the hieroglyphic race which dwelt upon the banks of the Nile.

Her arms, slender and spindle-shaped, like those of very young girls, were encircled by a peculiar kind of metal bands and bracelets of glass beads; her hair was all twisted into little cords; and she wore upon her bosom a little idol-figure of green paste, bearing a whip with seven lashes, which proved it to be an image of Isis: her brow was adorned with a shining plate of gold; and a few traces of paint relieved the coppery tint of her cheeks.

As for her costume, it was very odd indeed.

Fancy a *pagne* or skirt all formed of little strips of material bedizened with red and black hieroglyphics, stiffened with bitumen, and apparently belonging to a freshly unbandaged mummy.

In one of those sudden flights of thought so common in dreams I heard the hoarse falsetto of the *bric-à-brac* dealer, repeating like a monotonous refrain the phrase he had uttered in his shop with so enigmatical an intonation:

'Old Pharaoh will not be well pleased: he loved his daughter, the dear man!'

One strange circumstance, which was not at all calculated to restore my equanimity, was that the apparition had but one foot; the other was broken off at the ankle!

She approached the table where the foot was starting and fidgeting about more than ever, and there supported herself upon the edge of the desk. I saw her eyes fill with pearly-gleaming tears.

Although she had not as yet spoken, I fully comprehended the thoughts which agitated her: she looked at her foot – for it was indeed her own – with an exquisitely graceful expression of coquettish sadness; but the foot leaped and ran hither and thither, as though impelled on steel springs.

Twice or thrice she extended her hand to seize it, but could not succeed.

Then commenced between the Princess Hermonthis and her foot – which appeared to be endowed with a special life of its own – a very fantastic dialogue in a most ancient Coptic tongue, such as might have been spoken thirty centuries ago in the syrinxes of the land of Ser: luckily, I understood Coptic perfectly well that night.

The Princess Hermonthis cried, in a voice sweet and vibrant as the tones of a crystal bell:

'Well, my dear little foot, you always flee from me; yet I always took good care of you. I bathed you with perfumed water in a bowl of alabaster; I smoothed your heel with pumice-stone mixed with palm oil; your nails were cut with golden scissors and polished with a hippopotamus tooth; I was careful to select *tatbebs* for you, painted and embroidered and turned up at the toes, which were the envy of all the young girls in Egypt: you wore on your great toe rings bearing the device of the sacred Scarabaeus; and you supported one of the lightest bodies that a lazy foot could sustain.'

The foot replied, in a pouting and chagrined tone:

'You know well that I do not belong to myself any longer – I have been bought and paid for; the old merchant knew what he was about; he bore you a grudge for having refused to espouse him – this is an ill turn which he has done you. The Arab who violated your royal coffin in the subterranean pits of the necropolis of Thebes was sent thither by him: he desired to prevent you from being present at the reunion of the shadowy nations in the cities below. Have you five pieces of gold for my ransom?'

'Alas, no! – my jewels, my rings, my purses of gold and silver, they were stolen from me,' answered the Princess Hermonthis, with a sob.

'Princess,' I then exclaimed, 'I never retained anybody's foot unjustly – even though you have not got the five louis which it cost me, I present it to you gladly: I should feel unutterably wretched to think that I were the cause of so amiable a person as the Princess Hermonthis being lame.'

I delivered this discourse in a royally gallant, troubadour tone, which must have astonished the beautiful Egyptian girl.

She turned a look of deepest gratitude upon me; and her eyes shone with bluish gleams of light.

She took her foot – which surrendered itself willingly this time – like a woman about to put on her little shoe, and adjusted it to her leg with much skill.

This operation over, she took a few steps about the room, as though to assure herself that she was really no longer lame.

'Ah, how pleased my father will be! – he who was so unhappy because of my mutilation, and who from the moment of my birth set a whole nation at work to hollow me out a tomb so deep that he might preserve me intact until the last day, when souls must be weighed in the balance of Amenthi! Come with me to my father – he will receive you kindly; for you have given me back my foot.'

I thought this proposition natural enough. I arrayed myself in a dressing-gown of large-flowered pattern, which lent me a very Pharaonic aspect; hurriedly put on a pair of Turkish slippers, and informed the Princess Hermonthis that I was ready to follow her.

Before starting, Hermonthis took from her neck the little idol of green paste, and laid it on the scattered sheets of paper which covered the table.

'It is only fair,' she observed smilingly, 'that I should replace your paper-weight.'

She gave me her hand, which felt soft and cold, like the skin of a serpent; and we departed.

We passed for some time with the velocity of an arrow through a fluid and grayish expanse, in which half-formed silhouettes flitted swiftly by us, to right and left.

For an instant we saw only sky and sea.

A few moments later, obelisks commenced to tower in the distance: pylons and vast flights of steps guarded by sphinxes became clearly outlined against the horizon.

We had reached our destination.

The princess conducted me to the mountain of rose-coloured granite, in the face of which appeared an opening so narrow and low that it would have been difficult to distinguish it from the fissures in the rock, had not its location been marked by two stelae wrought with sculptures.

Hermonthis kindled a torch, and led the way before me.

We traversed corridors hewn through the living rock: their walls, covered with hieroglyphics and paintings of allegorical processions, might well have occupied thousands of arms for thousands of years in their formation – these corridors, of interminable length, opened into square chambers, in the midst of which pits had been contrived, through which we descended by cramp-irons or spiral stairways – these pits again conducted us into other chambers, opening into other corridors, likewise decorated with painted sparrow-hawks, serpents coiled in circles, the symbols of the *tau* and *pedum* prodigious works of art which no living eye can ever examine – interminable legends of granite which only the dead have time to read through all eternity.

At last we found ourselves in a hall so vast, so enormous, so immeasurable, that the eye could not reach its limits; files of monstrous columns stretched far out of sight on every side, between which twinkled livid stars of yellowish flame – points of light which revealed further depths incalculable in the darkness beyond.

The Princess Hermonthis still held my hand, and graciously saluted the mummies of her acquaintance.

My eyes became accustomed to the dim twilight, and objects became discernible.

I beheld the kings of the subterranean races seated upon thrones – grand old men, though dry, withered, wrinkled like parchment, and blackened with naphtha and bitumen – all wearing *pshents* of gold, and breastplates and gorgets glittering with precious stones; their eyes immovably fixed like the eyes of sphinxes, and their long beards whitened by the snow of centuries. Behind them stood their peoples, in the stiff and constrained posture enjoined by Egyptian art, all eternally preserving the attitude prescribed by the hieratic code. Behind these nations, the cats, ibises, and crocodiles contemporary with them – rendered monstrous of aspect by their swathing bands – mewed, flapped their wings, or extended their jaws in a saurian giggle.

All the Pharaohs were there – Cheops, Chephrenes, Psammetichus, Sesostris, Amenotaph – all the dark rulers of the pyramids and syrinxes – on yet higher thrones sat Chronos and Xixouthros – who was contemporary with the deluge; and Tubal Cain, who reigned before it.

The beard of King Xixouthros had grown seven times around the granite table, upon which he leaned, lost in deep reverie – and buried in dreams.

Further back, through a dusty cloud, I beheld dimly the seventy-two pre-Adamite Kings, with their seventy-two peoples – forever passed away.

After permitting me to gaze upon this bewildering spectacle a few moments, the Princess Hermonthis presented me to her father Pharaoh, who favoured me with a most gracious nod.

'I have found my foot again! – I have found my foot!' cried the Princess, clapping her little hands together with every sign of frantic joy: 'it was this gentleman who restored it to me.'

The races of Kemi, the races of Nahasi – all the black, bronzed, and copper-coloured nations repeated in chorus:

'The Princess Hermonthis has found her foot again!'

Even Xixouthros himself was visibly affected.

He raised his heavy eyelids, stroked his moustache with his fingers, and turned upon me a glance weighty with centuries.

'By Oms, the dog of Hell, and Tmei, daughter of the Sun and of Truth! this is a brave and worthy lad!' exclaimed Pharaoh, pointing to me with his sceptre, which was terminated with a lotus-flower.

'What recompense do you desire?'

Filled with that daring inspired by dreams in which nothing seems impossible, I asked him for the hand of the Princess Hermonthis – the hand seemed to me a very proper antithetic recompense for the foot.

Pharaoh opened wide his great eyes of glass in astonishment at my witty request.

'What country do you come from, and what is your age?'

'I am a Frenchman; and I am twenty-seven years old, venerable Pharaoh.'

'–Twenty-seven years old! and he wishes to espouse the Princess Hermonthis, who is thirty centuries old!' cried out at once all the Thrones and all the Circles of Nations.

Only Hermonthis herself did not seem to think my request unreasonable.

'If you were even only two thousand years old,' replied the ancient King, 'I would willingly give you the Princess; but the disproportion is too great; and, besides, we must give our daughters husbands who will last well: you do not know how to preserve yourselves any longer; even those who died only fifteen centuries ago are already no more than a handful of dust – behold! my flesh is solid as basalt; my bones are bars of steel!

'I shall be present on the last day of the world, with the same body and the same features which I had during my lifetime: my daughter Hermonthis will last longer than a statue of bronze.

'Then the last particles of your dust will have been scattered abroad by the winds; and even Isis herself, who was able to find the atoms of Osiris, would scarce be able to recompose your being.

'See how vigorous I yet remain, and how mighty is my grasp,' he added, shaking my hand in the English fashion with a strength that buried my rings in the flesh of my fingers.

He squeezed me so hard that I awoke, and found my friend Alfred shaking me by the arm to make me get up.

'Oh you everlasting sleeper! – must I have you carried out into the middle of the street, and fireworks exploded in your ears? It is after noon; don't you recollect your promise to take me with you to see M. Aguado's Spanish pictures?'

'God! I forgot all about it,' I answered, dressing myself hurriedly; 'we will go there at once; I have the permit lying on my desk.'

I started to find it – but fancy my astonishment when I beheld, instead of the mummy's foot I had purchased the evening before, the little green paste idol left in its place by the Princess Hermonthis!

Acknowledgements

The Publishers would like to thank the following authors, publishers and others for kindly granting them permission to reproduce the copyrighted extracts and stories included in this anthology.

THE PHANTOM SHIP by Jean Morris. Reprinted by permission of Jean Morris.

THE BLADES by Joan Aiken. © copyright Jean Aiken Enterprises Ltd 1984. Reprinted by permission of Jonathan Cape Ltd.

NULE from *Nothing to be Afraid of* by Jan Mark, published by Kestrel Books, 1980. © copyright 1977, 1980, 1981, 1982 Jan Mark. Reprinted by permission of Penguin Books Ltd.

SWEETS FROM A STRANGER by Nicholas Fisk. © copyright 1982 Nicholas Fisk.

THE HITCH-HIKER from *The Wonderful Story of Henry Sugar and Six More* by Roald Dahl. Reprinted by permission of Jonathan Cape Ltd.

THE DEVIL'S LAUGHTER by Jan Needle. © copyright Jan Needle 1984.

THE SAILOR BOY'S TALE by Karen Blixen. Reprinted by permission of Mrs. F. Feiler and the trustees of the estate of the late Karen Blixen.

Every effort has been made to clear copyrights and the publishers trust that their apologies will be accepted for any errors or omissions.